FICTION

OFFICER OF THE COURT

OFFICER
of the
COURT

BILL MESCE JR.

BANTAM BOOKS
New York   Toronto   London   Sydney   Auckland

3 9082 10603 4567

OFFICER OF THE COURT

A Bantam Book / September 2001

Copyright © 2001 by Bill Mesce Jr.

BOOK DESIGN BY GLEN M. EDELSTEIN

MAP BY HADEL STUDIO

Library of Congress Cataloging-in-Publication Data
Mesce, Bill.
Officer of the Court / Bill Mesce, Jr.
p.   cm.
ISBN 0-553-80178-3
I. Title.
PS3563.E74627 H4   2001
813'.54—dc21   00-045480

Published simultaneously in the United States and Canada

Bantam Books are published by Bantam Books, a division of Random House, Inc. Its trademark, consisting of the words "Bantam Books" and the portrayal of a rooster, is Registered in U.S. Patent and Trademark Office and in other countries. Marca Registrada. Bantam Books, 1540 Broadway, New York, New York 10036.

PRINTED IN THE UNITED STATES OF AMERICA

BVG   10   9   8   7   6   5   4   3   2   1

To the Family:

For taking me to a time and a place
I'd otherwise never have known

Prometheus ... had made Man's body to be like the gods;
and into him he put a speck of all the creatures on earth ...
There was a speck of the lion, and of the deer,
a speck of the cow and of the serpent,
a speck of the dog and of the fox,
of the monkey and of the owl,
the dove
and the vulture.

W.H.D. Rouse
Gods, Heroes and Men
of Ancient Greece

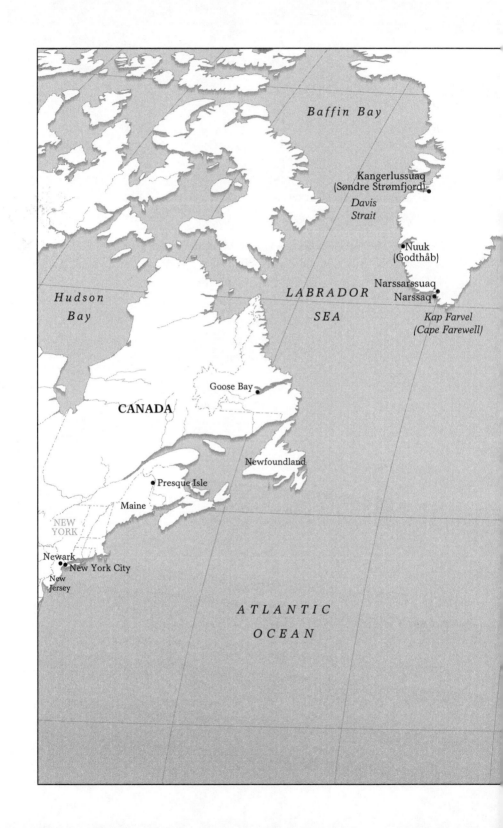

DECEMBER
1943

PART ONE

ARGONAUTS

CHAPTER ONE

ICARUS

"BLOODY ASININE," DECLARED FLIGHT LIEUTENANT LUCIAN "Paddy" Donlay.

"Eh? What's that? Blathering to yerself? First sign yer round the bend, mate, blathering to yerself." The diagnosis, delivered in a curt, unsympathetic Scots burr, was courtesy of Flight Lieutenant Alec "Taffy" Macnee.

Paddy Donlay peeped out the gap in the upturned collar of his fleece-lined Irvine flight jacket. "I said," and it emerged in his wry Dubliner's brogue, "bloody *asinine!*" Unsaid was whether he meant asinine Taffy Macnee or the asinine venture upon which Macnee had currently propelled them. The pair were shivering in a canvas-topped jeep that Macnee was wrestling through the ruts of the frozen mud track that curled out of the Bay of Firth and along the shoreline of Orkney Mainland.

Burrowed inside leather and fleece, Donlay could still hear what passed—in Macnee—for a laugh: a brief, gruff barking. "Har! What's bloody asinine was me thinking some soft Irish lass"—and here Macnee pinched Donlay's wind-reddened cheek—"had the stomach for exploration. The *guts*, if you will. Ya see, this is an *expedition!* An *adventure!* And all history knows there's no great explorers wi' an Irish name on 'em, Christian or otherwise. Remember: it was a gentleman carried the name *Scott* who trekked to the South Pole."

"Scott was an Englishman," Donlay told him.

"Aye, but his *name* was *Scott!*" shot back Taffy. "*Must* be a clansman's blood in 'im somewhere."

"Yer right, there was no Irishman nonsensical enough to freeze his

arse off with yer Mr. Scott," retorted Paddy. " 'Cause even some Sligo sot
on his worst night'd have enough sense to find his way home. Unlike yer
Mr. Scott."

At first glance, they seemed an odd coupling: Taffy Macnee, the scion
of an Uplands Scots laird who could trace the family title back fourteen
generations, and Paddy Donlay, whose sole knowledge of his lineage was
that his Da and his Da's Da both died coughing up coal dust before they
turned fifty. Yet in August of 1940 they were serving side by side in a
Hurricane squadron flying out of Manston, the Kingdom's most forward
spear point during the Battle of Britain. The skies over that part of Kent
grew so heavily combated by the two vying air armies that the Luftwaffe
would come to call it "Hell's Corner."

Macnee had come to the war out of patriotic fervor, Donlay for nothing more noble than an appetite for a good punch-up. It took only a short
time for their respective views to deteriorate to something more primal:
they fought simply to stay alive. After ten weeks of flying against the
German bombers and fighters of Luftflotte 2, not only were both the only
survivors of their squadron's original twelve-man roster, they were fair
on their way to being the sole survivors of the squadron's second generation.

They had begun as strangers; they ended the Blitz as brothers. They
had fought together and survived together; short of a blood tie, nothing
brings two men closer. And, having shared the strain of vaulting into the
sky six or seven times a day against an enemy regularly outnumbering
them several to one, living on coffee and Benzedrine in lieu of rest, they
also crumbled together.

Macnee snapped suddenly one October day, so battle-fatigued he tried
to land his Hurricane without remembering to lower his landing gear. As
his riggers attempted to pry him from the wreckage, he apologized for
crashing the aeroplane, then fell into uncontrollable sobs, bawling "I'm
sorry" over and over until he collapsed in exhaustion.

Donlay's crack-up lacked that single dramatic catharsis. Nightly, he
woke his barracks mates with screams as he violently tossed himself
about his bunk, trying to save the flying mates he'd already lost and to
dodge the Messerschmitts which, not content to joust with him in the
autumnal skies over Kent, now pursued him into his nightmares.

After the losses suffered during the Blitz, the RAF could ill afford to
debit off even pilots as spent as Taffy Macnee and Paddy Donlay. They
were transferred to Coastal Command and assigned to the air station in
the Orkneys flying a Short Sunderland (Macnee in the left-hand seat;
Donlay as copilot) out of the Bay of Firth on the less stressful routine of
antisubmarine patrol.

Each day Macnee and Donlay piloted their bulky flying boat on a leisurely patrol route, sometimes protectively circling over a passing convoy. If they saw a U-boat, they would alert the convoy escorts, and, if the opportunity presented itself, would descend on the submarine to rake it with the eight guns that earned the Sunderland the sobriquet "Flying Porcupine."

These patrols devolved into rather tedious exercises as convoy protection grew more effective (by summer '43, the German submarine fleet had been crippled to the point where it'd been withdrawn from the North Atlantic). Macnee and Donlay often spent hours each day floating over empty sea. Their only spark of excitement was the occasional spotting in the far distance of an FW-200 Condor out of the German fields in Norway, trolling for Allied convoys en route to Murmansk. To break the numbing drudgery of their patrol, Macnee would, over Donlay's objections, sometimes tilt the Sunderland in the FW's direction, though the more prudent German, once spotting them, would turn about straight for home.

Come winter, the boredom factor multiplied. The incessant foul weather whirled in off the North Atlantic to the west and the North Sea to the east, grounding aircraft. With the Home Fleet anchored in Scapa Flow, there were more servicemen about Orkney Mainland than inhabitants, so there was little in the way of social diversion beyond the usual bunkroom entertainments. Such tedium explains why either Macnee or Donlay would even contemplate the Scot's ludicrous proposal of an *expedition* and *adventure*.

Macnee's father, the laird, had honored his son's birthday two weeks previous by ordering him an elegant Purdy shotgun from Harrods. Macnee thought it such an object of beauty he was constantly brandishing the thing about to anyone he could corner. He would hold forth on the proud Purdy tradition, the weapon's exquisite balance, lovingly caress the polished walnut grips, and go on about how many coats of shellac it took to bring out the luster of the wood, flashing the brass butt plate upon which Daddy had had his son's name elaborately engraved beneath the family coat of arms.

"The way he touches her up ain't natcheral," Donlay complained to his mates. "Mate," he would declare to Macnee, "ya need yerself a woman."

Macnee got it into his head to christen the Purdy by potting some of the local fowl. He suggested a drive round the headland west of the bay toward the Atlantic side of the island, where he remembered seeing a colony of gulls. They'd spotted them often enough from the Sunderland; in fact, more than once they'd had to fly extreme evasive maneuvers to keep from running through the cloud of birds. This gave the two flyers even more incentive to pop off a few.

"Perhaps we can bring one down for dinner," the Scot suggested. "A wee variety in the mess, eh?"

Donlay grimaced. "I seen 'em birds down the bay eatin' the navy garbage."

"You heard o' grouse?" Macnee retorted. "Ptarmigan? Any o' you Celtic louts ever heard of squab, for the good Christ's sake? All they are is some kind or 'nother of pigeon."

Donlay shook his head stubbornly. "I thought we were talkin' sea-gulls."

"A seagull is just the ocean-going version of a pigeon."

"They're nothin' like a pigeon!"

"Well, no, ya silly git, they're not related. Of course it's not the same kind o' bird! I'm speaking thematically."

Still, after three days grounded by gales, Donlay had to agree with Macnee that any activity would be a welcome change from the Officers Mess. As the first gust of a shivering salt gale shook the jeep, however, the Irishman came to consider his agreeing to the escapade second only to his enlistment in the RAF as one of the major mistakes of his life.

The sky that day was a bleak, dark gray; the roiling overcast threatened snow or icy rain. The canvas top and sides of the jeep popped and cracked under a vicious thirty-knot wind.

"P'raps another day might be more in order," Donlay suggested. His teeth were chattering so hard he could scarcely get the words out.

"Problem is you Irish laddies are soft." Macnee wrestled with the wheel against not only the road but the buffeting winds.

"Oh, yeah," Donlay retorted. "We're all soft. Everyone knows Dublin's right balmy this time o' year."

They drove past the cottages of Stromness. The lighted windows sparked visions in Paddy Donlay of snug, shawled locals clustered round peat stoves, taking lulling nips of Highland Park whisky. "I s'pose the fine likes of a titled gentleman like yerself might consider the natives dead primitive," declared Paddy, "but they do seem to have sense enough to be inside today."

Macnee considered a response, could think of nothing particularly marked of wit, so placed his tongue between chapped lips and blew a vigorous raspberry.

"Quoting from the great Scots literary masters, eh?" taunted Donlay.

Not far past Stromness, Macnee pulled the jeep to a halt atop a low rise that looked down across the shingle beach to the surf. Here the gusts were particularly violent, whipping the slate-colored ocean to a froth and threatening to rip the canvas from the jeep.

Donlay squinted through the foggy plastic windows. A kilometer or so beyond the beach, across the Atlantic mouth of Scapa Flow, he could see the abrupt sandstone cliffs of the island Hoy.

"I don't see yer birds," he reported. "Maybe they got more sense in their little bird heads than a Scotsman's got. Sittin' someplace warm they are, I'll bet."

Macnee reached into the rear of the jeep for the leather Purdy case.

"Yer not serious 'bout still goin' out there in all that freeze, are ya?"

Macnee's answer was a determined smile and his barking "Har!"

Donlay'd seen the same cold, manic grin when Macnee turned the lumbering Sunderland after a Focke-Wulf running home to Norway. Donlay pulled himself deeper inside his Irvine jacket and steeled himself against the numbing blast that came when Macnee climbed out the flap.

He sat like that for some short while, though in that terrible cold his wait felt endless. Still, he heard no shots. Despite his shivering and quaking, Paddy Donlay managed a smile over the delicious irony that, for all the master craftsmanship Macnee boasted of as having been invested in his beloved Purdy, the firing works of the weapon had probably frozen.

There came another blast of frigid wind as Macnee's head slipped through the door flap.

"I grant yer a hardier soul than me," Donlay told him. "I surrender the point. Now can we go home?"

"There's someone down on the beach!"

Donlay began to protest, caught the urgent look on Macnee's face, and instantly understood that his mate meant more than a passing pedestrian.

The gusts off the Atlantic hit Paddy Donlay in the forehead like a knife, so sharp he grunted aloud in pain, and stopped in his tracks. He blinked, got a brief image of Macnee slipping and sliding below him on the shingle, bowed against the onshore wind. Macnee halted by a dull, low shape and looked back to the jeep; he gestured Donlay onward.

His boots crunched on the snow-crusted fescue, then the grass gave way to the stones of the shore, slippery with moss and garlands of ice. Donlay kept his eyes downward, both to save them from the wind and to pick his steps carefully.

Macnee was kneeling over a man facedown on the stones.

"Dead, I suppose," Donlay said flatly.

"I'm beginning to see why Ireland has produced no Louis Pasteurs," Macnee grumbled as he struggled to flop the awkward body onto its back. The dead man was shapeless inside the billows of a hooded parka glistening with sea spray and ice, feet bulky in arctic footwear—American "snow packs." Macnee nodded at the small, round hole in the parka hood. A filament of stuffing trailed from the hole, flapping insanely in the wind.

Donlay studied the brown trouser legs of a uniform extending below the hem of the parka. "Army?"

"Nor many great detectives," continued Macnee sourly. "No Sherlock Holmeses. No Sam Spades. By Jesus," he grunted, finally heaving the corpse over, "even the Chinamen have Charlie Chan. Oh, well, that would do it, wouldn't it?"

The bullet had made a tidy entry hole through the rear of the parka hood, but had left an exceedingly messy exit. A maroon spray of frozen blood and brain matter, stark against a face marble white with death and cold, radiated from a gaping wound low in the man's forehead.

It was a young face beneath the dappling of gore, with dark, tangled hair peeping out from the fur fringe of the hood. That was all Donlay saw in the hasty look he gave the dead man before turning away. He'd seen quite enough dead men, thank you, saw them in his dreams nightly.

Macnee fumbled for the zipper of the parka but couldn't get a good purchase because of the thick fingers of his flying gloves.

"You'll have to take 'em off," Donlay told him.

Macnee ignored him and continued to paw at the zipper.

"I said—" Donlay began.

"It'd be much appreciated if you'd shut yer gob," Macnee snapped. With a resigned "Oh, bollocks!" he grabbed the fingertips of his right glove in his teeth and tugged it clear. Cursing, he pulled the zipper down with his bare hand, then thrust it into his fleece-lined pocket.

"Wasn't that easier?" said Donlay. Macnee ignored the taunt and pushed the parka open with his other hand.

"Jesus!" Macnee said.

"Eh?"

"He's a *Yank*!"

"He's a *what*?"

"See for yerself!"

Donlay bent so he could peer into the open parka, see the dark brown tunic and American insignia. "What the bloody hell is a *Yank* doin' *here*?"

"Well, I'm the one to ask, aren't I?" Macnee whipped back. "Didn't wash up. Doesn't look like he's been in the water."

"What do you think? Since yesterday?" Donlay ventured.

"Maybe last night," Macnee replied. "But not before yesterday." He steeled himself, then pulled his bare hand from its sheltering pocket and swiftly shot it down the collar of the dead man to find his identification tags. The cold beat him on the first attempt.

"Yer Mr. Scott of the Antarctic would be ashamed, ya know."

"Piss off," Macnee snarled, reached into the collar a second time, found the tags, and laid them on the dead Yank's chest. " 'Grassi, A. G.,' " he read.

"What kind of name is Grassy?"

"American, I expect."

They ran back to the jeep and Macnee started the motor.

"Should we bring him back with us?" Donlay asked.

"Can't say I fancy wrestling him into the back," Macnee said. "Hardly room for him, is there?"

"Well, yeah, you wouldn't want him p'raps scratchin' yer loverly Purdy now, I s'pose."

Macnee slipped the jeep into gear. "We'll tell the CO, have them send a lorry."

Donlay squirmed round in his seat and squinted through the rear plastic window as the jeep jounced back the way it'd come. "Seems a shame to leave the lad out there like that."

"He didn't go anywhere all last night," Macnee replied. "I expect he won't be going anywhere now."

CHAPTER TWO

ODYSSEY

WE MET AT A CAFÉ SHE KNEW on the Strand, walking distance between where she was now working in Whitehall and my station on Fleet Street: neutral territory. It was a place very much to her taste, easy to pass by if you weren't looking for it. They had just drawn the blackout drapes, and I'd managed to cajole a second glass of dull port from the café's rationed cellar when the bell over the door jangled. I turned, saw her shaking the rain off her brolly, her wiry hair glistening with windblown drops. She gave a casual oh-there-you-are wave and a smile. She left her brolly in the stand, her splattered coat on the rack by the door, and waved at me to keep my seat.

I ordered her a port and something plain to eat. We passed ritualistic comments about the foul weather. She apologized for her lateness, fobbed it off on her new job at the War Ministry clerking for some grand panjandrum type. "Do you know him, Eddie? You know all the team, don't you?"

I shook my head. "Not all. It's a big team."

Her boss, she said, was one of the blokes responsible for leasing estate lands for military use. "Every time the Army joes need to practice blowing something up, we find them someplace safely removed."

"As much blowing up as there is these days, I wouldn't think they'd need much practice."

"Well," and she put on an air of mock seriousness, "there's blowing something up . . . and there's blowing something up *properly*."

The smile lines about her mouth were no longer reserved for merriment and had taken up permanent residence. Her eyes—always a clear bluish sort—now seemed watery, myopic. As her hair dried, I could see gray generously flecked throughout. She looked a bit older than I'd remembered. And tired. But, at that point, the war was into its fifth year: we all looked older and tired.

Our shepherd pies came and we poked at them a bit, neither of us seeming to have much interest.

"How long's it been, then?"

"A while."

"Still at the same game, then? The paper, I mean. Same paper, I mean."

"Still."

Her fork toyed at the edge of the plate, separating a bit of loose meat from the mass, then herding it back in. "Getting on all right? I mean all things considered."

"Fair. All things considered."

"I was sorry to hear . . ." She meant my leg.

"So was I."

"Seriously."

"If I gave it much serious thought, I'd spend the day in tears."

"Well, let's not have that, then."

"How did you know?"

Himself, of course. The Boss. She had only to smile and I knew it'd been him.

"I'd just as soon not have bothered you wi' it," I told her. "Not my idea, you know. Didn't mean to trouble."

"I'm glad he told me. Saves you having to tell a story. No sense you being cross with him over it. Not at this point."

"Can't afford to be. He signs the checks."

"Quite. How is the old boy?"

"He worries me." I tapped my chest. "I think he's not at all well."

She looked down at her plate, pensive. "I liked him. Always did."

"He is likable, as fire-breathing despots go."

Her smile flickered back, briefly. She pushed her plate away. "I thought I was hungry."

"Me, too." I flagged the waiter over but we'd reached our allotment on the wine. Cathryn settled for tea and I joined her.

"You're looking well, Cat."

"I'm looking like hell. And so are you."

I was unaccustomed to such bluntness from her, and took shelter behind a sip from my cup.

"Look, Eddie, I appreciate your ringing me up. It is nice to see you again, actually. It's nice to see you well and getting on—"

"You know me. I could always find a way to manage."

That pensive look again. "Yes. You always could. I daresay you always seemed to manage so much better alone."

"That's not true, Cat. I—"

"You're about to say something sweet and romantic about us, but . . ." She smiled sadly. "You were always a bit sweet, much as you tried to hide it, but you're no romantic. Save yourself a charming lie. You're just a touch lonely, I expect. That's all."

"You could give me the benefit of the doubt."

"How long have you been back in England, Eddie? Singapore was when? February '42? This is 1943, Eddie, and it's nearly Christmas. And when was the last time before you left for Singapore?"

There was a long, uncomfortable silence. I felt the teacup cooling in my hands. I wondered if the café had anything stronger than wine.

She sighed. "I'm not trying to fight. It's long done; there's no reason to fight. I'm glad you rang. It is nice to see you—"

"And how well I'm getting on. So you said."

"It got me thinking. It's been almost two years—more, if you go back before Singapore—"

"So you said."

She paused a moment, then pushed on. "Well, this may not be the best time, but I don't suppose there'll ever be a good time. We really need to . . . formalize this—" She was back to her usual delicacy, seeking the least abrading word.

"Situation?" I offered. "Condition? Circumstance?" For someone who'd downed only two glasses of wine—and a rather feeble wine at that—I was sounding quite acrid. "I think the legal term is separation, my dear."

"I've already been to the solicitor's. Filed quite some time ago, in fact."

"Well, aye, why not? Let's get on and be done wi' it, eh? It is two years now, isn't it? But if you've filed, there must be a villain, eh? There's got to be a villain for it to work, eh? That's the procedure, isn't it? And I'm to be the guilty party? Of course. Typecasting, I think they call it in the cine. And if I'm to be the villain, there must be a villainy. Can't process the paperwork wi'out a sin in the proper space. What's it to be, Cat? Did I flog you regularly? Gamble away the family antiquities? Ah! Infidelity! That's always a perennial favorite. Was I infidelitous, Cat?"

She was neither angry nor upset. As I said: merely tired. "I wouldn't put that down, Eddie. I never even imagined that. I'd wager that even since then—" She decided not to pursue that line. "Under the circumstances, he—my solicitor—suggested desertion. Abandonment. I agreed."

"Well," I said, and tapped my spoon alongside my cup, a slow cadence, a death knell. "Appropriate, I suppose. As you say, under the circumstances. More true than not, eh?"

"That was really your only sin, Eddie."

"Just the one?"

"Just the one. It was just that you practiced it so well."

To which I could say nothing.

"There won't be alimony," she went on, "nothing of that sort. You won't even need to go to the hearing. I'll have your copy of the decree sent round once it's executed."

I nodded a thank you.

"It is time we've got on with this. After all—"

"Aye, it's been two years. So you keep telling me." I had no right to be angry; at least, not with her. "Sorry."

She nodded and stood.

"Cat . . . I mean . . . I'm sorry about the whole bloody mess."

"I know."

She kissed me atop my head when she left, forgiving the errant schoolboy, then she was gone and I was alone at the table with cold tea and an uneaten meal. On the other side of the blackout drapes I could hear the rain rattle against the café windows.

"Well, what'd you expect, you silly sod?" He shook that large, grizzled head the way paters do over small sons whining that the cat scratched them after they've yanked its tail.

"Um, pardon, but I think an erratum is in order. Weren't you the wise old walrus who suggested I get back wi' her?"

His heavy brow rose, his eyes widened, fishlike behind the thick lenses of his spectacles. It was a stunning performance of ignorance. "Did I, now?"

"Just this summer, wasn't it? As I recall."

Completely ignoring the point, he eased back into the cracked leather of his chair, his thick fingers stretched across the wide expanse of his stomach, the deep furrows of his face transforming into something pensive. "Why is it if Jerry drops a wee bomb over Piccadilly, you're off like an Epsom Downs champion and there before it hits ground? But nearly four months ago I *suggest*—"

"Recommend."

"—suggest you try to patch it with the missus, and you wait until now—"

"I thought it'd make a nice Christmas surprise."

"Next time buy her a hat instead. My missus likes hats."

I'd intended to head back to my flat from the café, but found the idea of lying huddled under a comforter with a bottle of cheap Scots whisky and the BBC's mix of Christmas carols and war news a rather dim evening's entertainment. Instead, I clip-clopped through the rain back to the paper's office, pestered the night staff, loitered about the teleprinter scanning the bulletins: the opening of the Russian winter offensive against the German southern flank; Rommel pushing Tito's guerrillas back into the Yugoslav mountains; buoyant reports from the Pacific following the fall of the Gilbert Islands; the stalemate in Italy.

Himself, late in his office as per the usual, beckoned me from the door of his sanctum. "Why not leave the lads to their work, eh, Eddie? There's a good fellow. Now, in with you."

He'd closed the door behind us, dropped the blinds over the windows facing the newsroom, and reached into his desk drawer for two chipped teacups and a very fine bottle of the Irish stuff. I'd never understood what pretense the teacups supported, as the bottle frequently sat in plain sight.

He poured us each a dose. "For the rain, the chill, or what have you. Biscuit?" On his desk stood a sad-looking Christmas tree handmade of cardboard, one of his missus's home crafts projects. Next to it sat a Christmas tin filled with biscuits; as many as when the tin had first appeared several days earlier. "Now what's all this, then? All this glumming about?"

After which came the disavowal of responsibility and suggestion regarding headwear. "Good stuff, this," I concluded, raising my cup.

"Gift from Brannagh. I think he's heard we're going to pension off old Glatley next year and he fancies his seat on the city desk. This is his attempt to sway me."

"Is it working?"

"As you say, it is quite good. But you know I've always had you in mind for the chair."

"I'm not for a desk."

He poured himself a second splash. I frowned. His color had not been good of late, pasty and gray. The snarls he directed at the staff no longer seemed to have the same teeth behind them.

"Should you be having another? What's the doctor said?"

"I haven't been to the doctor."

"If you're not going to be sensible, at least go down to see Caffrey. He does the Medicine and Science column. That makes him almost a medical man."

"I thought you *were* divorced," he said, ignoring me. "Isn't that what you've always said?"

"That's how it felt. The good-byes at the time certainly seemed final enough. I just never got round to the paperwork."

"So, all this time you've been saying you're divorced, you were never really—"

"We were separated."

"Why would you say you were divorced, then?"

"Pour yourself another drink. To hell with the damned doctors."

"This business of the divorce—"

"Why'd you tell her about the leg?"

"She still loved you then, didn't she? I thought she'd want to know. She *should* know." He scowled into his cup, as if debating partaking of that second drink. "Probably still loves you. If they ever truly did, part of them always truly will. Even while they're throwing your bags at you and telling you to piss off. Why'd you ring her, then? All of a sudden?"

I shrugged.

"Holiday doldrums and all that? Listen, my son, have you anything on for Christmas? Not the time to be alone, particularly in your state. You should come round. The missus'd be happy for the company." He fondled one of the biscuits, rapped it against his desktop, tossed it back into the tin. The biscuits rattled together like gravel. "Don't see why I should suffer one of her Christmas feasts alone."

"We'll see. I should be off home." I headed for the door.

"One other thing, my son."

I turned. His glasses were on the blotter and he was rubbing his eyes. For years I'd believed he'd bury us all, but at that moment he seemed unutterably drained.

"You have me worried. You came back from points Far East and I doubted you. Thought with the leg and so forth, well, you know, thought you wouldn't be up to snuff and all that sort of rot. We—I—was very good about having you back, but very bad about putting you on the back bench. Well, I'm happy to say you proved me wrong with that business last summer, my son. Glad to put you back in harness, back on the first team. But of late . . . your stuff's all right, as good as anyone on the paper, but it, well, it's just off, eh? I know you, I *know* your stuff, and there may not be another eye in our circulation can see it, but I can. Someone in back of the string section out of tune, eh?"

"This business with Cathryn—"

He looked at me with a hard eye. "Please, my son. Tell that to yourself, but not to me. I'm thinking all this whatever-it-is is *why* you rang her. So what is it, my son? Any thoughts?"

I stepped back to the desk, picked up my cup, and held it out for another dash, then drained it. "Haven't a clue, frankly. Wish I did."

"Give it some thought, my son. Otherwise, you wake up one day and find it's devoured you and there's nothing left for me to abuse and exploit. Then where'll I be?"

I smiled and opened the door.

"It's our job to bear witness," the great man said, sounding immensely weary. "Sometimes we witness one war too many, Eddie. If that's it, then it's time to get out of the game."

It had been some time since I thought of poor old Harry Voss, but as I limped my way home, he came to mind. I thought it odd.

After all, we'd been on speaking terms for only a few days back in August, and even at that had had painfully little in common. I was a hard-barked Scot who'd lost count of my wars, and Harry was a homesick Yank whose tenure in London marked his only exposure to armed conflict. I was better acquainted with the weathered Gladstone that had accompanied me round the globe than with my wife, while Harry openly pined for the woman who dutifully waited for him.

Hardly friends. Just an accidental conjoining of a lonely soul and a sympathetic ear. Perhaps he came back to me then as I was feeling that same kind of loneliness—of feeling lost, unrooted—that he'd had. Perhaps right then I needed him to return the favor.

Back in August, we'd spent a long night over coffee and a bottle. It was a wake of sorts. Poor old Harry, cradling the cast of a broken right hand, was mourning a few dead ideals. It was dawn and I had invited him to stay, rest, join me for breakfast.

"I just want to go home," Harry had said, and took his leave.

I watched him from my window, shuffling along the bluish morning streets toward the court in Mayfair where he was quartered. A messenger waited for him in the orderly room of his billet, with orders that gave him just two hours to gather up his belongings and catch a train for Liverpool. By dusk, he'd been quartered on a Liberty ship, one of thirty-odd vessels making up an OB convoy that, by nightfall, was coursing through the North Channel and out into the North Atlantic heading for the States. Harry Voss had gotten his wish: He was going home.

The "cargo" of Harry's particular ship, I learned much later, was American soldiers being rotated Stateside, most of them wounded. Racks of bunks had been installed in the storage spaces; the companionways and compartments of the vessel were thick with the smell of gauze and disinfectant. To Harry's surprise, he found the men in those bunks and lurching about on crutches upbeat. They laughed, told jokes and stories; those with two good legs tried to dance in the confined spaces to records on the ship's phonograph. The swathes of bandages seemed to matter little to them. Whatever they had suffered—or were suffering—they were, after all, going home!

Their wounds seemed to matter more to Harry: the patches over missing eyes, the empty sleeves and trouser legs, the comatose mummified inside meters of gauze, rent bodies misshapen under blankets. There were hundreds of them on the ship, an army of the damaged and crippled, and so many of them painfully young.

After his first visit, Harry never returned belowdecks. When a few of the more ambulatory cases appeared in the wardroom, or braved the North Atlantic winds on deck, he kept his distance.

In recognition of his officer's status, Harry was allowed a level of privacy not afforded the enlisted ranks, who were quartered en masse. He was assigned a cabin which he shared with three lieutenants. Since Harry was a last-minute placement, one of the lieutenants had to give up his place in the three-tiered rack of bunks and sleep on a folding cot that, when open, occupied nearly all of the compartment's little deck space.

"It was like being in a box of puppies," Harry later reflected. The three lieutenants were friends, the pilot, copilot, and navigator from an Eighth Air Force B-17 Flying Fortress crew. They'd managed to get through their tour of twenty-five missions intact and now youthful, pockets brimming with back pay, intoxicated with survival, they were constantly laughing, endlessly prattling on about the enormous damage they intended to do to the stocks of liquor and unwary women Stateside.

"We're gonna swashbuckle through New York like the Three Musketeers!" declared the navigator.

"More like the Three Stooges," said the copilot.

Harry slid out the door lest the slapstick eye-pokings and hairpullings that followed inflict some collateral damage on him in the confined space.

Their second night at sea, Harry was awakened by the screaming of the navigator, thrashing about on the folding cot. All Harry could make out was the name "Jordy," shouted time and again.

Harry waited for the man's mates to climb down from the bunks above to wake and comfort the man, but other than the violent tossing of the tormented navigator and the usual rolling of the ship, the compartment remained silent.

The blackout curtain was drawn across the porthole, the only light switch on the bulkhead near the door. In the darkness, Harry started to fumble his way out from under his blankets to attend to the screaming young man, but a restraining hand lit on his shoulder.

"It's OK." The pilot's voice came to him softly out of the dark. "It'll pass in a bit."

The following morning, all three of the bomber crewmen—including the nightmare-plagued navigator—were back to their usual puppying about, as if nothing had occurred.

Harry spent as little time round the three whelps as he could, uncomfortable about the trio, feeling the weight of the differences in their ages and experiences. In the mornings, he would head straight for the wardroom, breakfast alone in a corner, and then, weather permitting, go on deck. He found himself an isolated spot forward, the gunwales of the bow gun tub an effective bulwark against the chill North Atlantic winds. The pilot found him there one morning and explained the situation concerning the navigator.

There had originally been four of them: the two pilots, the navigator, and "Jordy," the bombardier who'd shared their 17's cramped nose compartment with the navigator. They'd been together nearly a year since they'd trained as a crew back at Randolph Field in Texas. A few days earlier, on August 17, the bomber puppies had flown their last mission as part of Eighth Air Force's Mission No. 81 against the Germans' main ball-bearing plant at Schweinfurt.

The mission was a brutal running battle with German interceptors five miles above the earth, from the moment the bomber stream crossed the Belgian coast until it reached the target area ninety minutes later, growing even more ferocious after the American escort fighters reached their range limit near Aachen. Before the day was out, the force of 230 B-17's would lose 36 bombers and nearly 400 airmen.

The bomber puppies' ship was section leader, which meant Jordy was lead bombardier for the section. The other bombardiers in the section would watch the lead plane, releasing their bombs when the leader did. As they'd turned onto the bomb run, lining themselves up for their drop point, Jordy hunched over his Norden bombsight, trying to ignore the ugly black and red bursts of flak that jostled the aeroplane, sending shrapnel rattling against the aluminum hull.

"That's always the worst of it," the young pilot told Harry. "You're on the bomb run and there's nothing you can do. You can't climb or dive, you can't jink. You just have to sit there, sweat, and take it until you let your eggs go. And the bomb run at Schweinfurt was six minutes long."

Which was six minutes too long for the navigator. The flak thickened and he began screaming at Jordy to drop the bombs anywhere so they could get the hell out of there.

But Jordy kept to his post, coolly fiddling with the controls on his bombsight as he tried to put the cross hairs on his drop point through the heavy outpouring of flak blossoming all about them.

Then, over the bent shoulders of Jordy, the navigator could see an Me-109 bearing in on them.

"He had guts," the pilot told Harry, meaning the 109 pilot. Normally, the German fighters withdrew when the bombers reached the flak umbrella over the target, so as not to be struck by their own gunners. "But this kraut just plowed on through. Came at us head-on, 'cause he knew we're soft in the nose, no firepower up there. This guy was good, too, came in inverted." The sharper German pilots attacked upside down, explained the pilot, because it allowed them to dive away quickly after their pass.

The navigator shouted at Jordy to look up at the Messerschmitt rapidly growing larger outside the Perspex nose as the combined speeds of the two ships brought them together at over six hundred miles per hour. Jordy kept his attention on his bombsight, not looking up until he announced, "Bombs away!" He raised his head just as the 109 "gave us a little squirt." A 20-mm cannon shell crashed through the Perspex nose, decapitating Jordy. The pilot heard the navigator screaming on the interphone. When he climbed down into the nose he found the hysterical navigator splattered with the contents of Jordy's skull, blood and brain matter turning brittle as it froze in the cold, thin air howling through the holed nose at twenty thousand feet.

The pilot looked silently out at the rolling Atlantic for a moment before he turned to Harry with a sad smile. "Jordy was OK. Damn shame."

"How come you don't scream in the night?" Harry asked, earnestly amazed that anyone who'd been through such a horror wouldn't.

"Oh, I scream," the pilot answered, and flicked his sad smile again. "Every night. In here," and he tapped his forehead.

That late summer crossing was easier than Harry's first, back in January '43. The North Atlantic is famously inhospitable at any time of year, but more so during winter. Harry—and most of the other troops aboard ship—spent most of that first crossing vomiting in the loo, sinks, fire buckets, helmets, anything they could find as snow-filled gales whipped the ship about.

And, while such violent weather usually put a damper on the U-boats, everyone aboard was feeling jumpy. The wolfpacks had already sunk two dozen ships since New Year's Day. Harry's U-boat paranoia ratcheted so high that every whitecap seemed, at first glance, to be a periscope's wake.

But this was August. The U-boats were gone, at least for now, and the days were sunny; the Atlantic offered only a soothing swell. Harry enjoyed sitting out by the forward gun tub, sometimes exchanging a wave with someone on one of the other ships in the convoy. There were still exercises for the gun crews and boat drills, and the destroyers and corvettes in the escort screen cruised vigilantly round their charges. Occasionally, Harry would hear the distant, lulling buzz of aircraft—British Sunderlands from northern Scotland and the Orkneys, then later from the Shetlands and the Faeroes, and still later, American PBY Catalinas from Iceland—a protective canopy that would cover them across half the ocean. It all went to making Harry feel remarkably safe, and there were times when he could forget there was a war on somewhere miles behind him.

The convoy zigzagged its way northward, the seas grew rougher, the winds colder. They anchored in Reykjavik just long enough for the nimble little escort ships to refuel. At sea again, they continued north, to Kap Farvel in Greenland, and Harry could see, in the distance, the permanent ice cap draped across the inland heights. They turned southeast then, toward Newfoundland, and on this final leg, with every mile closer to home, the troops on board grew more restive and elated.

Most of them.

A day from the Labrador coast Harry was at his usual morning post by the forward gun tub. An announcement crackled over the ship's Tannoy system calling for the medical officer. Harry started when he heard his compartment number mentioned.

He hurried for the nearest hatch, made his way to his deck, and pushed his way through the curious GI's choking the companionway. The copilot was slumped on the companionway deck, arms round his knees, head bent, shoulders heaving with sobs. Through the door of his compartment Harry could see the MO, a comforting arm about the shoulders of the pilot, who was tearing at the bunk blankets in a blind rage.

On the folding cot in the middle of the compartment lay the body of the navigator.

"When does it fucking stop, Doc?" the pilot demanded of the MO. "When does it fucking *stop*?"

                    •   •   •

There was an ad hoc inquest; the ship's captain assigned one of his officers to interview each of the dead man's cabin mates. From the interviewer, Harry learned the navigator had overdosed on sleeping pills prescribed for him back in England. The goal of the inquest was to determine if the overdose had been accidental or otherwise.

"Do you know any reason he might have had to kill himself?" the officer had asked Harry.

"You've got to be kidding," Harry replied.

A burial service was arranged for that evening. Above, shimmering streamers of light rippled across the darkening sky: the aurora borealis. On the afterdeck, a crowd of crewmen and passengers gathered round the corpse, wrapped tightly in a binding of white canvas and draped with an American flag. They could not all have had the chance to know him, Harry thought, looking the crowd over. But he wore a uniform as did they, and that made him their brother.

"... until that day when the sea shall give up her dead."

The bier was upended; the body slid out from under the flag and disappeared into the wake of the ship. The crowd dispersed until Harry and his two cabin mates stood alone at the after rail, looking back at the propeller-churned foam beneath which their comrade now lay.

The copilot looked up at the changing colors of the aurora. "He woulda liked that."

Harry looked to the pilot, not speaking.

The pilot read the question in his eyes and shrugged. "He's sleeping OK now."

Two and a half weeks after leaving Liverpool, the escort ships, now assisted by Navy antisubmarine blimp patrols, herded the convoy past the minefields and submarine nets guarding New York Harbor. Harry stood with whooping and cheering soldiers along the rail of the main deck as they sailed past the Statue of Liberty and below the towers of Manhattan, the myriad windows fiery with the September morning sun.

He bid his two cabin mates good-bye, wished them luck, but before he could leave there was a rap on the door and a messenger appeared with orders for him. The pups saw the anxious look on Harry's face as he signed the delivery chit, and discreetly left him alone in the room.

Harry took a moment before he slowly tore open the manila envelope. He looked at the document's heading only long enough to make sure it was intended for him, then dropped his eyes to the text:

Your instructions upon arrival NYC are as follows:

(1) You are hereby assigned to the Judge Advocate General's section Ft. Dix NJ;

(2) You are to report to the senior JAG officer Ft. Dix for assignment no later than five (5) days subsequent your arrival NYC;

(3) You will follow all security restrictions regarding transmission of information not relevant to new assignment.

Harry read the blunt, typed sentences three times. He lay back on his bunk, first smiling, then laughing in both relief and glee.

Translated from the cold Army argot, Harry'd been given five days' leave before reporting for duty at his new station—Fort Dix—less than an hour's train ride from his home and Cynthia and his two boys. As for the closing paragraph, it was a rather obtuse way of telling him to keep his mouth shut about the matters that had transpired in England that summer and triggered his exile.

Harry Voss had a deserved reputation for being a drab plodder, a step-by-step-follow-the-prescribed-program swot, and a bit naïve to boot. All that comprised a rather lusterless air that people often mistook for intellectual dullness. But Harry was quite the clever fellow, doggedly and precisely analytical. He instantly recognized his new assignment for what it was.

It was a bribe.

From a table near the windows of the Horn & Hardart Automat at Broadway and Forty-sixth Street, Harry looked out across Times Square. There were uniforms everywhere—Navy white, Army khaki, the forest green of the Marines, even a sprinkling of the flat caps of the British Navy and the dashing blue of the Royal Canadian Air Force. But other than the fact that there were few automobiles (a consequence of petrol rationing), there was little other evidence of the war. People laden with shopping bags jostled each other on the sidewalks, queued in front of cines and theaters, ate from pushcarts on the streets as they always had.

Harry looked down at his bowl of clam chowder, wedge of cherry pie, cup of fresh-ground coffee on the marble tabletop before him, all smelling so rich, so *American*.

He knew then that the world beyond the glass could no more incorporate him than the shadow play on the projection screen of the Loew's Mayfair cine across the square. He could walk these streets, walk among these people, even act as one of them, but he could never again quite be one of them. If he ever spoke of what he'd seen on the other side of the ocean, and what he'd come to know, these people sitting round him sipping their egg creams and digging at plates spilling over with macaroni and cheese would look at him as if he were a lunatic, a madman speaking in tongues.

A uniform-packed train took him from Pennsylvania Station under the Hudson River, across the New Jersey marshes, and past the pig farms until he could see the belching smokestacks of the factories girdling Newark. From the Newark station he took a bus that deposited him just a few blocks from the street where he lived. But it was far enough that every half-block or so he had to set down his bags, catch his breath, and rest his aching arms.

Harry lived in the same neighborhood—the same building—in which he'd been born, on a street in Newark's First Ward. An immigrants' ghetto consisting of brick-topped streets crowded with aging tenements and small shops, it was predominantly populated by emigrant Italians and their progeny. Harry may have been the son of a Russian transplant, but these thickly peopled brick streets were still his home sod. The smells of boiling pasta and garlic crackling in a skillet of olive oil were as native to him as those of boiled potatoes and borscht.

The Newark Harry had left when he'd enlisted in early 1942 had been a manufacturing city still trying to shake off Depression doldrums, and the First Ward had especially suffered. Impoverished even before 1929, the Ward was home to peasant farmers who'd left behind even greater poverty in the Campania region of southern Italy and come to America with little more than what they could carry. But now Harry saw that everyone moved as if there were someplace they had to be; the shops and eateries that lined the streets brimmed with business.

It was unaccountable to him at first, but in the days to come Harry would learn this new activity was directly connected to all those belching smokestacks his train had passed on the way into Newark. Factories in Newark and the surrounding towns, like Kearney and Harrison, closed or partially idled during the Depression, were now open and thriving, nearly all converted to war industries. The plants were fully manned (or, more accurately, "womanned," as many of the new laborers were the wives and mothers of men off in service), and often running three shifts per day.

Every able-bodied person not in service was laboring at the Charms Candy plant, which was now minting munitions, or Spiotta Brothers, which had made men's suits before the war and was now spinning military uniforms, or any one of the other booming war plants in and around the city. The local shops were busy because there was more money than ever flowing through the neighborhood, although, ironically, with rationing there was less than ever to buy.

Harry trudged below the granite spires of Sacred Heart Cathedral, and if, perhaps, it didn't have the majesty of Wren's domed St. Paul's, this was his cathedral, and he felt a warmth in his chest St. Paul's could never have elicited. Then on along the border of Branch Brook Park, the oaks and elms and maples showing just a touch of their fall colors against a brilliant sky, past the derelict reservoir where he'd played baseball with his sons, and the public baths where Ward residents came for their showers.

He turned on to Seventh Avenue—his street.

With familiar sights came familiar faces. Some were feather-haired old men and women who had seen him grow from childhood. Many had come to him as clients, although knowing Harry, he had probably spent many an unbilled hour helping them through their legal affairs across their kitchen tables so they wouldn't have to make the onerous trek to his office cubby in the business district. He had helped them with their immigration paperwork, their deeds and mortgages and leases, the documentation and licenses for their little businesses, and with their final testaments.

In the neighborhood, they had called him "Roosk," an affectionate corruption of "Russkie." When they saw his face, sweaty and wilted from hauling his duffels along the street, they came out from behind their shop counters to greet him. Men and women welcomed him home with a hug. The older men clapped a hand almost painfully on the back of his neck, while the older women pinched his cheek as if he were still the wee child they remembered.

"Here, Roosk, you take this home, fresh tomat' like I bet you never see over there! You take this home for the family!"

"Here, Roosk, you take some fruit home, eh? I make a basket for you!"

Harry begged off. "I can barely carry my own bags, *comar'Rosa!*"

"You don't worry! I send the boy later!" And another hug, another kiss on the cheek.

"Hey, Roosk, you come in, I give you a welcome home haircut, huh?"

Harry tipped his cap and flashed his thinning pate. "I don't think there's much left for you to work with, *z'Emidio!*" And the old man who'd given him his first haircut a lifetime ago took his head between his spotted hands, bent it low, and kissed him on his pink scalp.

He crossed Garside Street, passing the chemist's shop on the corner, and the apron of stairs where the boys from the neighborhood had always loitered, the young ones bouncing rubber balls off the risers, the older boys puffed with adolescent pride, exchanging misinformation about womankind. The tykes were in attendance at Seventh Avenue School now, but the older boys were still there, only now some of them strutted like peacocks in newly issued Army khaki, home on leave from the training center at Fort Dix. They recognized Harry, gathered round him, querying him on what he'd seen of the war, making brave comments about their eagerness to be done with training and get on with "the real thing." The bravado masked a fear not of dying or injury but of what lay beyond the few city blocks where they'd spent their lives.

Past the stairs to the chemist's, another set of stairs, this leading to the men's social club in the cellar under the shop. It was one of the many such clubs in the area where the local men collected for rounds of cards and espresso. Hung near the door was a placard headed "In Memoriam," and below was a photo of a young, uniformed man, smiling, his Army cap so jauntily angled it threatened to slide off his brilliantined head. Harry took a moment, riffling his memory to see if he remembered the young man, then decided he didn't really want to know.

Past the dry goods shop, the hardware shop, then the tickling, tangy smells of salami and sausage and sawdust from Pennicho's butcher shop, where the Pennichos crushed grapes in the cellar every summer for a rough-edged homemade wine.

Across the street, children's voices sailed through the open windows of the school, warbling their way through "I'm a Little Teapot." His boys, Ricky and Jerry, were somewhere inside the drab pile of red brick. Perhaps one of them was among the choristers. Or were they too old for that sort of thing? It troubled him that he couldn't remember.

In the middle of the block sat another in the nondescript row of tenements, this one twelve flats squeezed onto four floors piled atop a fruit shop to one side of the entry, a grocery to the other. He set his bags down in front of the stoop, and looked up at the soot-streaked bricks, the face of the building crosshatched with a grillwork of fire escapes.

"*Heldish!*"

Before Harry even saw him, Philip Mayer sprang out of his grocery flinging his arms about Harry's shoulders. Like Harry, the wiry, gray-haired Mayer was one of the few non-Italians in the neighborhood, yet he spoke Italian as if he'd just stepped off the boat from Naples.

"Survival, *boychick*," Mayer had once explained to a much younger Harry when he had asked how Philip Mayer the Jew came to speak such proper Italian. "You can be a Jew, you can be a Republican, but you go out in the world you got to know survival. For survival, you got to have talent. And if you're a Jew out in the world, from the talent you got to make a art."

Young Harry said he didn't understand what any of that had to do with how Philip Mayer the Jew had come to speak such proper Italian. Mayer had pinched Harry's pudgy child's cheek and laughed. "You listen now. You learn later."

Mayer started pulling Harry toward the door of his shop. Harry pointed to his bags on the sidewalk.

"The bags got legs, they're gonna walk away?" Mayer tugged him inside. He shut the door and put the CLOSED sign in the window. "The world can do without me for five minutes while I welcome home the heldish. And I can do without the world for five minutes."

Mayer disappeared into the shop's back room and came back with two small glasses filled with a purplish wine. He handed Harry a glass, bowed his head and mumbled a brief prayer in Hebrew, then they clinked glasses. Mayer drained his, but the Jewish wine was so sweet Harry could partake only in sips.

"I should get upstairs," Harry said. "Get home . . ."

"You're already home. You look like you should sit." Before Harry could protest: "She's not home. She's working. All the women work now. She know you were coming?"

Harry shook his head.

"Then she's still working. You got time to sit." Mayer dragged two creaking wooden chairs together, freshened their glasses of wine. "You're not well?" he asked, leaning forward in his chair, scrutinizing Harry's face.

Harry hung his cap over his knee and dabbed at the sweat along his forehead. "Just tired."

"It's a long way."

"Very."

"A long way there. A long way home."

"Yes."

"It's good you make the round trip all in one piece."

"It's good."

Philip Mayer's eyes caught something in his study of Harry's face. In a well-practiced maneuver, he kicked his chair back until it leaned against the counter, its front legs clear of the floor. "Leave it back there, heldish."

"Leave what?"

"You know dybbuk?"

"What shelf do you keep that on?"

Philip Mayer chuckled. "It's like a ghost, except Jews don't have ghosts. We use the word sometimes to mean an evil spirit, a demon. But the word, what it really means, if you say it in English the way it is in Yiddish, it's to hang on to; to hold on tight."

"How do you get 'ghost' from 'hold on tight'?"

"It's how we use the word. A *dybbuk*, that's someone who dies, he feels you wronged him when he was alive, you made some sin against him, he comes back, he takes you, he possesses you. That's how he gets his revenge."

"You think I have a *dybbuk*?"

"I'm just saying you got those bags to carry upstairs. You don't need to be carrying nothing you should leave across the ocean, *heldish*."

"What's 'heldish'?"

Philip Mayer smiled and held his glass up in another salute. "Hero."

"I'm no hero."

"You came back, Harry. That's hero enough."

Harry grunted to his feet, walking the warped floorboards of the tiny shop. He smiled at the warm familiarity of the place.

"Hey, whatever happened to that little wisenheimer Irish kid you used to run with?" Philip Mayer asked him. "The family, they live over on Garside Street."

"Joe Ryan."

"Is he over there?"

"London."

"Is that what this is? You worried about Ryan?"

"I'm not worried about him." Harry took a sip of his wine. "So how do I get rid of this *dybbuk*?"

Philip Mayer smiled sympathetically and shrugged. "It's your *dybbuk*. Only you know what you got to do to make things right. I don't know your sin." He shook his head. "I know you a long time, my friend. I can't see no sin in you."

"Mr. Mayer, everybody sins."

They had a flat to the rear of the first floor. Harry stood a long time in front of the door. It had never occurred to him when he went into service that he should keep the key to his flat, but then he decided the door was probably open. Few in the neighborhood locked their doors.

He turned, passed through the creaking screen door at the end of the corridor that led out to the rear porch. Tenants came outside to sit in the cool of the evening, looking down at their children at play in the yard, a square of concrete hemmed on all sides by the walls of other tenements.

The porches were empty now, as was the yard. Harry sat in one of the chairs, used his bags as a hassock for his tired feet. Wash hung from lines strung from each porch to a pole across the way. Somehow, a breeze had found its way inside the walled yard, tickling the laundry. He took a deep breath and drew in the must of the old, dark corridors of the tenement, the taste of simmering tomato sauce, and minced meat flavored with Italian herbs sizzling in olive oil. Through one open window he could hear the voices of two old women chattering back and forth in tumbling Italian, and from another across the yard a Victrola played Caruso.

This is home, he thought, *and it is an absolutely lovely afternoon.* He dozed off.

It seemed such a little noise to wake him, but he heard footsteps in the corridor and they stopped near his flat. He stood and moved quietly to where he could look through the screen door into the hall.

He couldn't quite make her out through the metal scrim, but it was Cynthia, juggling her purse, a lunch pail, and a bag of groceries as she tried to fumble open the door. He watched her set the lunch pail and purse down, open the door, deposit the groceries inside, then return for her pail and purse. She pivoted at the sound of the creaking hinges of the screen door.

He had stood there all that time not knowing quite what to say, but then they were together, holding each other, both with tears in their eyes.

He found he didn't have to say anything.

CHAPTER THREE

THE POMEGRANATE SEED

IN THE FRIGID QUONSET SERVING AS Officers Mess stood a wretched-looking Christmas tree. Dwarfish, gnarled and twisted from the salt gales, it was more scrub than proper tree. A motley collection of colored balls, foil ornaments, and scruffy garlands had been draped on its scoliotic branches. These formal Yule garnishings were supplemented with more ad hoc adornments: an ammunition belt, sloppily daubed with silver paint, draped round the tree garland-fashion; empty cartridge casings, threads run through the apertures where the primer cap had been removed, hung from branches. On the tree's topmost place, normally reserved for a bright star or protective angel, someone had tacked a photograph of Winston Churchill, fingers of one hand raised in a V-for-Victory sign, ever-present cigar clasped in his other hand, bulldog jowls pulled back in a triumphant grin. Someone had pinned a set of pilot's wings to the photograph, affixing them on the front of Winnie's bowler. Disproportionately large against the image of the PM, the wings seemed of near-celestial span.

Harry stood before the tree, smiling in a small, respectful way.

Reluctantly, I left the circle of radiant warmth round the stove, limping across to the bar. I made a motion to Harry to see if he wanted his own drink freshened. He answered with a gesture indicating his stomach. I remembered that liquor and Harry's insides had always made rather poor mates.

I signaled the bartending corporal. "And let's have it *hot* this time, eh? That's why they call them *hot* toddies."

"I makes 'em 'ot, sar," he said. "They just don't *stays* 'ot."

I got Harry a mug of tea and joined him by the tree. The wind outside gusted and rattled the corrugated skin of the Quonset. I handed him his tea.

Harry looked pensive. "I wasn't home last Christmas. Looks like I'm going to miss this year, too."

"Well, that's war, isn't it?"

A queer little smile touched his face, then he turned back to the tree. "That's a *real* Christmas tree."

"How do you mean, 'real'?"

"This isn't like somebody ran down to the guy on the corner and just bought one. Somebody went out *there*"—he tilted his head at the snow slashing by the window—"and cut one down. Just like in the old days."

"And why does that make it more 'real' than the one you bought down the corner?"

Harry nodded at the tree. "These guys really meant it."

He was no doubt reflecting on a Saturday morning two weeks earlier when he'd been the chap running down to "the guy on the corner." In his small parlor, it was eight-year-old Jerry's job to hold the upper part of the trunk steady while Daddy struggled beneath the prickling lower branches trying to tighten the bolts that would steady the tree in its stand. Six-year-old Ricky was designated to traipse down to the tenement's cellar and haul back box after box of stored Christmas decorations.

Ricky's diligence faltered as soon as he returned to the flat. He up-ended a box of electric trains on the parlor rug. Not bothering with laying track, he grabbed the Lionel locomotive in his chubby fingers and shoved it across the rug, making engine and whistle noises until he crashed the engine into his brother's ankle. At that point Jerry tried to land a flying kick on Ricky's nose without losing hold of the tree.

"What're you two *doing*?" Harry bellowed from under the tree.

"It's Ricky! I'm gonna kill 'im!"

"It was a accident!" Ricky rebutted.

"I'm gonna give *you* an accident!" Jerry vowed.

"The two of you stop!" Harry declared.

"I didn't do anything!" Jerry protested.

"I didn't do anything!" Ricky protested.

"I said the two of you! Jerry, hold the tree! It's falling on my head! Does that look straight now?"

"It's crooked."

"Well, that's because the tree's crooked. There's nothing we can do about that."

"Mom's not gonna like it crooked," Jerry said.

"It's not crooked," Harry said. "The trunk is just—"

There was a knock at the door. Ricky screamed, "I'll get it!" and ran off into the kitchen.

Harry tried shimmying the trunk about in the stand. "What about now?" he asked Jerry.

"Nope."

"Well, that's just the way the tree is."

"It didn't look crooked when we bought it," Jerry pointed out.

"That guy must've been holding it wrong," Harry said.

"Hey, Dad!" Ricky screeched from the kitchen. "There's some Army guy here for you!"

Jerry was off like a cannon shot for a sight of a man in uniform, leaving Harry struggling alone with the still unanchored tree.

"Are you here for my dad?" Harry heard an eager Jerry demand.

A slow, drawling voice in reply: "If your dad's Major Harold Voss."

"Hold on a second!" Harry called out from under the tree. "I'm right here. I just need to, uh—"

"Hate to intrude," came the drawl, close by, "but you look like you could use a hand."

Through the branches Harry glimpsed gleaming brown shoes and olive drab trouser legs, then felt the tree steady above him.

"Thanks," Harry grunted as he tightened the tree stand screws. "Let me get these in a little more. . . ."

"Looks like it's kinda slanted a bit—"

"It's fine. There!"

As Harry crawled out from under the branches, the other man deferentially retreated back to the entry doorway, stooping to avoid the drying clothes Cynthia had left hanging from lines stretched across the kitchen. Harry followed, brushing pine needles from his shoulders.

"Captain Kneece." The tall young man in the Army overcoat introduced himself, displaying his AGO identification card. "Criminal Investigation Corps."

Harry studied the card, reading the name. " 'Derwood—' "

Kneece winced. "Well, sir, if it's gonna be something 'sides 'Captain Kneece,' I'd appreciate it if you'd make it 'Woody.' "

Twenty-four and lanky, Woody Kneece stooped his pomaded cap of rebellious wavy hair and kept his gangly arms close to him as if trying to physically intrude as little as possible. He spoke softly and shyly in that slow-dripping syrup Americans refer to as a "Southern drawl." Combined with his simian features—small, dark eyes too close-set; pugged nose; upper teeth a bit too extrusive—it gave him a slow-witted air.

"Sorry to bust in on you in your home like this," Kneece murmured, frowning at his own effrontery. He nervously fingered the folds of the garrison cap in his hands. "If it coulda waited, sir, I woulda." Then a late thought occurred to him and he looked up, concerned over a possibility. "You *are* Major Voss, aren't you, sir?"

Harry held up the captain's identification to remind the younger officer to take it back. "I'm Major Voss."

"I sure hate to make offense, sir, but you mind if I see some ID?"

Harry was wearing his usual Saturday morning garb: pajama bottoms, an undershirt, crushed slippers, and a faded, unknotted robe. For the first time it occurred to him he might not be at his presentable best. "Oh, sure, of course." He retreated to the bedroom, hastily tying up his robe.

"Hey!" Jerry demanded of the captain. "You been to Italy?"

"Nope," Kneece answered.

"Where you been fightin'?"

"Well, factually, son—"

"Leave the captain alone, please," Harry said as he returned to the kitchen and handed Kneece his own AGO card. "Why don't you sit down, Captain? Take your coat off. Coffee? It's already made. Still hot. You had breakfast yet?"

"Just coffee'll be fine, sir, appreciate it."

"Hey!" said Jerry. "If you didn't fight in Italy, wheredja get the fruit salad?"

"The what?"

Jerry stabbed a finger at the single, short line of service ribbons on the breast of Kneece's uniform jacket as the captain slid out of his coat. "That's what they call it," Jerry explained. "Fruit salad."

"They do?"

"*You're* supposed to know that! You're a *soldier!*"

"Didn't I just ask you to leave the captain alone?" Harry said, setting two cups of coffee down on the table. "He looks tired."

"I wanted to know about the fruit salad!" Jerry declared.

"Yeah, the fruit salad!" Ricky chimed in.

"I thought you were playing with your trains," Harry told Ricky. He smiled apologetically at Kneece, but the captain grabbed Jerry, sat him on his bony lap, and began pointing at his ribbons. "This one's for the American Campaign—"

"What's that?"

"Well, factually, it pretty much just means I was in the Army. This is for good conduct—"

"No battle ribbons?"

Harry rolled his eyes. "Kid's got a thing for blood like Bela Lugosi."

"No battle ribbons," Kneece said to Jerry with a sorry shake of his head.

"Howdja get to be a captain with no battle ribbons?"

"It's a mystery to me, too, little fella."

"But—"

"OK, OK," Harry cut in. "You've bothered this poor guy enough. Off, Jerry! Have you been down for the coal this morning? Before you think about telling me otherwise, that bucket looks awfully low, and if Mommy comes home and finds that stove cold—"

"What about him?" Jerry nodded at Ricky, who had returned to his trains.

"Him is supposed to be getting the decorations out of the cellar before him gets his fanny fanned!"

At that, "him" dropped his trains and scooted out the door, his older brother trudging along behind dragging a coal scuttle.

After the door closed behind the boys, Harry raised his cup in salute. "You deserve a battle ribbon just for surviving those two!"

"Aw, they're not so much," Kneece said. "I was a whole lot more of a handful when I was their age. That's what I get for bothering y'all at home, I guess. Wasn't sure I'd catch you. Figured maybe y'all'd be out Christmas shopping or something."

"Well, Saturdays, if I'm on leave, I'm on baby-sitting detail. My wife works on Saturdays."

"At one of these dee-fense plants?"

"She works in an office not far from here. They make artificial limbs. Business has been booming since the Sicily landings."

"I guess that would be the case," Kneece said. Self-consciously, he tried to stifle a yawn. "Sorry, sir. Put in a lotta miles this morning. Had to get up before dawn to catch the early train up from D.C., stepped off at Dix to check in with the JAG office there, then there was the train to the station downtown, then a cab here. Yessir, I am a mite beat."

"You said you've already been to Dix?"

"Yessir."

"I know most of the staff is on weekend leave, but wasn't Captain Megown on duty? He should've been able to help you. Unless you're here about something specific to one of my cases."

"The captain was a big help. If it wasn't for him, I wouldn'ta known where to track you down. But this isn't really any kinda JAG business. At least nothing's got to do with your office at Dix."

Harry's curiosity was suspended by a knock at the door. It was too soon to be the boys, and it would never occur to them to knock. He answered the door and there stood a splinter of a woman, middle-aged, no higher than Harry's chest (and Harry himself was of the short and squat variety). Her plain, handmade frock billowed round her skeletal frame, and her dark hair, heavily streaked with gray, was disciplined back in a severe bun.

" 'Scusa, Harry." Her dark button eyes looked past Harry and saw Kneece. She smiled a shy hello. " 'Scusa, signor." To Harry: "You know Carmella, she has the front apartment upstair'?" To Kneece: " 'At's Miz Rugolo, we live da same floor." To Harry: "She say she see da man from da Army—" To Kneece: "She see you come in da taxi. She tell me she see you." To Harry: "She come tell me da man from da Army, he come, she afraid maybe—"

Harry patted her gently on the arm. "It's OK, Regina. Captain Kneece is here for me. It's business from the fort. Didn't I promise you that as soon as I got word about Dominick I'd tell you?"

Her narrow little face grew concerned. "Good or bad, you tell me, remember?"

"I remember." Harry gave her a friendly hug. "Now stop worrying and go back upstairs. Scat."

She pinched his cheek, apologized again to them both, then departed.

"Must be hard living in a place like this," Kneece commented, "with everybody in everybody else's business."

"That's Mrs. Sisto," Harry said, taking his chair again. "Her youngest just finished up basic training for the Navy and is on his way to join up with his ship in Norfolk: antisubmarine patrol. Her middle boy's a B-24 gunner in India. Her oldest—Dominick—he went in with the infantry at Salerno back in September. So she's a little nervous. And the rest of us are a little nervous for her. She hasn't heard from Dominick in weeks. I told her I'd try to find out if he's OK."

Kneece nodded.

"A lot of the people in the neighborhood have boys in the service. What makes it doubly rough for them is most of these people come from the part of Italy where Salerno is. Every time she sees a Western Union scooter on the street she's scared to death it's either news about one of her sons, or word from the Red Cross that something happened to a relative on the other side."

Kneece looked at the closed door where Regina Sisto had been standing. "That's rough," the captain said. Harry could see from the look on his face that the captain was discovering the war was possibly a tad more complicated than it looked in the newsreels. "She seems like a nice lady."

"They're all nice ladies. Now, Captain, you said this didn't have anything to do with JAG business, so what is it I can do for you?"

Kneece seemed relieved to be off the subject of Mrs. Sisto. "Your wife does make good coffee. Hits the spot. A mite nippy out there." As he spoke, he reached inside his jacket pocket and drew out a small, well-creased notebook. He set it open on the table and thumbed through pages crammed with scribbling. He settled on a page bookmarked by a small photograph, the kind Harry instantly recognized as an ID photo from a serviceman's personnel file. Kneece slid the photo out of the notebook and set it down in front of Harry.

"Oh, Christ. Armando Grassi. What's he done now?"

"What makes you think Lootenant Grassi is in any kind of trouble?" Kneece asked.

"I don't think a guy from the Criminal Investigation Corps's office in Washington hunts me down all the way up in New Jersey to tell me Armando Grassi's been named Man of the Year."

"The lootenant worked for you when you were at the London JAG, didn't he?"

"Colonel Ryan—he was the London JAG CO—he had the office Table of Organization set up like a law firm. The senior officers—"

"Like you."

"—like me, they were the primary trial attorneys. The juniors—"

"Like Grassi."

"—right, mostly served as a pool of support staff. The seniors could draw on them as needed."

"Kinda rotated around to all the seniors."

Harry nodded.

"And Grassi rotated around to you a coupla times."

"Well, you tried to avoid drawing Armando, but yeah, he was on my team a few times."

"Rubbed you the wrong way, sir?"

"Let's just say Armando Grassi wasn't a team player."

"Grassi was working for you on your last case. Him and a—" Kneece consulted his scribbles. "Captain—"

"Ricks, Peter Ricks." Harry's gaze dropped to his coffee.

"That was your last London case, wasn't it, sir?"

"Not really a case," Harry answered quietly. "Just an investigation."

Kneece flipped to another page in his notebook. "Yessir, I see that. No charges. Mind if I ask why that was? Insufficient grounds? Or—"

"I'm afraid I'm not at liberty to discuss that case, Captain. You know

JAG investigations are privileged. More coffee?" Harry's cup was only down a few sips, but he turned to the stove, his back to the captain. "You can cable Colonel Ryan if you'd like. If he approves release of the information, fine. But I'm not—"

"At liberty, sir, yup, I understand how that is. I already cabled Colonel Ryan. Like you say: What happened in London's all privileged. When you were saying before about Lootenant Grassi not being a team player, I know you're not too comfortable talking about this . . ." Kneece craned sideways to peer at Harry around a pair of drying pillowcases.

Harry smiled at Kneece.

Kneece flushed.

At home on a Saturday morning, his ears filled with squabbling kids, Harry's legal acuity had not been what it should. But it was coming to him now. The CIC man's presence in his kitchen signified trouble, and Armando Grassi had always been a magnet for trouble.

Harry realized he was being gently, obliquely, but definitely grilled. He'd conducted enough similar interrogatories to know the drill: Keep it civil, keep it roundabout, give no clue as to the true purpose. This keeps the subject from raising his defenses. He'd caught Kneece at the game, and Kneece knew he'd been caught.

Harry returned to his chair. "OK, Captain, what exactly do you need to know?"

"You had some problems with Lootenant Grassi?"

Harry chuckled. "*Everybody* had problems with Lieutenant Grassi. Everybody has a talent, Captain. Some people play the violin, some people dance. Armando's talent was irritating the hell out of people."

"How'd he do that?"

Harry shrugged. Though no fan of Grassi, it was hard to reverse decades of living by the rule: If you have nothing nice to say about someone . . .

"Maybe I can help you out here," Kneece said. "See if any of this sounds right. You tell Grassi to go easy on something, he goes hard. You tell him to keep his trap shut, he opens it. You tell him there's something where his nose doesn't belong, he pokes it in."

"You've been asking around."

"I get the feeling this guy was as popular as a dog full of fleas."

"I wish I'd said that. *That's* Grassi!"

"He musta really rubbed you wrong on that last case."

"What makes you say that?"

Kneece leafed to another page of his notebook. "Well, sir, see, there's this medical record of you with a— Well, I can't read all these fancy Latin names for the bones, but you'd call it a busted hand. And that same day, there's this record for Lootenant Grassi and he's got this busted jaw. So, what I'm figuring, and you please tell me if I'm off base here . . ." He looked up at Harry, eyebrows raised in a question, as he laid his fist alongside his own jaw. "How's the hand, sir?"

Harry self-consciously flexed his right fist. "A little stiff, still."

"Bet the weather bothers it."

"Sometimes."

"Thought it might. Got an uncle, busted his hand in a fight in some honky-tonk years ago when he was a kid. Still gets an ache. Acts up on you, try some warm towels and a little shot of brandy. I don't know that the brandy does anything, but you just don't care as much."

"Is that what this is about? Is Grassi pressing charges—"

"Oh, no, no, sir, sorry if you got that idea, no, sir! Factually, his jaw, it's down here as him slipping in the shower. That was just me doing a little figuring about you two. See, sir, what I'm trying to do is figure out who the lootenant's enemies were."

"You'd do better to ask if he had any friends," Harry told him. "You won't have to take as many notes. Damned near everybody in the London JAG had a beef with Grassi."

"When was the last time you heard from the lootenant?"

"I haven't heard from him at all. Not since I left London."

"Not a word, sir?"

"Nothing."

"Maybe hear about him? Maybe this Peter Ricks fella dropped you a line—"

"I haven't been in touch with anybody from London since I left."

Kneece considered this a moment. "Know where Grassi's been all this time?"

"I presume he's still in England."

Kneece flipped to another page and shook his head. "Godthåb." He pronounced it slowly.

"Where the hell's that?"

"Greenland. So I figure somebody 'sides you in London musta been irritated as hell with Lootenant Grassi. They shipped him out as soon as he could travel. Still had his jaw wired up when they stuck him on the plane. Maybe that same person—or persons—was irritated as hell with you, too, Major, you don't mind my saying, sir."

"How do you figure?"

"Well, I can't get into that case file, that last business you were on in London, but I was told it was closed on twenty-third August. But your transfer orders were cut the morning of the twenty-second, and by that night you were on an OB ship home. Now, factually, that's not a lot to go on, but if I was guessing I'd say you got bumped off that case and somebody else closed it."

"That's a hell of a guess."

"I hope that's a compliment, sir."

"Like I said: I can't discuss—"

"I know, sir, sorry to keep poking at it. I'm just, um . . ." Kneece shook his head, baffled.

"You were asking about Armando's enemies."

"Yessir."

"That usually means . . ."

Kneece showed himself master of what American gamblers call a "poker face." He returned Harry's gaze, his face a model of whatever-could-you-mean innocence.

Harry looked down at the photo of Armando Grassi where it lay by his elbow. He pushed the photo back toward Kneece. "What happened to him?"

"Armando Grassi's dead."

"Yes." Harry took a breath. "I need to ask you a favor."

Kneece nodded.

"I'm sure my Jerry would like to hear every grisly detail."

"You'd like to take this outside, sir?"

Harry nodded. As Kneece drew on his overcoat, Harry pulled his on over his robe, topped their cups off with hot coffee, then led the captain out. In the hallway, he could already hear a clatter down in the stairwell, the coal scuttle clunking along the marble-treaded stairs, and Jerry and Ricky going back and forth:

"You're supposed to help me with this!"

"Nunh-unh. Daddy said for you to do it!"

"You're a stupid jerk!"

"Nunh-unh. You're a stupid jerk!"

"You!"

"You!"

Harry escorted Kneece out onto the porch overlooking the concrete-topped yard, and to the seats by the windows of his flat.

"Hey, Roosk!"

"Hey, Fredo!" Harry called back with a wave to the boy in the yard. He was a little older than Jerry, and playfully jostling for possession of a soccer ball with a man in an odd khaki fatigue uniform. Both were olive-skinned, dark-eyed, and dark-haired. The man looked up at Harry and waved.

"Signor Roosk, buongiórno!"

Little Fredo seized advantage of the man's momentary distraction to scoop the ball away with his foot. But the man swiftly reached out, grabbed Fredo by the waist of his trousers and lifted his feet clear of the ground. "You think I no see, huh?" The man looked back up to Harry. "Hey, Signor Roosk, you think this fish too small, huh? Maybe I throw him back, huh?"

"Maybe, Cosimo."

Cosimo laughed, Fredo laughed, Harry laughed. Cosimo set the boy down on the ground so the dueling over the soccer ball could continue.

Harry took one of the chairs. There were dustbins filled with food tins and bundles of tied newspapers nearby, saved for the salvage drives. Harry pulled a few of the newspaper bundles closer to use as a table and set his coffee cup down.

"These things don't do much for keeping you warm," Kneece said as he pulled on his garrison cap. He jammed his hands far down in his coat pockets, but it didn't stop his shivering.

"You should drink your coffee before it gets cold."

"I suppose you being from around here, you're inured to arctic temperatures. Before I got stationed in Washington, I'd never been any further north than Chapel Hill. Autumn came around, the trees started turning, and I got thinking, 'Well, you know, this is mighty nice. We really been missing something down home.' The air gets a little bite in it and that's all right. I'm thinking it's actually"—a grand delivery, complete with rolled r's—"rrrather brrrracing!" Kneece pulled up his coat collar and shivered again. "Well, then it started getting *cold*."

"You should come back around in February if you want to feel something *really* bracing."

"No, thanks." He looked away, the smile quickly fading.

"Something on your mind, Captain?"

"I was out of line before, making a remark about where you live, and about your neighbors and the like, and then to do it right in a fella's own home. . . . I don't want you thinking my people didn't raise me better. I apologize for any insult to your home or your neighbors."

"It's already forgotten, Captain. I presume Armando Grassi didn't fall in the bathroom this time, otherwise you wouldn't be here."

"Not unless you know some accidental way for somebody to put a bullet through the back of his own head."

It was Harry's turn to feel a chill. "When did this happen?"

"About a week ago."

"You've been on this all that time?"

Kneece frowned down at the man in the khaki fatigues playing with little Fredo. "What uniform is that?" he asked.

"Italian Army."

Kneece looked to Harry, eyebrows raised.

Harry smiled. "There's a holding center for Italian POW's down at Dix. Cosimo was taken in North Africa. He's a cousin to one of the families here in the building. If you're a relative, they'll let you take him home for the day."

"That's awfully free-thinking of them."

"He's no security risk. I don't think any of the POW's are. If Cosimo is any sign, they're a lot happier here than over there right now." Harry squinted up into the azure sky. It was going to be a brilliant December day. "Am I a suspect?"

"Sir?"

"Grassi's murder."

"What makes you think that, sir?"

"You were asking about enemies, when was the last time I heard from him, and so forth."

"Major, sorry if that was the idea you got. Factually, unless you found yourself a way to get out to the Orkney Islands and back without anybody noticing you being gone for a coupla days, I'd say you're in the clear."

"The Orkneys. Where's that?"

"Remember Scapa Flow?"

Harry shrugged.

"Remember when that U-boat torpedoed the *Royal Oak* back in '39? The war's not two weeks old, this kraut sub sneaks into the anchorage for the Royal Navy's home fleet at Scapa Flow and nails this big British bucket? Well, that's in the Orkneys. Just north of Scotland."

"I didn't know we had people stationed there."

"We don't."

"Then what was Grassi—"

Kneece's face took on an aye-there's-the-rub expression.

"Oh," said Harry.

"Yup," Kneece said. "Oh."

As Harry mulled over this new wrinkle, a thought came to him. "We could've done all this on the phone."

"The way it looks, I'm gonna have to go on up to Greenland, see what I can find out around Grassi's stomping grounds. Then I'm gonna have to go on to the Orkneys, see what I can sniff out there. Depending on what I find . . . Well, I've got authorization to go further."

"I hope they're paying you by the mile, Captain."

Kneece's eyes followed the Italian POW and young boy kicking the soccer ball in the yard below. "I went to college in North Carolina. That's where Chapel Hill is. Like I said, except for that, I'd never been out of South Carolina 'til I got posted to D.C. Never been in a plane. Before D.C., never been in a building higher than five stories. I guess that all sounds funny to you."

"I'm ready for the punch line, Captain."

Kneece turned to Harry. "I'd like you to come with me, sir."

Harry could only imagine the reaction on his face because the next thing Kneece said was, "No, I'm not joking, Major. It's already cleared. I've got the authority from Washington and permission from your CO at Dix, but it's up to you."

"Why the hell would you want me—"

"Because I may have this hotshot CIC identification card, but I'm just a country cop. Damn, Major, you're the second-highest-ranking person I've ever dealt with on this job, and I already put my foot in it with you. If I wind up poking around London HQ . . . Major, you know the ropes. You know who's who over there, how to deal with the big brass. You know all the right things to say, and what not to say, and to who and—"

"Hold on a second, Captain. Believe me, you're overestimating my—"

"OK, then, it's this simple." Kneece sounded urgent, desperate. "You've been there. I haven't. You knew Grassi. I didn't. I need your help."

Harry shook his head. The request was comical and pathetic at the same time. "Somebody must've put you up to this."

"No, sir, nobody."

"Did somebody 'suggest' me? Make a 'recommendation'?"

"This is my case, Major. I'm looking at what I know about this thing so far, and of the names that pop up, you look like the best bet to help me here."

"Captain, you're a conscientious SOB, I'll give you that." Harry sighed. "Well, as you say, I've been there. You haven't. So if you really want the benefit of my experience . . . I've been across the North Atlantic during winter once, Captain, and that's not an experience I want to repeat. I spent the whole trip being sick as a dog and sweating out the wolfpacks. When I shipped home in August, I just missed the U-boats being sent back out by a few weeks. My oldest boy thinks I missed having a hell of a story to tell, but I'll tell you just what I told him: I like being a bore."

"No convoy. Monday morning I pick up an ATC flight out of Newark ferrying cargo to Greenland and then on to Reykjavik. From there, I've got authorization to commandeer that transport as far as London."

"Somebody's putting an awful lot of muscle behind you, Captain."

Kneece nodded and Harry was intrigued: Kneece was as suspicious of that muscle as Harry. "My people are saying, 'Go get 'em,' so I'm going. I don't know anything for sure past that because nobody's saying anything past that. But if I was to guess, I'd figure our people are in a sweat because they can't figure out how some JAG looey who's supposed to be pulling his time in Greenland winds up shot dead a thousand miles away. That's a security hole you could drive a Sherman tank through. And the Brits are all het up 'cause that dead looey turns up on the front lawn of one of their biggest Navy installations. They're still looking over their shoulder from that business with the *Royal Oak.* I'm told both Scotland Yard and British counterintelligence are on this already. Maybe you're right: In the end, Grassi probably just rubbed some fella the wrong way and that's all there is to it. But brass on both sides of the water want to *know* before they let this thing rest. I know I'm asking a lot, Major."

You have no idea, Harry thought.

"I got a bunk at a BOQ at the airfield. I'm heading there now. Why don't you think it over, maybe give me a call sometime tomorrow." Kneece took a last slurp and nodded. "Ah, I let it get cold. Shame. I thank you for your time, Major. Sorry to have bothered you at home."

Glass shattered inside Harry's flat. Then the voices of the boys:

"Oh-oh! Dad's gonna kill you!"

"Nunh-unh! He's gonna kill *you!*"

Kneece smiled. "I think you better get on in there, sir." Then the captain's arm rose and fell in something between a salute and a wave good-bye before he disappeared into the hallway.

As Harry reentered his flat to break up his squabbling sons, he noticed that the identification photo of Armando Grassi still lay on the kitchen table. He picked up the small, cracked photo, regarded the halo of wild curls, the mischievous eyes.

Days later he shared his chagrin with me. "Dead a week and half a world away," Harry told me, shaking his head in amazement, "and the son of a bitch was still a pain in my arse."

Late that night, Harry quietly slipped out from under the bedclothes, careful not to disturb Cynthia, pulled on his robe and slippers, and tiptoed through the chilly rooms into a kitchen still shrouded with drying linens. He dropped a few coals on the lowering fire, poured himself a glass of milk from the icebox, and sat at the table in the darkened room.

Then, Cynthia was there, sitting across from him. He only then realized that she, too, had been lying awake. Earlier that day, he had told her of Kneece's visit, but not his request. Still, they'd had too many years together for her not to feel this *something* hanging over him all that day, and for the same reason, he knew she knew. But, as was her way, she didn't press him.

They exchanged a smile, his apologetic, hers understanding. She said nothing, simply held out her hand for his glass of milk and took a sip before handing it back.

He reached into his robe for his cigarettes, lit one. He watched the smoke curl upward into the shadows.

"Well." He sighed.

"Well," she said.

He reached into his bathrobe pocket for the photograph of Armando Grassi and set it on the table.

"That's him?"

He nodded. She took his matches from the table, struck one, and held the photo near the flame for study.

And then he told her.

He was about to explain those reasons Kneece had given him to justify the madness of leaving his safe home, and all those perfectly sane reasons for staying, when she leaned over, silenced him with a kiss, then led him by the hand back to bed.

PART TWO

COLCHIS

CHAPTER FOUR

THE GOLDEN BOAT

"Major, you really have got to look at this!"

"I don't think I do, really." Harry kept his eyes glued to the arched roof of the C-47 Dakota.

"You're missing something," Woody Kneece warned.

"I don't think so." The squares of sunlight coming through the aeroplane's windows wavered on the roof, then Harry felt one of the wings dip and the squares danced their way along the curve of the fuselage as his back pressed against the side of the ship. "Oooohhhh . . ."

"You OK, Major?" It was the flight mechanic, a sergeant less than half Harry's age.

Harry forced a smile and a nod, afraid that if he opened his mouth to respond he might vomit.

"Wow . . ." an awed Woody Kneece said, his voice hushed. Harry could feel the captain nearby on the bench that ran the length of the Dakota's cargo compartment, hunched round to press his face near one of the small fuselage windows. The pilot, once clear of the cinder runway, had steered the ship in a lazy, rising turn, taking it out over Port Newark, then back round the southern edge of Manhattan. The harbor waters had fallen away beneath them, becoming a distant rippled sheet flecked with whitecaps, marked by the curlicues of wakes from dozens of ships maneuvering in and out of their harbor slips, and the broad-shouldered tugs assisting them. Within the frame of gray water and porcupine frill of piers was the finger of southern Manhattan, its towers wreathed in ten-drils of vapor from countless steam vents, chimneys, and smokestacks.

"From up here kinda reminds me of the Emerald City," Kneece said. "He going to fly us over? That'd be something, flying over the Empire State."

"Too much cargo," the flight mechanic said. "We can't get that high."

"Man, that poor King Kong had a looong way to fall, didn't he?"

The aeroplane dipped its wing again; at the lurch, Harry squeezed his eyes shut and grabbed the bench, holding it so hard his fingertips hurt.

"Major?"

Harry felt a diplomatically light touch on his arm. He forced his eyes open: the flight mechanic stood over him. The sergeant's cherubic young face had a preternaturally sage air to it, as if he'd been through this many times, both Kneece's exuberance and Harry's rigid fear.

"You need a bucket or somethin', Major?"

"No, thanks, Sergeant, I'm fine."

"You let me know."

The craft leveled off, and the engines settled from the strain of the climb into a steady hum.

"Damn, I shoulda brought a camera!" Kneece moaned, almost in pain. He stumbled across Harry—"Excuse that, Major, sorry"—as he headed for the rear of the cargo compartment, threading his way among the packing crates to get a last glimpse of Manhattan falling behind.

"If man were meant to fly, huh, Major?" The sergeant said it without sarcasm or malice. "Tell you the truth, I'm not that crazy 'bout flyin' my-self." The flight mechanic saw the doubt on Harry's face and nodded. "No, really. I was just a gas jockey back home—that's Minnesota—and liked to mess with engines. How I got from messin' with Mr. Dobie's Model T to this, I'm not quite sure. I still like messin' with 'em, 'n' if it makes you feel better some, those Pratt and Whitneys are the best. But I'd just as soon mess with 'em on the ground."

"Where are we?" Kneece called from his vantage in the rear of the ship.

"That should be Connecticut down there."

"Man, it doesn't take long, does it? New York, then Connecticut, really covering some miles!"

The flight mechanic smiled his sage smile. "Well, Cap'n, we got a long ways to go yet."

Below were bands of barren trees, glades of faded grass, rivulets and streams sparkling with the early sun. There were patchwork squares of farms with their clapboard houses, weathered barns and fallow acres set off by low walls of piled fieldstone. The pastoral scenery gliding by a few thousand feet below reminded Harry of the miniature scenery he set along the rails of his sons' electric trains.

"How you feelin' now, sir?"

Harry smiled at the flight mechanic to let him know he was doing better.

"Bucket's always there if you need it, sir. Don't be afraid to call for it."

"Thank you, Sergeant."

"If you or the captain feel like it, there's a thermos of coffee up forward and some sandwiches. Now, if you don't mind, sir, I'm gonna catch some sack time. We haven't had a day on the ground since last week. Just yesterday we made the round trip to Presque Isle, and the day 'fore that we were hustling up and down Labrador way."

Harry nodded at Kneece, who was now bouncing from one side of the cargo compartment to the other, trying to see all there was to see. "I'll make sure he doesn't disturb you."

The Dakota carried auxiliary long-range rubber fuel tanks within the body of the aeroplane. A plywood table sat over the tanks, and from the charts splayed thereon Harry guessed it was used for navigational purposes. The sergeant cleared away the charts and clambered aboard, using a parachute pack for his pillow and his flight jacket as a blanket. Within seconds, the flight mechanic was—enviably, in Harry's view—asleep.

As the aeroplane continued northward without incident, and the Pratt & Whitney engines the flight mechanic took such pride in thrummed with a comforting steadiness, Harry's mood began to ease.

The ship's wireless operator, sitting before his set in his nest behind the pilot, brought out a guitar. The Air Transportation Command was a hybrid entity; military personnel wrapped round a core of civilian volunteers from the commercial airlines, which explained why the flight mechanic wore olive drab coveralls and sergeant stripes while the guitar-picking Sparks was attempting to stay warm inside a bulky Northwestern University pullover.

"You mind?" Woody Kneece asked, and Sparks handed the instrument over. "Let me show you." Kneece began running his fingers smoothly through the same chord progressions Sparks had been fumbling with.

Sparks shook his head, marveling at the captain's fluid movements. "My hand just won't go that way."

"It's fighting you because it doesn't know it can do this. You keep practicing and it'll learn the moves. After a while, you won't even have to think about it."

The Dakota's captain was a bear of a man named Doheeny, about Harry's age, and so big Harry couldn't see how he fit his broad-shouldered bulk into the cramped confines of the cockpit. Now Doheeny squeezed between the cockpit seats into the cargo compartment. "I thought I detected a musical improvement." In his plaid flannel shirt and twill work trousers, the captain seemed more roughneck lumberjack than aviator, the only symbol of his station being the crushed cap from his airline days. But his deep voice had an unexpected softness. Doheeny set one of his massive paws on Sparks's shoulder. "See what happens when you practice?"

"Well, I gotta be truthful," Kneece said. "Any good Southern family of means wants their kids to look cultured. Doesn't matter if they're dumb as cotton bales, as long as they look cultured. This way, when ladies and gents from Charleston society come to call, you can truck out the little fella and show 'im off."

"What's that?" Sparks asked as Kneece's random strumming turned into a melodic plucking.

"Some kinda Mozart, I think. Now me and my family had different ideas of culture. I'd get tired setting in that parlor playing for Miz Francie and Mr. Seville and whomsoever. So, late at night"—a dramatic strike of the strings—"when all are snuggled tight in their big ol' brass beds"—another strike—"Li'l Woody'd sneak out over to Buck Town, go down to them nasty ol' juke joints where the colored boys'll let you sit in if you can syncopate a little"—another strike, his voice lowering into something playfully lewd—"a little *boogie-woogie!*" Kneece's fingers began to jump about the guitar's strings, tickling up a boogie beat. Kneece was on his feet now, though he had to stoop his tall frame to accommodate the curved roof of the aeroplane. "If you can truck a little at the same time"—Kneece's feet began to move in jitterbug steps—"show 'em a little jig-walk, some short George, you got 'em clappin' with you now, they're sayin', 'Hey, that white boy ain't too bad, pour him a little hooch, why dontcha!'" Climaxing with a few hard strums, Kneece stood frozen with an absurd leer on his face. "And I'm thinkin' if Mama and Daddy could see me now, givin' some colored patootie the round-your-back . . ." A hand clutched at his chest as he fell to the deck of the cargo compartment making choking sounds, then kicking his feet in cartoon fashion before falling into an exaggerated rigor. After a dramatic beat, he sat up with a grin. "Then Li'l Woody gets his inheritance early."

Doheeny applauded—"Bravo!"—Sparks laughed, and even Harry forgot they were thousands of feet in the air long enough to smile. Kneece went back to helping Sparks work his way through his chord practice, and Doheeny made his way back toward Harry, stopping for a moment by the sleeping flight mechanic. There was something in the way Doheeny stood over the young sergeant that made Harry think he was going to caress the boy's head, much as Harry had often tousled the hair of his own sleeping sons.

"Shame he missed the show," Harry said.

"Stripes here taking good care of you?" Doheeny asked. Harry noticed that the Dakota captain rarely—if at all—called any of his crewmen by name.

"Fine. He's a good kid."

"It's a good crew." Doheeny lowered himself on the bench beside Harry. "How're you doing, Major? I couldn't help but notice when you climbed aboard you looked like somebody climbing the gallows."

Harry shrugged. "OK."

"We're about halfway to Presque Isle. When we touch down, I'd appreciate it if you fellas stay on the ship. I just want to check in at Ops, top off on fuel, and be off. I want to make White Pigeon—that's the call sign for the field at Goose Bay—I want to be there before dark."

"Is it that far?"

"This time of year it gets dark early up there. I'd like to avoid a night landing if I could."

"Difficult?"

"Let's just say at this stage of the game, me and my wife'd rather I keep my challenges to a minimum."

"Hey, is that snow? Look at it all!" Kneece was again glued to a window.

Harry turned. Below, bare, dark trees stood out like charcoal strokes against an undulating white blanket. Between pillowy drifts, creeks and streams and ponds shone like polished glass as their iced surfaces caught the midmorning sun.

"Where are we, Cap'n?" Kneece asked giddily.

"New Hampshire. We should be over Maine in a few minutes." Doheeny turned to Harry. "Excitable young fella, isn't he?"

Harry smiled. "First time seeing snow."

"What's going on down there?"

Far off, Harry saw the glittering circle of a frozen lake set snugly between soft banks of snow covered with firs. Small human figures, dark against the glowing ice, scrambled about, sometimes forming a heaving knot that would abruptly break apart, then the figures would dart to another spot on the ice, where they would repeat the process.

"Hockey," Doheeny said.

Kneece laughed. "Ice skaters? I feel like I'm flying into Currier and Ives!"

Doheeny straightened and set his hand on Kneece's shoulder with a smile. "Enjoy it, son, because I guarantee you the novelty of this moment will not last."

"I've got Presque Isle's beacon," Sparks announced, pressing his kapok-cushioned earphones close. "We're maybe a half hour out."

The terrain below had grown rougher: sharp hills forming a maze of twisted ravines, their flanks covered with scrub and hunched firs whose boughs sagged under snow. Icicled outcroppings of granite poked through the thick, white coating. And nowhere a sign of man: no stone-walled farms, no spire of a church poking above the treeline, not even the track of a rural lane through the forest.

It was an inhospitable place, whipped by gusts of wind Harry could feel rocking the C-47.

"Next stop, Presque Isle!" The copilot was a sleepy-eyed sort, almost dwarfish in stature. Harry thought he'd been paired with Doheeny be-cause only such a small person could fit in the cockpit space alongside the captain. "Show your ticket stubs for all meals and beverages!"

A band of ice, blazing like frozen fire under the winter sun, wandered down from the hills, guiding Harry's eyes to what he at first thought was nothing but a collection of snowdrifts along the riverbank. But curls of smoke from stubby little chimneys told him the drifts were the snow-covered roofs of a riverside hamlet.

"They cut down everything for firewood?" Kneece asked, noting the treeless hills.

"Potatoes," the flight mechanic answered. "They clear the ground for potato farms. All this part of the state, that's all it is is potatoes. Miles and miles of 'em."

Kneece chuckled. "Purple mountain majesties, amber waves of grain . . . and spuds."

The aerodrome stood near rail tracks just outside the collection of roofs. As the Dakota turned onto its landing path, Harry could see a rail engine, puffing black smoke, while a relay chain of small human figures off-loaded one of the attached freight cars straight into the cargo cabin of another Dakota.

There was a rumble and the Dakota shuddered—"Just the wheels comin' down, sir," the flight mechanic soothed—and then Doheeny set the ship down as tenderly as anyone can set down twenty tons of heavily laden metal on a narrow snow-cleared strip of tarmac. As the plane slowed, a jeep sped out from a cluster of clapboard buildings and Quonset huts nearby and took a position in front of the Dakota, leading it off to a parking area.

The plane halted, the crew pulled on parkas, and the flight mechanic was off to supervise refueling. Sparks went to check with the field's Communications shack, Doheeny and his copilot to the Operations shack for information on weather ahead. The interior of the Dakota chilled rapidly in a wind that pushed the frigid temperature below zero, and twenty minutes later, once airborne, the flight mechanic offered them something wonderfully warming and aromatic from a thermos.

"From the mess hall," he said. "Lobster bisque. Up here they know a dozen ways to make lobster, and a thousand things to do with potatoes."

As they sipped at their thermos cups of soup, the copilot turned round to call back: "As of now, you two guys are international travelers."

"We're in Canada?" Kneece twisted for another look out the windows.

"It's not gonna be much different, Cap'n," the flight mechanic told him. "Just colder."

The copilot was taking his turn on the cot-cum-navigation table, leaving Doheeny alone in the cockpit. The flight mechanic sat with Sparks, whiling away the flying time with hands of gin rummy.

A bored Woody Kneece sat across the cabin from Harry, absently picking at the strings of Sparks's guitar. "How many times you hear me say today I wished I had a camera?"

"I lost track after one hundred and sixty-two."

"Right now I'd trade that camera for a magazine or a book or something. Still, I'll bet this is better than your boat ride, huh, Major?"

"It's dryer."

Kneece chuckled. He tilted his head back against the fuselage, musing. "I keep thinking they skedaddled you out of London so fast to make that boat home, I'll bet you barely had time to pack."

"Barely."

"That last case, that file was still open when you left. That didn't bother you, leaving an open case like that?"

"I had other things on my mind just then."

"Did you know somebody else was going to sign off on it?"

"When I got around to thinking about it, I assumed as much."

"That didn't bother you? Somebody else closing your case?"

"A case closes. You go on to the next one. Captain, the file may have been open when I left London, but that case was *over*."

"Investigation kinda dead-ended?"

August came back to Harry for a passing, mordant moment. "That's a good way of putting it. Dead end."

"I wonder what Grassi and this fella Ricks thought about that? If they felt the same way as you? The way everybody makes Grassi out, I can't see him quitting on anything, even if all the cards were played out."

"I don't know what Grassi and Ricks thought. I never asked them."

"You guys all served together. I figured you'd at least drop a line to say hello. Not about the case or anything. Just, well, you know."

A memory, very specific now: Peter Ricks, sitting with Harry in his darkened quarters, Harry much further into a liter of scotch than was good for him, Ricks's face an unhappy combination of frustration, resignation, defeat.

"When I left," Harry told Kneece, "I don't think any of us had anything to say to each other. You keep going back to that case, Captain."

"I haven't asked you about the case, sir. That's privileged, you said."

"You're asking me about everything about that damned case but that damned case, Captain."

Kneece struck a final chord on the guitar and let the notes hang in the air until they faded into the drone of the engines. Carefully, he set the guitar on the bench, then stepped across the cabin and sat beside Harry. "I'm just trying my best to figure this thing out. I got this uncle—"

"The one with the broken hand?"

"Yup, same one. He's with the po-lice back home. There's a view that that kind of truck is a little *déclassé* for family hands." Kneece made as if to flick soot from his fingertips. "But, seeing as Uncle Ray—that's his name, Ray—Uncle Ray's from my mama's side, not in the bloodline, they live with it. Even let him sit in the front room when he comes by. But, see, I like ol' Uncle Ray. Sometimes in the summer he'd take me around in his patrol car. And I guess watching him at work, it kinda took with me, enough so's I left North Carolina for what we call the State Constabulary, which didn't make Daddy or Mama too happy. I learned a lot about how to do the job from Uncle Ray. I mean, it's not like we were big-city cops or G-men or something. Somebody gets drunk, throws a punch, somebody pulls down somebody's fence because he figures it's on his side of the line, somebody's running a little shine—"

"Shine?"

"Moonshine."

"I thought that went out with Prohibition."

"People still like the taste of shine when it's cheaper than taxed likker, Major. But what I'm saying is maybe the worst that happens is once in a while, somebody grabs his rabbit gun and peppers some fella's bee-hind he found out is diddling his sweetie. But even when it's small-time, Uncle Ray taught me there's always three pieces to the puzzle: who did it, why'd he do it, and—"

"What'd he do."

Kneece grinned. "Now, according to Uncle Ray, the *what* is usually pretty easy. Somebody broke in and took the family silver, that's a *what*. And if you know *who*, Uncle Ray says you can pretty much figure out *why*. But if you don't know *who*—"

"*Why* gives you *who*."

"You sure you don't know Uncle Ray? Sounds like you heard this before. Well, Uncle Ray's formula doesn't work every time, but it's a good way to start."

"This is all a roundabout way of saying what? That you think your 'why' is in my case back in August?"

"I figure you, and Armando Grassi, and this Captain Peter Ricks musta got some pretty high-up people awful riled. And scared, too."

"Scared? How do you figure that?"

"Look at how fast they shot you out of England. Did you know they had Ricks on a troop transport into the Mediterranean within twenty-four hours of shipping you out?"

"No, I didn't."

"And soon as Grassi was well enough to travel—zip! Ricks into the Mediterranean; Grassi to Greenland; you back to the States. They put y'all where y'all couldn't cause any more trouble. And they put a lotta space between you, like they didn't want you talking to each other."

"I wouldn't think the States is a place to send someone where you don't want him to make trouble. Awfully close to Washington." He wasn't trying to shut Kneece's musing down now, just testing the theorem.

"Unless that someone is so happy to be Stateside. You were happy to be Stateside, weren't you, sir? I mean, if I had a wife, a coupla kids . . ."

"That's a lot of impressive supposition, Captain."

"We've got a lotta miles to go yet, Major, and calling me 'Captain' all that time is gonna rub me like a stiff collar. What say you make it 'Woody.' "

"OK, Woody. Good thinking. But you're wrong. Let me tell you something about the case in August you don't know. It was over before I ever climbed on that boat. You think maybe Armando Grassi got himself killed trying to pick up a loose end from that case? There were no loose ends. That case had as dead an end as you can get."

"White Pigeon"—the aerodrome at Goose Bay—sat approximately one hundred fifty miles from the Labrador coast, near where the head of the Hamilton Inlet narrowed to become the Hamilton River. The airfield was a single, busy landing strip and a scattering of clapboard buildings.

Bound on all sides by pine forest and snow from one horizon to the other, Goose Bay promised even fewer creature comforts and distractions than Presque Isle, six hundred miles south.

Harry looked at his watch, then back out the window to the rapidly advancing dusk. "This can't be right," he said, tapping his watch. "This says it's not even four."

"You ever hear that bit about the Land of the Midnight Sun, Major? Well, that's in the summer. In the winter, it's just the Land of Midnight. Summer, the sun hardly goes down; winter, it hardly comes up."

The Dakota fell into a lazy circle above the landing strip. On the runway below, Harry saw another Dakota, its propellers revving to invisibility before it began rolling down the tarmac.

As Harry's C-47 circled the far side of the field, he noticed a jumble of scrap wood, tins, and the multicolored spreads he assumed were food trash. The camp dump, he guessed, and moving through it were burly shapes, paradoxically hulking and pillowy white. It wasn't until one of the shapes sat back on its hindquarters and buried its blunt snout in an upended packing crate that Harry could make them out.

"They like to go through the garbage," the flight mechanic told him. "It's like a smorgasbord for them."

"Polar bears?" It was Kneece, returning to his earlier enthusiasm. "Are those real polar bears? Funnier looking than I'd've figured."

"Yeah, they look kinda cute from up here, Captain. But do yourself a favor and don't go bumpin' into one."

The other Dakota rose slowly to an altitude close to where Harry's ship was circling, then made a shallow bank to the south. "Headin' home," the flight mechanic explained.

A few minutes later they were on the ground. The flight mechanic was reaching for the hatch, but Doheeny stopped him with a shout as he hauled himself out of the cockpit. "Stripes! Don't you dare open that door until you're in uniform!"

Grumbling, Doheeny's crew followed the captain's example, reaching into their parka pockets and coming out with Santa Claus caps: red, a trim of faux white fur, a furry white ball attached to each flopping peak. Doheeny went them all one better, attaching a tatty Santa Claus beard to his ears.

"C'mon, Sarge, get that headgear on. And hand me the mailbag!" Doheeny took a stand by the hatchway, mailbag on shoulder, a thick-leafed sprig in his other hand.

"What's that?" his flight mechanic asked.

"Mistletoe!" Doheeny grinned. "Real mistletoe! I picked it up back at

Presque Isle!" He beckoned the flight mechanic to swing open the door. Though a blast of frigid air nearly took away his ragged prop beard and sent Harry and Kneece deep into their overcoats, Doheeny stood in the doorway with his Christmas cheer unperturbed.

"Ho! Ho! Ho!" Doheeny declared, holding the mistletoe over his head. "Which one of you good little boys has a kiss for Santa?"

A voice from outside: "Hey, Sanny Claus! Kiss this!"

The Negro cook in the mess hall offered them a choice of breakfast, lunch, or dinner: this was clearly a twenty-four-hour operation. The air crews and field personnel now eating—some in civilian garb, some in the uniform of the U.S. Army, and some wearing Royal Canadian Air Force blue—ranged from the bright-eyed and fresh-shaven to the red-eyed and bewhiskered, some almost dozing over their plates.

Above the mess counter was a row of drawings, crayon-rendered holiday pictorials in the splashy style of young children. Most featured a stick-figure family waving hullo before the living room Christmas tree, though there were more fanciful artistic endeavors, such as one featuring Father Christmas astraddle an Army cargo aeroplane being tugged through the skies by the requisite complement of reindeer. Most were addressed to "Daddy," though there was one to "Cousin Sonny," another to "Uncle Bob," and one to "THE BEST BRUTHER IN THE WURLD!!!!"

"Come wit' da Christmas mail!" the cook informed Harry. He pointed to a drawing featuring a man with his face colored in brown crayon, a massive mushroom-shaped appendage on his head, standing next to a more recognizable depiction of Father Christmas. "Das from my daughter 'Lores. See dat? She thinks I'm all a way up at da North Pole wit' Sanny Claus!"

Harry and Kneece, each carrying a bowl of the dinner stew, joined Doheeny where he sat with his crew. Despite the ovens and the potbellied stove at the other end of the mess, Harry and Kneece kept their coats on. The flyers had shucked their parkas, but still wore their leather aviator jackets.

Kneece smacked his lips over his first taste of the stew. "Damn, this is good!" His eyes narrowed in calculation. "What is that? Tastes a little like venison."

"Probably caribou," Doheeny replied. "They trade the Eskimos for it."

"Those polar bear steaks they get sometimes are good eatin', too," the second pilot said. "Especially the way Sambo there fixes 'em," and he nodded at the cook.

Kneece leaned over to Doheeny and discreetly whispered, nodding at the copilot, who munched on a thick wimpy as he paced round and round the table. "Is there some reason he won't sit with us?"

"Hey, Junior!" Doheeny called to the circling copilot. "The captain here wants to know why you don't sit down."

The copilot licked at the grease bleeding from the sandwich onto his hand. "I spend the better part of every day with my arse in a cockpit seat. I'm not sitting now."

"My fellas are going to be hitting the sack early," Doheeny told Harry and Kneece. "We're going for takeoff at 0300. You fellas can always catch up on your sleep on the plane."

"Why so early?" Kneece groaned.

"Where we're going, they've only got a couple of hours' light each day. So, we have a choice. Take off in the light, land in the dark, take off in the dark, land in the light, but there's no way to do both. And Bluie-West-One—that's the field we're going for—it's kind of dicey getting in there on a good day. If I can, I prefer going in there with daylight, particularly since we don't know what the weather's going to be like."

"Which, this being winter, is pretty crappy a lot of the time," the copilot contributed.

Doheeny nodded. "I checked in with Ops and they've been out of radio contact with Bluie-West-One for four days, and haven't been able to raise anybody in Greenland in two. Could be weather interference, or maybe some of the transmission towers are down. This time of year . . ." He shrugged, as if to say such circumstances were the norm. "I'd prefer to wait until we heard from them, but since this is a priority flight, well . . ."

"So it's an early reveille," Kneece concluded good-naturedly.

They could hear the cough and sputter of an engine start-up outside, then another, setting the tableware rattling on the table.

"Where do they all go?" Kneece asked.

"East is Greenland. Some go west, making for Alaska. Some north; there's other fields up the Labrador coast."

"Captain," Harry asked, "I don't know if it's a security thing or not, but can I ask what you're carrying that makes our flight a priority?"

Doheeny smiled broadly. "You and your captain."

Harry turned to Kneece, seeking clarification, but Kneece's attention seemed to be on his bowl of caribou stew.

"Cap'n, that cargo we got is pretty important, too," Sparks said.

"Vital to the war effort," the copilot said.

"Couldn't fight the war without it," Sparks said. "Why don't you tell these guys what they're sharing their urgent priority with?"

Doheeny chuckled and turned to his flight bag. "I happen to have the manifest right here. Let's see," and he flipped through the flimsies on a clipboard. "Desks, desk chairs, twelve typewriters, and the rest of this considerable poundage is miscellaneous office supplies: pens, pencils, erasers, typewriter ribbons, paper, and, let's see, six, seven, hm, twelve different forms."

"Forms?" Kneece asked.

"Can't fight a war without having the right requisition forms, Captain. Didn't they teach you that in officer's training? That's why we're also carrying all this carbon paper."

"You need those triplicate copies," Sparks said.

"I thought they wanted quintuples now," the copilot said.

"I must've missed that memo," Sparks said. "Didn't get my copy."

"That's because they were only doing triplicates," the copilot said.

The three flyers shared a teammates' laugh.

The second pilot and Sparks drifted off to their sleeping quarters; Kneece soon followed. "I'm not used to an evening nap, but I'll see if I can force my eyes closed for a couple hours."

Doheeny swabbed the last of his bacon and eggs clean with a last bit of toast, then leaned back in his chair and lit a cigarette. "No bed for you, Major Voss? You a fellow night owl?"

"Sometimes it's hard for me to sleep when I'm away from home."

Doheeny nodded. "Can I get you a cup of coffee?" He fetched two cups from the urn at the mess counter. "This your first time going over?" He extended a lit match as Harry drew one of his own cigarettes.

"First time by plane," Harry answered. "I was in London for a while."

"You don't look like the kind of guy who's off hunting medals. How'd they sucker you into going back?"

"Business."

Doheeny nodded. He'd been carting military personnel long enough to know not to pry when information wasn't volunteered. "There's no reason we can't make this a little less formal." He held out a hand. "Jim."

"Harry. Can I ask you something, Jim? How'd they sucker you?"

"You mean into this Army aerial bus service?" Doheeny smiled. "You fly for the airlines, pushing bodies here to there, that's just being a flying cabbie. Remember: it wasn't so long ago, a lot of these fellas had a stick in their hands when flying was still more an adventure than a business. Some of them miss that kind of fun. And some of them . . . I don't like to use the word mercenary. The airlines have a seniority system. This gets the younger guys out from under, gives them a chance to command their own ship. And you're wondering which of those is me."

"A man always looking to minimize his challenges doesn't strike me as someone who misses barnstorming. And you look like you've been around long enough not to worry about seniority."

"I'd been flying with the line almost ten years. I'm pretty secure."

"So is it patriotism?"

Doheeny let out a curt laugh. "I lost my patriotic fervor a long time ago, Harry. Don't get me wrong. I'm all for America winning and apple pie. I was a flyer in the first war, the Great War. I was with Rickenbacker in the old hat-in-the-ring squadron."

"You're kidding!"

"Sounds more impressive than it was. I only made the last few weeks of the war. Not long enough to do any damage or get any damage done to me. But it *was* long enough to get the bejeebers scared out of me. After that, I thought, 'Next time, I'll go if they ask me, but I'm not volunteering.' "

"And this time they asked you?"

"You have any children, Harry?"

"Two."

Doheeny fumbled out his billfold, pulled out a small photograph. "Michael Sean. We named him after my father, and my wife's father. That was taken when he was nineteen." Harry saw a slight but handsome young man in Navy whites. Doheeny nodded. "I know. You'd never guess he was my boy. Those are his mom's looks."

"Same with me. Ricky and Jerry." Harry turned over a photo of his own two.

Doheeny was careful to wipe his hands clean before touching the photo. "Good-looking boys, Harry. Miss 'em?"

"A lot."

"Michael Sean always had a bug in his ear about flying. Why not? I was flying the mail when he was born, then I was with the airline. He even took some trips with me. And he knew about my days with Rickenbacker. You know how that kind of thing makes an impression on a kid. Well, when the war broke out, he wanted to be like his old man and be a dashing young fighter pilot. But he couldn't cut the vision test. I can't say me and his mom weren't relieved over that. But Michael was determined. Stubborn like his mom, too. When the Air Corps turned him down, he tried the Marines, then the Navy. He couldn't make it into the pilot's seat, but his eyes *were* good enough for him to make radio/gunner on a Devastator. He was with one of *Saratoga's* torpedo squadrons at Coral Sea." Doheeny took the photo back from Harry and slid it carefully back into its place in his billfold. He held the billfold in his hand, the thumb caressing the cracked leather. "Even after a year and a half Mary Margaret keeps thinking he'll turn up somehow. Missing isn't dead, she thinks. So, he was at Coral Sea while I was bussing businessmen to Cleveland. Now I do this. It helps me live with that."

Harry looked down at the photo of his own two boys a long time before he slid it back into his billfold.

"How old are they?" Doheeny asked.

"Eight and six."

"Pray for a short war, Harry."

The Dakota followed the Hamilton Inlet to the coast, a strip of glossy blackness between two shadowy shoulders of forest. Over the Atlantic, the aeroplane banked into a more north-northeasterly track. Once settled in on course, Doheeny turned the controls over to his copilot and went back to the cargo cabin.

Kneece was sitting with Sparks, passing the time on another guitar lesson. The flight mechanic was, again, snoring on the navigation table.

"When did that poor guy get to sleep?" Harry asked.

"Probably not until five minutes after takeoff." Doheeny shivered. "Little chilly, hm? Afraid not much heat gets back here, and it's not going to get better. I see my little guy took care of you." He meant their parkas, procured for them from the Goose Bay stores.

"It was no fun stripping down to climb into the long johns he got us."

"Let me get you guys something to warm your insides." Doheeny poured them each a mug of something steaming from a thermos by the navigation table.

Harry caught a sweet whiff. "Hot chocolate?"

"Where the hell did you get this?" Kneece demanded, his face, in closed-eye trance, lingering over the aromatic vapors curling out of his cup. "I don't think I've seen even a Tootsie Roll in six months."

Doheeny nodded at the snoring flight mechanic. "I don't know where he scrounges it, I don't know how, and I don't ask. I just always make sure to say thank you and let him know it's appreciated. If you want to see more of this, I recommend you do the same." He sat next to Harry. "Sleep well?"

They shared a chuckle. "Probably about as well as you."

"The place seemed pretty busy last night," Doheeny mused.

"It's not always like that?"

"Not like last night. That was a lot of traffic in and out. Something's up somewhere." Doheeny let the subject go with a shrug, and turned back to Sparks. "Hey, Junior, bravo!" he called out, nodding as the wireless operator forced his fingers into unaccustomed curls round the neck of the guitar. "You're sounding a hundred percent better already! Good work, kiddo!"

Sparks bowed his head sharply, a cartoon of a Philharmonic soloist acknowledging applause.

"Very nice," Doheeny said. "What is it?"

"Another 'some kinda Mozart'?" Harry asked.

"Some kinda Bach this time," Kneece said.

Doheeny shook his head appreciatively. "By the time we get where we're going, we're going to be the most cultured sons of bitches in the North Atlantic!"

The flight mechanic was still prostrate on the navigation table, and now Sparks was dozing in his chair in front of his set and Kneece was stretched out on the bench seat. The only noise in the cargo cabin was the humming of the engines, and Kneece's snoring.

Harry sat with a pad of foolscap in his lap. In his law studies days, he had developed a trick of analysis for himself. He would boil each component of the issue at hand—a known fact, a rumor, a speculation, even questions—down to some elemental phrase, write it on an index card, and continue until the entire matter was thus reduced to its basal parts. He could then—literally—lay the case out in front of him, like a puzzle, taking it all in at a glance. He would move a piece here and there until sections of the picture began to form.

Index cards were a bit impractical in the cargo cabin, but foolscap would suffice. On the paper he had written:

GRASSI/GREENLAND

GREENLAND DUTIES?

GREENLAND CONTACTS?

LEFT WHEN/HOW?

GRASSI DEAD ORKNEYS

ORKNEY CONTACTS?

RICKS

After a moment's hesitation, he penned one more note:

LONDON AUGUST

For some time he stared at the notations on the page, but there were too few pieces to toy with, and too many of those contained question marks.

"What's so distracting is all the racket he's making!" Doheeny was crouched over Kneece's sprawled shape, trying to sight his octant through one of the aeroplane's windows. "This is hard enough, and I've never exactly been an ace at it."

Harry looked for a sign that this was intended humorously. To his dismay, he saw none. "What happens if we miss?"

"I don't have to get us on the money, Harry. Just close enough to pick up a radio beacon. Providing the beacon's working and the tower hasn't been blown down. You want to see something that takes the mystique out of celestial navigation?" Doheeny explained that he could only spy Sirius—his third star sighting—through the small window above the chemical toilet in the rear of the plane. "I wonder if Magellan did his navigating in the can."

Finished with his star shootings, Doheeny spread a navigational chart on the floor so as not to disturb the sleeping flight mechanic.

"How're we doing?" Harry asked.

"About seven hundred miles to go. Hey, look, Short Stuff"—meaning his copilot—"is going to sack out for a bit. Want to sit up front?"

"It looks different in the movies," Harry commented once he'd squeezed into the right-hand seat. He and Doheeny sat nearly shoulder to shoulder in the cockpit seats, and there seemed precious little room between Harry and any other point in the cockpit. The only light was the glow of the control panel dials.

Doheeny nodded. "One time they were running some John Garfield movie in the mess at Presque Isle. I had to laugh. I forget the name of it, but he's on a B-17. They made the damned thing look like the Queen Mary. The way they had them walking around in that thing, you'd think it was a ballroom with wings. I pity the kid who saw that movie and thought, 'Oh, boy! I want to fly one of those!' That hotshot got a real unpleasant surprise."

To one side of the Dakota, the sea fleetingly mirrored the pale light of the moon as it slipped behind one cloud after another in the heavily patched sky, just enough to hint at the heaving surface, oily in the night. But to Harry's side, looking away from the moon, the North Atlantic rollers had disappeared into a dimensionless blackness. No horizon line demarcated sea from sky.

"How do you tell where the water is?" Harry asked.

"When you see a fish go by the window, we're too low. Just kidding, Harry. Actually, one of these gizmos on the panel tells me. I think. Which one is it now? Boy, I hope it's working. Harry, I'm kidding. We've got to work on your sense of humor. Hey, would you like to fly her a little bit?"

"Is this another joke?"

"It'll be fine. I won't let you get us into any trouble."

"I'll pass, thanks. You could ask Captain Kneece."

Doheeny laughed. "Kid looks like he'd try to put us through a loop just for the fun of it."

They talked only sporadically, and of little things: family, food, a favorite program on the wireless back home. But for the most part they let the time slip by quietly. Back in the cargo cabin, the world glimpsed only in fragments through the small windows, Harry had felt the ship vulnerable, at the whim of winds, hilltops, and spearing trees. But here, seeing the world in panorama gave him, paradoxically, a greater sense of stability, a sureness of his place, however insignificant he and the ship might be suspended in the fathomless dark. And there was a security seeing Doheeny's massive hands on the control yoke, the humming aeroplane obviously and easily in his thrall.

"Sir? Semitak Island, sir."

Harry stirred from his sleep. "What?" Rubbing his eyes, he looked up to see the flight mechanic hovering over him.

"Semitak Island, sir. I thought you'd want to know."

Harry, again, tried to rise. This time, the flight mechanic took him by the arm and helped him upright. Harry arched his back and groaned.

"Shoulda woke me up, sir," the flight mechanic said. "I woulda given you the table." In atonement, he held out a mug. "That's the last of it, Major, and it's not that warm."

Harry took a sip of the chocolate, which was not warm at all, but he appreciated the token. "What's Semitak Island?"

"That's where the radio beacon is. It means we're close. The beacon's like a road sign. It gets kinda easy from here on in."

Harry shivered and pulled on the parka he'd been using as a blanket. Across the cabin, a sleep-tousled Kneece was making smacking noises with his tongue. "Jesus, I'd give a day on the beach at Edisto to be able to brush my teeth," the young man grumbled.

The flight crew were all awake now, and at their stations. The sky had lightened to a gunmetal gray. The patchwork of clouds of the night before had now knit into an unbroken blanket the color of dirty linen.

The flight mechanic looked at the cloud cover with a studying eye. "I don't like that."

The ocean had the same dull, metallic cast as the sky, broken by white tips that exploded in spray as they were caught by a wicked wind, dotted by growlers bobbing among the waves, and statuesque bergs of dingy ice, their cathedral spires swaying in the heavy seas.

"Are we ahead of schedule?" Harry asked the flight mechanic.

"No, sir. Just about right on. Why?"

"I know your captain was trying to time our arrival to daylight. It looks like he's going to come in ahead of sunup."

"This *is* sunup, Major. The sun never really gets much higher this time of year."

"Hey," the copilot called back, "there's a door prize for anybody who can tell me why they call this ice cube Green-land."

Kneece twisted about, trying to see ahead through the windows. His eyes went wide, his jaw dropped. "Jeeeeesuuuuuusssss . . ."

In August, as Harry's Liberty ship had rounded Kap Farvel, there had been a jewel-like quality to the place, the ice cap glaring under the summer sun, girdled by a lowland band of green pastures, the beaches sloping into emerald water. But this was now winter's kingdom. Through the window Harry saw a wall of ice that ran towering and unbroken from one horizon to the other. The winter snows seemed to extend the cap all the way to the stony beach and even farther, in a berg-speckled sheet of ice extending a mile or more from the shore.

The Dakota slid into a northward course, following the coast. Then, "Clubhouse turn, Harry!" Doheeny warned, and the plane banked sickeningly right.

As the Dakota leveled off, the bluffs became a solid wall of rock. The Dakota rose and Harry could see that the two walls were the sides of an inlet. The fjord's waters were host to a parade of bergs, large and small, steepled and flat-topped, all fixed in the inlet's solid cover of ice. Doheeny flew a straight course that intersected the winding fjord below.

"Here we go," Harry heard the flight mechanic say. Harry looked up from his window to see the sergeant staring outside. The mechanic had made this flight innumerable times, but evidently this was a sight that still enthralled him.

Harry could see why. The walls of the fjord pulled back to reveal an enormous geologic bowl, an arena for titans set at the feet of guardian mountains. The vast base of the bowl was a bay filled with frozen sea, at the head of which Harry could see the Quonsets and control tower of an aerodrome clustered against the base of the mountains. A C-47 was lifting off the aerodrome's single runway, while another aeroplane—this one a small, single-engined craft—was just touching down.

"Your captain said landing here was kind of tricky," Harry said. "This doesn't look much different than the other fields."

"Take a good look at that runway, Major. It's on a slope. We have to land uphill."

Harry knew too little about the science of aviation to understand the difficulties of such a landing, but his feeling was that if it was a concern to Doheeny and to the usually blithe flight mechanic, then it was going to be a concern for poor old Harry.

Doheeny lined the Dakota up over the bay for his landing; Harry heard the landing gear come down. He looked to the flight mechanic for some cue as to how to prepare himself (and what to prepare himself for): The mechanic offered nothing more than a reassuring smile. But as the ship neared the ground, the mechanic's face twisted into the grimace of someone expecting a sharp jar, and that's exactly what followed.

The ship hit the ground uncommonly hard and Harry heard a disturbing—loud—metallic clatter. His first panicked thought was that parts of the aeroplane were coming loose.

"It's OK," the flight mechanic called over the din. "We're down."

"What's all that racket?"

"Runway's steel matting. Always sounds like that."

The tail of the Dakota set down lightly and the ship rolled to a slowing taxi.

Kneece let out a sigh of relief and turned to Harry with a grin. "Any landing you can walk, crawl, or limp away from, right?"

The Dakota taxied to a parking area; the engines windmilled to silence. Doheeny cheerily donned his Father Christmas cap and beard, tossed a mailbag over his shoulder, and waited for the flight mechanic to crack the door.

"Ho! Ho! Ho!" Doheeny bellowed into the frigid Greenland air. "Say hello to Santa Claus, kids!"

Outside, a voice snarled: "Just gimme the fuckin' mail 'fore I freeze my fuckin' nuts off!"

CHAPTER FIVE

EREBUS

" 'FRAID I HAVE TO CLOSE UP the bar, sar," the Officers Mess barman said.

If there's a sadder pronouncement, I've yet to hear it.

"The mess'll be open for them joes what's on the night flights," the barman said, "so's you and the other gennelman can stay and be comfy. Anythin' else I can do for you sars 'fore I close 'er up?"

"Polly, put the kettle on, Polly, put the kettle on."

" 'Scuse, sar?"

I took a deep breath, hoping to clear my head. There'd been one toddy too many, I suppose. "Another cuppa for my friend, if you please, my good fellow, and I'll have one as well. Make 'em steaming, there's the good lad, laddie."

Maybe it'd been more than *one* toddy too many.

I laid a fiver on the bar in gratuity for the barman's evening ministrations, generosity that was, perhaps, another product of the superfluous toddies. Little matter; it was the paper's money.

The barman locked up his cabinets and cubbies, switched off the overhead lights, and left us with the cozy glow of a few table lamps round the lounging area near the stove. It was a typical RAF mess, a motley collection of furniture that looked to be leave-behinds at a church jumble sale: leather chairs and a sofa, their split hides heavily patched with adhesive tape; fabric chairs bleeding stuffing. I handed Harry his tea and nestled with mine on a particularly dilapidated piece where one had to sit just so to avoid the attentions of an overaroused cushion spring.

Harry was standing by the window, his billfold open in his hand. I heard a crackle as his thumb caressed one of the cellophane photograph sleeves.

There were two pictures there, one a blurry photo showing two youngsters playing about their sled on a field of snow. So heavily wrapped in winter outerwear, their faces so small and undistinguished in the field of view, they could've been Eskimo children. It was the last picture Harry had taken of his sons, shot the previous winter before he'd shipped out.

The other photo was several years older, taken at some sort of party-like gathering. The woman at its center was seated at a dinner table, looking over her shoulder at the camera. A warm, wide smile enlivened otherwise unexceptional features. In the unadorned way she drew back her light hair, in the simple cut of what I'm sure was her one posh frock, the lack of jewelry except for a pair of small earrings and a gold band on her left ring finger, one saw not a plain woman, but one of simple grace. It drew one to her, a woman who, paradoxically, one might pass on the street without a second glance.

"If you're wondering if she'll forgive your going, I'd be thinking aye," I said.

"Did your wife forgive you?"

"Different kettle of fish, old man. You've hardly ever been away. I was hardly ever home."

"Do you know what a *dybbuk* is?"

"Pardon?"

Something outside the rime-ringed windowpanes drew his attention. "They're coming back. They're carrying guns."

"Tut-tut, Harry. I believe the soldiery prefer the appellation 'weapon.' Little boys play with 'guns.' Big boys play with 'weapons.' "

"Play?"

"There's an old epigram, one of those classical Greek things, though for the life of me I can't remember the attribution just now. Bloody toddies. Or age."

"You were saying."

" 'The boys throw stones at the frogs in fun; but the frogs, they die in earnest.' Or words to that effect."

Harry looked back out into the falling snow. "Are we the boys or the frogs?"

"We'll know in a few hours, won't we? Perhaps we're the stones."

"How do I invest in this place?" Kneece asked. "Business looks good."

Woody Kneece was commenting on the whirl in the Søndre Strømfjord Operations shack. The cramped tin-sided hut buzzed with men flitting round maps on tables and walks, chalking data on a gridded slate giving operational information, hovering before a bank of communications equipment. Doheeny shepherded Harry and Kneece to a corner out of the flow of traffic.

"The dispatcher says it's been like this for a couple of weeks now, and the same down at Cape Farewell," Doheeny told them. "With that much cargo moving through this fast, I'm guessing something major's cooking in the ETO. They're also racing a storm front coming down from the north. They shoved one plane out of here just before we got in, and there's another one five minutes behind us they want out before the snow hits. You guys are going to have to hotfoot it if you want to beat the storm. The strip at Godthåb's too small for us, so we'll sit it out here for you. That little puddle-jumper you saw on the runway is for you. They're already putting your bags on it. So . . ." The captain held out his hand. "Happy trails, fellas."

"If you guys never landed on skis before," the pilot cautioned, "brace yourselves."

The "landing strip" was nothing more than an area of tamped-down snow marked off with flares, outside the meager cluster of snow-topped buildings that was Godthåb. The Britannica will tell you that Godthåb is the provincial capital for South Greenland. However grandiose that may sound, it looked no more than a hamlet to Harry. The pilot hadn't exaggerated; the landing was a teeth-jarring experience, even after the plane was taxiing toward a large shed and the man in the parka trudged over and pulled open the cabin door. Harry gasped at the incredible cold that whooshed in. The moisture in his nostrils instantly froze.

"What the hell'sa matter with you, Fred?" the parka-clad man snapped. He gestured at the falling snow. "You think you could cut it any closer?"

"Fred" patted the man on his fur-covered cheek. "You worry too much, Mother."

While the pilot and the man in the parka hooked a towline from a tracked "Weasel" to the plane to tow it into the shed, another man in winter furs came lumbering up to the plane.

"Captain Kneece? Major Voss? I'm Corporal Olinsky. Want to follow me?"

Harry and Kneece zipped up their parkas and tugged up their fur-lined hoods, then followed Olinsky toward a nest of Quonsets linked to each other by a network of waist-high trenches dug in the snow.

Olinsky pointed beyond the Quonsets to low squat houses half buried in the snow, windows yellow with firelight peeping out from under snow-laden eaves. A winding road—really just an open strip of snow twisting between the buildings—seemed to mark the center of town, passing beneath the guardian steeple of the church.

"You fellas ever been through before?" Olinsky called over his shoulder. "That's the town over there."

Slogging through the snow, bent against the wind, Harry had no breath to spare for a comment, but Kneece did: "So that'd be downtown Godthåb?"

Olinsky laughed. "Yeah! Downtown! Downtown Goddamn's more like it. Dance halls, fine dining, and the Bijou! Too bad for you guys we got none of that! A hot night in downtown Goddamn is watchin' the clock hands go around! Get a good look at 'er, such as she is, 'cause after this storm, there's not even gonna be that much to see!" He helped them down into one of the trenches. "Wanna see somethin'? New guys get a kick out of this." Olinsky pulled the fur trim of his hood away from his mouth and spat. Even with the wind in his ears, Harry heard a small but distinct snap: The glob of saliva landed on the snow as a solid projectile. "Froze 'fore it hit the damn ground! How goddamn cold is that?"

Harry needed no such colorful demonstrations to concede the brutal temperature. Less than five minutes, and the small areas of Harry's forehead and cheek open to the air already throbbed with pain. A merciless stinging plagued his extremities.

"G'ahead," Olinsky said. "Try it."

Kneece pulled back his hood enough to spit clear of the fringe of fur. Again came the snap. "My Uncle Ray would say it's colder 'n' a brass toilet seat on the shady side of an iceberg," he said, delighted. "And he was talking about it being forty degrees."

"Above zero?" Olinsky said in good-natured amazement. "Damn, Cap'n, I'd be happy if the windchill around here bottomed out at forty below! Forty above? That's not cold! That's the damn tropics!"

"What's all this guff I hear about them making Veronica Lake pin her hair back?" Despite the worsening storm, and the fact that a member of his command had been murdered a thousand miles across the North Atlantic, confronted with two officers who'd just come another thousand miles to query him on the matter, the only issue in which Captain Israel Blume seemed to express any acute interest was that of Miss Lake's new coif.

"I heard it was the War Department asked her to do it," Kneece replied obligingly. "All the ladies are working in the dee-fense plants. A lot of them were wearing that peekaboo number Veronica had. And it seems the ladies' hair kept getting tangled in the machinery. So the War Department asked ol' Veronica if she'd do something different with her hair."

"Veronica Lake without the peekaboo." Blume shook his head glumly. "I can't see where that would still look like Veronica Lake."

Kneece nodded in somber agreement. "Well, factually, she doesn't."

Olinsky, who, out of his parka, carried a soft babyish roundness to his face, had led them to the Quonset serving as mess and rec hall. There had been a halfhearted attempt to bring some Christmas cheer to the drab room by draping sickly garlands round the windows. An equally feeble Yuletide tableau was set on a table against one wall. It consisted of a plastic Coca-Cola-bearing Father Christmas and pieces of wood nailed together in the approximate skeletal shape of a Christmas tree. The "tree" was festooned with strips of the same poor garland as the windows and some makeshift ornaments: tableware, pieces of scrap wood and paper cut into stars and circles childishly daubed with paint. Two dozen soldiers were scattered round the tables eating, playing cards or checkers, flipping through magazines with the look of men who'd already flipped through those magazines a dozen times. A Victrola had been playing "You'll Never Know" as Harry and the others had entered. By the time they had finished peeling off their parkas and flight jackets, the record had finished. No one bothered to stop the Victrola from resetting and beginning the record again.

Olinsky had led them to a dark-complected, curly-haired fellow, thirtyish or so, with a heavy brow over large, dark eyes that gave him a fixed look of intense study. Israel Blume was trying to stay warm inside a West Point varsity sweater pulled over a West Point sweatshirt and under a very civilian-looking plaid blanket draped round his shoulders. Blume had looked casually up from his meal and offered neither salute nor greeting. His gaze flicked over Harry and Kneece. The wind had escalated to a howl and the windows were white with blowing snow. "Seems like you guys made it just under the wire. Help yourselves to some chow."

The cook dished them each a plate of two fleshy lamb chops, a slab of bread, a hill of mashed potatoes, and a microscopic portion of sliced carrots and peas. Blume fixed Olinsky with that intense look of his when they'd returned to his table and said, "Grown-up stuff," nodding the corporal to another table. Soon thereafter came the elocution on Veronica Lake and her new hairstyle.

Kneece looked respectfully down at the meat on his plate. "Lamb chops. You guys are living pretty high."

"Oh, yeah," Blume said flatly. "We're living in the lap of luxury. I may move here permanently after the war."

"I'm just thinking what my wife has to go through to get a pound of hamburger these days," Harry said.

"The rationing getting that bad?" Blume asked.

"This year meat, cheese, and fat went on the list. Ground beef was hitting twenty cents a pound *before* I went into the Army."

Blume's lips pursed appreciatively. "The locals, they raise sheep. These chops are like hamburger around here. Spend a month or two here. These chops won't seem so special. And not every part of a sheep is chops. You ever have mutton?"

Harry and Kneece shook their heads.

"Don't."

Kneece nodded. "We had a hell of a fine cook back home, so I know what a good chop tastes like. This ol' boy you have in the kitchen knows what he's doing."

"He should. He cost me six gallons of peaches, a canned ham, and a Dorothy Lamour movie. I traded Bluie-West-Eight for him. That's a weather station up on the north coast. The boys were sorry to lose Dorothy Lamour, but we'd seen it a hundred times. I think they were sorrier to lose the peaches. But this guy earns his keep. You pull duty in a place like this, a good cook makes it a bit more bearable."

"I'll give you that," Kneece grinned through a mouthful of lamb.

"You'll Never Know" ended again. The Victrola reset.

"Either put another record on," Blume said loudly, without looking up from his plate, "or turn it off, because if I hear that goddamned thing one more time today somebody's gonna eat it for dessert!"

The Victrola was turned off.

Blume sighed. "That thing must've played a hundred times today. One more time and I would've went completely batty—instead of half-batty, which this place makes you on a good day."

"Captain, you do know why we're here?" Kneece asked, producing his little notebook and setting it open on the table in front of him.

"Tourist season's over. So I'll say Grassi."

"How much do you know about what happened to him? What've you been told?"

"All I know is he showed up in England somewhere—"

"The Orkneys," Kneece supplied.

"—wherever. And he's dead. Then I heard somebody was going to stop by for a talk about him which, I suppose, is you. I'm guessing you guys wouldn't be here if he just slipped on a banana peel and cracked his nut."

Kneece cleared his throat. "Well, factually, we can't discuss the details—"

Blume waved this away with his fork. "Fine. It's said. What're you looking for here? Suspects?"

"Why? Do you think you have any?"

The corner of Blume's mouth flickered. "Just everybody here."

"Including you?"

"Sure. Why not?" Blume noticed the smile of recognition on Harry's face. "That's the look of a fellow sufferer."

"Grassi and I were in the same unit in England," Harry said.

"For how long?"

"Six months."

Blume set down his knife and fork and held out a hand, which Harry took. "Welcome to the lodge, brother. You've got my sympathies."

"Every time I talk to somebody about this fella," Kneece interjected, "I get the impression he was not a guy you'd want to be stuck on a raft with."

"You know what the two worst days of my life were?" Blume demanded. "The day I wound up with a Baptist mother-in-law, and the day Armando Grassi's jaw healed up enough for him to talk. I'm not sure which is number one. Two days like that in one life nobody should have." Blume went back to his lamb chops, but after the first forkful thinking about Grassi had vexed him so that he put his utensils down and pushed his plate away.

"Let me explain a couple of things. Look around. A pull here is no picnic. You're going to spend a good part of the year snowed in with your buddies. That being the case, it helps if your buddies can act buddy-like."

Kneece gestured at Blume's plate. "You gonna finish that? This stuff's really good."

Blume pushed his plate in Kneece's direction. "So I try to keep things loose. Why not? This is no combat post. You hear anybody shooting at us here? The Navy is down at the Cape running antisub patrols. We don't run antisub patrols. The day I tell my men to grab their weapons, I've got six men in the hospital because they can't find the business end of an M1 without hurting themselves. This isn't even a place like the Cape or Bluie-West-One, where you've got transports going through so you still feel like you're part of the rest of the world. Half the time, I'm not sure anybody remembers us. We're just out here."

"What is it you *do* do?" Harry asked.

"Weather. From Rommel and Patton my people don't know *bubkes*, but I've got the Sergeant Yorks of weather-predicting here." Blume pulled his plaid blanket closer round his shoulders. "You guys aren't cold?"

"After being outside this is practically a sauna," Harry said.

"Give it an hour. Wait for the novelty to wear off." Blume took a sip of his coffee and made a face. "Hey, Olinsky!" He held up his cup. "Be a good soldier and get your captain something hot in here, OK? What I'm saying is you should try to make things easier here. Not harder."

"And Grassi made things harder?" Kneece asked.

Blume turned a wry face to Harry. "What would be your guess, lodge brother?"

"Unbelievably harder. No, make that *excruciatingly* harder."

Blume turned back to Kneece. "We all know it's cold here. And boring. And miserable. We should all be someplace—*anyplace*—else. So, who needs to hear that every day? And me, I should *especially* hear this from one of my officers? Some guy who's supposed to help me keep these poor bastards together by setting an example? The minute Grassi stepped off the plane, I said to myself, 'Izzy, here comes a pain in your head.' "

"How'd you know that?" Kneece asked.

"Because he was *here*. Captain, let me explain another something to you. You're in the Army. You ask for something, you fill out your requisitions and all those damned copies, that thing you ask for is what you *don't* get. I didn't want this guy. I didn't ask for this guy. I didn't ask for *anybody*. I didn't have any personnel requisitions in; I didn't have any holes in my T.O. to fill. I didn't even know this guy was coming until he showed up."

"What did his orders say?"

"What did his orders say? They said, 'Look, here, this is for you! An extra body! Enjoy! Happy Hanukkah!' "

Kneece blinked, puzzled. "Happy what?"

"Happy—" Blume frowned. "I take it there's not too many of the Chosen People where you come from."

"The what?"

"Jews, Kneece. The Thirteen Tribes. Moses and The Guys. The Old Testament Gang."

Kneece looked uncomfortable. "Oh, uh, no. None I know of, anyway."

Blume nodded, unsurprised.

"Hanukkah is a Jewish holiday," Harry explained. "It comes around the same time as Christmas. '*Dreidel dreidel dreidel*,' " he sang, " '*Dreidel made of clay …*' "

For the first time, Blume's face softened and he permitted himself—with a certain reluctance—a smile. "I didn't think 'Voss' was a—"

"It's not," Harry told him. "I have a neighbor—a good friend, really. He's Jewish. I've picked up a few things from him."

"Where was that?" Blume asked, warming. "Where're you from, if you don't mind my asking?"

"Newark."

"Over in Jersey? We're practically neighbors! I'm a little south and across the Delaware: Philly."

"No kidding." Harry saw the impatience on Kneece's face. "About Grassi: you said you knew he was trouble from the beginning."

"A lieutenant I didn't ask for appears—presto—with no specific orders and a busted jaw. I should think this is a gift? That somebody's not dumping their own headache on me? Look around. Short of Leavenworth, can you think of a better place to stick somebody who's trouble?"

"Grassi ever talk about why he was sent here?" Kneece asked. "Mention this trouble he got himself into?"

Blume shook his head, sat silent as Olinsky returned with his cup. Blume waited until Olinsky returned to his own table. "The only thing Grassi'd do is whine about how he'd been screwed. He seemed to have a pretty strong opinion that he'd been screwed."

"But he didn't mention any particulars? Or any names of parties he thought were involved in his getting screwed?"

Blume studied Kneece for a moment. "Tell me something: You get special training for this kind of job?"

"Some."

"In all of that special training, did you ever think you'd be asking an official interrogation question about the particulars of a screwing?"

"Come to think of it, no."

"Well, so you have an answer, no, he never said anything specific. Just about how—"

"He'd been screwed." Kneece let his eyes roam around the soldiers in the mess hall. "Is everybody here because they got screwed?"

"Not everybody."

"How about you?"

"Oh, I was screwed all right."

"Mind if I ask what you did to piss off somebody enough to get yourself sent here?"

Blume's face grew cold. "What did I do? I was born with the name Israel Blume and I finished in the top twenty of my class at The Point. That's what I did. And somebody decided that was a damned sin."

"What exactly were Grassi's responsibilities?" Harry asked.

"When you find out, let me know."

"What'd he get sent here as?" Kneece asked. "What'd his orders say?"

"His orders? I told you. His orders said, 'Here he is.' No classification, no assignment. They didn't even forward his 66-1 to me until he'd already been here a couple weeks. Maybe they were afraid I wouldn't let him off the plane if I'd already seen his file."

"So what did he do here?" Harry asked.

"He spent a lot of time trying to figure out how to get the hell out of here is what he did. Besides that? I went easy for the first week or so because of his jaw. I figured I'd run some administrative stuff through him." Blume shook his head grimly.

"Useless, hm?" Harry suggested.

"I'd ask him to work up a duty roster for me. He looks at me like I'm speaking in Yiddish. 'A what? How's that work?' It took me an hour to explain to him what a duty roster was. 'Take care of these manpower reports, Grassi.' 'Where's that readiness report?' 'I need a rotation watch schedule for the radio shack.' 'A what? What's a rotation? How does that work?' I think half the work I got from that guy—maybe *all* the work— came from poor Olinsky there. You want to hear something funny? On top of everything else Grassi did to annoy the hell out of people, he was an outrageous slob." To Harry: "You know *chozzer?*"

"Pig?"

Blume nodded. "But go into his office—"

"Neat as a pin," Harry said. "Clear desk."

Blume nodded, still marveling over the discrepancy. "You know why?"

"Because he didn't do anything."

"At least nothing I gave him to do. Then, when his mouth got working really well again . . ." Blume put his hands to his head, reliving the headache. " '*Oy gevalt,*' as my Nana would say. Every time I turned around, Grassi's in my ear *nudzhing* about how he's an Army lawyer, not some clerk, and he wants to do Army lawyer stuff."

"Noodging?" Kneece asked.

"A *nudzh* is like a pest," Harry translated.

"Noodge." Kneece grinned, enjoying the word. "Noodge!"

"Every time he got into that jazz," Blume groused on, "I'd point out the obvious to him. I'd say, 'Lieutenant, I appreciate you want to use all that law school training; I'm sure your mother's so proud you're a lawyer. But maybe you should notice we don't have a great demand for a JAG bureau here.' " He sighed gustily. "I got two guys, one gets a little cabin fever, the other says the wrong thing, somebody throws a punch, the next thing I know Grassi's squawking about a full-blown court-martial. A couple of the guys sneak into town one night and steal some local yokel's sheep, Grassi wants to turn it into a major JAG investigation. One time—I swear, this is the truth—we got a bad can of spinach, Grassi's hot to trace it all the way back to the Quartermaster General. I told him, 'Lieutenant,' I said, 'if one of these guys even threw a punch at *me* I wouldn't bust him; I'd give him a medal for breaking up the boredom.' "

"Sounds like he was after anything that could get him back to the States," Kneece concluded.

"That's what I thought in the beginning. But after having this guy in my ear for a couple months, I started thinking it was something else. He didn't just want to get out of here; he wanted to—"

"Get back in the game," Harry offered.

Blume brightened. "Yeah. For him, getting sent here was like getting benched."

"I already know the answer," Kneece said, "but I'm gonna ask: Did he have any friends on the post?"

"Look around. Do you see anybody beating their chests in grief over his death? Olinsky was his clerk. He spent as much time with Grassi as anybody. If there's something personal you want to know about the lieutenant's stay with us, ask him."

"What about any of the locals? Maybe a girl—"

"The civilians didn't find him any less a *nudzh* than we did. Besides, once the thermometer started dipping, he didn't go far. Not a hardy type."

"How long was he gone before you noticed he was missing?"

"I didn't know he was missing until I got the message they'd found him dead in England."

"The Orkneys."

Blume shrugged. "The Orkneys. Is he more dead because it's the Orkneys?"

"Captain," Harry interposed, "nobody has to tell me how off-putting Armando Grassi could be. And I understand you'd probably avoid him day-to-day as much as you could. God knows, I would've. But I'd think you'd notice—especially in a small post like this—if any one of your men, and especially a *nudzh* like Grassi, had dropped out of sight."

"You'd think that, wouldn't you? Except Grassi didn't drop out of sight."

"I'm getting confused," Kneece said.

"We're both getting confused," Harry said.

"About a week before Grassi turned up in the Orkneys, we got a signal from the Cape. Some C-47 pilot crashed on takeoff, and there was some kind of jurisdictional squabble. See, the Cape is Navy, but the transport, the crew, they were Army. And it looked like something wasn't kosher about the crash. Scuttlebutt had it the pilot was boozed up or something like that. So the Cape signaled us, and they wanted us to buck the word up to our senior at Bluie-West-One. He was the one with the authority, the one who had to make the decision about what to do with this pilot. Well, Grassi got wind of this; next thing I know, he's all around my head like a bunch of gnats."

"Noodging," Kneece said.

"Noodging."

"He wanted the case," Harry said.

"He says this is what he does, this is what he's trained to do—on and on, you know."

"I know," Harry said sympathetically.

"He was after me all the time on this. You know how he could get. You wanted to smack him."

"I *know*," Harry said.

"Only this time, maybe he had a point, I was thinking. We have misconduct maybe, maybe drunk on duty, something not nice with this pilot. And here we have a bona fide JAG officer on hand. Why not?"

"It also got Grassi out of your hair," Kneece pointed out.

"Hey, the Navy shouldn't suffer, too? Comrades-in-arms? Let him be somebody else's headache for a couple days. I get the OK from Bluie-West-One, I give the word to Grassi, and for him this was Hanukkah *gelt*." To Kneece: "A gift. Not that he'd say thank you or anything, it would kill him to express some gratitude, then he's off. He wasn't gone an hour, this pain in my head I've had for three months mysteriously disappears. Go figure."

Kneece flipped back to an earlier note he'd made in his pad. "You said he was gone a week?"

"Something like that. I can check the date with my office files."

"And he never checked in with you? Not the whole time he was down at the Cape? No report of his findings? Or the progress of his investigation?"

Blume shook his head.

"He didn't send a signal about leaving the country?"

"Nope."

"And *you* never checked in with *him*?"

"Nope."

"Even when the couple of days turned into a week?"

"He could've been down there a month, I would've let it be. Does the phrase 'Don't look a gift horse' and so on mean anything to you? The last I saw of him, the last anybody here heard from him, was the day he left. Amen."

"So you don't have any idea of why Grassi left Greenland? Why he wound up a thousand miles away? What he was on to?"

"Not a clue."

"You said before you didn't think he was just aiming to find himself a way out of here. So you don't think maybe this was just him going AWOL? Somebody like Grassi, ants in his pants, stuck in a place like this—"

"He could've hopped any transport any time. Stopping him is not something people on this end would've thought of. 'Please, Captain, sir, can I go down to the Cape?' That's not how you slip out unnoticed. Look: I'm the last guy to give that pain-in-the-arse credit for anything, but I don't think Grassi was going over the hill; I don't think he'd do that. What I *do* think is he got his beak into something and got slapped, which would be like him."

Kneece propped an elbow on the table and rubbed his chin meditatively. "It looks like a visit to the Cape is gonna be our next stop." He nodded at the window. "How long does that usually last?"

"A day. Couple of days. A week. I'll check in with my crack weather team and let you know. Anything else?"

"We've been traveling all day," Harry said. "Where can we bunk?"

"Grassi's quarters are the only spare accommodations I've got. Nobody's been in his room since he left." To Kneece: "That's how cops like it, right? Don't touch anything? If he left anything useful to you, it's still there. Olinsky'll take you over. I'll assign him to you. When you're ready, he'll take you over to Grassi's office and show you whatever you need. If you need to talk to anybody else on the post, Olinsky'll set it up."

They said their good nights. As Harry pulled himself into his parka he nodded at Blume's plate. "Would your rabbi approve?"

Blume smiled. "It gets harder to keep kosher the further north of the forty-ninth parallel you get. God should understand. I hear He's on our side."

"Your captain told us nobody's been in here since the lieutenant left."

"Nobody has, sir."

Kneece stood fixed in the doorway, unable to force himself through. "Are you telling me *this* is how he left it?"

Olinsky chuckled and slid past Kneece to deposit their baggage inside. "Captain, sir, this is how he *lived* in it. Lieutenant Engstrom—that was Lieutenant Grassi's roomie—he moved out a month ago. He said he'd rather sleep on the floor squeezed in with some of the other officers than put up with this. The latrine's down that end of the hall, sirs, coal's at the other. Damn, it's freezin' in here! Let me get the fire goin' for you, sirs." Olinsky trotted off toward the coal bin with a bucket from the room.

The junior officers' billet was a Quonset with a corridor along one side, and the other side divided into small rooms, each just big enough for two bunks, a pair of upright lockers, and a chair and small table serving as a shared desk. One of the bunks in Grassi's quarters—presumably that of the vacated Lieutenant Engstrom—was bare with a stack of fresh

sheets and blankets neatly folded at the foot. On the bunk opposite, bedclothes were a tangle. Across both bunks and the floor was strewn a soldier's full issue of clothing, from fatigues to underthings, ties to socks.
The room was chill enough to elicit vapor when they spoke, yet even in
that cold their noses wrinkled at an odor indicating it had been some
time since any of the litter had been through the post laundry. At the base
of Grassi's bunk sat an open footlocker, its interior a jumble of toilet articles, more clothing, footwear, and personal items. The upright locker also
overflowed with more jumble, including an insanely crimson dressing
gown more suitable for wear in a Hong Kong brothel than a remote sub-
arctic military outpost.

"Was he like this back in London?" Kneece spoke in the hushed voice
of a witness to a great disaster.

"He was legendary," Harry said. He cleared the empty bunk of stray
Grassi items, flicking them away with his gloved fingertips. "For the art-
work, too." He nodded at the display over Grassi's bunk: a collage of girlie
photographs clipped from magazines and newspapers. Some were extracted from clothing advertisements, while others were familiar
Hollywood-produced images: publicity photos for Betty Grable, Rita
Hayworth, et al.

"A rawther ec-lectic collection, I must say." Kneece's eyes were appre-
ciative as they ranged across the display.

"Yeah, eclectic," Harry said, tucking fresh sheets round the bunk's
mattress. "If she breathed, she was eligible. That's what Grassi meant by
eclectic."

"I see he rawther fancied the expressionists, rawther. And, pray tell,
good fellow, perchance how did you come into possession of the clean
bunk?"

"Privilege of rank."

Kneece frowned at the other bunk. "I think these sheets out-rank us
both. Why don't you let the corporal fix that bunk up for you?"

"This is keeping me warm."

Kneece picked about the linens of his own bunk. "Damn. I wonder
when the last time was he changed these sheets?"

"You'll be OK. I remember reading somewhere that germs can't sur-
vive extreme cold."

Kneece moved to the upright locker and shook his head over the
crimson dressing gown. The locker's top shelf was jammed with colored
bottles and jars: a noxious assembly of lotions, creams, scents, toilet
waters, balms, elixirs, and every other potion intended to enhance the ap-
peal of the human male. Kneece sniffed at one of the bottles and recoiled

as if he'd been struck. "Good Christ! Who was he trying to impress with all this? The Eskimos? Don't light any matches around this stuff, Major. You'll take out a wall. I guess these died of loneliness." He held up a few wrapped prophylactics.

Olinsky returned, his bucket filled with coal, and began to stoke the room's brazier.

"Captain Blume says you were Lieutenant Grassi's clerk," Kneece put to him.

Olinsky grunted an assent.

"Not a big fan of the lieutenant?"

Another grunt.

"Do you know why we're here, Corporal?" Harry asked.

"Everybody knows what happened to the lieutenant. So everybody figgers—"

" 'Everybody'?"

"Well, Cap'n, this is kind of a small place. Word goes around."

"Everybody figures it's something about Lieutenant Grassi," Harry supplied, and Olinsky nodded. "It's been my experience, Corporal, that people get a little shy about speaking ill of the dead. Even if they know the dead was a total son of a bitch."

Olinsky laughed. "I guess that's so, sir, yeah."

Harry finished making his bunk and started fishing through his travel bag for his notepad. "What I'm saying, Corporal, is don't be shy."

"OK, yessir."

"Captain Blume thought if Lieutenant Grassi had any friends you'd know who they were," Kneece said.

"I suppose that's true, if he had any. The lieutenant didn't have that kind of knack, makin' friends."

"You worked for him. The two of you must've talked. You know, just . . . chatted."

The word amused Olinsky. "Well, yeah, you'd think that, but I tried to avoid having 'chats' with the lieutenant if I could. He wasn't much for conversation."

"I can't believe that," Harry said.

"Oh, not that he wasn't gabby."

"OK, *that* I can believe."

"He was always—I mean *always*—goin' on and on about what a crummy place this is. Well, tell me somethin' nobody here don't already know! You know, sirs, maybe you gotta be here a while to understand, but after a bit, you don't really want to hear it no more. So, instead of him bendin' my ear all the time 'bout how bad we got it 'n' how bad everything is, I tried to stay out of range as much as I could. Sometimes he'd buttonhole me, try to pump me about women in town, or if there was someplace he could get his hands on some good hooch."

"And what would you tell him?" Kneece asked.

"I wouldn't tell him nothin'. Anybody else I'd put on to somethin', you know, just to be polite, but him, I'd just say, 'Lieutenant, I don't know nothin' 'bout that kind of thing, sir.' To me, it's not like I could see this guy sayin', 'Thanks for the tip, Corp.' More like he'd come back pissin' 'n' moanin' 'bout maybe how not-too-pretty the local dames were, or how he'd had better booze in his time. Like I said, who needs to hear it?"

"Captain Blume says Grassi didn't seem to understand most of his duties."

Olinsky's face wrinkled. "I think he just put on like that to get out of it. The cap'n'd come in 'n' maybe say, 'Hey, Lieutenant, do this or do that,' 'n' Lieutenant Grassi, he'd get all dumb, then the cap'n'd leave 'n' there it is on my desk, 'n' the lieutenant sayin', 'Hey, Olinsky, take care of that.' If it was you, how hard'd you work for a guy keeps doin' that to ya? Even if he is your boss? There, that brazier's goin' good now. Oughta keep you warm for a bit. You're gonna have to keep feedin' this thing. I told you where the coal bin was?"

"Yes, Corporal, thanks," Kneece said. "What about these cases Grassi was always trying to make?"

"Cases?"

"Captain Blume says the lieutenant was always trying to turn certain incidents into legal issues—"

"Oh, *cases*, like a *legal* case. Oh, *yeah*, he was always tryin' to turn every this 'n' that thing into some kinda Federal case. Hey, is that a pun? A Federal case?"

"Not really, no."

"Oh. Well, anyway, like the time with those guys stole the sheep. The cap'n tell you 'bout that?"

"A little."

"No big deal, really. These two guys—I don't got to give you no names, do I?—they bought some torpedo juice off some Navy guys at the Cape, they got a little tight one night, they were a little bored—well, hell, everybody's *always* bored. Anyway, all it was was this joke. They snuck down into town, got into this guy's pens, 'n' stole one of his sheep."

"I got the impression from Captain Blume that there was no shortage of lamb chops at the mess."

"Oh, this wasn't for eatin', sir. It was just a joke! They took the sheep, dressed it up in fatigues—how they got that thing in them clothes, I guess they had to be *real* drunk 'n' *real* bored—they got it all dressed up 'n' left it sittin' in the cap'n's jeep in the mornin'. Even the cap'n thought it was funny. But Lieutenant Grassi, he starts goin' on that this is some kind of stealin', 'mistreatin' the civilian populace,' I think he said. I mean, this guy, he got his sheep back, I don't know what the big deal was. I don't think it was a big deal. And the lieutenant, I figgered him a guy to be just as likely as any other joker to pull a stunt like that if he wasn't tryin' so hard to work his way outta this place. So then the lieutenant, he's grabbin' people, sayin', 'Do you know anythin' 'bout this?' "

"He asked you."

"Yeah, sure. Do I know these guys? he asked me."

"But you didn't tell him."

Olinsky nodded.

"You were thinking, to hell with him, right?"

Olinsky shrugged, a little red-faced.

"It's OK," Harry put in. "I worked with the guy. I would've done the same thing."

Olinsky looked relieved. "The way I worked it with the lieutenant was whenever he got on his horse 'bout somethin' like this, like with the sheep, if it was somebody I knew 'n' he didn't, I'd just say I didn't know nothin' 'bout it. If it was somebody I knew 'n' he knew I knew 'em, then I'd say, 'Well, that's funny, sir, he always seemed a right guy to me.' "

"I guess, then, Lieutenant Grassi didn't share any confidences with you about what he was going down to the Cape for?" Kneece asked.

"The lieutenant didn't share confidences with me 'bout nothin', sir. I didn't even know he was goin' down there 'til he stuck his head in the office, said he was flyin' out in ten minutes 'n' for me to watch the fort for him. 'Watch the fort.' I was *always* watchin' that guy's fort."

"Had you heard anything about what happened at the Cape?"

"I heard what everybody else heard. Some flyboy crunched a C-47. You seen what this place is like: it's not like that don't happen. I just figgered this was another one of those things where the lieutenant was gonna try to turn it into a big deal. When you sirs want me to come wake you up tomorrow?"

"When's reveille?"

"The cap'n doesn't go for an official reveille. They keep the kitchen open for breakfast from 0630 to 0830."

"Split the difference and make it 0730."

Olinsky said good night and left.

Kneece surveyed the debris, kicked at a pair of wrinkled pants, and stood over the brazier, stripping off his arctic mittens and warming his hands over the coals. "What was that word, Major? That Jew word? For pig?"

"Chozzer."

"Yeah. Chozzer."

Harry, still wrapped in his parka, settled on his bunk, back to the wall, notepad propped against his upraised knees. He was making notes not only of the conversation with Olinsky, but from the earlier interrogatory with Captain Blume.

"We should go through this crap," Kneece said. "Maybe there's something here." He knelt by the footlocker and started sifting through the mishmash of contents. "Hey, who do you think this is?"

Harry looked over his reading glasses at Kneece, who was holding up a small photograph in a simple oval frame. Kneece tossed it and it landed on the mattress close to Harry. A broad-shouldered, plain-faced woman sat in a chair in a high-necked dress that ran to the floor, her hair pinned up round her head. Standing behind her, his hand on her shoulder, was a slight, small-eyed man, his hair greased flat and parted razor-straight down the center of his head. From the woman's dress and the man's vested suit and celluloid collar, Harry guessed the date of the photo as being from the 19-teens. In the fashion of the time, both man and woman wore stony expressions.

"What do you think?" Kneece asked. "Dear old Mom and Dad?"

Harry nodded.

"Here's some more." Kneece tossed over an envelope filled with small Brownie box photos of more recent vintage.

Harry thumbed through them, careful to hold them only by the white-framed edges. There was the man from the framed photo, now paunchy and gray-haired, sitting at the end of a table, a cake lost in the glare of a host of birthday candles in front of him. Crowded about him were smiling faces and at his shoulder, the broad-shouldered woman who was his wife, heavier and grayer, her cheek held close to his as he prepared to blow out the candles. Then another photo of the woman, older still, holding some kind of small dog up to her face, laughing, the dog squirming so much as to be nothing more than a toothy blur in her hands. Another picture of the man and woman seated at the same table, dressed in what were probably their only good sets of clothes, once again surrounded by well-wishers. Above their heads the photographer had caught the tail of a hand-painted banner:

PY

SARY

Harry didn't look at the rest of the photos. He slid them back into their envelope and tossed it back to Kneece. "Do you know if the War Department has notified his folks yet?"

"You know, I don't know."

"I wonder how that telegram's going to read."

"Hey, I got some letters here!" Kneece sat near Harry on his bunk and began working through a bundle of V-mail envelopes, maybe two dozen in all. "All from the same address in Chicago. Is this Eye-talian?" He turned the first mail piece over to Harry. "You live with those folk, Major. Can you savvy any of that?"

"A little." Harry skipped quickly through the first small piece of paper, then the next V-mail piece. "They all look like letters from his folks."

"What do they say?"

"The usual stuff. 'How are you?' 'We're worried about you, hoping you'll come home soon.' 'Do you need anything?' " Harry felt a heaviness in his chest, the same heaviness he'd felt days before when he'd first seen Grassi's ID photo lying on his kitchen table. Only now the feeling had more to it, a tangible oppressiveness.

"Do you think he might've said anything to his folks about what he was doing out here?"

"He was enough of a blabbermouth, I wouldn't put it past him. But the latest one here is from November. That's weeks before the crash down at the Cape."

"We should go through all these letters just in case."

"All?"

"At least the last couple of months."

"You mean at least as far back as August."

Kneece said nothing, but returned to poking round the footlocker's interior. "I was right to ask you to come along. Like the way you handled that Blume fella . . ."

"I didn't 'handle' him, Woody. I just talked to him."

"But the *way* you talked to him . . . Was all that true? About you having this Jew neighbor?"

"Friend, Woody. An old friend. He runs one of the stores on my street."

"I don't know any Jews, not personally. I couldn't even tell you if we have any in Charleston. When I was a kid, all I knew about 'em was what my daddy had to say. You remember that newspaper Henry Ford used to put out? Mr. Ford was always running those pieces about the 'International Jewish Conspiracy,' and how they were all commies? Well, Daddy was very big on that stuff. He was all with Mr. Ford when Mr.

Ford's paper was saying how jazz was some kind of Jew plot to make all the niggers crazy and make 'em make trouble. When he found out I was going down to the juke joints at night, I don't know what he was more worried about: that I'd wind up with some colored gal, or that I'd go commie."

"Did you go down to those places because you didn't believe your daddy and Mr. Henry Ford? Or did you do it just to aggravate him?"

Kneece smiled slyly. "At this point, I couldn't factually tell you. Now, can I get you to help me with the rest of these letters?"

"Woody, there's nothing in those letters for us."

"I'd still like to—"

"I'm pretty tired. I'm turning in."

When Olinsky awakened Harry and Kneece, it was as dark outside as when they'd arrived. The blizzard continued unabated, and the temperature had dropped far enough below zero that even with the brazier aglow their quarters remained frigid. "You fellas bein' first-timers, I figgered you're probably short on what you need," Olinsky said as Harry and Kneece wriggled into the cold-weather garments he'd brought.

There were long woolen underwear and woolen socks, woolen shirts and trousers, armored-force coveralls, and woolen pullovers. Over these, Harry and Kneece tugged the flight jackets and woolen caps given them by Doheeny's flight mechanic, scarves to cover the lower portion of their faces, goggles, then their hooded parkas. On their hands they wore woolen gloves inside mittens.

"You can't see nothin' out there," the corporal warned before escorting them to the mess hall. "There's guide ropes tied from one building to the next. Hold on to them and don't let go. Not even to scratch your nose. The rope breaks, you just follow it back to where it's tied on. If it's broke at both ends, don't move. I'll come get you. Please, sirs, don't go off on your own. There was this guy last year thought he was a real arctic explorer. He let go. I guess he figgered he was gonna shortcut his way somewhere. We didn't find his body 'til spring."

After breakfast, they settled in Grassi's office, a suffocatingly minute cubicle squeezed among others in the Quonset serving as post HQ. As Blume had promised, the office was immaculate, a startling contrast to Grassi's living quarters. Yet the Grassi touch manifested itself nonetheless. Although there were few dossiers in the one stack of drawers, they had been filed in no particular order, lacking any identifying tabs. Their respective contents had been laid out in similarly haphazard fashion. Paradoxically, the handwritten notes within those files were succinct, followed orderly progressions, and were written in a brilliantly clear hand.

"He might've been 4-F on personal hygiene," Kneece commented, "but I give him an A for penmanship."

"Remember the other officer who worked with me on that case in August?" Harry asked.

"That Ricks fella?"

"Peter Ricks. He and Grassi were such opposites you'd think they'd burst into flame just being in the same room. Ricks was one of those clean-cut types that looked like he'd stepped off a recruiting poster. Very big on good manners, the kind of young fellow mothers hope their daughters are going to bring home. But his notes . . ." Harry took a blank piece of paper from the desk, made some scribbled lines representing writing, then made more scribbles jammed in the margins. He drew a dizzying series of writhing arrows whirling among the scribbles. "That's what a page of Ricks's notes looked like."

Kneece looked from the faux Ricks page to the Grassi file open on the desk. The captain smiled slowly, tapping the Ricks page. "Nothing got by him."

"Ricks was like a net. He grabbed everything, every connection, every possibility."

Kneece nodded at the Grassi folder. "This guy just went straight for the jugular."

"Right instincts, I guess. But lousy lawyering."

They went through each of the few files, breaking up their reading by interviewing post personnel who'd had contact with Grassi. Recalling those interviews later, Harry shook his head. "The polite ones tried to say as little as they could. A lot of them weren't polite."

"Armando Grassi had me thinking they must be giving away lieutenant's bars with a tank of gas back home," said one of the other headquarters officers.

And from another: "After Grassi, I guess next they'll be drafting monkeys."

By afternoon's end, they'd questioned everyone there was to question, and had exhausted the scant paperwork Grassi had left behind. Blume, shaking snow off his parka, found them working out the cricks in their backs from hours in wooden chairs. "Productive day?"

"As one of my relations might say," Kneece replied, "we got us a whole lotta not much."

"That wouldn't be your Uncle Ray, would it?" Harry asked.

Kneece laughed. "I guess you get an ear for him after a bit."

Blume reached inside his parka for a crumpled piece of paper: a message from the outpost's wireless shack. "Captain, last night you were saying something about going down to the Cape? This blizzard is part of a storm blanket running from here nearly all the way to Bluie-West-Eight. According to this—and the analysis of my weather team—it's really two storms dovetailing. The storm centers seem to be pulling apart, and the prediction is for a gap to open wide enough to give us a couple hours' flying weather. That might be long enough to get you two down there. This is not a thing I would recommend. That air's going to be pretty rough and we're talking about a pretty tight hole. But if badly is how you want to get down there—"

"When would we have to leave?" Kneece asked.

"The weather guys are ball-parking we could get you airborne by 0400 tomorrow morning. That is if you're done here."

"How about it, Major? You game?"

"I don't like the way these early wake-ups are getting to be a habit," Harry said. "Is 'badly' how we want to get down there?"

"The trail gets colder every day. No pun intended. You can stay, Major, but if I read Captain Blume right, if you do there's no telling when you'll be able to get a ride out. That about the size of it, Blume?"

"That's about the size of it," Blume said.

"What about Doheeny?" Harry asked.

"This window won't open until the seam between the fronts passes Strømfjord," Blume replied. "They won't be able to take advantage of it. But I'll pass the word to them to rendezvous with you—"

"Rendezvous earliest possible," Kneece said. "How about it, Major?"

"I have a feeling it's not going to be the smartest thing I ever do." But Harry sighed and nodded his acquiescence.

Kneece smiled, pleased. "Blume, do you have communications with the States? Can you reach D.C.?"

"We have to relay through Goose Bay."

"I'm going to code a transmission for you, Captain. As soon as you can get through . . ."

"Sure." Blume looked at his watch. "If I were you two, I'd get some chow and see if I could grab some snooze time."

"What about Grassi's effects?" Harry asked Kneece. "All that stuff in his quarters? Are you done going through it?"

Kneece nodded. "I guess Captain Blume here can pack it all up and send it to Grassi's folks."

"Before you do . . . That message you're going to send out . . ."

"Just a routine status report for my CO."

"Could you ask your CO to check and see if Grassi's next of kin have been notified? The first word they get that their son is dead shouldn't be his things showing up on their doorstep," Harry said.

. . .

"Well," Lieutenant Commander George Zagottis said with a certain resignation. Harry could see the Navy officer steel himself inside the deep layers of his arctic gear before pulling away from their warm huddle and hauling himself above the rim of the half-track's rear compartment. Zagottis lit up the vehicle's mounted searchlight and swiveled it face forward. "There it is."

Girding themselves as Zagottis had, Harry and Kneece likewise pulled themselves up.

The snow was coming down steadily, but without the fierce winds they had experienced in their stay two hundred and fifty miles north at Godthåb. Caught in the searchlight, the snowflakes glittered against the darkness of the arctic morning. Harry squinted beyond the glare of the beam to the oblong mound where Zagottis directed his light.

At first it appeared no different from the other piles of snow plowed clear of the metal matting and left alongside the runway of the naval air station. But then Zagottis's light found bits of a C-47's charred fuselage. One of the horizontal stabilizers jutted at an angle up through the snow. The Dakota had come to rest belly-up; the rudder was invisible, crushed beneath the inverted tail.

Zagottis was a short, bandy-legged fellow, stout like a wrestler. He had jet-black hair molded into a helmet by long hours inside a parka's hood, and a broad, pleasant face creased by weather lines and reddened and chapped by a cold replete with watery eyes, sneezing, and hacking cough. He had been waiting for them in the half-track at the Narssarssuaq runway. No sooner had introductions been made when Kneece announced he'd like to visit the site of the crash that had drawn Armando Grassi to this place.

Zagottis had snuffled and sighed. "Then we need to go now. If we don't, by the end of this storm, it's gonna be a chore just to find the damn thing."

Now, peering at the wreck, Zagottis's illness-soured mood turned still more bitter. "The pilot, this rooster of a first looey named McKesson, he figures he's a real Mr. Hotshot. He's practically fresh from ninety days of flight school so now he thinks he's a regular Lindbergh. I see him, his whole crew, they got eyes red like stoplights, they been flyin' all night, probably more. They're runnin' on pep pills. I tell him 's a squall comin' up from the south off the water, got these leading gusts o' wind tunneling through the offshore islands. I tell Lindbergh, Mr. Hotshot, I say, why not stand down a day or two, let it blow by, catch some sack time? Doesn't listen, says this is a red-ball priority. Snaps his gum, says, 'Gas me up and get me outta here, pal,' thinks he can beat the storm outta here. My pilots, Navy combat flyers, I got them standin' down, but Mr. Hotshot—"

"Doesn't listen," Kneece said.

"I even put it down in the tower log, which I'm not supposed to, but I see this is a disaster comin' and I want it on the record I talked to this McKesson, that it was Mr. Hotshot's call not to sit it out. His wheels just clear the mat two hundred yards that way"—Zagottis pointed into the darkness past the C-47's tail—"and that bitch-evil wind gets up under his starboard wing. Mr. Hotshot can't bring 'er back, she flips, lands on 'er head. She tears up a nice stretch of my runway, skids off, her tanks go up, and here she sits."

"When was this?" Harry asked.

"Two weeks yesterday. December first."

"Can we get inside?" Kneece asked. "I'm going to want a look."

"I was afraid you were gonna say that." Zagottis sneezed, then instructed the half-track driver to keep the engine running so it wouldn't freeze up, and to leave the vehicle's headlamps and searchlight directed at the wreckage.

They clambered out the rear door, then waded through the powdery snow. The walk became a struggle as they neared the aeroplane and the drifts grew waist-deep. The lieutenant commander floundered about until he managed to push through the snow and past the ajar fuselage door. He reached back to help pull a gasping Harry and Kneece clear of the snow. "Watch your step, fellas. Watch your head, too: low bridge."

With the plane on its back, the door sat high above the curved "floor" of the cabin, making for a long step down. The force of the impact had buckled most of the fuselage ribs.

Its windows covered by banked snow, the C-47's cabin was pitch dark except for the column of light through the door from the half-track. In that narrow swath Harry could see the interior of the cabin was as fire-blackened as the outside of the ship. Two weeks in Greenland's winter gales hadn't purged the interior of the reek of burnt petrol, charred wood, and scorched metal. The stench set Harry's always problematic stomach roiling.

Zagottis produced a torch, which he handed over to Kneece. Kneece began poking his way forward, tripping over the tangle of blackened debris scattered through the ship's body, the ray from the torch sweeping this way and that. The litter on the floor was comprised of the burnt wood of packing crates heavily dappled with sparkling crystals of broken glass.

Zagottis sneezed. "Damn . . ." He pulled his hood clear of his face to spit out a wad of phlegm: *snap!* "My family is fishermen, we have a boat we run out of San Francisco, all the way back to my grandpa. I'm on that boat since I'm a kid: rain, cold, wind, that bitch-evil San Francisco fog that goes right in your bones. All that time I don't get a sniffle, all my life. Your pal Grassi shows up—"

"I wouldn't call him my—"

"—and *bang*, I'm sick as a dog. It's not enough the guy's a pain in the ass, he's a germ carrier to boot. Typhoid Mary." Zagottis sneezed gustily.

"Somehow it doesn't surprise me." Perhaps it was because they were inside the ship, out of the elements, that Harry'd stopped shivering. Finally getting used to the cold, he decided. *Harry* (and this he said to himself with an uncharacteristic touch of jaunty bravado), *you are becoming an arctic veteran.*

"How about the crew?" It was Kneece crunching his way back to them from the cockpit.

"Mr. Hotshot McKesson, he didn't make it out. You saw that cockpit? Took us three hours to cut his body outta there. In the dummy seat a shavetail named Coster. I don't know how he got outta here—*he* doesn't know—but he must be in good with God somehow. 'Cept for some bumps and bruises, Coster come out OK. Two E-6's back here. Marquez on the radio; he doesn't make it. Bell, the flight mechanic, the crash crew gets him out but he's in bad shape: busted bones, cracked skull, burned up bad. Third degree all over here." Zagottis waved his mittened hand round his torso and face. He shivered, though Harry didn't think it was because of the cold. "A guy in that kinda shape goin' home, sometimes you think he's better off he doesn't make it."

"All Army," Harry noted of the crew.

"Yeah. I pulled their serial numbers from their dog tags if you need 'em. This wasn't an ATC flight. Diplomatic."

"What does that mean? Diplomatic?"

"You know, like they're sendin' a pouch to some embassy in the ETO, or a courier, like FDR wants Harry Hopkins to go shake Churchill's hand, let 'em know he's still a pal. Most times, somebody like that goes by Navy ship, unless it's a red ball, then you throw 'em on a C-87 and send 'em transatlantic direct. Unless it *is* Harry Hopkins, then he gets to go by Pan Am clipper, first class, him and the Rockefellers."

"But some of it *does* go through you," Kneece said.

"Some. No Rockefellers."

"Grassi's CO says you reported the crew might've been drinking."

"That's what we thought, 'cause we get in here, the place smells like a distillery. Coster, McKesson, it's like they're swimmin' in the stuff. But we goofed." Zagottis shrugged apologetically. He beckoned for the torch, led them farther aft, and knelt. Kneeling by the Navy man, Harry caught a sweet scent hovering above the floor, something more welcoming than the deathly smell permeating the rest of the gutted ship. Zagottis flashed the light about the jumble between the arched fuselage ribs, flipped burnt bits of packing crate out of the way. Something glittered under the light on the floor between them: a hard mass several inches across.

"Ice?" asked Kneece.

"Glass," Zagottis said. "Melted in the fire, then hardened again."

"My God, how hot did it get in here?" Harry asked.

"Hot," Zagottis said.

"A lot of glass," Kneece observed.

"A lot," Zagottis agreed. He crab-walked a few feet, reached down into the debris, and picked up a fire-blackened piece of paper a few inches square. One side of the paper glittered with crystals of broken glass. "This look about the size of a bottle label to you? You can't read it, the fire took care of that, but take a sniff. On the adhesive side."

Kneece took the label from Zagottis, held it to his face and sniffed. He turned to Harry and smiled, handing him the label. Harry sniffed. That sweet smell again, stronger.

"Liquor?" Harry guessed.

"Whisky," Kneece declared.

"I'm figurin' a coupla dozen bottles," Zagottis said. "That's why everythin' smelled like booze."

"And every*body*," Kneece said.

"By the time we know better, Grassi is already on his way here. There's somethin' else." Zagottis stumbled his way farther aft, the light flashing round at his feet. "Where the hell . . . ? Ahh, here we go." His beam rested on another glossy mass nearly eighteen inches across, this more a pile than a pool, rising to a thickened middle. At first Harry thought it was more melted glass, but this had a milkier color. Zagottis pulled off a mitten with his teeth, reached into his parka with his gloved hand, drew out a penknife. He scraped at the substance, then shook the powder onto the palm of Harry's mitten. "Taste."

Tentatively, Harry flicked his tongue at the white powder. "Sugar!"

"Sugar." Zagottis swept his light round the debris. "Also melted in the fire. *Pounds* of it. That stuff over there looks like dirt? Coffee. More pounds. See those?" He shone the light on a pile of what looked like smoked, deflated cricket balls spilling from the remains of a smashed packing crate. "Like your grapefruit barbecued? Eat up. Poke through all this crap you're gonna find maple syrup, butter, canned hams, fresh fruit . . . A whole restaurant in here." Zagottis scowled at the incinerated delectables. "My name's not Eisenhower, I'm not a priority, so I gotta jump through hoops to get stuff I need. Aviation gas, vacuum tubes for radios. I got planes out here so overdue for engine overhauls it's not funny, but I can't get parts. Not even spark plugs. Antifreeze, shovels, chow for my guys don't come out of a can smellin' like dog food. Blankets, electric flyin' suits, long johns, socks, snowshoes, snow packs, gloves, cigarettes, knives, forks, pens, pencils, paper clips, every other goddamn thing. I gotta fill out requisitions in triplicate to get toilet paper—"

"Quintuplicate," Harry said.

"—but we're always down to wipin' our asses with old copies of *Stars & Stripes* before we get it." Zagottis kicked at a piece of packing crate. The crack of splintering wood was sharp inside the hull of the Dakota. "My guys eat powdered eggs, wash it down with powdered milk, wipe their asses with newspapers, fly on bad plugs. But some son of a bitch somewheres is gettin' fresh grapefruit with his breakfast."

"Where was this load headed?" Kneece asked.

Zagottis sneezed and swept his sleeve at his nose. "Dunno."

"Where was it flying in from?"

Zagottis shrugged.

"I'm all in suspense about how you logged the flight."

"No log. I told you, I wasn't even suppose' to put down about me warnin' Mr. Hotshot to stand down. That's how it is with a night train."

"A what?"

Zagottis smiled at the consternation on Kneece's face. "That's what we call 'em—an off-log diplomatic flight. I don't know about you, Captain, but I'm freezin' my ass off. If you're done lookin', we can conversate in my office where it's eighty degrees warmer. That poor bastard in the track's probably froze to his seat by now."

The air station was squeezed on a narrow plain between the interior highlands and the jagged, ice-blocked coast of Kap Farvel. It was the biggest and most elaborate aerodrome Harry had seen since he and Kneece had left Newark, 2800 miles away. Near the half-mile-long runway were fuel storage tanks, munitions stores, a machine shop, the wide bulk of a repair hangar. As the half-track clanked along the runway, Harry saw, in the sweep of the headlamps, like troops lined up at parade dress, a mixed squadron of blocky four-engined B-24 Liberators alongside ungainly PBY Catalina flying boats. The open faces of each ship's engines were shielded from the weather by tightly wrapped tarpaulins.

"You called this flight a 'night train,'" Harry heard Kneece say to Zagottis. "Something about 'off-log'—"

"We call 'em night trains 'cause that's how they are—they slip in, slip out, you hardly know they're there. They show up with orders sayin' we're not supposed to log 'em. I figure—well, what I used to figure before the bar car from the Super Chief cracked up here—was they wanted these runs off-log 'cause it was some kind of secret mission or somethin'. That's why they were goin' this route, out of the way. Now?" Zagottis shrugged. "I figure they just didn't want to share the goodies."

"How long's this been going on? These night-train flights?"

"Well, I'm here eight months. Some hands I got go back a year or better, they remember them comin' even back then. Sometimes we get a couple a month, then maybe you go a month or more with none."

"They just come in from nowhere, go out to nowhere? Seems like a hell of a way to run a railroad."

Zagottis laughed. "You gotta understand how it works here. I get flights comin' in here all the time I don't know who they are. Army, Navy, sometimes Canucks, sometimes even limeys. Come outta the east, west. Communications as bad as they are—especially this time of year—half the time I don't know a plane's comin' in 'til it touches down on my runway. These are military transport planes, Captain, not your papa's Ford. You don't just pick up the keys, say I'm goin' for a spin, and wind up here. I figure you don't get here unless you're supposed to be here. And where you wind up is for your dispatcher and the guy at the other end to worry about. I gas 'em up, I give 'em hot chow, a bunk if they need sack time, but my job's to get 'em outta my way fast as I can." Zagottis pointed at the phalanx of aircraft parked near the runway. "Those are my priority. Anytime I got half a sky, my planes're up nursemaidin' convoys in and out the Denmark Strait. No convoy? They're still up there, huntin'. They go huntin' U-boats, Captain, and when they find 'em they kill 'em. Anythin' else is just a distractin' pain in my ass."

Harry knew all this was important, but at the moment couldn't think why. Snowflakes danced down into the open rear of the half-track. The thickening blanket of snow muted the sound of the vehicle's treads on the runway matting. For the first time since he'd shakily climbed out of the plane that had brought them to Narssarssuaq, he felt at ease. Even the cold dropped away.

"What?" He was suddenly aware of Zagottis speaking to him, shaking him by the arm.

"You awright, Major? Looks like you're fadin' there."

"Fine, fine," Harry said, and thought it curious how thick his tongue felt. "Just tired. We had to get up early . . ." He lost his train of thought. "Just tired."

"Feelin' pretty good?"

Harry smiled and nodded.

"Want to just nod off, huh?"

Harry nodded again.

"Oh, Christ. Hey, Kneece, help me get him on his feet. C'mon, Major, let's go."

"What's the matter?" Kneece asked.

"He's been out here too long. Hypothermia."

Harry found himself on his feet, propped against the rim of the compartment. He felt someone—Zagottis, probably—pull the fur trim of his parka hood away from his face. "Let that wind in there, Major."

"Is this how it happens?" Harry heard Kneece ask.

"It can sneak up on you like that," Zagottis said. "First you're cold, shiver the teeth right outta your head. Then you feel pretty good, like you had a few. It starts seemin' like a good idea to just lie down in the snow, catch forty winks. 'Cept you don't wake up. Tell you the truth, Kneece, it's not a bad way to go."

"How you doin', Major?" Zagottis asked.

"I'm cold again," Harry said through chattering teeth. He pulled the woolen Army blanket Zagottis had provided closer round his shoulders.

"Believe it or not, that's a good sign." Shrouded in another blanket, Zagottis was standing by his office coal stove stirring a pair of mugs filled with steaming water from a kettle on the stove. He turned away from the mugs to sneeze. "Oh, mannnn," he groaned after the explosion. "I wish your pal Grassi was still alive—"

"He wasn't my—"

"—so I could kill 'im for givin' me this goddamn bug." Zagottis handed Harry one of the mugs. "Hope you don't mind sharin' a tea bag; gotta make 'em stretch. How about you, Kneece? I got water for tea, I got a pot of coffee warmin' up here, too."

Kneece was slouched in one of the chairs across from Zagottis's littered desk, flipping back and forth through his small notebook. "Coffee."

"What's that taste?" Harry asked, smiling up from his mug. "Honey?"

"Yeah. I got an uncle up in Monterey with his own bees sends it to me."

Even with a few swallows of honey-sweetened hot tea inside and a blanket tight round him, Harry shivered. The Navy lieutenant commander had been right when he'd said his office was eighty degrees warmer than outside, but that still left it chill enough to maintain a crust of frost on the one window.

Zagottis may have been the air station's commander, but his office was no more well appointed than the other cubicles in the headquarters Quonset: cramped, the few pieces of furniture scuffed, an uncurtained window offering a monotonous view of falling and fallen snow. Behind the desk a row of pegs lined the wall with clipboards filled with rosters, status reports, and the like. The wall to his left was covered with a variety of sector and area maps, some under acetate overlays heavily done with grease pencil markings indicating air routes, patrol sweeps, weather conditions. The opposite wall Zagottis referred to warmly as his "gallery."

There were, Harry guessed, at least two dozen photos tacked to the plywood partition from small Brownie box–produced images to larger eight-by-tens. Most were typical family photos: groupings of smiling folk Harry presumed to be friends and relatives, from aged elder to cherubic newborn, posed against sundry dining rooms, playgrounds, parlors, picnics in the park, the aforementioned family fishing vessel.

Harry's eyes settled on a photo showing a young, laughing, sloe-eyed woman on a porch swing with an equally elated Zagottis alongside wearing the Navy whites of an ensign. In the photo Zagottis was holding aloft between them a jolly pile of baby garbed in nothing but a baggy diaper, its pumpkin grin showing the first nubs of new incisors. Harry looked from the illness-dogged features of the lieutenant commander to the smooth-faced lad in the photo. He needed to revise his estimate of the commander's age: no more than thirty, probably younger.

Zagottis nodded at the photos. "My wife is always sending me pictures. Says they gotta be better to look at than the view I got."

"She's got that right." Kneece was stonily regarding the incessant snow outside the window.

"The novelty of winter wonderlands wearing off, Woody?" Harry poked.

The young captain smiled ruefully. "That kinda come back to bite me, didn't it?"

Harry turned back to the photo. "A boy?"

Zagottis nodded. "That's right after I got out of OCS. He turned one ten days later, just after I shipped out. Been another birthday go by since then. This'll be his second Christmas I'm not there."

"Me, too." They smiled at each other, sharing the same sense of home.

"Commander." Kneece cleared his throat. "The two men who survived the crash—"

"Coster and Bell."

"I'd like to talk to them. I realize Bell might not be in any shape—"

"Kneece, you can talk to 'em all you want, but first you gotta find 'em." Zagottis gave a last look at his son. He topped his mug of tea with more hot water, then slipped one of the clipboards from its peg, flipped to a particular page, and turned the board over to Kneece. "Communications log," he explained. "Coster's a little out of his head after the crash. He sees his cockpit partner get squished like an egg, comes damn close to the same treatment, no surprise he starts to unravel. Takes the sick bay doc a while to calm him down, slip him some dope to get him more or less on an even keel. Soon's Coster can think clear he's at me he's got to send a signal back to the States, very important, top priority. The signal goes to Army GHQ in D.C., some light colonel named Edghill. I don't know what he does for a livin', but it looks like he was McKesson's boss. Turn the page; doesn't take long for Edghill to come back to him."

Kneece held the clipboard up for Harry. Harry took his seat and flipped through the carbon copies of message forms. As I later saw, they read as follows:

FROM: LT A COSTER
       ARMY FLT 103 XRAY
TO: LT COL EDGHILL DC ARMY GHQ
       XRAY DISPATCH
DATE: 12-1-43
ARMY FLT 103 XRAY CRASHED CAPE [sic] FARVEL AIR STATION STOP
CO MCKESSON TSGT MARQUEZ KILLED TSGT BELL HURT CARGO DE-
STROYED STOP PLS ADVISE ASAP END MESSAGE

Harry turned the page for the reply:

FROM: EDGHILL
TO: CO KAP FARVEL
DATE: 12-1-43
REPLACEMENT FLT 121 XRAY TO ARRIVE YOUR STATION SOME TIME
12-2-43 STOP HANDLE AS TOP PRIORITY STOP ADVISE COSTER TO
BOARD ORDERS AWAITING AT TERMINUS STOP BELL MCKESSON MAR-
QUEZ ALL EFFECTS TO BOARD ON RETURN LEG 12-3-43 END MES-
SAGE

"They wanted McKesson's and Marquez's bodies returned?" Harry asked Zagottis.

"And all their effects. I see this, I shoot one right back. Poor bastard Bell's in a coma, my doc tells me it's pretty shaky the kid makin' it at all, let alone bumpin' around in a C-47 for a thousand miles. But . . ." Zagottis nodded Harry back to the communications log:

FROM: LT CMDR ZAGOTTIS
       NARSSARSSUAQ AIR STATION
TO: LT COL EDGHILL ARMY GHQ
DATE: 12-1-43
M[edical] O[fficer] STRONGLY AGAINST BELL TRANSPORT STOP CON-
DITION GRAVE STOP RECOMMEND DELAY IF UNTIL STATUS IM-
PROVES STOP ADVISE END MESSAGE

FROM: EDGHILL
TO: CO ZAGOTTIS KAP FARVEL
DATE: 12-1-43
COMPLY BELL TRANSPORT AS ORDERED END MESSAGE

"That read like they're lookin' for an argument?" Zagottis asked.

Harry flipped back to the first message, to the entry on the Time of Transmission line. Coster had sent his signal at 0132 hours on December first. Edghill's reply had been received thirty-four minutes later, at 0206. Zagottis had sent his caution to Edghill just a few minutes later, at 0214, with the lieutenant colonel coming back nearly as fast with his rebuff at 0223.

"This second night train," Kneece said.

"One-twenty-one X-ray," Zagottis wheezed.

"It did arrive the following day? December second?"

"Comes in around 1200 hours, sits just long enough to refuel, then she's gone. She's back the next day, midafternoon sometime. Same deal: top off 'er tanks and off."

"The eastbound leg: that's where Grassi hitched his ride to the Orkneys?"

Zagottis shrugged. "That's how I figure it."

"You're not sure?"

"Hell, Kneece, I didn't know where Grassi was 'til I get told they found 'im croaked in the Orkneys. The night train pinwheels that mornin'. By that night, I got Grassi down here, and the second his boots hit the ground he is in my ear."

"About what?"

"Same stuff as you guys, only he's not as polite. He doesn't let up, ei-ther. You tell 'im somethin' he doesn't want to hear, somethin' goes click in his head and he doesn't hear it. You gotta tell him sixty-two times. 'You sure there's no record of night trains?' 'That's why they're night trains, dummy.' What're the cargoes? Where do they come from? Where do they go? Where do I think they go? Sittin' with him over coffee's worse than cops goin' at you with bright lights and a rubber hose."

"A noodge," Kneece said.

"What?"

"You were saying," Harry interposed.

"When Grassi's not on me about the night trains and the crash, he's cryin' about the cold, he doesn't like his quarters, what's wrong with the food . . ." Zagottis rolled his eyes. "I got a real sympathy for Captain Blume puttin' up with him all the time. Did you know the guy, Kneece? Major? Then you know what I'm talkin' about. I'm not surprised he give me a head cold. That guy *was* a head cold! All this time, makin' it worse, I got my hands full. There's somethin' goin' on in the ETO, or somethin' ready to pop, 'cause I got transports comin' in like this is the corner fillin' station."

Harry nodded. "I heard up at Bluie-West-One your traffic's been heavy lately."

"Heavy?" Zagottis laughed at the understatement, sparking a series of hacks. Again he spat mucus into his wastebasket. "I had six other transports come through the day the night train plowed. Had eight the next day. I'm tryin' to get them in and out, fix this hole that bonehead McKesson put in my runway, I got my birds to worry about, then I got your pal Grassi . . ."

"I wish you wouldn't call him our pal," Harry said.

"When was the last time you saw Grassi?" Kneece asked.

"Grassi wound up spendin' a lotta time in the sick bay botherin' Coster, which couldn'ta been a treat for Coster. I was just glad Grassi was leavin' my people alone. This second night train, 121 X-ray, like I said, she touches down around 1200. I stick my head in sick bay, tell Coster his ride's here, which doesn't make him look too happy, wish 'im luck. Grassi was with 'im so I didn't hang around."

"Did anybody see Grassi board the night train?"

"If anybody did it'd be the ground crew. I'll show you the duty roster, you can ask around. That night, evenin' mess, I finally notice Grassi's not around—far be it from him to miss a meal even if all he's gonna do is bitch about how lousy it is. He's gone, I just figure he got whatever he could get and went back to Godthåb." Zagottis slumped in his chair and rubbed the warm side of his tea mug along his forehead.

"Do you know what Coster told him?"

"I'm not his CO. Grassi makes a report, he doesn't make it to me. What I know is after his first round with Coster that night he comes to me, wants me to send a signal." Zagottis took the communications log from Kneece, flipped to a fresh page, and handed it back.

Kneece held the log to where Harry could lean over and they could read the carbons together. There were two:

```
FROM:   LT A GRASSI
        JAG NARSARSAK [sic]
TO:     LT COL EDGHILL DC ARMY GHQ
        XRAY DISPATCH
DATE:   12-1-43
```
RE FLT 103 XRAY DISPATCHED BY YOU LT MCKESSON CO STOP PLS
ADVISE FOLLOWING STOP ITEM ONE NATURE OF CARGO ITEM TWO
DESTINATION ITEM THREE PURPOSE OF FLIGHT ITEM FOUR FLIGHT
AUTHORIZATION STOP ALSO REQUEST 103 XRAY COPILOT COSTER
DETAINED NARSARSAK [sic] FOR JAG INQUIRY END MESSAGE

Again Harry noted the time the message had been sent: 1110. He flipped
to the response received at 1142:

```
FROM:   EDGHILL
TO:     GRASSI
        NARSSARSSUAQ AIR STATION
DATE:   12-1-43
```
YOUR REQUEST PASSED ON TO HIGHER AUTHORITY STOP WILL RE-
SPOND EARLIEST END MESSAGE

"Higher authority?" Kneece asked.

"You're lookin' at me like you think I'm gonna know what that
means," Zagottis said.

Harry flipped through the communications log. "Did you ever get another message from Edghill regarding Grassi's request? Or from anyone
else in D.C.?"

Zagottis shook his head. "Never thought about it once Grassi was
gone. Then when I heard he was dead . . ."

"The night-train crews," Kneece persisted, "were they always the
same personnel? Was it a rotating pool of pilots? Did you know any of the
names of the other—"

Tiredly, Zagottis sighed. "Kneece, you got any idea how many pilots
come through here? It's like askin' the doorman at the St. Francis if he
knows all the cabbies at the hack stand. You recognize some faces, some
of the same guys come through more than once, but I don't know who
they are. I don't know who most of the regular ATC pilots are. Hell, most
the time, I never deal with 'em; the ground crews do. If they don't lay
over for the night, I hardly see 'em. McKesson, though, he hit me as a
new face. Musta been new to the route."

"What makes you think so?"

" 'Cause only a rookie who doesn't know how bitch-evil this place can be'd be that much of a bonehead. The only thing I remember about all the night trains was they always had an X-ray designation in the flight number. That's how we knew, when they radioed their approach, that it was a night train and not to log it."

Kneece flipped back to a page in his notebook. "And they radioed Edghill as 'X-ray Dispatch.' "

Harry grunted himself out of his chair and went back to Zagottis's gallery wall. He stood by the photo of Zagottis with his wife and baby boy. "Commander, how much did this little muscle man weigh when he was born?"

Zagottis's face brightened. "Eight pounds and an ounce."

"My first was seven and a half pounds. My second was close to eight. Planning on any more?"

"Big families run in the family. Soon's I get home, I'm goin' to work on it."

Harry caught the look on Kneece's face, something best described as polite impatience. Harry looked back at the smiling baby. "Commander, how big a cargo was that night train carrying? The one that crashed."

"The crash, the fire, hard to tell. Maybe a thousand pounds. No more than two thousand."

Harry turned to Kneece. He raised his eyebrows and dipped his head, signaling that his participation was now concluded.

"Commander, did you do any kind of follow-up on any of this?" Kneece asked Zagottis.

"Follow-up? I was so damn happy to have this mess off my desk. . . . Look, when I saw Grassi was gone, I'm done. What's that look, Captain? You look like you don't believe me."

"It's not that, Commander, I just remember how upset you seemed over the cargo this night-train flight was carrying. I'd've thought you'd want to—"

"Want to *what*, Captain?" Zagottis looked to Harry as if to say, *I know you understand.* He turned back to Kneece. "Am I p.o.'d about that cargo? Sure. Do I think it's a waste of valuable Army transport? You betcha. An unnecessary risk of personnel? Damn right. Who's the ambassador they got in England? The one come in after they pulled Joe Kennedy out?"

"Winant," Kneece said. "John Winant."

"OK, so Mr. Ambassador Winant, he wants to throw a dinner party for the Queen, he gets Mr. Roosevelt on the blower and orders up some goodies. Maybe Winant wants to have a surprise party for Eisenhower. Stupid? Yeah. A fuckin' waste? Sure. You think there's anythin' in there the

Army's gonna consider a fileable charge?" Zagottis gravely closed his eyes and solemnly moved his head from one side to the other in a nonverbal proclamation of NO!

"Look, Kneece," the commander continued, "there *was* one guy I would've loved to nail: McKesson, 'cause he was the asshole got people hurt and put a hole in my runway. Screw a court-martial, I'da pinned his ears back myself! But I saw 'em pull the kid's body outta that plane one piece at a time. You don't get more punished than that. He did it to himself, too, which makes it some kind of poetry."

I can picture Harry sitting on the edge of his bunk, an Army blanket draped round his shoulders, head tilted back to keep his reading glasses in place as he stares down at squares of paper arrayed on the floor, upon each of which is a single line of bold printing. Harry's lips are pursed in study as his eyes dart from one bit of paper to another, his canted chin parked in palms, splayed fingers enveloping his sagging jowls.

Harry seemed so much the image of the contemplative muse that Kneece, to gain his attention, deferentially cleared his throat as if disturbing a man at prayer. It required a second "ahem" to turn Harry's head. Kneece was on his own bunk, his own note tablet in his hands. "What's all that, Major? What's with the bits of paper?"

"Nothing," Harry said. "I'm tired. I'm turning in."

Harry slid off his glasses and began to burrow, fully dressed, under the several blankets on his bunk. Kneece reached for his parka.

"Where're you off to?" Harry asked.

"We never had breakfast. Why don't you come get something to eat with me?"

"We also didn't get a whole night's sleep. I'm fine right here. Besides, I'm almost thawed. I'm not going back out there." Harry pointed to Kneece's writing tablet. "Message to Edghill? Asking what's going on here?"

Kneece shook his head admiringly at Harry's intuitiveness. "Something like that. I also want to know where Coster and Bell are stashed. You got a look on, Major, that says I'm wasting my time."

"I have a *look*?"

"Yes, Major. A look."

"Every time I roll to a new spot it's cold. You have any cigarettes?"

Kneece reached inside his flight jacket and tossed the pack to Harry. Harry sat up, lit one, looked for a place to toss the expired match.

"I wouldn't be too afraid of messing these finely appointed apartments," Kneece said. "The maid'll be by later."

Harry smiled. He stood, looking like some Himalayan vagabond as he shuffled, swathed in blankets, across the room to toss the match into the stove. "What do you think's going on, Woody? With these night trains?"

"I'm thinking black market. That's why they keep the flights off the record. They're running stuff through here, off the beaten airways you might say."

Harry nodded. He'd considered the same thing himself. "Remember what Zagottis said? An Army transport can't get here unless it's supposed to. It takes a lot of coordination to put together a crew and a plane, load cargo, get the necessary flight clearances. That's a lot of overhead for a criminal enterprise."

"You know what they say. You have to spend money to make money."

"I believe the trick is to make more than you spend. There wasn't enough cargo on that plane to pay for the trip."

"Come on, Major, I hear a bottle of even bad booze overseas can bring—"

"A planeload of booze would've been worth it. Not a couple of dozen bottles. Most of the stuff on that plane—the sugar, the coffee, all that stuff—is easier, simpler, and cheaper to steal out of the Quartermaster stores right in the British Isles. One of the reasons you said you wanted me on this trip is because I've been there and you haven't. Take it from me then: Grapefruit is not that big a black-market draw. There wasn't enough money at stake on that plane for Grassi to wind up dead."

Kneece weighed Harry's point. Then: "I don't know about that, Major. Spend some time with Uncle Ray and you wind up thinking there's folks'll shoot you for a shiny button. OK, let's let the dog run a bit. The stuff's not black market. What then?"

"I don't know what it is, but I'm getting an idea about what it isn't. I don't see this having anything to do with what happened with Grassi, Peter Ricks, and me in England last August. It looks to me like this business started here, with that wreck."

"You don't give up," Kneece chuckled.

"You still think it does?"

Kneece jutted out his chin, narrowed his eyes, scratched the top of his head with his fingertips and in a voice that was a fair approximation of Stan Laurel's, announced, "I'm not sure, Ollie."

"You ought to get your own show on the radio."

"Factually, Grassi's death having something to do with August is a good theory, and I do hate to put away a good theory without a good reason. Since I don't know what happened in August, I don't know there still isn't a connection between this and that."

Harry sighed in frustration, but he couldn't help but smile. The captain was a terrier—not all that unlike Harry—unwilling to let go. "If you want to find out about Edghill, don't go to Edghill."

"You think he's involved?"

"Or maybe somebody who works for or with him. It's only a possibility, but it *is* a possibility."

"Why do you think that?"

"When were you told about Grassi's murder?"

Kneece studied Harry a moment. "Let's see, it would've been that Wednesday: the eighth."

"About a week from the time Grassi signaled Edghill."

"They had a hell of a time running Grassi down, once his body turned up. The Brits assumed, like anybody would, that he must've belonged to one of our units in the British Isles. There was a lot of running around trying to find him on duty rolls. It was only during a cross-check they came across the record of his transfer to Greenland. Then there was some more running around trying to figure out why it was he was a stiff on a beach in the Orkneys instead of annoying people in Greenland."

"The upshot being that it took a few days for Washington to get notified. Even if you take off the time the Washington brass spent—a day, let's say a couple of days—trying to figure out what to do with this mess before it landed on your desk, that still means Edghill had Grassi's request in his hands for at least a couple of days *before* Washington was notified Grassi was dead."

"So?"

Harry took a last draw before pushing the remains of his cigarette through the openings of the grate. "Edghill responded to Coster's message within a half hour. He came back to Zagottis about moving Bell even faster. Edghill put together a plane, a crew, and a replacement cargo and had them here inside of a day. Grassi had a very simple request: Where'd this plane come from, and where was it going? We know Edghill got the request; he acknowledged it about thirty minutes later; another fast reply. But Edghill never sent Grassi a response."

"Grassi was out of here the next day."

Harry returned to his bunk, lay down, and rearranged his blankets into a snug cocoon. "Edghill didn't know that. For all he knew, Grassi was still here waiting for an answer. Unless Edghill had a private pipeline to the Orkneys and knew, before anybody else on his side of the Atlantic, that Grassi wasn't going to be in Greenland to receive an answer. You want to find out about Edghill, ask somebody you know in CIC. I mean somebody you know personally, somebody you can trust, somebody who won't blab about it to everybody in your office."

"You're sounding a little paranoid, Major," Kneece said.

Harry closed his eyes. "You told me you wanted me around because I know the ropes. That's one of the ropes I know."

He heard the door to the room open. "You want me to bring something back?"

"It'd be cold by the time you got it here."

"I used that word 'noodge' right, didn't I?"

"Like a Hebrew scholar, Woody."

"You get your shut-eye, Major. I'll see you later."

The door closed. It was some time before Harry's thoughts quieted.

Harry slowly rose to consciousness, aware of flashes of light and dark on the other side of his closed lids. His irritation at being thus stirred was compounded by reveille, a piece of music composed by some militaristic sadist for the express purpose of transforming peaceful slumbers into wakeful vexation. The nettling value of reveille was, in this case, multiplied manyfold in that it was here not being tooted by a skilled bugler but by a grinning Jim Doheeny. The pilot was vocalizing the tune through the cupped fingers of one hand in an annoyingly wretched semblance of a bugle while flicking the room lights with his other hand.

Harry allowed one eye to crawl open. On seeing Doheeny by the door, his happiness over the pilot's reappearance did not preclude him from flinging his pillow at him.

Doheeny easily caught the pillow. "Music hater." He tossed the pillow back and moved toward the heating stove.

Keeping his blankets close about him, Harry sat upright. Kneece's bunk was empty. The blankets were undisturbed: Kneece had never come to bed. The captain's writing tablet lay on the bunk, its first sheet blank.

"So," Doheeny said, "have you enjoyed your stay in the tropics?"

"The tropics?" Harry yawned.

Doheeny was shoveling lumps of fresh coal from a nearby scuttle atop the dying embers inside the grate. "Compared to where we've been, this is a sunny day on the beach."

"When did you get in?"

"Few minutes ago. The weather cleared Strømfjord late this morning. We took a swing west over the ocean, marking time until it cleared here."

"What time is it now?" Harry squinted at his watch but couldn't get the luminous face in focus.

"A little after three."

Harry looked out the window into darkness. "A.M. or P.M.?"

Doheeny laughed. "P.M."

Harry had been asleep five hours.

Doheeny slipped off his heavy mittens as he dropped onto Kneece's bunk. He unzipped his parka and fiddled inside his outer garments until he produced a pack of cigarettes. He placed two in his mouth, lit them, then handed one over to Harry.

"Listen, Harry. Your pal Kneece is talking about us flying out of here today—"

"That's got to be a joke. We just got here."

Doheeny seemed amused at Harry's shock. "You didn't know?"

"The reveille thing was funnier."

"The clan is gathering over at the mess hall right now. I've got my orders, and my orders say Kneece's the boss. But leaving today isn't a good idea. You have the rank on him, Harry."

"I may outrank him, but I have no authority over him. This is his party."

Doheeny nodded glumly, understanding. He stubbed his cigarette out on the metal frame of the bunk, stood, and zipped up his parka. "I'd appreciate it if you'd try to talk some sense to that kid, Harry, because he's not using a whole hell of a lot of it. He's got *that* mental disease."

"Which mental disease is that?"

"The one we all had at his age. He thinks he's going to live forever."

Only Kneece was eating. The others—Doheeny and his crew, and Zagottis—ignored the plates of food in front of them. Even Doheeny's copilot, circling the table as was his usual inclination, held a sandwich with only one bite missing.

Kneece seemed oblivious to the frustration directed toward him. His attention was completely dedicated to the serving of the ubiquitous Greenland lamb chops and a scoop of less appetizing powdered eggs.

"It's not like I don't appreciate your concerns," Kneece was saying. Harry wasn't sure who he was saying it to as Kneece had yet to look up from his plate.

"Oh, I think it is," Zagottis snapped back, "otherwise we wouldn't be havin' this talk!"

Harry filled a cup of coffee at the serving counter and turned for the table. The flight mechanic flashed a quick smile of hullo before turning back to the discussion at hand. Harry saw that his right hand was heavily wrapped in gauze.

"Let me put something else out to consider," Doheeny said. "I'm tired. My crew is tired. We were flying hard before we picked you up in

Newark, we've been flying hard ever since. If you'd sent word you were going to be flying out today—"

"Mr. Doheeny," Kneece said, emphasizing the gulf between his military rank and Doheeny's civilian status, "it was my understanding that 'flying hard' is what you ATC fellas do. Besides, you had a day lay-up with the storm. Look, I'm not trying to be a pain in anybody's arse here, but I've got my priorities. Your crew can catch sack time on the plane. I don't know why that should be a problem. They've been doing that since we left New York."

Zagottis sneezed into his napkin. "Captain Kneece, you know I got to put this in the log. I got to put this down I warned you against this."

"Fair enough, Commander."

"Warned him against what?" Harry slid into a chair at the table.

"I'm tryin' to explain to the captain there's bad weather buildin' south of us," Zagottis told him glumly. "We're gettin' headwinds whippin' through the offshore islands. If that sounds familiar, it's 'cause the last guy thinks he can outfly those winds ends up on my runway lookin' like this." He poked his fork into Kneece's pile of powdered eggs and let the runny stuff slough off the tines.

"The weather's better than when we got here." Kneece looked distastefully at the spot where Zagottis's fork had stirred into his eggs.

"Let me tell you somethin' about Greenland weather, Captain," Zagottis shot back. "It's bitch-evil even when it's not snowin'. You don't believe me, ask Hotshot McKesson. Oh, that's right. You can't! 'Cause Hotshot McKesson got himself permanently indisposed!"

"Commander, you told me McKesson was a rookie and he messed up like one. Mr. Doheeny is a veteran on this route. I guess I have more faith in him than you do."

"Well, that just flatters me all to hell," Doheeny said. "But this route veteran still says lay over for the night. Is twelve hours going to make that much of a difference?"

Kneece set down his fork and knife, dabbed at his mouth with his napkin. He looked from Doheeny to Zagottis. "Commander, can you guarantee me that this bad weather off the Cape is going to be gone in twelve hours?"

Zagottis turned to Doheeny with an I'm-sorry look; answered Kneece with a negative shake of his head.

"Thirteen hours? Twenty-four?" Kneece looked to Doheeny and shrugged. It was decided. "How long before we can be in the air?"

The way Doheeny was fingering the handle of his fork Harry thought the pilot might lunge across the table and stab Kneece with it. "We've got some cargo to unload. Then refuel. No later than 1800. Let's go, fellas. We've got work to do." Doheeny rose.

Zagottis did, too. "I'll see about havin' somethin' hot put on the plane for you to eat before you roll."

Doheeny thanked him. As he passed by Harry, the pilot stooped over, rested a hand on Harry's shoulder, and whispered, "If you don't talk him out of this, don't get on that plane." He gave Harry's shoulder a pat, then followed his crew out into the cold.

They sat with the length of table between them, Harry studying Kneece across the tongues of vapor from his mug, the captain returning industriously to his plate.

"Ahem," Harry said.

Kneece looked over. He folded his face into a vague impression of Clark Gable jauntiness, affected the King's voice (as much as he could through a mouthful of food), and asked, "So! Come here often?"

"What've you been up to while I've been asleep, to work up such an appetite?"

"Oh, I've been busy, sir."

"I'm sure."

"I don't know if you know it, Major, but you don't sleep right. You throw yourself around on that mattress like you got a bee in your britches. Did you know that, sir? Why is that?"

"You talked to the ground crew like Zagottis suggested."

Kneece nodded. "And the docs at the hospital where they had Coster."

"Did the ground crew see Grassi get on that second night train?"

Kneece shook his head and slurped his coffee. "Man, nothing stays hot here for long. The way everybody's dressed like Eskimos around here the ground crew couldn't tell who was who around that plane. But the doc who was duty officer at the hospital when the night train came in, he remembers Zagottis coming in to say good-bye to Coster and leaving, he remembers Coster leaving. He remembers Grassi leaving with him. And something else— He says Coster didn't look happy when Zagottis brought him those orders to fly east on the night train. The doc says this was more than Coster just being shook up from the crash. He says Coster looked pretty damned *scared*. And mad. Doc says Grassi spent the better part of the night with him, talking. Whatever it was Coster was telling him, it looked to be getting Grassi all het up. So I read it like this and you tell me if I sound like I'm off in the trees or not: Coster's so unhappy about where he's going, he does a bunch of tattling to Grassi."

"Knowing Armando, he probably smelled blood: a big, fat court-martial with him as a crusading prosecutor. That'd be enough to get him all het up," Harry agreed.

"Coster's so p.o.'d at Edghill—or whomsoever—that he helps Grassi b.s. his way onto that second night train. But when they get to the Orkneys, whoever's waiting there knows Grassi doesn't belong on that plane."

"And by then they have to assume he knows too much."

Kneece made a pistol of his fingers. "Pop! goes the weasel."

"This doctor, did he manage to overhear anything that Coster and Grassi talked about?"

"Nope. Those two managed to keep it between themselves."

"I'm surprised it wasn't the strain of being discreet that killed Armando." Harry cleared his throat, firmly announcing a change of subject. "I would think after seeing that wrecked C-47 you wouldn't need Zagottis warning you more than once about winding up like McKesson."

"I have to calculate maybe Zagottis is right about the weather. But I also calculate maybe it's just he's overscared on account of he wound up with two corpses on his hands and a big hole in his precious runway. Doheeny, well, I calculate maybe he's just looking for a break. I'm not saying he doesn't need it and I wish there was the time to give it to him. So, I add all that up to one side."

"And on the other side? I know you've been concerned about the trail going cold—"

"I *was* concerned. But now I'm damned scared about it, thanks to you, sir."

"Thanks to . . . ?"

"You're the one who pointed out to me just how fast these people can work. That's the other side of the calculation. Somebody—or more than one somebody—got McKesson's plane replaced, left Armando Grassi dead in the Orkneys, and put up Coster and Bell in two days. All that done in just *two days*, without leaving a whole lot of sign about the whos and whys and wheres. They've had almost *three weeks* since then to cover their tracks." Kneece's face grew pensive. "I have a lot of respect for you, sir. It'd bother me if you thought I was pushing like this just to—" He looked up. "This isn't about a box of black-market grapefruit, Major. There's three men lying graveyard dead, maybe four. I'm not going to give the sonsabitches who did that any more lead on me than they've got now."

Harry unhappily had to admit that Kneece's disquisition made estimable tactical sense. It also provided a hard-to-dispute compelling moral cause.

"Look, Major," the younger man said, "I'd like to hear you're making the ride with me, but if you don't want to climb on that plane tonight, fine, I understand. I don't have a problem with that. Hell, you left your family and came all this way . . . I asked you for more than a fella should, and you put in a lot more than I had a right to expect. You've been a big, big help, sir. My thinking is I *owe* you the trip home."

"I wasn't talking about going home. I was talking about—"

"Following me later? With all respect, Major, I have to be a little hard here. I can't go trying to run the bad guys to ground all the time having to worry about you catching up to me."

"What if I decide to follow on my own?"

"Your travel authorization is under my orders. If you're not with me, you're going to have to get your own clearance from Stateside."

By which time, Harry thought, Woody Kneece would be in Burma if that's where the trail led.

Kneece pushed his empty plate away. "The cook they got here's got nothing on Blume's man." He poked at a morsel stuck between his teeth with his tongue. "Thoon's 'at p'ane's 'eady to go, if you're not aboard . . . en'oy your Chri'ma' a' home."

Harry sipped down the last of his cold coffee. "All right, Captain." Harry rose from his seat and parked a haunch on the table where he could look down at Kneece. "I'll leave with you."

Kneece brightened. "I'm glad to—"

"But I want a promise from you."

"Sure."

"If, God forbid, something happens and you make it and I don't . . . *you* tell it to my wife. Not the Army. Not by Western Union or telephone. You *go* to her, you look her in the eye, and you tell her."

Kneece smiled coolly. "Awright, sir. You got yourself a deal."

"Hey, Sarge! What's he waiting for?" The oscillations sent throughout the body of the aeroplane by the twin engines gave Kneece's voice a tremulous vibrato that was all too appropriate for the circumstances.

The flight mechanic, sitting across the cargo cabin from Harry and Kneece, was turned round, peering out a cabin window into the night. "Waitin' for the wind to fall off a bit, I think."

Above the idling growl of the Pratt & Whitneys, their voices had a tinny resonance rebounding off the walls of the near-empty cargo cabin. Most of the Dakota's cargo had been off-loaded at Strømfjord and at the Narssarssuaq aerodrome. The cabin now seemed barren with just a few small items and one four-foot-square crate lashed to the deck.

Kneece crossed the cabin to sit by the flight mechanic and look through a neighboring window. Harry looked out his own side. The snow along the runway matting glowed and faded as the moon blinked through gaps in scudding clouds. The Dakota rocked uneasily, wind slipping off the water and across the ice of the Cape to wrap about the ship with a shudder. With each buffet, spindrifts of snow whipped up from the snowbanks, pinwheeling with dizzying speed before settling to rest again.

True to his word, Doheeny had had the Dakota ready for departure before 1800 hours. As the pilot climbed aboard he'd been obviously unhappy to see Harry seated in the cargo cabin. There had been a rapid exchange of silent communication—a glum look from Doheeny that transmitted "What the hell are you doing here?" responded to by Harry with a fatalistic shrug. Doheeny had inserted himself in the cockpit, starters whined, engines coughed and turned over. Once the engines settled into an even hum, Doheeny had conducted the ship to the end of the runway.

Which was where, some ten minutes later, it continued to sit. Each tick of the clock cultivated a seed of anxiety in Harry planted by Zagottis several hours earlier, when he'd warned of the danger of the flight.

"What happened to your hand?" Harry asked the flight mechanic, trying to sound casual.

The sergeant seemed glad for a reason to turn away from the window. "Stupid," he said, brandishing the bandage. "I was poking around that port engine last night, cleaning the gaps on the plugs. Couldn't reach in far enough with my gloves on. Wrench froze to my hand. I should know better."

"Does it hurt?"

The flight mechanic smiled. "Like a son of a bitch, sir."

The Dakota continued to idle.

"You know . . ." Harry began to say, intending to suggest that perhaps a departure at this time wasn't such a good idea.

"What?" Kneece called back. "You say something, sir?"

Harry let it go; they were moving.

He looked forward, saw but couldn't hear Doheeny say something to his copilot who then set his left hand down atop Doheeny's right which sat straddling the throttle controls. There was something so personal in the act that Harry turned away.

The engines picked up a notch, then began a steady increase in pitch and volume as the Dakota clattered and bumped its way ever faster down the runway matting. Harry could still feel the wind bounding against the fuselage, but the ship was moving steadily. Any attempt to find cause for comfort in this evaporated with one look at the flight mechanic.

This was not the young sergeant he remembered who had treated each takeoff and landing with the offhanded air of someone embarking on his morning commute to work. This time, the flight mechanic sat utterly still, his face hard, eyes closed, his good hand cradled protectively about his bandaged one.

The rearward cant of the deck evened as the tail wheel rose from the runway.

"Here we go!" Kneece called out. His exuberance sounded forced.

The transit of the Dakota grew suddenly smooth as the wheels cleared the runway.

"See, Harry?" Kneece called out. "It was worse flying down here from—"

"JesusJesusJesus!" The explosion of oath/prayer was from the copilot. Windshear—solid as a bus or cannonball—slammed into the Dakota.

The aeroplane lurched to port, rolling violently until it stood almost on its port wingtip. The movement flung Harry backward, knocking the wind out of him and sending the back of his head rebounding off the aluminum hull. Still, he fared better than Woody Kneece, who was catapulted across the cargo cabin. His forehead collided with one of the fuselage ribs and he fell back to the deck, dazed.

Stunned himself, Harry was dimly aware of Jim Doheeny yelling in the cockpit: "Gear up! Gear UP!"

The engines howled in a full-throttle agony as Doheeny fought the turbulence. On his back, Harry had a glimpse through the upside windows; clouds backlit by the moon streaming past the windows from top to bottom: the wind was not only pushing the ship up on her wing, but sideways as well. He rolled to his side, trying to get his feet under him. Another glimpse, this through the windows below him—the ground closer than he thought it could be without colliding with it, snowdrifts blurring by; he was sure they were being pushed directly over the burial mound of Hotshot McKesson's shattered aeroplane.

"Major!" It was the flight mechanic. The initial lurch of the ship had sprung the lashings on the cargo crate. With the steep bank of the ship, the crate was no longer sitting on the deck but on the rim of the passenger bench: it was now sliding toward Harry, shifting the ship's center of gravity dangerously forward and threatening to easily crush Harry in the process.

"Get the nose up!" Doheeny yelled toward the cabin. The flight mechanic threw himself between Harry and the crate. He straddled the up-angled edge of the bench, braced a foot against one of the fuselage ribs and put his back against the 600 lb crate, slowing it enough for Harry to scramble to safety.

Still short of breath, and dizzy from the blow to the head and violent motion of the ship, Harry's stomach began to spasm. Another gust rocked the Dakota and the crate crashed to the deck and began sliding rearward. Harry found himself thrown to his feet. But before he could gather his wits about him and assess their new situation, he felt the deck tilt again, this time in a climb.

"*JesusJesusJesus!*"

"Gimme a hand!" the flight mechanic screamed. This time he was behind the crate, his shoulder against the wood slats fighting desperately to keep it from sliding into the tail, trying to shove the crate back into its place. Harry joined him and found Woody Kneece by his side. A spider-web of blood snaked across Kneece's face.

Side by side they somehow kept the crate in place, even as the slant of the deck sharpened beneath their slipping feet, rising in the nose. The engines screamed with every ounce of power and Harry heard the aluminum sinews of the Dakota moan with strain.

"*JesusJesusJESUS!*"

And then it was over. The C-47 found itself free of the death-grip of turbulence, flying evenly through a calm and quiet sky. Yet the engines were still bellowing at full throttle and Harry saw the flight mechanic with his face turned away from the window; his face screwed tight as if expecting something horrible and inevitable.

Then there was a smooth banking turn to port, the engines quieted, and the flight mechanic's face opened in an unwinding sigh.

It would not be until some time after, over some comforting cups of coffee and cigarettes lit with shaking hands, that the men on the Dakota would manage to exchange tales of their individual participation and the whole story would come together. It was only then Harry could appreciate how close—and in how many ways—they had come to dying.

Doheeny had expected trouble from the outset. He had told the copilot to set his hand over his on the throttles to keep his hand from bouncing free should the worst occur. Though their landing gear was still extended when the windshear hit, they were already too far along their take-off to abort. He could only hope the Dakota could bull through the turbulence.

But the bullet of wind was too strong to fight. The initial impact rocked the Dakota, bringing up the starboard wing. Doheeny called to the copilot to raise the landing gear, reducing the ship's drag and giving him more thrust to work with as he wrestled with the control yoke. But with the ship on the edge of inverting completely, the copilot needed both hands on the control yoke to help Doheeny bring the aircraft to heel. With an altitude of less than a hundred feet, the roll of the ship had already pushed the port wing dangerously close to the ground.

"I swear," Doheeny recounted later, "that port wingtip was shoveling snow."

It may very well have been. With a 120-knot takeoff speed, the plane's wing could probably have knifed through the loose surface powder without consequence, but if it encountered something solid—or pushed into the terra firma beneath—the ship would have pitched forward and finished its journey as an exploding cartwheel tumbling alongside the runway of the Narssarssuaq aerodrome.

It took only seconds for Doheeny to recognize that the Dakota, already at near-stalling speed, couldn't buck the turbulence. He'd sensed the shift forward in the ship's center of gravity as the heavy crate in the cargo cabin slid loose, keeping him from getting the tail down to climb.

Despite the frantic flavor of the copilot's chant of "JesusJesusJesus," he knew what he had to do. With one hand still clutching the control yoke, the other frantically brought up the landing gear then darted about the throttle and mixture controls, the flap settings, trying to give the ship every possible bit of power and lift. The flight mechanic knew what he had to do as well: keep the loose cargo from dropping into the tail, forcing the plane into a climb and stall.

But when the ship had first leveled out and Harry had thought them finally safe, they were actually facing another dire problem: the one that had caused the flight mechanic to so obviously brace for imminent doom. They had been taken by a second current, this one pushing them inland. Lacking the horsepower to fight it, Doheeny had taken a gamble and ceded to Nature, turning with the new current to port, hoping to move with it. The maneuver had given him back control of the ship, but had put them in a frightful race. The port turn had put the aeroplane on a collision heading with the high ground that bordered the inland side of the airstrip. Could Doheeny clear the high ground before the tail-riding turbulence smashed them into it?

"If we'd had one more coat of paint on the belly of that plane," Doheeny said later, "we would've hit."

Referring back to their flight log and the time the copilot had registered for their takeoff, Doheeny later calculated that the whole incident had taken no longer than twenty to thirty seconds to transpire.

"How're you feeling, Sarnoff?" Jim Doheeny asked the wireless operator.

"I'd rather not do that again, Captain."

"How's Ol' Betsy?"

Sparks smiled down at the guitar. "Couple new dents but she's OK. Maybe they'll make 'er sound better than I do."

Doheeny slumped on the passenger bench near the wireless set. He looked too exhausted to stand. "How about this thing?" he said, nodding at the set. "This in one piece, too?"

"First thing I checked, Captain."

"Get on your key. If the boys downstairs saw any of that, their hearts are probably in their mouths."

"Mine, too."

"Then it's unanimous. Let them know we're OK and on course for Iceland."

In the rear of the cargo cabin a shaken Harry was trying to nurse his jangled nerves with a Lucky Strike. Across the cabin the flight mechanic, hobbled with his bandaged hand, was clumsily applying a strip of gauze to the ugly gash that ran the breadth of Woody Kneece's forehead. The flight mechanic's awkward ministrations prompted winces and grimaces of pain from Kneece, but he voiced no complaint. Penance, Harry thought.

Harry heard a moan—half from fatigue, the rest from disgruntlement—from Doheeny as he tiredly pulled himself to his feet. Kneece saw the pilot heading his way and prepared to take his medicine. Kneece was as tall as Doheeny, but his more spindly physique looked eminently more fragile, particularly as Doheeny stood over him, glaring down with a repressed fury more intimidating than any pyrotechnic display of shouts and blows.

"Everybody OK back here?" Doheeny asked, although his eyes remained on Kneece.

"More or less, Captain," the flight mechanic answered. "The captain—" Doheeny cut him off. "I see."

"We had a problem with the big crate, Captain. I guess I must've messed up the tie-downs back at—"

"It's OK, Junior." Doheeny took a breath that seemed to grow his shoulders a few inches in every direction. "Captain Kneece."

Kneece nodded and began to stand. But Doheeny rested one of his bearlike paws heavily on the captain's shoulder, forcing him back into his seat. Doheeny turned to the flight mechanic and with a motion of his eyes sent the sergeant toward the cockpit, leaving Doheeny alone with Kneece and Harry.

"Captain Doheeny," Kneece began, his voice apologetic. Harry noted the return of "Captain" to Kneece's address of the pilot. "I don't know how to—"

"You're damned right you don't," Doheeny said curtly. "Just in case that knock on the head left things a little fuzzy for you, let me lay it out for you nice and clear. You almost got us all killed today, Captain. We were one stroke of dumb luck away from getting spread all over that runway like margarine. Call me thin-skinned, but I'm a little perturbed about that.

"As soon as we set down in Reykjavik I'm sending a dispatch to your boss back in Washington. It's going to say you ought to be hauled up on charges and that I'd love to be the person to press them. It's going to say you don't have any more right wearing captain's bars than my Aunt Fanny does. It's also going to ask that me and my crew be relieved of this assignment because you're a hazard, Kneece. You will get somebody killed."

Harry could tell from Kneece's face that the pilot's declamation stung; all the more because even Kneece recognized the truth of it.

"Don't get in a sweat, Captain," Doheeny continued. "I've been flying for the Army long enough to know it'll be a good day if you even get a slap on the wrist. They're going to figure, well, as long as nobody got hurt . . . It'll be on the record that I squawked, but you and me are going to be stuck with each other until you get to wherever you need to go. But there's going to be a change in how it's going to work on this aircraft from here on out—"

One of Doheeny's meaty hands grabbed a fistful of Kneece's flight jacket and raised him to his feet, pressing his back painfully into the arch of the fuselage. "You and me, we're going to have an agreement. I agree that I'm not going to give you any advice on how to do whatever it is you're here to do. And you are going to leave all decisions about flying this aircraft to me. All righty?" Doheeny pressed Kneece harder against the metal hull. "And if you do anything to bring any of my people even close to being hurt . . ." Doheeny released Kneece and the captain slid back into his seat. "I don't care if we're five thousand feet up and over the North Atlantic, Kneece, I swear to God I'll boot your ass through that door myself."

CHAPTER SIX

DELOS

HARRY STOOD OVER THE OFFICERS MESS billiard table. They had laid the weapons out on the green felt: four carbines, four holstered automatic pistols, spare ammunition.

"Eddie? When you . . ."

"Aye?"

"What was it like when . . . when you were hurt?"

I smiled at his discomfiture. "You're a good and sweet lad, Harry, but the tact is wasted on the likes of me. I do know the ol' thingie is gone, you know. Sparing my feelings is a moot point, old boy."

"When I was in the plane, when we took off from the field in Greenland . . ."

"When you thought you were going to crash."

"Yes. I wasn't afraid. Not then, not while it was happening. I was sure we were going to crash, but I wasn't afraid. That's funny, isn't it? I felt . . ."

"Cool. Detached. Every bit of it happened with astonishing clarity."

"Yes."

"But then comes the afterward. . . ."

"I wasn't even thinking about it anymore, and that's when the shakes came. I went into the toilet on the plane—"

"You may omit further details in that regard."

"It's funny, isn't it? That it happens that way?"

"You need time to be afraid, Harry. The more time you have to think, the more opportunity you have to be afraid. Fear ages much like wine."

Harry reached out to touch one of the carbines with his fingertips. As if the weapon radiated a searing heat, they recoiled from the gleaming varnish of the walnut stock. "So, with you . . ."

"Was it like that for me? Not a bit. In fact, I can't say I recall all that much of it. I remember the sound of the Nip planes, the sound of the bombs coming down. I was running—we all were—and then it's lights out. I woke six days later on a hospital ship heading home, the last out of Singapore. Woke up and the little bugger was off. I felt like I had just closed my eyes. Like a magic trick: Close your eyes, then"—I whirled my hands above the contrivance affixed to my stump—"Presto! Disappeared!"

"That's a hell of a trick."

"Oh, yes," I said. "I was quite impressed."

Harry paused in the doorway of the chemical toilet. He took a deep draught of the chill air of the cargo cabin, purging the nausea, firming his legs beneath him. The flight mechanic sat huddled forward with Sparks, while Woody Kneece was in the after part of the cabin very much the errant schoolboy exiled to the dunce chair; slumped in his seat, sullen, and furious at his own stupidity.

"You made your first command decision," Harry said, sitting beside him. "How does it feel?"

"You have these daydreams of being the guy who takes charge. Young Teddy Roosevelt." Kneece bared his teeth in a mock T.R. grin. "Charge!" The levity swiftly faded. "In the dream you're always right. . . . There was this time back home, fella come in under another fella's fence and stole some chickens. Well, Uncle Ray and I drive out, this old boy still has the stolen chickens in a bag on his porch, we make him give 'em back and apologize, make 'em both shake hands. They're acting like everything's fine, but on the ride back Uncle Ray says to me"—here Woody Kneece's accent thickened until it had the quality of molasses—"'Derwooood, I'll bet you a cold drink an' a bag o' goobers we all're comin' on back here.' Sure enough, next day there we are, because that chicken farmer peppered that other old boy's bee-hind with birdshot. I ask Uncle Ray how he knew. They both looked square the day before. He just looks at me and shakes his head, Uncle Ray does, like he can't believe how you could fit so much stupid in one head. And he says to me, 'Derwooood, some no-'count carpet-baggin' white trash burns down yore house, runs off with yore wife, and shoots yore stud bull, then comes back to apologize. Yore damn guaranteed that old boy's gon' wind up facedown in a ditch 'cause, son, sometimes I'm sorry jus' don' cut it.' " Kneece looked toward the cockpit and added glumly, "But what else do you say?"

"I'd like to keep you from making another mistake, Woody. Actually, three of them. If you keep trying to make a connection between Grassi's killing and what happened in London back in August, one, you're going to waste a lot of time; two, you're going to get some very important people very annoyed with you—"

"You think I'm worried about ruffling some feathers?"

"How far do you think you're going to get irritating the hell out of the people whose help you're going to need to get your questions answered?"

"You said three mistakes."

"If we're going to work together, we have to be going in the same direction. If we're not, besides the wasted effort . . . somebody's going to get hurt. I made that mistake once. I'm not going to make it again. If we can't get together on this, I will get off this plane and catch the next ride home."

"I'm still listening."

"About what happened in London last summer— We're going to leave it on this plane tonight, right now."

"If you have a case to make, Major—"

"It's simple, Woody. The soldiers we were investigating in that case were lost in action. They were dead before I even got to New York."

"That's what you meant: dead-ended."

"Dead-ended. That case is over because there's nothing left."

"What about . . . ?" As he had in Harry's kitchen, he laid his fist alongside his jaw.

Harry felt a twinge in his hand only moderately less sharp than the one in his heart. "There was a woman involved. A girl, really. Grassi went to her, tried to use her to get me to take the case a certain way. That was Grassi going his own way; that was his command decision. And his miscalculation. The girl didn't come to me. She took a bottle of sleeping pills."

"Oh." Kneece let a long moment go by. "Did she . . . ?"

"I don't know. She was still in the hospital when I shipped out. Grassi wasn't even sorry. I think he felt worse that he got caught going behind my back than over what he did. When I belted him . . . Woody, I felt like that was the only thing I'd done right in the whole mess."

They sat together for a while listening to the drone of the Dakota's engines as the cold waters of the Denmark Strait slipped by below them. Kneece leaned over to look out the window.

"Gonna be a clear night all the rest of the way, looks like."

Harry hadn't heard him. He was sitting much as he'd found Woody Kneece earlier, sour-faced and angry with himself. His hand had begun to throb.

"OK, Major, you made your case," Kneece said. "Unless something pops up contrariwise, this case starts in Greenland. London had nothing to do with it."

Harry nodded approvingly. Gratefully.

"You mind me asking something personal, sir? There's a lot you're obviously not telling me, OK, that's how you have to play it and I'll take your word for it that it's over. But there's something about that case still dogs you. The guys you were after are dead. This thing with the girl, that sounds like it was Grassi's fault, not yours. So what is it?"

"It's like you were telling me, Woody," Harry said. " 'Sorry just don't cut it.' "

The wind tearing at the airstrip at Keflavik was brutal; the gusts had blown great stretches of the aerodrome clear of snow, revealing a ground that, under the bleaching moon, seemed lifeless and bare.

Harry wasted no time jogging after Jim Doheeny, hurrying across the windswept grounds for the warmth of the Ops shack. He felt immense pity for the souls trying to tough out the frigid night in tents whose canvas walls whipped so hard they cracked like gunshots.

In the Ops shack, "talkers" stood before maps, grease pencils in hand, following the movements of their trolling Catalinas, while another talker tracked what Harry thought to be a major outbound convoy as it passed the Outer Hebrides. Periodically, the rumble of aeroplane engines, as Catalinas taxied close by, joined with the wind gusts to rattle the corrugated walls and windows of the shack.

While Doheeny conferred with the Ops staff, Harry placed himself out of everyone's way by the heating stove. He poured two cups of coffee and handed one to Doheeny.

"How's it look?" Harry asked him.

"Same story here we heard back at Bluie-West-One; before the weather broke bad, a lot of air traffic was coming through. They're expecting it to pick up again once Kap Farvel clears. But for now, we look good. We've got the eastbound route all to ourselves, and they're expecting as much as thirty-six hours' decent weather between here and the Isles. You can give your pushy little Southern buddy the good news that I'll probably have him in the Orkneys a little after midnight."

"Listen," Harry said, "my pushy little Southern buddy says don't rush to get airborne. Upon reflection, it has occurred to him that no matter how early we get to the Orkneys, nothing productive is going to happen before morning. So, he says lay over for the night. Your crew can get some rest in real beds, get some decent food. If a takeoff at 0800 is good—"

Doheeny had, at first, looked baffled over this largesse, but now he grinned skeptically. "This is his version of candy and flowers."

"He *is* sorry, you know."

"He should be. I'm not letting him off the hook, Harry. This isn't like stepping on Mom's fresh-mopped floor; you get a whack on the fanny and she cleans up your mess. There wouldn't've been any cleaning up this guy's mess."

"I know."

"I'm still sending that dispatch to Kneece's CO. The next time Kneece gets another half-assed notion, I want him to remember this. Maybe he'll keep his bright ideas to himself."

"I'm not arguing with you, Jim."

Having vented, Doheeny calmed. "Oh-eight-hundred is good."

"Can I ask you something? Kind of official."

Doheeny's eyes narrowed. "Are you talking for him?"

"We're on the case together."

"As long as *you're* doing the asking, I'll answer."

"Do you know any of the pilots flying diplomatic courier planes?"

"Most of the guys I know in the service are from my airline days. For the most part, they're all flying for ATC."

"Where do these ATC flights end up?"

"Well, you have the transatlantic direct flights; those can end up any-where—"

"Forget those. The planes that fly this northern route."

Doheeny beckoned Harry to follow him to a map covering the North Atlantic from the Labrador coast to the European mainland. "Presque Isle is the western crossroads. From there, flights jump off across the States, across Canada to Alaska, over the Atlantic to Bluie-West-One or Kap Farvel, and from there hopping to Iceland and then the British Isles. The eastern terminus is Prestwick." Doheeny pointed to a spot on the west coast of Scotland, thirty miles southwest of Glasgow.

"Do the flights ever go on from Prestwick?"

"If it's a rush cargo, some kind of priority deal, maybe a plane flies on to London or something. I never have. As a rule, the run ends at Prestwick. The cargo is off-loaded and gets carried wherever it needs to go by local air or overland."

"Ever fly to the Orkneys?"

Eyes on the tight-knit smattering of dots across the Pentland Firth,

Doheeny shook his head. "That's a British base. Anything that needs to be flown in, the RAF takes care of."

"Would you ever have reason to land there? Let's say an emergency—"

"When a pilot works up his flight plan, he's supposed to consider 'alternates'—a place where he can put down if he has a problem. The first time a pilot flies the northern route, he learns thinking up an emergency alternate is a waste of time. Look at the map, Harry. The British have landing strips on the Faeroes, the Shetlands, the Orkneys, but they're all so far off the normal flight path. . . . If you can't make Prestwick, you're not making any of them, either. You make Scotland or you start rowing." Doheeny yawned. "This coffee's like battery acid. I'm going to hit the sack before you-know-who changes his mind. You coming?"

"Later." Harry continued to stare at the map.

"Harry, you mind if I ask you a question?"

"Shoot."

"Why'd you get on that plane tonight?"

"At about the time that plane of yours felt like it was standing on one wing, I was asking myself the same question."

"What time is it?" Woody Kneece moaned, pulling himself upright on the passenger bench. He squinted out the window at the oppressive grayness of the arctic morning, and the rolling North Atlantic below.

"Oh-nine-forty Greenwich, sirs," the flight mechanic said, appearing with a thermos of hot coffee.

"I woke up this morning, didn't look like your bed had been slept in," Harry told Kneece. "Is there that much of a nightlife in Iceland?"

"Hardly." Kneece stood, stretched, waiting for the mechanic to withdraw to the company of Sparks, who had recommenced exploring his guitar-strumming with mixed success. Kneece sat beside Harry. He held a finger upright and announced, in a voice reminiscent of the narrator of a radio serial, "While our plucky troops slept the night away in blissful comfort, our youthful hero braved arctic temperatures in his dogged pursuit of truth, justice, and the American Way!"

"Is that Superman's way of telling me you were snooping?"

"*Investigating*," Kneece corrected. "Did you talk to Doheeny?"

Harry relayed the substance of his conversation of the night before with the pilot. "I had Reykjavik radio a query to Prestwick about these X-ray flights. I got an answer just before we took off. Wherever these planes are setting down, it's not there. OK, your turn."

"I checked with the guys in the control tower, communications, ground crews, asked the same questions we've been asking and got pretty much the same answers. They've been getting these off-log flights at least since the Americans landed in '42. Same deal we heard from Zagottis: The radio call from each flight includes an X-ray designation, so the field knows not to log it. Nobody knows what the cargoes are. Nobody's sure they could identify the pilots. Most times the planes just set down long enough to gas up and go."

"What about this last flight? The one that replaced McKesson's?"

Kneece pulled out his notebook. "Army flight 121 X-ray. It came through, all right. They remember it."

"Did anybody see Grassi on it?"

"People in these parts wear too much fur to tell each other apart. But there was somebody sounds like it had to be him. A couple guys remember somebody from the plane bothering the ground crew with a lot of questions: Have these kinds of flights come through before, do they know what's on them, that kind of thing. They remember him especially because they thought it was funny him asking those questions. They figured he was on the plane; he ought to know. Now, another funny thing about this 121 X-ray, it didn't just gas up and go: it sat out there on the runway for six hours. The crew was holed up in the layover barracks all that time, didn't even come into the mess hall. They just kept to themselves—"

"Except for Grassi the noodge."

"Except for Grassi the noodge."

"The weather hold them up?"

"Weather was no worse than it usually is around here."

"Then why the hell—"

"It didn't make any sense to me either, Major, but I think I have a bead on it. Even with a refueling stop in Iceland, a C-47 can make the trip from Kap Farvel to the Orkneys in four, five hours if there's no bad headwinds. I know, I checked with the Operations staff at Reykjavik. So, if 121 X-ray left Farvel a little after noon, that'd put it in the Orkneys between four and five P.M. Greenland time. But there's a big time difference between Greenland and the Orkneys: four hours. It still would've been between one and two in the afternoon there."

This was sounding uncomfortably like those arithmetic problems that Harry had detested as a schoolchild: If one train leaves the station at one o'clock traveling at sixty miles an hour, and another train leaves at two o'clock moving at thirty miles an hour . . .

"One-twenty-one X-ray sits at Keflavik for six hours. It's another two hours' flight time to the Orkneys. That plane didn't reach the island until 2000 or later which, in the Orkneys at this time of year, means not until way after dark. One-twenty-one X-ray didn't fly in, Major. It snuck in."

"Hey!" Sparks called from his station. "You guys ever see a Spitfire? Keep your eyes out starboard."

The flight mechanic came aft and said, "The RAF station at Scapa Flow picked us up on their radar a couple minutes ago. They scrambled a Spit to check us over and make sure we're who we say we are."

"Awfully suspicious on their part." Kneece's eyes had the eagerness of a child about to receive a new toy.

"Well, they don't get many Americans flyin' out this way," the flight mechanic said. "There he is! Down there about eleven o'clock low."

Harry caught the sleek silhouette and British bull's-eye insignias against the leaden seas. The fighter nimbly chandelled, bringing itself several hundred feet above the Dakota, then throttled back on a parallel course above them. Evidently satisfied with its identification of the C-47, the Spitfire dropped alongside and waggled its wings in greeting. Doheeny answered with a more sluggish wave from his larger aeroplane. Kneece moaned.

"I swear to God, first chance I get, I'm getting a camera! I don't care if I have to steal one from a reconnaissance plane! I can't believe I'm not going to have a picture of this!"

"Captain!" It was Sparks, alarmed. "Down off the starboard wing! In the water! Is that a sub?"

"Hold on, everybody!" Doheeny called out calmly, and put the C-47 into a sharply banked circle. Below, Harry could see the shape, a long, dark oblong wallowing in the swells marked by a halo of hovering terns. Harry heard the flight mechanic take a tense breath. "What's the matter?" he asked.

"Well, the word is that when the krauts sent their U-boats back into the Atlantic, they gave 'em more deck guns and told 'em not to run from aircraft. They want 'em to fight it out."

"That doesn't look like a sub," Kneece objected. "Does it?"

"Funny-looking sub," the flight mechanic said.

Harry guessed they were now three hundred feet above the water, and in as tight a circle as Doheeny could hold his ship. The object didn't seem to be moving in any direction, just idly rolling in the swells. Harry saw no conning tower, no deck guns or any of the other appurtenances one would expect.

"Damn . . ." The sergeant sighed and handed a pair of field glasses to Harry.

Harry got the binoculars sighted. The object below had the slick, shiny quality of wet rubber. Occasionally, one of the circling seabirds would drop down and tear at the hulk with its hooked beak. A particularly high swell nudged the thing into a roll. Harry recoiled from the sudden appearance of a hole—a wound—several feet across, jagged around the edges, revealing an interior of pink meat bright against the pewter ocean. Shadowy shapes just beneath the surface of the water darted clear of the rolling body until it again settled with its damaged side turned into the water and the carrion fish could resume feeding.

"What the hell is that?" Kneece was still trying to get a look through the window.

"Some kinda whale," the flight mechanic said. "Probably hit one of the mines they got around Scapa Flow. Well, that's kind of a waste, huh?"

An RAF corporal led Harry and Woody Kneece along the aerodrome's manicured gravel paths, the well-ordered lanes swept clear of snow with typical British tidiness. From this high ground near Kirkwall on Orkney Mainland, they had a panoramic view of the base and the waters of Scapa Flow. A major British military installation since the first Great War, the base had concrete combat information centers, clapboard barracks and administration buildings, concrete-bolstered gun emplacements guarding the sea approaches, and massive waterfront hangars for the patrolling Sunderlands. Still farther, scattered at their moorings, their drab battle paint intentionally blending with the gray water, were the ships of the Home Fleet.

Kneece stopped in his tracks and pointed down toward the water. "What's that huge thing out there! It's like a mountain of guns!"

The corporal maintained a blasé English reserve. "Oh, yes, sir, well, that'd be Duke of York, sir, battleship she is. The carrier—flattop, you Yanks like to say—that'd be Victorious. Please, sir, my officer's waiting."

At the Officers Mess they were led to a table tucked in a corner where a pot of tea and a tray of cups and biscuits were laid on. The RAF major at the table stood as they approached.

"Major Astin Moncrief, gentlemen. A pleasure. You must be Captain Kneece? And that would make you Major Voss. Please make yourselves comfortable. I'm adjutant at the airfield here. The CO thought as I'd acted as liaison with all the investigative types inquiring about your unfortunate colleague Lieutenant Grassi, I should take the duty on again." He pronounced Grassi's rank in the British manner: Leftenant. "I wasn't sure if you've had a chance to eat in your travels. You're a bit early for luncheon, I'm afraid, but I thought some tea and biscuits might tide you over."

Harry guessed Moncrief to be in his late twenties, though, like nearly everyone he'd met in the northern climes, he had a face weathered beyond his years. The major was smallish, handsome in a mousy way, his polite smile permanently carved into his chapped cheeks.

Moncrief's eyes fixed on the square of bloody gauze on Kneece's forehead. "Hard traveling, wot? Need our doc to have a look there?"

Kneece shrugged the attention off. "About our flight crew . . ."

"Quarters are already arranged, they'll be quite well taken care of, I can assure you. Any idea how long you'll be with us?"

"A day or two," Kneece replied. "At most."

"We should be able to accommodate that with no problem. How do you gentlemen like your tea?"

After the tea had been poured and the biscuits doled out, Moncrief reclined slightly in his chair, crossed his legs very precisely, and drew a silver cigarette case from his blouse. "Do you gentlemen mind? Care to partake? No? Now, what is it I can do for you? I'd thought that between our intelligence services and yours, all the questions that needed to be asked had been asked. Even Scotland Yard sent a delegation to dig and delve. Have they not forwarded their report on to you?"

"Report?" Kneece said.

"We've been on the road for a few days," Harry explained. "It might be behind us in Washington."

"More milk for your tea? I presume that you'll be off to London next?"

"Possibly." Harry caught a look from Kneece. "Probably," he amended.

Moncrief withdrew a small leather-bound agenda from his blouse pocket and scratched a quick note. "A reminder to myself," he explained. "I'll see to it that the Yard's report is made available to you when you arrive in London."

"Thanks."

Kneece looked to Harry. Aside from the caricatures he'd seen in American films, Kneece's first Englishman obviously constituted a being quite beyond his ken. Like most Americans on such a first meeting, he vacillated between a feeling of superiority over English stuffiness and inferiority under English decorum. His look asked that Harry take the lead, as the latter was probably better acquainted with the customs and language of the natives.

"Major," Harry put in, "we don't want to bore you asking questions you've been asked a dozen times already."

"No bother, really. With all respect to Lieutenant Grassi's tragic demise, I do quite enjoy all the skullduggery. Shades of Sherlock Holmes and all that. Don't think me too callous, gentlemen. Please understand, the standard program for Orkney Mainland is frightfully tedious. Any change in the routine, even this unfortunate circumstance, is to be appreciated." Moncrief's smile assumed an apologetic air.

"Quite," Kneece said, and Moncrief's smile flickered, unsure whether or not he was being mocked.

"What I was going to say," Harry interposed, "is maybe it'd be easier for you just to summarize what all these other parties came up with."

"Oh, well, yes, let's see. Naturally, all were quite keen on discovering how the poor chap got here in the first place. How're those biscuits? Not quite from Mother's oven I should imagine, but I trust they're passable."

"Fine, thanks," Harry replied. "What we found on our end is it looks like Grassi hitched a ride on an American cargo plane. Obviously it must have landed here."

Moncrief's smile flickered again. " 'Obviously'?"

"How else could he have gotten here?"

"Well, that's the question, then, isn't it? But we'd know about a plane, now wouldn't we? Pick it up on RDF and all that—that's radar to you Americans. Where would he put down if not at the airfield, eh? And if he didn't arrive by air transport, what then? Fall off a passing ship perhaps? We've no record of any convoys in the area at the time, no reports from any of our patrol vessels of any craft sightings. If you'd like, I can arrange interviews with station and shipboard personnel to corroborate."

"You're saying no American aircraft has put in here recently."

The smile became one of satisfaction. "What I'm saying, Major Voss, is that no American aircraft has lit on the Kirkwall tarmac since I began service here last year."

"And none of your personnel saw Grassi around until they found his body? Not in town—and I'm guessing there must be some kind of town around here—not on the base? Some stranger nosing around—"

"I'm afraid not, Major. As I said, MI 5, MI 6, Scotland Yard, they've all been through here and had a go at this. A puzzlement, eh?"

"I've got a relation that would call this an 'arse-buster,' " Kneece interjected.

"Quite." Moncrief took a draught on his cigarette. "Seems a pity you've come all this way for so little."

"Who found the body?" Kneece asked.

"Actually, there were two of them, two of our Sunderland flyers off on a lark."

"We should talk to them."

"Of course."

"Have them show us where they found the corpse."

"Not a problem." There was a hesitancy to Moncrief's smile.

"Something the matter?" Harry asked.

"Just a forewarning, gentlemen. These two flyers, good chaps both, I can assure you, but it's been a long war for them, I'm afraid. They might strike you as a bit, well . . . perhaps just a touch potty, if you gather my meaning."

Kneece glanced over at Harry, puzzled. " 'Potty'?"

Harry laughed. "I think Major Moncrief is telling us they're a little nuts. Right, Major?"

"Quite," Moncrief said.

"Quite," Kneece agreed.

[handwritten annotation: NEXT FEW PAGES FUNNY AS BENNY HILL]

BOOM!

Kneece was the first to straighten and look back up the shingle to where Taffy Macnee stood with his Purdy, shaking a pair of spent shotgun casings clear of the breech. Nearby Paddy Donlay wore a pained look. Behind them, up near where the two jeeps were parked, stood Moncrief, his smile sorrowful, his face semaphoring that well, yes, I did warn you about these two.

"What the hell're you shooting at?" Kneece barked.

Calmly Macnee slid two more shells into the Purdy. "That one there." He nodded at the sky.

Kneece and Harry looked up.

"Those?" Harry asked, pointing at the terns whirling about fifty yards down the beach.

"Not those," Macnee corrected. "Him!" He made a motion with the muzzle of the Purdy in the direction of the birds. "That one there! The one's laughing!"

"That's yer Scotsman's brain for yer, Cap'n Yank," Donlay said. "Thinks a bloody bird is laughin' at him! It's this kind o' brainstormin' explains the lack o' yer great Scottish empires!"

"That one there, Paddy." Macnee raised the Purdy to his shoulder. "He's the one almost went into the props yesterday, that bird did."

"Oh, you reckanize him, do yer?"

"Aye, almost brought the whole business down! Now he's followed me here, he's up there laughing at me! Keep laughing, ya bloody bag o' bird shit!" The Purdy thundered again.

As far as an Orkney December went, it was not so bad a day. None of the many clouds puffing along were threatening, and in their interstices flashed bits of blue sky and a yellow—if unwarming—sun. The wind along the shingle beach was chill and steady, but tolerable.

BOOM!

"Does he have to do that?" Kneece called up to Moncrief. The RAF major shrugged helplessly.

The freshly expended shells rattled on the shingle. Macnee thrust the Purdy out to Kneece. "You'd appreciate this, Yank. Feel the balance on that. You'll not feel a curve that nice against yer hand short o' some bird's bosom, and I am not meaning the feathered kind!"

"Feel free to throw some cold water on him, Cap'n Yank. He gets like this about his bloody gun, makes me skin crawl! Next he'll be marryin' the bloody thing."

"Piss off, Paddy. He's a Yank! From the American South, isn't that right, Cap'n? Hooligans and cowboys! All Yanks appreciate a good firearm, eh, Cap'n? Blazing six-guns and the like! Wisht yer had one o' these to do in the red men, eh?"

Moncrief strode down the shingle. "Perhaps if we get on to the matter at hand . . ." He laid a firm hand on the Purdy, lowering its muzzle. "Taffy, I believe our visitor has some questions. Do be a good fellow and pay attention, wot?"

Macnee nodded and cradled the shotgun in the crook of his arm. He waggled a warning finger at the terns. "Don't you be off nowheres, mate! I'll be back to ya! Right-o, Cap'n Yank, let's have at it!"

Kneece plunged in. "Where did you find Lootenant Grassi?"

"We're there, Yank. Hereabouts."

"I know that. I mean exactly."

"Har! Exactly, he wants to know, Paddy. Were ya making maps that day, Paddy? Oh, I'm sorry. Yer can't be drawing maps unless ya can *read*."

Kneece turned to Moncrief. "That report you told us about; will that include the crime scene photos?"

"Afraid not, Captain. There weren't any. At least none with your lieutenant in them. The people from the Yard didn't arrive for three days after Lieutenant Grassi was found. We couldn't very well leave him be all that time. When these two discovered the lieutenant, we had him brought back to the air station."

"Nobody here thought to take any pictures? I'd think your local security people would've thought—"

"We're soldiers, Captain Kneece, not forensic specialists."

"Where's the body now?" Kneece persisted.

"First, it went to the Yard for a postmortem, I believe. After that I think it was transferred into the hands of your people in London."

"It was here."

Kneece turned: Paddy Donlay stood a few yards away, pointing to the gravel at his feet. "You're sure?"

"There, over there, over here," Taffy Macnee muttered. "What's the difference, Cap'n Yank? He'd be no less dead if yer found him on the other end of the island."

"Pretty sure," Donlay insisted. "It looks right."

"Where's the high-tide line?"

Donlay pointed to a jagged line of kelp, dried sea salt, and broken shells running along the beach five yards below them.

"How'd you find him? How was he lying?"

"Horizontal!" Macnee said, punctuating the witticism with an explosive "Har!"

"On his face," Donlay answered.

"Then you turned him over? Was the ground wet under him?"

"It's always damp here, Captain," Moncrief said. "Look round. The wind carries the spray from the ocean nearly to the road."

But Kneece ignored Moncrief, focused on Donlay. "Was it wet under him?"

Donlay was trying to remember. "We're talkin' weeks ago, Cap'n Yank."

Kneece immediately dropped to the beach, pressing his cheek against the stones. "Was he lying like this?"

"Not quite."

"How?"

Donlay obligingly adjusted Kneece's limbs to approximate the way he'd found the late Armando Grassi.

Puzzled at the performance, Moncrief looked to Harry. Harry was smiling. He understood. It was a trick—like Harry's note-card device—to kindle the brain.

"OK," Kneece said. "You find the body—"

"What ho!" Macnee chimed in. "Paddy, do yer see it? Oh, my, it's some deceased *person*—"

"Steady on, Taffy," Moncrief warned.

"Apologies, Adj. Sorry, Cap'n Yank. As you were; yer dead, we discover your *corpus*."

"You moved the body?" Kneece asked.

"We wanted to find out who he was. So I turned the body over like so."

"It *wasn't* wet under him like everywhere else," Donlay said abruptly. "It was fresh wet all round, but not under him."

Kneece put his arms under his head. The look of beachside repose was comically incongruous to Harry amid the context of parkas, Irvine jackets, ice-flecked shingle, and numbing cold. "Was the front of his body as wet as the back?"

"No." Donlay shook his head.

"If yer want to know if he was in the drink, just ask us," Macnee said.

"We've pinched enough out of the punch bowl to know," Donlay added. "He hadn't been in the water."

"Was his body rigid?" Kneece asked. "Was it stiff?"

"Yer talking yer rigor mortis, eh? Yer not dealing with the ignorant here, except maybe for that dense Irish sod. Just ask it plain out."

"He may be a berserker," Donlay told them, nodding at Macnee, "but he's a well-read berserker."

"I was the one who turned him," Macnee reported. "Not a fresh fish, but not all stiff."

Kneece sat up. "How about his face?"

"Not a bad-looking blighter," Macnee said. "But not my type at all. How about you, Paddy? Ya let him chat ya up, did ya? Aye, for a whisky and a plum pudding you'd do the whole naughty business with any half-handsome bloke in a uniform, wouldn't ya, ya terrible little tramp?"

"I mean did his face look bruised?" Kneece pressed. "Any black-and-blue marks?"

"He did have a nice-sized hole in the middle of his forehead," Macnee mused. "What do you think, Paddy? Moths?"

Donlay reached down and picked up a nugget of ocean-polished sandstone. He tossed it to Kneece. "Except for the bullet hole, pale and smooth as that."

"Was the bullet hole an exit wound?"

"In here"—Donlay tapped the back of his head—"out here." Another tap low on the forehead.

"I want to thank you gentlemen," Kneece said as he got to his feet. "You've been a big help."

"Right," Moncrief said. "Off you lot. Back home. And try not to get into any mischief on the way." As Macnee and Donlay trudged up the shingle to their jeep, he asked Kneece, "Done, are we, then, Captain?"

"I think—"

BOOM!

"—so."

"I'm not moving from this spot until those two fruitcakes are a safe distance away," Harry said.

"Quite," Moncrief said.

Moncrief and Harry returned to the other jeep, leaving Kneece—at his request—alone on the beach.

In the shelter of the canvas-topped jeep, Moncrief offered Harry a cup of still-warm tea from a thermos. "We should save some for your colleague. He's rather astute, isn't he?" Moncrief watched Kneece pace idly back and forth on the beach, hefting the smooth stone Donlay had tossed him. Kneece brought out his notebook and began to flip through the pages. "I mean, he's a bit misleading on first meeting, one's thrown off by those rough edges, but he does seem to know what he's about, eh?"

Harry said nothing, watched Kneece hurl the stone out into the frothing surf.

"They're good joes really," the RAF major told him. "Macnee and Donlay, that is. Hope they didn't put you off. Blitz veterans, you know. Two of the few to whom so much is owed by so many. Put in the hours upstairs, each got their well-deserved gong. One hesitates to take too stern a line with them. As I say, so much is owed and so on. I put in for the flying service myself in those first days. Not quite up to the mark, I'm afraid. Seems admin's more my line of country, my forte, one might say. Need the paper pushed? Give the bumf to Old Adj, he'll put the paper right. But we also serve who sit and type, eh, Voss?"

Moncrief prattled politely on, but Harry's focus remained on the low, gray form of a corvette a half-mile distant. The ship turned a white-trimmed wake as it made its sentinel's rounds off Scapa Flow's western access. Beyond that, the North Atlantic. Beyond that . . . home.

That drifting thought was interrupted by a crash as Woody Kneece climbed atop the hood of the jeep and called out: "Hey, Major Moncrief! What's that?"

The rise upon which the jeep was parked provided a view a mile or more in any direction. Behind them to the east was Stromness. Immediately below them, the shingle beach began its turn away from Scapa Flow and then north up the Atlantic side of Mainland, changing from shingle into piled sandstone rocks. On their northern hand, the ground fell away into a snow-crusted field that, in better weather, served as pastureland for cattle and sheep. A half-mile beyond, the pasture was bordered by a thick wood running from the rocky oceanfront to a mile or more inland. It was to this wood that Kneece, from his perch on the jeep's hood, now pointed.

"We call them trees," Moncrief said dryly. "What do they call them in America?"

Kneece smiled and pointed again. "That fence. Is that one of your bases?"

Harry squinted. Almost lost in the thick underbrush that skirted the wood he could see an eight-foot-high steel fence topped by strands of barbed wire.

"That would be Sir Johnnie's estate," Moncrief said.

"Sir who?"

"Sir John Duff."

"What's he? Some kind of duke or something?"

Moncrief politely hid his amused smile behind his gloved hand. "Baronet, actually. Sir John's a business wallah of sorts in England. Quite wealthy, I understand."

"And he lives *here*?" Kneece sounded disbelieving.

"Oh, no," Moncrief answered. "I don't think he's been here since the war. As I recall hearing, Sir John was supposed to build a manufacturing something-or-other down there. Never came about. The war, I suppose."

"I guess that's where he was going to put it; that open space," Harry said, pointing to a large gap among the close-set trees.

"I imagine." Moncrief glanced at his watch. "They'll be serving luncheon by the time we get back. I'm told the Officers Mess has come into some fine salmon purchased from the local fishermen. Our cook may not be the head chef at Maxim's, but I think you'll enjoy it."

"Somebody *does* live down there," Kneece insisted, still atop the jeep, still pointing. "Isn't that smoke?"

A thin, white tendril rippled up from the trees near the ocean.

"Oh, yes," Moncrief said. "That'll be Old Ted."

"Who?"

"Sir John's groundsman."

Kneece hopped down. "A groundsman, huh? Can we talk to him?"

"If he's of a mind to talk to us. You think he might know something?"

"That's what I'd like to find out, Major."

Moncrief started the engine and steered them along a track that was no more than a lane of frozen mud. The jeep bounced horribly over the narrow wagon ruts etched into the ground until it pulled to a stop in front of a gate set in the fence. Through the fence Harry could see thirty yards along the track as it wound through the woods. He could make out the shape of a small cottage, and beyond that a larger building.

Moncrief sounded the horn. It was a minute or more before a stubby form emerged from one of the outbuildings. Clad in macintosh, woolen watch cap, and mud-splattered boots, the figure threaded his way carefully among the icy ruts to the gate. He was a stooped fellow, a white-haired sixtyish, with a face crowded with age, hard labor, and unforgiving weather.

"Oy!" the old man called from the gate.

Moncrief swung open the canvas door of the jeep and stood where the man at the gate could see him. "Old Ted, hullo!"

"Moncrief, is it? What brings the RAF round, eh?"

"I've some guests with me, Ted. Some Yanks who'd like to ask you about the lad found on the beach a few weeks past. Mightn't we come in?"

Old Ted shrugged. He unlatched a padlock, unraveled a chain, and swung the gate open. Moncrief rolled the jeep forward, braking just inside while Ted closed and refastened the gate. The old man sat atop the jeep's hood and beckoned Moncrief to proceed.

The track ended at a clearing under the canopy of bare tree branches. There was a tidy cottage of fieldstone, a few smaller outbuildings that looked to be for storage, and a large, stout building of corrugated metal, all looking fresh-built. The clearing ran to the rocks piled along the oceanfront. Through a gap in the rocks Harry saw a wooden dock extending out into the ocean.

"Ted Bowles, this is Captain Kneece and Major Voss of the American Army."

Bowles touched a finger to his brow. "Mornin', gennulmen. Sorry took so long gettin' down t' the gate. Didn't hear ye right away. I was oop inna barn there." He indicated the corrugated metal building. "One o' them damn wagon 'orses o' mine got loose, gettin' into where he ain't s'pose t' be. Moncrief 'ere says you got soompin' ye wanna ast me?"

"I don't see why we have to do this out here, do you, Ted?" Moncrief asked politely. "Why don't you put on a cuppa and we'll make ourselves comfortable."

"I'm all fer comfortable," Old Ted declared, and led the way to the cottage. He stopped and looked back. Kneece had remained behind, staring down into the frozen mud of the clearing. "Young gennulman! Are ye wi' us?"

Kneece looked up and flashed a smile. "I'm sorry. It's nice and quiet here. Very relaxing. I guess my mind wandered. You're kind of far from everything out here, aren't you?"

"On Mainland yer not far from noothin', young squire," the old man said.

Harry looked down at the ground where Kneece had stood. In its thawed moments, the earth had been turned by horse hooves, and flat, treadless wheels Harry guessed to be from a wagon. But there were also the treads of wide tires, and some of them led to the foot of the dock.

"How do you get to town?" Kneece asked, joining them.

"Got ever'thin' I need here," Old Ted stated. "But I gots me wagon, me 'orses if I needs 'em."

The cottage was snug inside. There was a small front room with a stove, wooden table and chairs. Packing boxes of food tins were piled here and there, as well as peat for the stove. There was also a phonograph, and a commercial wireless, its varnished cathedral housing scuffed, some of the knobs missing. Two doors led off to still smaller rooms. Through one partly open door Harry could see a narrow bed, and through the other more boxes and food tins.

There was also a small army of cats. They seemed draped everywhere: perched on the piles of rations, on the one shelf that contained Old Ted's few pots and pans, prowling among the roof beams.

"Make yerselves comfortable." Old Ted stirred the embers in the stove and threw in some fresh blocks of peat. "T'ain't mooch but I think there's enoof places for ever'body."

There were, in fact, only two chairs. Moncrief diplomatically nodded to Kneece and Harry to avail themselves while he brushed a cat off a box and sat himself down.

"You have yourself a nice little lodge here, Mr. Bowles," Kneece observed.

"Aye, well . . ." Old Ted set a kettle to boil on the stove. "It's enoof fer me, 'tis. Never 'ad this mooch to meself before, so I got no complaints. That one's not botherin' ye, is 'e?" He indicated the cat sprawled on the table before Harry, showing him his belly. " 'E wants a roob, that one does. Ye mind cats, Yank?"

Harry tentatively reached out a fingertip to rub the cat's chest.

"Well, me, it's noothin' like a good dog, I gives ye that, but I'm gettin' use t' this lot. Started coomin' round soon's I set in. Beggars all, only in it fer the food. That's right, eh, mates?" He bellowed this at the cats in the rafters.

The cat under Harry's finger began to purr. Its claws slid out of their sheaths and round Harry's hand, threatening a painful scratching if Harry tried to pull away.

"Ye got yerself a friend there, Yank. 'E nips ye, just nip 'im back." Old Ted disappeared into the storeroom and returned with two tins of kippers. At the sound of his twisting the tin keys, the cats—from wherever they were positioned in the room—descended on the old man. He chuckled as he set the tins down on the floor and the dozen or so cats crowded against each other, each trying to get its muzzle into a tin. "That'll keep 'em busy for a bit, it will."

"Ted," Moncrief began, "I was telling them how this all belongs to Sir Johnnie."

"Oh, aye, the squire, all this is 'is, aye."

"Nice spread," Kneece said. "I don't remember seeing another stand of trees anywhere on the island."

"Orkney's not much fer yer trees, noope. There's another wood on Mainland, the one at Binscarth over at Firth parish, but this is the only other one 'n' it belongs to Sir Johnnie." Old Ted said this last with pride.

"Why's he have it fenced in?"

"It's 'is, i'n't it?" The kettle began to whistle. "Don't mind the coops, gennulmen, I'm not armed for many guests." Old Ted gestured at the motley set of drinking implements: a teacup, two mugs, a tin cup. "Use all the sugar ye need, Yanks, I gots plenny 'ere, 'n' the milk, too. That's from me own cow out there inna barn."

"I was asking about the fence," Kneece persisted.

Old Ted went back into the storeroom. "Would ye want soompin' in that tea for the chill?" He returned with a bottle of Black & White.

"Little early in the day for us, I should say," Moncrief commented.

Old Ted poured a healthy splash into his own cup. "I shouldn't neither, but it's rhoomatism fer me," he said and flexed his fingers painfully. "Gots to oil the gears, I do."

"The fence," Kneece repeated.

"Likes I was sayin', the squire does as 'e likes wi' 'is own property, dun 'e? That fence, it went oop when 'e buys the place, 'cause 'e was suppose' t' put oop one o' 'is shops 'ere, 'e was, one o' 'is fact'ries."

"What kind of factory?" Harry asked. "We don't know Sir John. What exactly is it he builds?"

" 'E's Johnnie Dooff, i'n't 'e? 'E's in lots of things, i'n't 'e? Got himself fact'ries all round the isles, 'e does."

"How come he didn't build this one?" Kneece was sounding impatient.

"Yer astin' a wrong man, ye is, young gennulman. That's a business thing, 'n' what's the likes o' me know 'bout business things?"

"The war, I suspect," ventured Moncrief. "I mean, it was before I was posted here, but once the war began I would expect the difficulties of establishing a manufacturing plant in a remote place like this . . ."

"You know, back in the States," Harry said, "in the boondocks outside Newark—that's where I live—Curtiss-Wright built a propeller factory. They made a big deal about it; they were very proud because from the time they broke ground to the time they opened the doors it was only ninety-six days."

"Perhaps Sir Johnnie didn't intend to build propellers," Moncrief said.

"Excuse me, Mr. Bowles," said Kneece, "do you mind if I use your bathroom?"

"Ya mean the toilet, do ye? Welp, that's one thing the squire 'asn't got to yet. No runnin' water. There's a closet round the back if ye don't mind the chill."

Kneece nodded a thanks and headed for the door.

"Oh, Yank, don't be wand'rin' off. No offense, like, but the squire don't like nobody just wand'rin' round his property."

Kneece smiled his acknowledgment, then flashed a look to Harry. While Harry wasn't quite sure what the look meant, he had a feeling about what it was he had to do.

He reached into his parka for his notebook. "Mr. Bowles, you don't mind if I jot all this down as we talk, do you? For the record. You know how it is. When we get back to our bosses, we're going to have to type up an official report."

"Ah, ye can keep yer office jobses, ye can. Not fer me. This is more to my likin', what I gots 'ere."

"Mr. Bowles, what exactly is it you do for Sir John?"

"I just watches the place is all. 'E's worried 'bout poachers and such-like. Not mooch game on the island. Ain't that right, Moncrief? If ye had to live on whats ye catch ye'd starve. 'Cause the squire's gots 'is woods 'ere, the 'untin' is a little better, but it all belongs to the squire then, dun it? So I keeps the poachers out, tends to mendin' whatever needs mendin'. Ye know; just general lookin' out fer the place."

"But he doesn't come up here, does he? Major Moncrief told us that Sir John hasn't been up here since the war began."

"Welp, natcherly, not with the war, would 'e? 'Ard to get round it is, eh? From the big isles up to 'ere, I mean. 'Sides, the squire's got 'is business to tend to, big business with the war."

"So he's in war industries?"

"Like I told you, 'e's Sir Johnnie Doof. 'E's into whatever there is to be into."

"How'd you get this job, Mr. Bowles?"

Moncrief cleared his throat. "I hate to interrupt, and certainly this sort of thing is hardly my bailiwick so I don't mean to tell you your business, Major, but what does this have to do with Lieutenant Grassi?"

Harry smiled and let his eyes drift away from Moncrief to the window. Woody Kneece was squatting by the foot of the dock, peering at something in the swirls of frozen mud.

"It's just background, Major," he replied. "Your bosses are probably like our bosses; they like to see you fill up a certain amount of paper. They're not convinced you're on the job unless you're filling up paper. You're in 'admin' yourself, you understand how it is."

Moncrief's smile turned sympathetic. "I quite see your point."

"Besides, Mr. Bowles doesn't mind, do you, Mr. Bowles?"

"Gives me soomebody t' talk to 'sides the kitties, it does. All I ever sees in the way of hooman beans is soometimes the major 'ere coomes 'n' sets wi' me for a round o' cribbage, pass the time, 'e does."

"Do you think I could get another cup of tea?" Harry asked. Outside, Kneece was moving out onto the dock, examining the boards.

"Sure enoof, Yank. There's some water left, I think."

"I was asking how you got this job."

"I worked in one o' Sir Johnnie's fact'ries, didn't I? Most o' me life

standin' at 'em machines, stampin' out machine parts I did, down in
Birmingham. That was one o' the squire's first shops it was, 'n' I was
there almost from the day it opened. I was just a tyke when I started, a
boy, makin' a few pence sweepin' the floors. Wi' 'im all that time, 'e
coome to know me personal, the squire did." Again the tone of pride.
"Then it coomes I'm not so yoong, am I? Gets hard gettin' round, dun it?
'Specially now I got this rhoomatism." Old Ted held out his splayed fingers for Harry. "A day like this, even that mooch hurts. Anybody else, any
o' these other bastards, 'em bosses in 'em trilby 'ats, 'ey sees ye moovin'
a mite slower, 'ey give ye a look likes yer pootin' 'em t' sleep is how
mooch 'ey care. 'Not oop to it anymore, eh, Old Ted? Thanks for all 'em
years but 'em machines got to get fed, so piss off! 'Ere's a door, ye old
sod, it's the dole for ye now.' "

"But not good old Sir John Duff."

"Gimme this position, 'e did, didn't 'e? Livin' better 'n' when I was
on the job, I am." He pointed to the piles of food tins, the bottle of Black
& White. "Takes as good a care o' me as ye can, dun 'e? 'Sides, it's
soompin' t' do, keep me useful. Ye gotta feel useful, eh?"

The water was boiling. Old Ted took Harry's mug and prepared a fresh
cup of tea.

"How long have you been here, Ted?"

"Oh, welp, let's see."

"You were here when I got here, Ted," Moncrief offered, "and that
was August '41."

"Hm, aye, but it was after that Christmas afore. So, early that year,
early 1941."

Harry could see Kneece at the end of the dock, on his knees, studying
the pilings. "When Major Moncrief's people found the dead American—"

"That was a bloody shame, eh? Young bloke, I 'ear. Know any more
'bout that, do ye?"

"Not yet. Did you hear anything that night?"

"You mean like a shot?"

"Well, anything."

"Noothin'. Would ya like some biscuits wi' that? The squire sent oop
some very tasty bits, 'e did." Old Ted shambled off into the storeroom.

"I was asking—"

"Oh, right, welp, no, noothin' comes t' mind."

"You mean you don't remember hearing a shot? Or you didn't hear
anything?"

"I didn't 'ear noothin', Yank."

"How far away would you say that stretch of the beach is?" Harry
asked Moncrief. "Half a mile? That doesn't seem very far."

"Might be a little more. But the weather here can be quite harsh. This is a relatively mild day. Tell him how bad it can be, Ted."

Old Ted pried open the top of a tin of biscuits and set it down in front of Harry. "I likes t' dunk meself. Moncrief there, 'e's too bloody polite t' enjoy 'imself, but if ye wants to dunk 'em in there, don't mind me."

Harry dipped the end of a biscuit in his tea before taking a bite, and this seemed to please the old man. One of the cats was on the table now, and nosing toward the tin.

"Out o' it, you!" Old Ted said and the feline leapt for safety. "Ye 'ad yer kippers! Don't be a bloody swine now! What were we sayin'? Oh, aye, like Moncrief there says, if the wind was oop that night, 'n' blowin' away from 'ere, ye coulda been settin' off cannons 'n' I coulda not 'eard 'em."

"Do you remember seeing anybody around that day who wasn't familiar?"

"Nope— 'Ere! What's 'e up to?" Old Ted caught sight of Kneece standing at the end of the dock and rushed out the cottage door. Harry and Moncrief followed.

When they reached the dock, Kneece was sitting on one of the pilings, affecting a relaxed air as he lit a cigarette. He maintained that attitude even in the face of Old Ted's red-faced bluster.

"You was just s'pose' t' use the toilet, eh? Whatcher doin' out 'ere, then, eh? I told you the squire don't want nobody roamin' all 'ere 'n' there, didn't I?"

"I'm sorry, Mr. Bowles. I just thought I'd step out here for a little fresh air, have a smoke—"

"I can *see* ye 'avin' yer smoke, Yank! But I *told* ye—"

"Here now, Old Ted, no harm's been done," Moncrief interposed, stepping forward, his voice conciliatory. "So the lad came out for a taste of the sea air."

"I *told* 'im—"

"Yes, yes, old boy, we all heard what you'd told him. But it's done, then, eh? Why don't you go on about your business and we'll be off. We're done here, yes, gentlemen?"

Harry and Kneece agreed, Kneece apologized again, and they climbed back into the jeep and drove off, the old man balefully glaring at them from one of the cottage's windows.

"I know it seems petty and all that, all this fuss from Old Ted, but you have to understand he takes his responsibilities to Sir Johnnie very seriously," Moncrief explained.

"He was right," Kneece said. "I mean, factually, it *wasn't* a big deal, but when you're a guest in somebody's house, you should honor the rules of the house."

"Why, that's quite civil of you, Kneece." Moncrief sounded impressed. "My experience with Americans is they seem to prefer a more . . . *informal* attitude. They seem to treat every home as if it's their own. Mind you, it's little bother to me, a fellow wants to throw a leg over the arm of his chair and all that, it can be quite refreshing, quite cavalier and so forth. But, be that as it may, as you say, when you're a guest in someone's house . . . I wish more of you Yanks were cut from the same cloth."

"Well, Major, you have to understand." Kneece, Harry thought, seemed oddly intent on the scenery passing by beyond the plastic windows. "We may all be Yanks, but those *Yankees* are another thing. In my part of America, we get raised right." Kneece gave Harry a mocking smirk. "Isn't that so, Major?"

"So, you're done with us then?" Moncrief asked. "Will you be off to London? Not until after lunch, of course, we should still be in time for that. Or will you be with us for supper as well?"

"We still have some odds and ends to tidy up," Kneece replied cheerily. "Besides, we've been traveling pretty hard the last couple of days. It wouldn't hurt us to lay over for the night and fly out in the morning. What do you think, Major? Could you use a good night's sleep?"

"Always," Harry said, truthfully.

"Get off!"

The shout woke him, and he was startled to hear it was his own voice, here in the real world. He thrashed about his bunk, yet still felt that force, that great suffocating hand from his nightmare, on his chest forcing him down.

"Shhh." It was hissed in his ear.

Harry's hands reached for his chest. The hand *was* real.

"It's me," the whisperer said. Harry recognized Kneece.

"You all right, Harry?" Jim Doheeny called out of the dark, from the other side of the bunk room.

"Say you're all right," Kneece whispered.

"I'm OK, Jim. Just a bad dream."

"Pick up your clothes," Kneece instructed. "Tell him you're going out for some air."

"I'm going outside for a cigarette," Harry said.

"You want company?" Doheeny asked.

"No, thanks, Jim. I just need a few minutes to myself."

Harry waited for the sound of Doheeny resettling himself on his bunk. "Now what?" he asked Kneece softly.

"Now we go."

. . .

It was after midnight, but the aerodrome at Kirkwall was hardly silent. Below them Harry could hear the thunder of a Sunderland's engines pulling it from the waters of Scapa Flow into the night sky. The patrolling and hunting never stopped.

Kneece led Harry to a jeep parked by the barracks where they'd been billeted. "Get in."

"Where'd you get the jeep?"

"Let's just leave it at I *got* it."

Then they were through the aerodrome gates and off down the road.

"I hope I remember the way." Kneece peered through the windscreen, trying to divine landmarks in the feeble beams of the cat's-eye headlamps.

"Remember the way *where?*" But as soon as he'd asked, Harry answered his own question. "You saw something out there today."

"Pardon my enthusiastic language, Major, but you're goddamned right I saw something today."

"Why didn't you say something before?"

"I didn't want to bring it up in front of Moncrief. That Brit was on us like a tick on a bloodhound all day. I thought he was going to follow me into the latrine, I swear to God."

And indeed, ever since they'd left Old Ted that morning, Moncrief had hovered close about them, as if the major felt it was his obligation to host them through every moment of their stay. He'd conducted them on a tour of the air and naval facilities, stood at Kneece's shoulder as the captain had questioned airstrip, communications, and radar personnel to corroborate what Moncrief had told them, kept up an incessant and incessantly banal conversation all through dinner, and hadn't seemed of a mind to leave them to themselves until they'd retired to their billet.

Kneece gestured out at the moon-washed pastureland. "This place reminds me of the low country back home. I don't mean it looks the same, but just like home it's farmers, most of 'em not having a lot of cash money. They need a fence, they split some wood and they got a fence. What's a fence? Uncle Ray used to say all you need is enough to keep the cows out of the corn and let people know this is somebody's property. After that, you let two barrels of double-aught shot do your fencing for you."

Harry was irritable with the cold, and with still being half asleep. For the moment, his customary civility failed. "What the hell're you talking about?"

"Major, look around. Fella makes a fence of split rails, or he makes a wall of fieldstone. It costs a lot of money to do something more, because the material's got to come up all that way from England or Scotland or wherever. But Mr. Sir Lord High-and-Mighty Johnnie Duff paid to put in a coupla miles of steel fence here. For what? To keep people out of a factory he didn't build?"

"Maybe he's just funny about his property. He doesn't like to share. That old guy said something about poachers—"

"Pardon my French, Major, but that sounded like a pile of pigshit to me. You know how much blood you got in your body?"

The sudden change in subject left Harry bewildered. "How much blood—?"

"Factually, five to six quarts. A quarter of that is all jammed up in your head."

And Harry finally knew what Kneece knew. "There would've been blood under Grassi's body," he said.

"Shot from the back, he falls forward. Even with all that gassing Moncrief did about the wind and such, as much blood as would've come out that bullet hole, there still would've been a good bit under him, protected by his body. Even those two Looney Tunes Macnee and Donlay would've seen it, there would've been so much. And it didn't just wash away."

"He was above the high-tide mark, drier underneath than on top."

"I don't know how much you know about what happens when you die, Major, but when you're dead the blood settles in the low spots. The blood would've settled in Grassi's front, in his face. You'd be able to see it, blue under his skin."

"Like a bruise! He wasn't killed on the beach. *He wasn't killed on the beach!*"

"The only place close by where a plane could come in and land unseen—"

"Is Johnnie Duff's lovely little forest."

"It had to be someplace close. That's what I was looking for when I climbed up on the jeep. We figured his plane probably didn't get here until after 2000 hours. Stands to reason Grassi must've been killed soon after. The blood had had time to settle in the body, but in the morning when they found him rigor was just coming on. It usually takes four hours to set in, but if he was outside all that time, with cold like this, it's like keeping a body in an icebox; rigor would be delayed by hours. Grassi's body had to have been out on the beach most of the night."

The jeep bounced past the dark windows of the village of Stromness and toward the beach where Grassi had been found.

"You saw something out at old Bowles's place," Harry said. "What?"

"You saw it, too."

"Those tire tracks? So? *We* left tracks. Moncrief's been out there before. *He* would've left tracks."

"With his jeep, yeah. But those weren't jeep tracks leading out to the dock, Major. Those tracks were wide and heavy, like a truck. That old fart's telling us he toodles around on a horse and buggy, but he's got tire tracks from a truck out to the dock. The ground out there has been thawed and froze up so many times I can't tell real well how old those tracks are, but maybe a coupla weeks, I'd guess."

"How can you tell that?"

By the sickly light of the dashboard Kneece's grin looked sinister. "I'm a good Southern boy, Major. Every good Southern boy has done his fair share of raccoon hunting, and every good 'coon hunter knows how to read sign."

"Did you find anything out on the dock?"

"Rub marks on the piles, like from a rope. Somebody's been tying up there. I can't read that kind of sign, but those marks don't look that old."

"You're not going to tell me you learned all this criminology at the elbow of Uncle Ray?"

"Dick Tracy's Crime Stoppers."

They had reached the crest where they parked that morning. To their left were the calm waters of Scapa Flow. In front of them, the moonlit Atlantic heaved restlessly under the relentless wind. Kneece turned off the headlamps and tried navigating the rutted track that led to the wood by the light of the waning moon.

"You think Moncrief is involved," Harry said. "Otherwise we'd be doing this with him and a squad of his MP's."

"I don't know that he is, I don't know who else here might be connected, but somebody is. Somebody *has* to be, besides the old fart. You said this thing needed somebody to organize it at our end, and you're figuring maybe Edghill in D.C. Wouldn't they need somebody at this end, too?"

"Somebody who knows the routes and schedules of the air and navy patrols."

"The plane comes in after dark, in the grass, under their radar, flying down the seam between the patrols. It leaves the same way. They truck the cargo to the dock and it goes out by boat while the patrols have their backs turned."

Kneece turned the jeep off the track, killed the engine, and let it coast across the icy pasture to a stop.

"Which brings us up to now." Harry looked apprehensively at the dark wood ahead. "The question of the moment is, what is it we're doing here?"

"You remember much of your basic training?"

"I remember not liking it much."

"I hope it comes back to you." Kneece climbed out of the jeep.

Reluctantly, Harry followed.

Despite the bulk of his parka and heavy boots, the captain seemed to glide easily and silently through the tangled underbrush. Every footfall of Harry's brought the crack of ice and rustle of dead leaves, the betraying snap of fallen branches. The rustles and snaps seemed to cut through the whiffle of the night wind with a deafening clarity that Harry was certain carried all the miles back to Kirkwall.

Kneece stopped. "Do you think you could try not to make so much noise?"

Harry trod still slower, still more carefully, yet could never match the near-silent tread of Kneece.

Kneece halted at the fence. He extracted a fence cutter from his coat pocket and snipped his way slowly through the links of the fence from the ground up until he'd opened a slit three feet high along one of the support poles. He peeled back one side of the slit and nodded at Harry to crawl through. Kneece followed, then bent the flap back into place. In the dark, with the opening made so close to the pole, no one walking by would see the gap in the fence. Or so Harry hoped.

Through the dense wood, Harry could see the glow of a lit window from the cottage. Mingled with the groans of swaying branches and puffing wind were the muffled strains of music, something orchestral with a low, crooning voice in the lead. Kneece stopped so abruptly that Harry bumped into him.

"What's the matter?" he whispered, panicked.

Kneece pointed to his ear and then in the direction of the cottage.

Harry listened more intently. He almost laughed. Old Ted was listening to a recording of Tommy Dorsey's orchestra, with Frank Sinatra singing "Fools Rush In."

At the edge of the clearing, Kneece motioned Harry to stay, slipped across the clear space to the stone walls, then crept along until he reached the cottage window. Kneece snuck a look inside, then beckoned Harry to join him. Beyond the panes, Harry could see Old Ted slouched in one of the chairs, head back, mouth sagging, eyes closed. On the table in front of him was a plate, a few orts of supper nosed round by a pair of cats. A third feline was curled in Ted's lap, a fourth on the old man's rising and falling chest. The phonograph had completed its emission of "Fools Rush

In." Harry could hear the hiss of empty vinyl regularly punctuated by the thump of the needle against the hub of the record.

Kneece slipped along the wall, then across the clearing to the barn. There he again signaled Harry to join him. Kneece drew a torch from his parka pocket and handed it to Harry. He pointed to the ground. By the light Harry saw the same wide tire treads he'd seen leading to the cottage's dock.

"Hold the light on the lock," Kneece said. "Move around here to block it."

Under the beam Harry saw Kneece take a small leather case similar to a manicure kit from his pocket. Kneece unzipped the case and had Harry hold it open for him. The captain took off his gloves and drew several needlelike instruments from the case, the stainless steel winking in the torchlight. Kneece inserted the needles into the padlock on the barn door and began to finesse them about.

"Where'd you learn how to pick locks?" Harry whispered.

"A fox gets in your henhouse, you don't learn to catch him by thinking like one of the hens." Kneece paused a moment to warm his fingertips with his breath.

"You and your Uncle Ray really ought to send these little gems of wisdom to *Reader's Digest.*"

"There we go!" Kneece slipped the padlock clear of its loops, then took the torch from Harry. He started to ease the door open. One of the hinges squeaked. Kneece killed the torch and froze. They both looked to the cottage. Stillness.

Kneece spat on the offending hinge several times, rubbing the saliva into the metal parts. This time the door opened quietly. He ushered Harry inside, closing the door behind them.

The barn was rife with the smells of must and damp hay, leather tack and animals. Harry heard hooves nervously paw the ground. The torch blinked on; Kneece sent the beam to the right, then left.

There were stalls along either side. Immediately to Harry's left, the torch beam fell on the bony posterior of a cow. The tail flicked anxiously, and Harry had a glimpse of large, nervous eyes, uncannily like his own. He affected what he thought would be a disarming smile and waved a casual hullo to the cow.

"You're not around animals much, are you?" Kneece muttered. On the captain's side of the barn were two stalls inhabited by broad-backed dray horses. One of them tossed its head, snorted. Kneece stroked its flank, moving forward to where he could cup the animal's cheek. "There, there," he crooned. "Easy, boy. Easy." The horse grew still.

Immediately in front of them, blocking their way farther into the barn, sat a stout dray equipped with a hayrack.

"If he uses the wagon to get around with," Kneece grumbled, "what's this supposed to be? His spare?"

Harry pushed past the wagon. Kneece now stood beside a hulking shape that, even concealed under a large tarpaulin, Harry easily recognized as a sizable lorry, perhaps weighing in at as much as a ton. Kneece flashed his light at the tires. All were crusted in dried mud. He leaned close for a better look at their treads. Kneece slipped under the tarp and into the cab. Then, finding nothing of note, he slid out and climbed up into the cargo bed. "Major . . . C'mere and have a look at this."

Harry slipped under the tarp and stood on the hub of a rear wheel to look up into the truck bed. Kneece was kneeling over several boxlike objects.

"What're those?"

In answer, Kneece fiddled along the side of one of the boxes, Harry heard the click of a switch, then Kneece slid open a panel on the top of the box and a blindingly brilliant light shot upward.

"What the hell—!"

"Pathfinders use these to signal aircraft for paratroop drops, glider landings—"

"Or what have you."

"Around here I'd say the 'what have you' looks to be the thing."

Outside the barn, Kneece reclosed the padlock, but instead of leading Harry back the way they'd come, to Harry's consternation the younger man headed away, skirting the clearing round the cottage in a direction opposite the oceanfront.

"We're not going back?" Harry whispered, hurrying after Kneece.

"We're not done yet," the young man replied grimly.

The lorry tracks led them to a gap in the trees, a narrow lane that had been concealed by the canopy of tree branches so tightly knit little of the moonlight seeped through. They followed the tire marks for several minutes, then the wood fell away and they found themselves at the edge of the large clearing Harry had spied earlier that day, the supposed site for Johnnie Duff's unbuilt manufactory.

A hundred yards or so from the trees, Kneece called to Harry and pointed at the ground. Here, the tire tracks appeared to circle and cross themselves.

"This is where he stopped and turned around so he could back up," Kneece explained.

"Back up to what?"

"Should be right along here. Here we go." Kneece's light had fallen on another tire imprint, this larger and running at a right angle to those of the lorry.

Harry was impressed at the width of the tire mark, nearly twice that of the lorry. "What kind of truck is that?"

"The kind that flies. Keep going and y'all're going to find another one parallel to this one, and in between them a smaller one."

"Left landing gear, right landing gear, tail wheel in the middle."

"Oy!" The shout echoed across the field.

Harry and Kneece froze. Kneece switched off his torch.

" 'Oo's out there, eh?" Harry heard the voice of Old Ted Bowles. The old man was invisible against the shadows of the trees.

"What do we do?" Harry whispered to Kneece.

"Get down."

"What?"

"*Down!*"

BOOM!

Harry instantly recognized the blast of a shotgun. Old Ted no doubt had nothing in his hands as elegant as Taffy Macnee's Purdy, but the weapon sounded just as lethal.

"Jesus!" Harry hissed and clawed the hard earth, trying to pull himself closer to it. He closed his eyes, the equivalent under those circumstances of a terrified child pulling the bedclothes over his head so as not to see the monsters rising up out of the dark to devour him. "What now?" he asked Kneece.

"Now we run!"

"Where?" poor Harry demanded.

But Kneece was already bolting across the field. Hearing the clatter of Old Ted reloading the shotgun in the dark behind him, Harry scrambled to his feet and took off after the fading footsteps of Kneece.

The captain was soon lost in the shadows of the woods. Harry ran blindly. For the moment, he opted for simply trying to put as much distance between himself and Old Ted as possible.

"Woody!" he hissed out into the gloom ahead of him. "*Woody!*" He crashed into the underbrush, fending off branches that tore at his eyes, caroming off tree trunks in his path. Bulling his way through the woods, he collided with the barrier fence, bounced off its springy links, and fell painfully onto his backside.

BOOM! The pellets from the double-barreled blast ripped through the brush behind him.

Harry pulled himself to his feet and instantly fell victim to another collision, this time with Woody Kneece, who'd been running along the line of fence.

"I can't find the hole!" Kneece said.

"*What?*"

"The place where I cut through! I can't find it! I don't even see the jeep!"

The captain continued along the fence, running his gloved fingers along the links, trying to find the gap. Harry followed at his heels.

They could hear Old Ted slogging through the brush behind them, sounding terribly close and horribly angry, swearing oath after oath at the brambles and branches pulling at him.

"We've gotta go over!" Kneece told Harry.

"What do you mean—"

Kneece went into a squat, his hands together in a stirrup. "C'mon, Major! Unless you think you can climb it!"

The nearing sound of Old Ted erased any hesitancy Harry felt. He stuck his boot into Kneece's clasped hands and pulled himself up the fence as Kneece shoved him upward. The topping strands of barbed wire bit into his gloved hands as he stepped free of Kneece's laced fingers, but the toes of his boots slipped on the links, too big to find purchase in the narrow apertures.

"Dammit, Major," Kneece growled and leapt onto the fence like a fly. He scrambled upward, perched himself at the top to haul Harry up. The two men, awkwardly engaged, teetered atop the fence. "Jump!" Kneece bellowed, then pushed Harry over the top.

BOOM!

It was less a leap than a fall: Harry barely managed to get his feet under him before slamming into the ground. His ankles buckled under the impact and he toppled over.

"There's the jeep!" Kneece called out.

Harry saw nothing but stars of pain. He felt Kneece grab him under one arm and jerk him to his feet. The stars multiplied. Harry felt himself sliding free of Kneece, then he was prone on the ground.

"Woody? Woody!"

Kneece was gone.

BOOM! The metal fence sang as the lead shot whined off the links.

Somewhere ahead, quite close by, the gears of an engine ground, a motor roared, and then brakes squealed as the jeep pulled to a stop beside him, shielding him temporarily from the fence, the passenger door open above him. Somehow, Harry found the strength to pull himself inside. While his feet were still dangling in the night, Kneece whipped the jeep into gear. The vehicle bounded across the moonlit pasture, leaving the cursing Old Ted and his menacing shotgun behind.

Even after Kneece found the road, he didn't turn on the headlamps until they were almost to Stromness. Harry was surprised—and not a little unnerved—to see, in the light of the dashboard, that Kneece was smiling.

"Was that something?" the captain said, sounding giddy. "I swear, Major, I swear that old sumbitch damn near parted our hair with that shot at us on top of the fence. It couldn't get any closer!" Kneece chortled over this, evidently assuming this brush with death to be some sort of coup.

Harry had neither the strength nor breath to tell Woody Kneece how little he thought of his exuberance. "You know, Woody, I've been a lawyer almost fifteen years without getting anything more serious than a paper cut. You've almost gotten me killed twice in the last two days!"

"It's nice to get out from behind the desk once in a while, right, Major? Hey, you think their mess hall is open this late? I could really use something to eat after all that skedaddling around. How about you?"

"There's something wrong with you, Woody. Something really wrong."

Woody Kneece laughed again. Dropping his voice into a Bing Crosby bass, he began crooning "Fools Rush In."

CHAPTER SEVEN

TARTARUS

HARRY WAS STANDING OVER THE OFFICERS Mess billiard table weighing one
of the .45's in his fist. The gun looked as unnatural in his hand as a second thumb. His fingers flexed about the grip, his index finger held cau-
tiously clear of the trigger. "Somebody's going to have to show me how
to use this," he said.

Though England sits as far north as Canada's Goose Bay, by grace of that
phenomenon known as the Atlantic Drift, Harry stepped onto the tarmac
of the American bomber base at Duxford and turned his face skyward,
basking in the warmth. Saturday, December 18th was a particularly pleasant day in East Anglia. The sun was a vivid yellow orb in a sky of winter
cobalt, tinting the mud and harvested wheat fields into squares of the
muted brown and amber Gainsborough favored in his days there.

An Army staff car and driver waited for Harry and Kneece by the
lollipop-shaped hardstand where Doheeny's aeroplane was directed to
park. The staff car driver brushed by them to load their bags in the car's
boot. Harry sighed happily, feeling like a knight-errant shedding the load
of his armor.

"We'll probably be in London for a couple of days, Captain," Kneece
told Doheeny. "There's no reason you and your men can't enjoy some
stand-down time. I just ask that wherever you are you check in with
Operations twice a day. If we're going to need transport, that's where I'll

leave a message. I promise no more at-a-minute's-notice stuff." And he was off for the car.

"Well," Harry said to Doheeny.

"Well," said Doheeny. He held out his hand to Harry. "Seems like this trip is all hullos and good-byes."

Harry grasped the pilot's hand. "Until the next hullo, then."

"Everything looks smaller than I thought it would." The sentiment did not keep Kneece from avidly pressing his face against the staff car's window as the humble shops and flats of Camden gave way to the Victorian poshness of Mayfair. "Where's all the famous stuff? Like Big Ben and Piccadilly Circus?" He didn't wait for an answer. "Everything looks pretty good. I mean, I thought with all the bombing . . ."

"You'll see more damage closer to the river, down in Westminster. The worst of it came down on the other side of the Thames."

This was all as new to Kneece as the snows of Massachusetts and Goose Bay's polar bears. His bright eyes devoured each brick, each passerby's countenance, the pubs and greasy-smelling fish-and-chip shops, the restaurants with canopied entrances and liveried doormen.

Harry fidgeted stiffly. They'd had to pull over three times on the narrow country road to make way for convoys of American Army lorries. The aerodromes on their route all buzzed with the bombers and fighters of the 8th Air Force, and one stretch of farmland had been turned into a sea of Army tents, rolling on acre after acre. When Harry'd first arrived in England a year earlier, those same fields had still been home to wheat and cows. Now, with its sixty air bases and swelling complement of Army camps, so many of his countrymen were stationed in East Anglia alone that American and Englishman alike had begun calling it Little America.

They were slowing to pass through a bottleneck caused by the blockading of a side street. Royal Army Bedford trucks were clustered by the blockade, and Home Guardsmen were directing traffic. As they passed, Harry saw the posted sign: UXB. Past the Guardsmen, the uniform facades of row houses had been violently disrupted.

"What's UXB?" Kneece asked.

"Unexploded bomb."

Among the strewn bricks spilling into the street sat a cushioned rocking chair, surprisingly intact. Royal Engineers gathered round a crater punched into the cobbled street. "Looks like there's a team in there trying to dig it out."

"Really?" Kneece craned his head this way and that. "They're working on a live bomb right now?"

"Must've been a stray. It doesn't look like anything else around here was hit." Harry turned to the driver. "Was there a raid last night?"

"Couple of nights ago," the driver replied. "But you never know when they're from; they're still digging up duds from the Blitz. They'll be digging bombs outta this place for a hunnerd years."

They crossed Oxford Street. "There we are," Harry told Kneece. "Right up ahead."

The captain leaned forward to look out the windscreen. "It sure doesn't look like much."

It was hard to disagree. Until one went round Rosewood Court's front gate, one was treated to featureless walls, penurious windows, blank-faced doors set deep in the stone. These uninviting entrances were reserved for servants, deliverymen, and other common laborers, not residents. The architectural premise at work behind this in-turned enclave was that the only fitting association for the families of position who inhabited the Court were other Court residents. To that end, the stately granite facades and balustraded verandas of the town houses and pieds-à-terre faced each other across a cobbled square. The yard itself was invested with rose-dressed trellises and a two-tiered fountain of expectorating nymphs. Each veranda was dressed with garlands of ivy and colorful flowers set in boxes and standing urns. The interiors of the various residences, Harry knew, were appointed with equal grace: oak staircases, mahogany wainscoting, parquet floors, and doors veneered with the rosewood that had lent the Court its name.

Since the coming of the Americans in early 1942, the Rosewoodarians had retreated to country estates scrupulously out of German bomber range. The rose trellises and fountain had been removed and the yard turned into a car park. The flower boxes and urns collected stubs of Lucky Strike and Camel cigarettes. By the gate, obscuring the brass plate that announced ROSEWOOD COURT, now stood a large olive drab sign with white lettering reading:

UNITED STATES ARMY GENERAL HEADQUARTERS

ADMINISTRATION ANNEX

(AIR CORPS INCLUSIVE)

LONDON

Still, as the staff car turned the last corner and drew up to the gates, the Court retained enough of its Victoria Regina majesty to squelch Woody Kneece's initial disappointment. He smiled up at the gargoyled cornices. "Oh, my . . ."

Two white-helmeted Military Policemen stood sentinel. While one studied their identification, the other swung open the gates. Kneece peered upward at the ormolu lions sitting atop the gateposts. "Oh, my my . . ."

The driver held the door for them as they climbed out. As he began to unload their bags, Kneece pivoted, soaking in all of Rosewood Court. "You used to live here? Not exactly the Fort Dix barracks, Major!"

"Lived and worked," Harry said. "My office used to be over there." He pointed to one of the town houses now marked with another olive-drab-and-white sign reading JUDGE ADVOCATE GENERAL—BUILDING B. He pointed to the top floor of another building, a narrow one tucked in the corner. "Those were my quarters."

"Real plush, sir. You must've hated to leave."

"You would think," Harry said noncommittally.

Harry signaled to the driver not to disappear with their bags just yet. He began rooting through his gear until he found his officer's peaked cap.

"What're you doing?" Kneece asked.

"I want to check in with the JAG chief." Harry frowned. At some point in their travels, the crown of his cap had been crushed. No amount of poking and prodding at the interior was able to resuscitate it.

"Let me see that," Kneece said, and without waiting for Harry to offer it, reached inside the crown and deftly removed the buckled wire grommet. "If you don't mind my saying so, sir, before you go nose-to-nosing with senior brass, you could use—as the rank and file like to say—a shit, shower, and shave."

"It'll be OK. The Chief and I are pals."

"Here you go." Without the grommet, Harry's cap had the soft, crushed look of a flying veteran's cap, like Doheeny's; what combat airmen referred to as a "fifty-mission hat." "You look like a regular Doolittle now. I believe the word is 'jaunty.' And jaunty as you may look, sir, I'd still think at least about a shave if I were you."

"I am thinking about it," Harry said, parking the cap on his head and heading across the yard for the town house billed as JUDGE ADVOCATE GENERAL—BUILDING A.

Harry could hear Kneece calling to him, in his best impression of a Warner Brothers cartoon character: "You'll be sorrrrreeeeee!"

The corporal sitting at the reception desk in the entry hall was clear-skinned, well-groomed, his uniform pressed, his shoes spit-shined. "Su-sir?" It was less a query than an apprehensive puzzlement from the corporal as to why this hairy, smelly thing—of intimidating bulk in its crumpled coveralls and leather flight jacket—stood over his desk.

"Is Colonel Ryan in?"

"The colonel? Oh, yessir, the colonel—"

"Tell him Major Voss would like to see him."

"I'm afraid the colonel's busy—"

"Tell him Major Voss would like to see him *now.*"

The corporal licked his lips nervously, torn between offending his commanding officer and provoking the savage looming over him.

"*Now,* Corporal."

The corporal gratefully left his desk, retreating to a set of sliding oak doors leading off the main corridor of the house. He stuck his head between the doors, Harry heard some murmuring, then the corporal beckoned him to come along, standing well clear as Harry passed by and sliding the doors shut behind him.

It was a spacious, high-ceilinged room, originally a parlor of some sort, Harry guessed. The current occupant had kept the room much as the previous tenants had left it, with Persian carpets, overstuffed lion's-paw furniture, globe lamps, crystal chandelier, and other such effulgent displays. Joe Ryan, as anyone acquainted with him knew, was always one to treat himself indulgently. Ryan, *sans* jacket and shoes, was standing on an ottoman, wobbling on the needleworked fabric, while a white-haired gentleman in a vested suit, his mouth bristling with pins, prowled round him making marks on his Army trousers with a tailor's chalk.

"Harry-boy!" Ryan flashed his movie-star smile at Harry's appearance. "Harry-boy, you look like the Wild Man of Borneo! Did you *walk* all the way from the States?"

"Can't walk. All that water."

"Make yourself comfortable," Ryan said, his smile taking on a doubtful twitch. "You just get in?"

"Just."

"You look beat."

"It's been a long couple of days." Harry let his eyes wander round the appurtenances. "Looks like you found a pretty nice home in the Army."

"If they put this place in the recruiting movies the draft boards'd have to beat kids off with a stick. Ouch! Mr. Cockburn, you caught me with that last pin."

"Sorry, sir," the white-haired gentleman mumbled.

"Didn't your office used to be . . ." Harry nodded in the direction of a smaller building across the Court.

"A lot of these poor bastards had to go with Eisenhower when he moved his headquarters to Algiers, the ones Ike figured were 'essential' to combat operations."

"How lucky for you to be nonessential."

"We needed the room anyway," Ryan replied cheerfully. "The more GI's they pack into England, the more GI mischief we have to deal with. I've had to add two lawyers to my staff since you left, and I have a request in for a third."

"Bully."

They were the same age, though one wouldn't know to look at them. Ryan was—and always had been, all the way back to their school-chum days—trim and athletic-looking, with square-jawed good looks and an outgoing charm. But Harry noticed subtle differences from the Ryan he'd left in London four months before. Ryan's middle was thicker, the sharp line of his jaw softer. Despite his beaming smile, his green eyes had lost their playful sparkle. The flesh round them was puffy and shadowed.

"There's cigarettes on my desk, Harry. Help yourself."

Ryan's "desk" was a large, cherry-stained dining table set before the brick-faced fireplace and its low, warming blaze. Harry found a brass cigarette box and a cup of tapers among the papers littering the desk. He tamped a cigarette on the tabletop, lit one of the tapers from the fire and took a long draught, then slouched in the deep-cushioned chair behind the desk.

The elderly man with the tailor's chalk was busying himself with Ryan's inseam. "You dress to the left as I recall, sir?"

"That's a kick, isn't it, Harry? They even ask you which leg you run your hose down. But they ask so nicely. To the left, Mr. Cockburn. Make a big allowance! What about this waist, Mr. Cockburn? It feels kind of snug."

"Yes, sir, I was of the same mind. But that was the measurement of your last pair."

"Jesus, am I going to have to diet now?"

"I can adjust them, sir."

"The point is, Mr. Cockburn, that I don't want you to have to adjust them. I shouldn't be having a belly!"

"Live like a lord, look like a lord, sir."

"That's very poetic, Mr. Cockburn, very Shakespearean."

"Thank you, sir."

"What do you think, Harry? You think I'm getting a little round in the middle?"

"Everybody says fat people are jolly. Look at me. See how jolly I am?"

For the first time, Joe Ryan did look at Harry, shrewdly measuring the man slouched in his chair. His smile faded. "Are we done, Mr. Cockburn?" Ryan raised his arms so that Mr. Cockburn could unbuckle his trousers and remove them.

Cockburn folded up the trousers, along with the other pair and two jackets lying across a settee. "I'll see to that waist situation," he told Ryan, and with a nod of farewell to both of them, backed out the sliding doors and closed them behind him.

"Hungry, Harry? I think there's something left there. Or I can have something sent up."

On a tea cart's tray sat a plate with a sandwich with less than half gone. Whatever was putting the softness to Ryan's physique wasn't food. There was also a silver coffeepot and an unused porcelain cup. "This is fine. You don't look all that surprised to see me."

"I knew you were coming." Ryan grunted as he bent over to pull on his trousers and shoes. "Listen to me. I sound like an old man."

"How did you know?"

"Colonel McCutcheon across the yard—he's the CID commander. He got the word you were coming in with some CID investigator named Kneece who's investigating this business about Armando Grassi. McCutcheon remembered you used to be on my staff—"

"And passed you the word."

"We're all friends here, Harry. Colleagues."

"Teammates."

"Yes."

"All for one, et cetera."

"Yup." Ryan came round the desk for a cigarette of his own. Harry moved away, sitting on the most distant end of the settee. Ryan smiled sadly at the maneuver. "How's Cynthia?"

"Fine."

"The kids?"

"Fine. Cynthia says hello. Philip Mayer—"

"The guy with the store?"

"He says hi, too."

"How's the neighborhood?"

"The same. But different."

Ryan sighed and lowered himself into his chair. "You're still angry about—"

"I wouldn't bring that up."

Ryan nodded at the warning. "What the hell are you doing here, Harry? How did this CIC joker rope you into this expedition?"

"He asked."

"That's all?"

"You've been away from the neighborhood a long time. Maybe you forgot. Back there, when somebody asked you for help, you helped. Kneece asked for help. I'm a helpful guy."

"You're a regular Boy Scout, Harry. What're you doing here?"

"I told you. I want to find out who murdered Armando Grassi and why."

"That's why Kneece is here. Why are you here?"

"Kneece thought I might be good to have on hand because I knew Grassi."

"You worked with him a couple of times. You hated him each time."

"I explained that to Kneece. He thought because I'd been stationed here—"

"And because of all the loads of mutual affection and respect between you and the brass here in London—"

"—that I'd have some connections."

"You tell him how off-base he was on that, too?"

"I did. Kneece never said it up front, but I think the real reason he wanted me along was that he had this idea that Grassi's murder had something to do with what happened here back in August."

Ryan's eyes narrowed. "I have to wonder what put that idea in his head."

"So do I. It wasn't me."

"How much does he know about August?"

"Now?"

"You told him."

"Just a little. To persuade him that he was wasting his time; that whatever happened to Grassi had nothing to do with August."

Ryan smiled coldly. "This wouldn't be one of those reverse-psychology routines where you say, 'It doesn't,' to get him to say, 'It does'?"

"I'm not that clever, Joe. You know that. You were always telling me how smart I wasn't."

Ryan stood, turned his back to Harry, and tossed his cigarette into the fire. There was a pair of brandy snifters and a nearly empty carafe on the liquor stand near the fire. Ryan lifted the carafe in offering. "How's your stomach these days?"

Harry held up his coffee cup. "I'm fine."

Ryan poured a small splash into one of the snifters and returned to his seat. He took a small sip. "The headquarters move to Algiers gave us a lot of new office space, but we're still tight on bunk room. The only space they could find you and your traveling buddy is down in the junior officers' quarters. Sorry."

"We'll be fine."

"What do you think?" Ryan asked. "About Grassi?"

"I don't think it had anything to do with August."

"You told Kneece that? Does he believe it?"

"I think so."

"If I were in your shoes, I wouldn't've told him that. I would've said this smells to high heaven of a connection to August."

"Is that what you think?"

"No. But I would've said that just to get him to dig around, pick at everybody's sore spots. That's what I would've done. But then, I'm not you. Sweet, pure Sir Harold the True."

Harry crossed the carpet to set his empty cup down on Ryan's desk. "You don't have to believe this, but I want to put that business behind me as much as you do."

"Look at that!" Ryan mocked. "We still agree on something!" He took another sip from his glass. "What're you doing here, Harry? I don't mean in England. You're not here in any official capacity; you're just part of Kneece's luggage, so you didn't have to check in with me."

"I just wanted to say hello to an old friend."

Ryan's eyes went cold. He set his glass down on the table so hard, Harry feared the frail crystal would shatter. "You came in here wanting to make some kind of impression. OK, I'm impressed. You're not the old Harry. You're a tough guy now. Man of the world. You're a shark. You're a barracuda. Is that what you want to hear?"

Only at that moment did it occur to Harry that he didn't know what he wanted from Ryan. "Cynthia and Philip Mayer wanted me to give you their regards. Consider their regards given." He reached for the handles of the sliding doors.

"Harry! Harry, wait!" Ryan was standing, imploring. "We should talk."

Harry slid open the doors.

"Harry! How about dinner tonight? I've got things to do this afternoon, otherwise we could go right now, but tonight—"

"Colonel Ryan, what in the hell could you possibly have to say that I could possibly want to hear?" And he left.

RE YOUR INQUIRY G-1 RECORDS ALL CONCERNED
UNAVAILABLE STOP

"That was waiting for me at Colonel McCutcheon's office," Kneece said when Harry looked up from the message in his hands. "You know him? McCutcheon? London CID boss?"

Harry shook his head. "He must've transferred in after I left."

"You should've seen this guy's office, Major! Are they all like that? You know—like . . ." Kneece sought the word.

"Like something out of *Little Lord Fauntleroy*."

Kneece pointed at the message. "Don't ask me what 'unavailable' means. There's not too many reasons personnel records wouldn't be available to a CIC investigator. Factually, I can't think of one, leastways a *good* one."

At that moment, Harry and Kneece were working their way through lunches of tuna sandwiches and coffee in the Rosewood Court canteen. It had been nearly a week since Harry had seen the young captain clean-shaven and in his Class A's. Kneece now seemed almost unfamiliar.

Harry continued reading:

CASUALTY LIST SHOWS YOUR WESTBOUND E-6
NONCOMBAT DEATH PRESQUE ISLE INFIRMARY 12-4
STOP NO LEAD ON REST OF FLIGHT CREW STOP

"That'd be Bell, the flight mechanic," Kneece explained. "I told my buddy not to use any names in his communications. Going by what you've been saying, I didn't know whose eyes this'd get in front of."

"Zagottis was right," Harry said bleakly.

"About what?"

"Bell couldn't take the trip." Harry returned to the message.

EDGHILL ASSIGNED G-4 TRANSPORT SECTION 12-40
SPECIFICALLY AIR SUPPORT US DIPLOMATS BRITISH
ISLES STOP RUMOR POLITICAL CONNECTIONS STOP
STILL HUNTING HOPE MORE TO FOLLOW STOP YOU OWE
ME VERY BIG END MESSAGE

The young captain wiped his fingers clean on a napkin, took the message from Harry, gave it a last glance, then tucked it inside his jacket. "What do you make of that? 'Political connections.' "

"Edghill's in Washington. All connections are political there."

"When I wired ahead to let CID here know I was coming, I included a query on the whereabouts of that copilot that survived the crash. Coster. I asked Colonel McCutcheon how that was going—"

"Unavailable."

Kneece nodded. "I'm starting to think 'unavailable' means 'Whatever we know, we're not telling.' You going to eat the rest of that?"

Harry pushed his plate across.

"I've got some other not-so-good news," Kneece said through a mouthful of Harry's sandwich. "Remember how Major hoity-toity Moncrief said he was going to rrrring up the chaps at the Yahd and have all that rrrrahther dull paperwork forwarded to your lads for your pe-rrrrusal, eh? Well, it ain't here. When I asked McCutcheon about it, he says he don't know nothing nohow no way about it. He says he'll put in a call to Scotland Yard about it, but I'm getting the bad suspicion it's going to be 'unavailable.' You ever run over a skunk, Major? Well, things are smelling like we ran over a big, fat one. Anyway, that's how my meeting went. How did *yours* go?"

"I said hi. He said hi."

"Somebody you remember from when you—"

"Yeah."

"Can he help us?"

"I wouldn't hold my breath."

"With how high a lot of the boys around here seem to be living, I want to go on record as taking umbrage at our *egregious* accommodations! Which brings up a matter in which I don't want to be too indelicate. You *are* going to take a shower sometime, aren't you? Sir?"

"Is that a question, Woody? Or a plea?"

"Well, see, sir, factually, I didn't notice before because it'd been just as long between soapsuds for me, but, well, we're going to be sharing a pretty small room . . ."

"Woody, are you saying I stink?"

"Not as a person, mind you, sir, but speaking in a strictly hygienic sense . . ."

Harry bowed his head and sniffed at his own person. His nose wrinkled. "First thing after lunch," he promised.

Woody Kneece sat cross-legged on his bunk, dressed in long underwear. He poked at the keyboard of a typewriter set on a pillow in front of him, the letters coming with the slowness of a midnight drip of a leaky faucet. Despite his painstaking technique, he was still capable of a misplaced digit, accompanied by a whispered "Damn . . . ," followed by the rasp of eraser on paper.

"What's all that?" Harry pointed at the the balls of crumpled paper on the floor round Kneece's bunk. He was fresh and still dripping from the shower stalls of the junior officers' quarters.

"McCutcheon had a wire from my CO back in D.C. He wants a full written report bringing him up to date. McCutcheon wants to send it out on a courier plane tonight."

"I take it one thing Uncle Ray didn't teach you was typing."

"Damn . . ." Kneece reached for his eraser.

Harry rubbed his neck, still tingling from a shave. "You were right. That hot shower felt nice, right up until the time I stepped out and my feet hit that cold concrete floor."

Kneece grunted. "That do make one's balls jump. Damn!" He looked at his wristwatch and moaned. "I was hoping we'd get a chance to see the sights, maybe grab some chow somewhere off-campus. You know: see how the natives live. I'm never going to get this thing done in time for that flight."

Harry tried to adjust his few strands of hair to cover the maximum area with the aid of the paltry view offered by the pocket mirror mounted inside the door of one of the room's two small lockers. "McCutcheon couldn't find you a typist?"

"He couldn't even get me an empty office. He says I'm lucky I got the typewriter. Well, there's no sense you being stuck here, Major. You go see the sights."

"I've seen them," Harry said.

"So how will you while away all these hours you're going to have to your lonesome while I slave away here?"

"I was thinking of looking up an old friend."

"Another old friend? Can he type?"

There came three solemn knocks on the door. Before either Harry or Kneece could respond, the door swung open, nudged by a toe. There stood a young officer, hands buried in the pockets of his greatcoat, a stub of cigarette hanging from his lips, his garrison cap pulled low on his brow in exaggerated jauntiness. "Who the Sam fucking Hill did you piss off to get sent to this dungeon?"

Even with his face partially obscured by his upturned collar and the lowered cap, as well as a large square of gauze taped over his left eye, it took Harry only a heartbeat to recognize him. His face exploded in a smile, he shot across the room and gripped the officer's hand in his. "Dammit, Pete! Pete!"

"Hello, Major."

"Come in, come in!"

"Do you think you can fit another body in this phone booth?"

"We'll shoehorn you in. What're you doing here? I thought you put in for—"

"Italy, yeah. Up until two weeks ago, that's where I was."

Harry's smile wilted as he nodded at the gauze. "Is it . . . Is it serious?"

Ricks dismissed Harry's concern with a shrug and a smile. He reached into one of those deep coat pockets and withdrew a fifth of Black & White. "I remember you didn't have much taste for this, but as Mater taught me, 'Good guests always bring a gift.' " He tossed the bottle to Kneece. "If you're not up for it, Major, I'll just have to force myself to imbibe your share." He shrugged off his coat and the crossed muskets of the infantry glinted on his collar tab. He pushed past Harry to study his bandaged visage in the small locker mirror. "Dramatic, isn't it? My own damned fault. I had my head up where it wasn't supposed to be and a slug kicked up some crap into my eye. The best ophthalmic guys were here in London, but once they got a good look at it, it turned out not to be such a big deal; just a little scratch on the eyeball. This thing's actually going to come off soon." Ricks took a last drag on his cigarette, drawing the red glow so near Harry feared he'd burn his lip, stubbed the cigarette out on the locker door, drew the last of a pack of Lucky Strikes, crumpled the pack, and let it fall among Kneece's typing discards. "Anyway, I was over visiting some of the old JAG gang yesterday and heard you were coming in today. You guys look a little worse for wear yourselves. You get that shaving, Junior?" He pointed at the bandage on Kneece's forehead.

"I got it being a dumb-ass."

"Join the club. Hey, anybody got a match?" To Harry: "Going to introduce me to your bunkie?"

"Captain Woody Kneece," Kneece said, climbing off his bunk and striking a match. "CIC-Washington. You're Peter Ricks. You used to work with the major."

"My fame precedes me."

Kneece indicated the silver first lieutenant's bars on Ricks's shoulders. "Wasn't it *Captain* Ricks?"

Ricks leaned forward to light his cigarette, though his eyes remained on Kneece's face. His cigarette lit, he flopped onto Harry's bunk. "The Army doesn't consider a year in the JAG suitable preparation for combat command. After three months in Italy—and this particular stupidity"— he pointed to his bandage—"I'm disinclined to take issue. So, they bumped me down to second looie."

"You got some of it back," Harry observed.

Ricks smiled ruefully. "The krauts are extremely conscientious about providing regular room for the advancement of junior officers."

"Captain Kneece here came to see me about Grassi," Harry told him.

"I heard about Grassi." Ricks said it flatly. "I'm told when they got the news, several of his neighbors from these very rooms knelt out in the courtyard and offered up thanks."

"Woody thought maybe I could help since I knew him."

"You're a better man than me, Major. I knew the little prick better than you and I wouldn't've *wanted* to help. *Because* I knew him better than you."

"That's a little hard," Kneece said.

"Did you know Grassi?" Ricks demanded.

"Just what I've heard from folks who did."

"Then it shouldn't surprise you that with half the world shooting at the other half, somebody would take advantage of the crossfire to put a pill in Armando Grassi's head or stuff a pineapple up his arse. Didn't he get shipped to the North Pole or something? You cracked his jaw a good one, Major, and he was still wired up when they ran him out of town. You should've seen it, Captain—what is it?"

"Kneece."

"The major here may seem like a big teddy bear, but when Harry laid it on Grassi the little son of a bitch's feet left the ground."

"Greenland," Harry said, reddening. "They sent him to Greenland."

"Who the hell shot him? Santa Claus? I believe Grassi could move Santa to homicide. All those frigging elves, too."

"It's what we're trying to find out," Harry said.

What little interest Peter Ricks displayed in Armando Grassi's fatal misfortune evaporated abruptly. "Did I hear right, Major? You were sent home?"

Harry nodded and turned to fiddle with something in his locker.

"How're things back in the States?"

At that point, Harry deferred to Woody Kneece, the ready raconteur. The captain regaled Peter Ricks with tales of rising hemlines, sports standings, and rationing tales. "My daddy's got six good running horses in his stables," Kneece prattled on, fueled by some of the Black & White. "But the horses know how much my daddy likes his meat, and with all the beef rationing, those nags are starting to get nervous. They're so twitchy that all Daddy's got to do to get a winning run out of them is stand at the starting gate with a spit and a bag of barbecue charcoal."

Ricks, with his own cup of whisky, laughed so hard—too hard, Harry thought—he began to choke.

Harry stood in a corner of the tiny room, nursing his cup through the second and third doses the younger men downed. He provided Ricks with a fresh cigarette, which the lieutenant lit from the stub of his previous smoke. He offered little to the conversation; in fact, he barely heard most of it.

I had actually had the pleasure of sitting with Peter Ricks during those closing August days. Where Armando Grassi was short, spidery, unable to sit still, erect, or silent, providing an uninvited and incessant mix of opinion, argot, and King's English, Ricks was tall and square, with the good looks a mother always wishes for in the husband of her daughter. Grassi splashed across a chair; Ricks set himself at such sharp angles one would have thought him positioned by level and T-square. This was not military discipline, but the product of his patrician Nob Hill upbringing, as was his manner of speech: soft, proper, civil.

And thus Harry's great interest this December eve in the young man on his bunk, for he could not envision the Peter Ricks of the previous summer introducing himself with the statement, "Who the Sam fucking Hill did you piss off to get sent to this dungeon?" Nor could he see that same Peter Ricks slouched across his bunk, chain-smoking cigarettes, swilling down whisky, and trading raspy laughs with the likes of Woody Kneece.

In the shadows beneath Peter Ricks's green eyes was a deep exhaustion that no amount of rest would heal. And like most profoundly weary men, what had seemed of great concern to him before now seemed so obscenely pointless.

"It was getting claustrophobic in there," Ricks muttered around his cigarette.

"Yes," Harry said.

It was an early twilight, and the cobbles and Georgian homes and even the air in the streets of the blacked-out city had the blue of old stone. Kneece had finally shooed them out with a pained look at his watch and the pile of handwritten notes yet to find their way onto a typed page.

Ricks shivered. "Aren't you cold?"

"You've been spoiled by your time in sunny Italy."

Ricks laughed. "It is *winter* in sunny Italy. When it is winter in sunny Italy it does not snow. It rains. And rains. And rains. Guys in my outfit do not worry about getting killed. They worry about getting wounded and going down in the mud where they will suffocate and remain undiscovered until some other poor doughfoot trips over them." Ricks grinned at Harry's doubtful look. "No joke. You have any more butts, Major?"

Harry pulled a pack out of his jacket pocket and handed it over.

"It's your last one."

"It's OK." They stopped and bent together to shelter the flame as Harry struck a match. Ricks reached inside his coat and brought out a flat silver flask. He held it up so that Harry could see the ornately engraved PR on the side. "A gift from Pater before I shipped over. I found it at the bottom of my duffel bag. It'd been sitting there for over a year; never used." Ricks unscrewed the top and held it up to Harry. "Want a belt? Take the chill off?"

Harry shook his head.

Ricks took a swig, recapped the flask, and slipped it into his coat pocket. "I know. I'm drinking too much. I'm smoking too much."

Harry wanted to ask why.

Ricks saw this and smiled grimly. "Sunny Italy is one hill after another. On top of each hill is a kraut machine-gun nest, or a kraut field piece, or a kraut tank, or some other goddamned kraut thingamabob. You and your guys fight your way to the top of the hill, and when you get there you find that the krauts have scrammed and dug in on the next hill. There is always a next hill. The word 'Sisyphean' comes to mind. I was the third acting CO my company's had since we landed at Salerno in September. I only lasted three days before I got this." He gestured at his bandaged eye. Ricks halted, looked up and down the sidewalk, and sighed. "Major, I'm in the infantry, which means I walk for a living. I'm off the clock now; could we find a place to sit?"

They were not far from Hyde Park. Harry led them through Curzon Gate and toward the Serpentine. There was a small café on the bank of the pond, closed for the evening. They sat at one of the wrought-iron tables on a terrace by the water. Ricks treated himself to another sip from his flask. This time, he did not return it to his pocket, but set it carefully on the table before him. "Hey, whatever happened to that girl?"

"What girl?"

"What was her name? That pilot's girlfriend."

"Elisabeth McAnn. I don't know what happened to her."

"It's a shame she doesn't know about Armando. She might feel that evened up the scales. Does that sound a little cold on my part?" He shrugged. "I've buried too many good kids in the last three months to shed a tear over a weaselly shit like Grassi." He sighed. "I feel like I've been over here a million years. Did it matter to you so much to come all this way? About Grassi?"

"I'm here."

"Did you stop by to see Ryan? I would've loved to have been a fly on the wall for that. How'd it go?"

"There wasn't any hitting."

Ricks chuckled. "Feel like getting something to eat?"

"I was on my way out when you showed up. Come around tomorrow. We'll have breakfast."

"I'd like that."

"I'm really glad to see you, Pete. I followed the news about Italy when I was home, I knew you were there . . . I'm just glad . . ." Harry shrugged apologetically.

Ricks nodded. He reached for his flask to pocket it.

"Pete . . ." Without having planned it, without even knowing why,

Harry told him everything, the entire tale from Kneece's arriving at his home to the telegram that had been waiting for the CIC captain when they'd arrived in London. It felt good to be able to share the burden with someone he felt he could trust; someone he *knew*. When he was done he looked to Ricks for his opinion, his insight, his verdict.

But Peter Ricks sat blank-faced, perhaps—and in the growing darkness, Harry wasn't sure—even somewhat annoyed. "Major, I'm not in the JAG anymore. None of this is my business."

"Last summer, when you told me you were putting in for combat duty, you told me you were looking for 'clarity.' Is this your way of telling me you found it?"

Ricks's hand had been fingering the silver flask. The polished sides caught light from the rising moon, and Harry saw it flash briefly in the one sad, tired eye of the young man across from him. "The poop is that Mark Clark wants to be the first American army commander to liberate a European capital, and it looks like he'll spend every man in the Fifth Army to do it. We've had fifteen thousand casualties since September, we're hung up on the Gustav Line fifty miles from Rome, and we're all going to die for a headline. So, moral clarity? But life is *simpler* out there. You don't think about much, you don't think about *anything* but what you need to do to get through the day, the next hour. The next two minutes. Everything else is just so much crap you can't fit in your pack." He rose from the table, slowly, wearily, leaving the flask on the table. "I'll bet this place is beautiful when the lights are on. Be careful with this Kneece kid, Major," he warned, without turning.

"Why?"

"What do you know about him?"

"He likes to pretend he's this wide-eyed yokel, but there's more to him. He's playing a lot of cards very close."

"You're goddamned right he is. They give him a plane and *carte blanche* to nose around in this stuff . . . this guy must have a power line from his hip pocket straight to Washington, and that's not standard for your typical CIC dick. The brass aren't jumping through hoops because of Armando Grassi."

"I was going to ask you for some help."

"You were."

"We don't know everybody that's involved, but we're obviously talking about people on both sides of the Atlantic. They know Kneece, they know me."

"They see you coming and up goes the drawbridge. No information. This has a horribly familiar ring to it, Major."

"Like you said, you're not JAG anymore, Pete. You have no tie to us.

You're just some infantry officer on medical leave trying to find an old friend."

"What's my old friend's name?"

Harry produced a notebook and pen from his inside jacket pocket, scribbled on a page, tore off the sheet, and handed it to Ricks. Ricks tried to read it by the moonlight. "What's this? Caster?"

"Coster. That's his name and his serial number. He was the copilot of a plane that went down on December first in Greenland. He flew out of Kap Farvel with Grassi. The wire in Greenland said there'd be orders waiting for him on this end."

"How do you know they didn't just put a pill in this guy's head, too?"

"I don't. I think the decision to kill Armando was made in the Orkneys. I don't think it was planned in advance."

"And from what evidence do you derive these intriguing suppositions?"

"If they'd planned all along to kill Armando, why not dump him out over the North Atlantic? Nobody would ever have found the body. No, I think somebody local was surprised when Grassi showed up three weeks ago. So, if the higher powers in this thing weren't planning on killing Armando Grassi, I'm guessing they weren't planning any harm for Coster, either. That means he could be intact somewhere, that they really did cut orders for him."

"So, you think if I just wander casually over to G-1, and in an offhanded, quite unofficial way ask if they know where my old chum Flyboy Coster is . . ." Ricks shook his head. "Do you know how many bodies get processed through here every—"

"They'll remember him."

"He had that distinctive a personality?"

"It would've been recent."

"The last troopship was recent. Do you know how many men—"

"He would've shown up alone, without his file, no written orders, not even any gear. G-1 would've gotten his assignment orders from an authority high enough where they would've passed him through as fast as they could without asking questions."

Ricks lifted his flask from the table. "I don't know what you think you're doing here, Major. Maybe you feel bad about how things turned out for that girl, maybe you really do feel bad about Grassi. But you can't undo anything. If you came back because you think that somehow this'll even the score for what happened last summer . . ." Ricks uncorked the flask and drank deeply. He looked out at the dark water of the Serpentine, the placid surface iced with the cold light of the new moon. "You can do everything right and somebody's still going to get hurt."

They were both silent.

"I'll ask a few questions over there," Ricks told him resignedly, after a time. "But I'm not going to drive myself crazy."

"Thanks."

Ricks took a last sip and slipped the flask back into his coat. "I'm getting out of here before you get me writing briefs next." He started to walk away, following the curve of the lake, but then stopped and called back: "We know each other a while now, Major; can I say something in the clear?"

"Sure."

"You had to be out of your frigging mind to come back here."

"I *was* out of my mind."

Peter Ricks disappeared into the shadows. Twilight had become evening. Harry sat alone at the dark café. He wished he hadn't given Ricks his last cigarette.

My affection for the Rose & Crown public house grew with each freshly poured drink. Halfway through a pitcher of bitters, the dowdy, dark interior of the pub became a cozy womb, the sullen duffers hunched over their pints and chessboards fine old English sods who appreciated the exquisite flavor of quiet and the need for an introspective body to be left alone with his thoughts.

"Yer o'er the line," Lil said from the bar.

I ignored her, leaving her to busy herself behind the bar. Instead, I focused—as much as my ale-fogged intellect could—on the dartboard. I loosed the projectile along what I considered an immaculate parabola toward the board and watched it gracelessly crash sidelong into the cork and clatter to the floor.

"There seems to be some fault in your equipment. I find it structurally unsound."

"There seems to be some fault with yer bein' a drunken old sod," Lil told me.

"I am not old," I objected, cocking my arm with a fresh dart. "I am venerable."

"And yer venerable foot's still o'er the line. Cheat yerself, it's no mind to me, Eddie, but I thought you might care to know."

"Och, a foul, you say? Which leg is it, Lil? Please, point out the transgressor to me! What leg has sinned and stands in foul?"

Her ruddy cheeks were crisscrossed with a filigree of veins, her hair a scratchy tuft of gray-streaked brown. Her husband was fighting the Japs in Burma under Wingate, her son in Baghdad keeping Raschid Ali's people from going over to the Nazis, and little that occurred in the pub she now managed alone warranted more from her than mild interest.

"No, I beg thee, Lilith my treasure, be this the offending limb? I offer my suffering in amends. If thine eye deceiveth thee, pluck it out . . ."

"Oh, Christ," Lil muttered, rolling her eyes tiredly.

"If thy foot missteps—" At that, I brought the dart in my hand with full force down upon my leg, stabbing again and again. "*There*, you damned rotter! And again, you most foul fouling fouler!" The dart made a solid thunk as it sunk deep into my wooden limb.

Perhaps if I'd imbibed a little less of that pitcher I would have remembered that this was a too oft repeated jape, no longer deliciously grotesque but stale.

"That's got to be a little hard on the pants."

I had not had so much to drink that I did not instantly recognize the accent as American. The cloud I'd been under since August, and had sought shelter from almost nightly in the somber confines of the Rose & Crown, scudded away.

"Bugger all!" I declared. "*Harry!*" I swung the leg round, clasped his hand in mine, and threw my other round his neck. "Lil, my sweet, have you ever seen a sorrier-looking bastard than this Yank?"

She gave me a droll look. "Haven't I?"

I leaned close to Harry's ear. "There's nothing as cruel as the tongue of a woman seeking to conceal her affections."

Lil rolled her eyes again. "The muck that comes out of that gob of yours . . ."

"Uh, careful you don't stick me with that thing," Harry said. He was looking at the dart still embedded in my leg.

"I should leave it, don't you think?" I took my snap-brim from where it'd been resting on the back of my head and hung it from the tail of the dart. "Useful, eh?"

"Ya've got the taste of a ghoul, have yer been told that, dearie?" Lil said.

"She's a love, isn't she, Harry? Have you eaten? Victuals for my mate, woman! Give her leave, Harry; Lil's a proper barkeep, but a bloody barbarian in the kitchen: no hot food here. Lil, this poor man's traveled all the way from the Colonies to sample some fine English cuisine. What can you lay on for my chum?"

"I can do you a plate of some cold meats and cheeses."

"That'll see him right, won't it, Harry? Bring it to my private dining quarters when it's ready, Lil. My God, you're a sight, Harry!"

I led him by the arm to a corner booth, carrying the remaining half of the pitcher and a pair of mugs with me. I sat him across from me and poured two pints. His face was drawn and more weathered than I remembered; he looked very much the world-weary traveler with his crushed officer's cap and flying jacket. But I sensed it was more than mileage that had seasoned Harry Voss.

He toyed with the handle of his pint. I suddenly remembered how badly drink used to sit on his stomach.

"You don't have to drink it just to be polite, Harry. Leave it and it'll be twice as much for me."

He laughed.

I wiggled the dart free of my leg, jabbed it into the scuffed tabletop, and set my hat over it. "There. Done and done."

I could see in his eyes—so much more shrewdly appraising than they used to be—that he saw a change in me as well; the mien and sickly pallor of someone spending too much time entombed in the Rose & Crown.

I asked after his family, and was surprised when he responded with the terse reticence of an interrogation subject. Harry's family had, as I remembered, been his touchstone; he'd never before been hesitant over an opportunity to revisit the thought of them. Now, with uncharacteristic abruptness, he deflected my course. "Did you see Elisabeth McAnn like I asked?"

"Soon as she was well enough to receive visitors."

"How is she?"

"She seemed right enough when she left hospital. Not particularly amicable, mind you, but then what should one expect under the circumstances?"

"What about after she left the hospital?"

"She applied for travel papers to Ireland. Old family relations still there, I understand. There was some fuss over her application. Talk of security and all that. Some of the military nabobs fretting the poor little lass might open her pouty lips to some anti-British Dublin rag and rekindle the whole business. But I talked to a few people I knew at the Foreign Office, did some of my best convincing, made the point she was as eager to have it all behind her as anyone else. She was seen right, Harry. She made it home with no trouble. After that . . ." I shrugged. "I suppose we could find her if you're of a mind."

He shook his head, but seemed to consider it a few moments, his face clouding.

"I did go to my editor with the story," I told him.

"I thought you said they'd never print it."

"They didn't. You haven't said what brings you back to London. Have you been reassigned here?"

"I need you to do something for me, Eddie." He fell silent as Lil brought the plate of food, waiting until she'd withdrawn.

"A favor?" I asked. "You need a favor?"

He frowned at the plate of food. "Eddie. Can you be a friend?"

"I'm not sure I understand—"

"As opposed to a reporter."

"Ah. You mean off-the-record and so on."

"I need this, Eddie."

"Aye, Harry. I can be a friend."

He paused, still unsure.

I drained my glass, poured another pint. "When I'm writing a piece, if I don't quite know how to start it, I just sit at the typewriter and bang away. Eventually, it works its way."

"Have you ever heard of a man—a big businessman supposedly— named John Duff? He's got a title—"

"Sir Johnnie, of course. I'd be a rather poor member of the guild if I didn't."

"He's that famous?"

"I wouldn't say 'famous.' 'Well-known within certain circles,' if one aspires to a certain journalistic specificity. Don't feel a complete ignoramus, Harry. Duff's a name for the Brit cognoscenti, not American venues."

"So, what's the cognoscenti word on this guy?"

"Well, as you say, Sir Johnnie's a rather prosperous industrialist. Quite a few military contracts. Well connected socially."

"How well connected?"

"Well, I wouldn't call him a bosom friend, but he's been known to sit for tea with the almost–Edward VIII."

"Who?"

"Windsor, man. The duke? The one-time Prince of Wales? Wally Simpson, the abdication, and all that?"

"Sir John Duff is friends with the Duke of Windsor?"

"Before you go all agog, Harry, understand that people in those circles don't have friends as you and I mean the word. Friends for them are people who come for cucumber sandwiches and discuss the affairs of the day. Good friends come for dinner. Amongst that ilk, your friendship is only as valued as your conversation. On that basis, Sir Johnnie must be quite the silver-tongued dinner companion judging by his chumminess with those of official and titled rank—most particularly those with the power and position to help or hinder his various enterprises. And I don't just mean those native to the British Isles. He became quite social with your Mr. Kennedy when Kennedy was ambassador here. It's good that Sir Johnnie has such well-placed friends, because our military types have always felt him a bit, oh, suspect."

"Why's that?"

"Well, he's a bit of a paradox. Here's Sir Johnnie, a major supplier of royal arms, yet he was a regular attendee of the Cliveden set."

Harry's nose wrinkled and he reached for a slice of cheddar, avoiding the Spam on the plate. "What's this Cliveden thing?"

"All right, then, here's a short brief on recent British social history. Ready? Before the war—that is, before all the shooting and blowing up of much of Europe made political discourse academic—not everyone held an antagonistic stance against Herr Hitler. There were several minds on the subject. You had your peace-at-any-cost tribe; they were still heartily sick enough of the last great war to want to avoid another."

"I can understand that."

"But then there were more esoteric views. There were English blue-bloods to whom Hitler was just another form of king—a vulgar, ill-mannered king, but a monarch nonetheless, and kingship is an office and authority which our aristocracy is both familiar with and accustomed to. In fact, this camp harbored a certain admiration for a chap who, wielding absolute power in the grand old European tradition, brought a prostrate Germany back from defeat and depression to ironfisted strength in just a few short years. To hell with Parliament and the Magna Carta, laddies! Leave us to a right proper monarch with star chambers and public beheadings and the lot!

"Your own Mr. Lindbergh was quite public in expressing respect for the Reich. He seemed to fancy all that marching in step. After seeing the Condor Legion's performance in Spain during the Civil War, Lindbergh proposed—with a certain undisguised admiration—peaceful coexistence with Germany on the simple basis that, militarily speaking, Jerry was obviously unbeatable.

"It also didn't hurt that many of these people—your Mr. Lindbergh included—shared, to some degree or another, the Reich's anti-Semitic bent. In other words, to them, anyone who hated Jews couldn't be all bad.

"Then there were the, oh, what shall we call them? Let's call them capitalist pragmatists. They felt that whether they admired Hitler—as some did—or thought him a rather uncouth upstart—which some also did—he was merely looking to carve Germany a share of the European economic pie. The unlamented Neville Chamberlain held that view, as did Mr. Kennedy. They, and a number of like minds, were regularly invited by Lady Astor and her husband to their Cliveden estate—"

"The Cliveden set."

"—precisely—where they would chat over dinner and brandies about what bone could be thrown to Mr. Hitler. The idea was to keep the peace so everyone could go on doing business with everyone else and making mountains of loot, including the Germans, which, in turn, would be an incentive for them to remain at peace. It was a reasonable view espoused by reasonable people. The flaw in the theory was its proponents never quite understood they were dealing with someone who considered reason a character weakness."

"So, Sir John Duff was one of these Cliveden people."

"Sir Johnnie, being a bit shrewder than most, managed to keep a presence in *all* camps. *Par exemple*, he was, as I said, an acquaintance of the Duke of Windsor. Windsor was, in those days, something of an idealogue, always on about getting along with the Germans, how Hitler wasn't such a bad chap and was more concerned about the Russians than moving against the West, and some other astoundingly naive claptrap. When with the duke, Sir Johnnie loudly proclaimed his support for the duke's views. But when he sat at table with Mr. Kennedy, whom the duke could not abide, he was equally adamant in his agreement with the ambassador's particular interpretation."

"And at the same time, Duff's making guns or whatever for the military."

"Well, call me a cynic, Harry, but one could harbor a suspicion that Sir Johnnie's interest in keeping global peace was more commercial than altruistic. A Germany at peace is a customer. A Germany at war . . . To be fair, I'm not sure Sir Johnnie's interest in the sundry peace lobbies was completely mercenary. He'd had two sons."

" 'Had'?"

"Lost them both to the first war. You know; the one that was supposed to end them all."

He had, up until then, listened to my disquisition with a growing air of distaste for the parties concerned. But at the mention of Sir John Duff's loss, his face grew suddenly soft. "*Two* sons, you said?"

I nodded.

For a moment, it looked as if he had changed his mind about going forward. I prodded: "What does this have to do with the favor you wanted?"

He took a breath, seemed to make a commitment. "What do you know about Duff's holdings in the Orkneys?"

"I didn't know he had holdings—" And then the lights went on for me. "Och! You're here about the Yank soldier they found dead up there!"

"You know about that?"

"Harry, any self-respecting London newspaperman who doesn't have a set of cooperative ears at Scotland Yard should chuck it in."

"What'd you hear?"

"Not much. An American soldier found dead near Scapa Flow, the apparent victim of some foul play. I got the impression it was a true Agatha Christie program, all mystery and such."

"That's all?"

"After the body was brought down to the Yard for a postmortem, someone turned off the info spigot. That was all there was to get."

Harry smiled incredulously. "And you let it go at that? You must be mellowing."

I poured the last of the pitcher into my glass. "To be perfectly honest, Harry, there didn't seem much of a story worth pursuing. Giving it thought, one's thinking goes to a falling-out between allies over a questionable play of cards, or a high-spirited GI paying the consequences for relieving some farmer of one of his prize sows or his daughter's virtue."

"Hardly worth your time." It might have been a criticism.

"Aye." I patted my pockets. "You wouldn't happen to have any of those fine American fags about your person, would you?"

He shook his head. "Harry, I can't believe they brought you all this way over the deceasing of a single wayward GI. Considering the nature of your parting in August, I'm hard put to imagine Colonel Joseph P. Ryan issuing a call for Harry Voss."

"London didn't ask for me. JAG didn't ask for me. I'm here with a fellow from the Criminal Investigation Corps in Washington. He asked me to come along. He thought I might be able to help."

"All the way from Washington? And why would a Washington criminal investigator come to you, Harry? Are your deductive powers so highly regarded amongst the highest circles of your government?"

He reached into his jacket and brought out a small square of paper. This he laid on the table. I turned it round so the photograph faced me.

"Armando Grassi," he declared.

It is odd how one man's death can outweigh that of a hundred, if you knew him. Even if you disliked him, a shadow passes over your soul.

"My recollection is that he'd been transferred to Greenland, wasn't it? Aye, Greenland. In point of fact, his jaw was still—"

"Yes." Harry scooped the photo up and slipped it inside his jacket.

"That must have been quite a blow you delivered, Mr. Dempsey," I joshed.

"By all rights Armando Grassi should still be in Greenland annoying the hell out of people."

"Why isn't he?"

"Be my friend just now, Eddie. Please."

For all the bonhomie, we hardly knew each other, Harry and I. Yet he had asked for a friend. I nodded; I needed a friend, just then, as badly as he did.

Briefly, but fully, he told me what he and Woody Kneece had thus far uncovered.

"I agree with you," I said at his conclusion, "that I doubt it's some variety of black-market smuggling."

"John Duff is that well off?"

"Sir John Duff, Harry. I wouldn't say the man has more money than God, but I'd hate to referee a count. Have you talked to him yet? To Sir Johnnie?"

"I suppose that's our next thing to do." There was an odd, sheepish look to him when he said it. Again the lights went on for me.

"That's the favor! You're hoping I can provide you with some sort of entrée."

Still sheepish, he nodded.

"As it happens, I have the phone number of Sir Johnnie's appointments secretary. She is an unbearably officious and snooty-sounding lass with whom you will not enjoy dealing. After several unreturned calls she will find you several minutes to meet with him in his offices, perhaps a week or more hence. At that meeting Sir John will do everything he can to make you feel this is a great imposition, provide you little useful information, and then politely but firmly show you the door."

Harry smiled suspiciously. "But there's an alternative."

"Are you going to drink that?" I pointed to his pint. He pushed the glass to me. "He may be blasphemously rich, Harry, and his house a grand one, but it still has a front door and a knocker."

"Just drop in on him?"

"Take a page from the unfortunate experience of your countrymen at Pearl Harbor. Sometimes one can accomplish so much more when one is uninvited."

It was not the way Harry Voss did things, afflicted as he was with an almost fatal sense of propriety. It took him a few moments to persuade himself. "How can I find him?"

"Sir Johnnie is news. And I am in the news business. He has a place here in London, but he normally weekends at one of his country estates. I can find him."

"When?"

"By tomorrow. You'll need to take me with you."

"I don't know that Kneece is going to like that."

"Captain Kneece will not get you past that front door and its fine brass knocker."

Harry took my glass, poured half of what was left into his glass, then beckoned me to hold it up in toast. We clinked glasses.

"Tomorrow, then," he said.

At Rosewood Court, Woody Kneece was absent, leaving behind a litter of balled-up paper and his typewriter. Propped on Harry's blankets was the text of a radio message addressed to Harry from Israel Blume:

PER YOUR INQUIRY BUPERS WASHINGTON REPORTS
KIN A GRASSI NOTIFIED 12-8 STOP BODY SHIPPED
HOME VIA OB CONVOY 12-8 ARRIVING NY 12-23 STOP
ARRIVE CHICAGO BY TRAIN 12-25 STOP HAVE SENT
GRASSI EFFECTS STATESIDE THIS DATE END MESSAGE

Harry balled the message up in his hand and let it drop to the floor among Woody Kneece's literary mistakes. He lay back on his bunk and stared up at the exposed timbers of the cellar roof.

"Merry Christmas, Mr. and Mrs. Grassi," he murmured, then closed his eyes and hoped for sleep.

"Sir John Duff maintains a number of residences," I explained, shifting round in the front seat of the Army sedan to face Harry and Peter Ricks. "His corporate headquarters is in London, and he has major factories in Birmingham and Sheffield, so he keeps flats in those cities. There's another in Cardiff for when he's administering his coal holdings in Wales, another in Southampton where he does most of his shipping, and on his rare holiday, he summers at a cottage in Brighton."

Woody Kneece whistled. "This guy's like Esso. He's got a station in every town."

"Captain Kneece, not to criticize, but I'd much appreciate it if you'd drive on the proper side of the road, which, in this country, happens to be the left."

"I'm on the left. This mule path is so skinny this tank takes up both sides."

Indeed, the country lanes of the Kent Downs, crowded by overhanging trees and hedgerows, provided an ill fit for the blocky American Chevrolet.

"Providing the captain doesn't put us into a farm wagon, we're heading for the Duff family estate of Belleville outside Canterbury," I continued. "When Sir Johnnie is attending to his London affairs, he usually weekends there. Finally, he has one additional residence I think you'll find of particular interest. He has a hunting lodge on the coast of Solway Firth in Galloway—the west coast, facing the Irish Sea."

"What's a firth?" Kneece asked.

"Like an inlet," Harry said.

"In geologic point of fact, an estuary," I said. "It's rather rustic up there. Hills, forests. A bonnie empty stretch of coast. No near neighbors."

"Nice and private," Ricks noted.

"Aye, and here's something else of note."

Like any good newspaper, my rag kept obituary files on the socially prominent, constantly updating them so they could be drawn on posthaste upon any sudden loss among the ruling class. By token of his title and ungodly wealth, Sir Johnnie qualified for membership in the obit club. I extracted a photograph from his file and held it up for Woody Kneece to take a quick glance before I handed it over to Harry and Ricks for study.

"It's a couple of boats," Kneece said.

"Big boats," Ricks amplified.

The photograph was a stern-on shot of two vessels, side by side. Behind them one could see the curve of the hotel-lined white beach of Cannes. The larger ship was the *Nahlin*, the 250-foot yacht upon which Windsor had squired Wallis Simpson round the Mediterranean during his ill-advised 1936 cruise. Alongside was a smaller vessel, a cabin cruiser a quarter the size of the *Nahlin*, yet no less impressive with its polished teakwood deck and sparkling brass fixtures. Small, festive parties clustered on the afterdeck of each craft. Although the photo was taken from some distance, it was easy to pick out the lean form of the duke on the larger ship, quite dashing and fit in white ducks and white open-necked shirt. The dark female form at his side, turned in conversation to someone in the crowd, one presumed to be Wallis Simpson. Windsor was waving at the camera with one hand, and with the other holding a paper streamer, the sort one sees stretched from ship to shore during dockside *bon voyage* festivities. This particular streamer stretched down to the hand of a strapping, white-haired fellow on the smaller vessel. Close by him, also smiling, stood a man with owlish dark-rimmed glasses and a high forehead. Across the stern of the craft was the word *Rascal*.

"The *Nahlin*," I explained, "is Windsor's yacht."

"The Duke of Windsor?"

"As I told Harry here, he and Sir Johnnie are friends. The other—"

"Sir Johnnie has a boat," Ricks said, stating the obvious.

"A big boat," I said. "And this lodge of his in Scotland has its own boat slip."

"How far is it to Orkney Mainland from his place in Galloway?"

"I would guess some four hundred fifty miles or so. Sir Johnnie's yacht could easily make the trip in a day or two."

"That's Duff on his boat? The guy with the white hair? Who's that with him? He looks kind of familiar."

"That's the then recently appointed ambassador to the Court of St. James: Joseph P. Kennedy. Notice how he and the duke are studiously trying not to look in each other's direction. I told you they weren't taken with each other. This was at Cannes, the first summer after Kennedy arrived in '38. Windsor had already abdicated and resituated himself in France. Sir Johnnie offered the excursion to Mr. Kennedy, with the approval of Chamberlain's government, as a token of Britain's appreciation for Kennedy's efforts on behalf of 'peace in our time.' It also gave Sir Johnnie ample time to ingratiate himself with the ambassador."

Following my briefing, Ricks announced he had located Second Lieutenant Andrew Charles Coster.

"You were right, Major," he told Harry. "The G-1 clerks remembered him immediately. Coster showed up with no record package, no written orders, just the clothes on his back. But there were orders waiting for him, by cable straight from Washington, highest priority, expedite."

"To where did they expedite him?"

"Italy. Right up on the line. Attached to a battalion in the sector next to where my battalion was disposed. The assignment is under the guise that he's a Forward Observer coordinating close air support."

"They sure got him hidden away as far as they could," Kneece said.

"I don't think they're trying to hide him," Ricks said. "Put this guy up on the line with no background in FO operations, no infantry orientation? I think they're trying to find a clean way to get the poor bastard killed. Coster's on the line almost two weeks—he's probably dead already."

We rode silently thereafter. It had been some time since I'd escaped the confines of London. There was a sense of clean breath to the barren fields that purged the stale atmosphere of the Rose & Crown from one's lungs. It made it all the more a shame to say that even here were the makings of war.

Kneece had to force the staff car up a hedgerow to make way for some farmer on a dog cart, then round a bend in the road, make way again for a convoy of Army lorries. Out on the downs, a flock of sheep would slide down the side of a hillock like a foaming wave, then the next mile or so would find the grasslands covered with a blanket of tents, or an RAF or American aerodrome.

"Now there's a view!" Kneece pulled the car to a halt, climbed out, and scampered up a hillock for better vantage. Just a few miles distant were the roofs of Canterbury, the spires of the cathedral standing over them like sentinels. Beyond them, a squadron of black crosses glided across the sky: American B-17's returning from a morning mission. They were coming out of the east, and more than one ship was trailing smoke.

"I can't believe I still haven't gotten myself a camera!" we heard young Kneece exclaim.

Peter Ricks looked up at the B-17's and their streams of oily black smoke, his flask in his hand again. " 'Will no one rid me of this meddlesome priest?' " He leaned back against the seat, drew his garrison cap down over his eyes, and took a pull from his flask.

The manse at Belleville was a humble digs by the standards of the peerage. Still, at thirty rooms or so, it was comfortable enough.

Woody Kneece steered the Army sedan past gateposts wound with strands of Yuletide evergreen, down a gravel drive lined with ancient elm trees. He shook his head at the fields rolling away on either side of the drive. "Who does he get to cut the grass?"

"Five thousand acres' worth," I said.

"What's that?" Halfway up the drive, Kneece pulled the car to the side. Perhaps a quarter-mile off, the heather had been turned over in a scar of dark earth, the furrow ending in the fire-blackened hulk of a crumpled B-17. It was a weathered wreck, old. "Back home we just put a birdbath and a statue of a colored jockey on the lawn."

"Let's do this," Peter Ricks said.

At the end of the drive, Kneece killed the engine. "You know," he said, "we haven't talked about how we're going to do this."

"Whatever I say from here on," I instructed, "don't contradict me. Let me have first innings. You'll hear your cues."

Peter Ricks shrugged. "Well, that's more of a plan than I've got," and he stepped out onto the drive.

We stood at the foot of the front steps as the Americans took in the tall windows, the ivy-clad walls, the gilded dome that topped the house. The double doors were garlanded with fir branches and large red bows were fixed to each door. I grabbed the bell pull and tugged, then firmly rapped the brass knocker for good measure.

An aged waistcoated butler answered the door.

"For Sir John Duff, there's the good fellow," I announced.

The butler blinked twice through his thick glasses at the row of uniforms gathered behind me. "Excuse me?"

"I say we're here for Sir John, man. Would he be about?"

"Um, actually, no, sir. If you'd like to leave a message—"

"I wouldn't like to leave a message, thank you. Is there anyone else we could talk to? It's terribly important."

He glanced again at the row of uniforms. "Well, perhaps Mr. Fordyce—"

"Fordyce is here?"

"Mr. Fordyce, yes—"

I held up a finger to silence him, drew out my notepad. "Pass that to Mr. Fordyce, mate. He'll speak with us."

My assurance seemed to irritate him. He took the note I'd scribbled and closed the door in my face.

"Mr. Owen," Woody Kneece said. "I'm just a poor, miseducated country boy so maybe I didn't savvy it right. Did you tell Major Voss you could get us in the door? Or just to the door?"

A moment later, the door swung open. "Gordon Fordyce. I'm Sir John's confidential secretary." He looked from the bit of paper in his hand—my note—to me, and his eyes unhappily narrowed.

I touched a finger to my chin and pushed my face upward as if modeling it. "Hard to forget such Olympian beauty, eh, Mr. Fordyce?"

"Oh, I remember the face." He spoke with a bored intolerance. "But I don't believe there was opportunity for formal introduction at the time."

"My exit was a bit rushed, as you might recall."

Fordyce was good at his game; he betrayed no emotion (other than his obvious wish that I was not on his doorstep), not even curiosity.

"I had always understood Sir Johnnie's house to be a hospitable one," I said.

"And so it is."

"Then why are visitors left to freeze in the winter's cold on the front steps?"

His eyes moved among us, then he stood back from the door. As I passed by him, he handed me back my note, then rubbed his fingertips together as if my scrap of paper had left some greasy residue behind.

Despite his patrician coolness and pinched upper-house speech, Gordon Fordyce had begun life the son of a working-class Birmingham couple living in a soot-streaked walk-up. Fordyce would possibly have ended his days in similar circumstances had he not caught the eye of Sir John soon after taking work in one of the laird's factories. Perhaps the attraction had been Fordyce's fierce aspiration to make something of himself—an ambition with which the self-made Sir John could surely empathize. Or, as one tale went, the older man saw something in Fordyce that brought to mind the men his sons might have become had they survived the Great War. Sir John must have had an extraordinarily discerning eye to see such traits, because to most, Gordon Fordyce displayed none of the charm and athletic looks that Sir John's sons were remembered for.

Soft, pale, his shoulders hunched, his outsized head marked by a weak chin and small eyes, in his tweeds he called to mind nothing as much as Mr. Carroll's White Rabbit. The carefully cultivated pronunciations, the fastidiousness in his pomaded hair, parted with geometrical precision, and the mustache trimmed so narrowly it clung precariously to the edge of his lip, indicated someone making a great effort to distance himself from humble beginnings. The common perception in my trade was that Fordyce, like so many other apparatchiks the world over, being a moon incapable of producing its own heat and light, had found a satisfying orbit about Sir John, officiously wielding the reflected power and authority of his master.

Fordyce requested we take care to wipe our feet on the entrance mat lest we sully the parquet inlay floor of the vestibule.

"I understand Sir John's out and about," I said.

"He's still at Sunday service."

"Then he should be back shortly, eh?"

"Is this something Sir John really needs to be bothered with?"

"Oh, I should think, aye. I'm writing a particular story and it looks to mention Sir John in possible connection. It's about a jolly ghastly murder up round the good sir's Orkney patch."

"Ah. The soldier."

"So you've heard."

"Sir John has a gentleman in his employ at the Orkney house. He passed the news to us. He also mentioned a visit by some American military officers. Would these be . . . ?"

"Well, the poor fellow was an American, you know."

"I didn't know. How does this relate to Sir John?"

"Might I call you Gordon? As we do know each other." Before he could object, "Understand, Gordon, the fellow was killed practically at Sir Johnnie's door."

"I'm not aware that anyone has made any connection with Sir John—"

"Ah, well, Gordon, one thing leads to another, eh? And in the course of the investigation into the poor lad's fate, it appears that someone may be misusing Sir Johnnie's property thereabouts."

"Really."

"It's not hard to suppose that maybe the one has something to do with the other."

"Actually, I find it quite hard to suppose that, and even more difficult to see you bringing Sir John into the affair. Sir John hasn't been to the Orkney property since it was acquired years ago. How is it, Mr. Owen, that you and your publication have come to be involved?"

"Well, it's a juicy story, isn't it? Someone of Sir Johnnie's—"

"Sir John, please."

"—apologies, Sir John, someone of Sir John's position involved—"

"As I said, I don't think the circumstances constitute involvement."

"Well, that'll be for our readers to decide, eh, Gordon?"

Gordon Fordyce allowed a slight wrinkling of his brow. He turned to the Yanks, sighted Harry's major's leaves, and addressed him, assuming him, as senior officer, to be leader of the gang. "Major, I wasn't aware that your service had become so lax in sharing military information."

"Well, you see, Gordon, in a strict manner of speaking, this is not exactly a military matter," I explained. "Our American friends are looking at this as a criminal matter. No different from some American johnnie getting himself knocked dead in a pub brawl. No reason for Official Secrets and all that. I heard about the lad from one of my contacts at the Yard. A good reporter has an ear everywhere, Gordon, you should know that. In the process of looking into it, I bumped into these gentlemen who were pursuing the same line of inquiry; we thought we'd pool our resources, and voilà."

"Voilà." Fordyce sighed. "There seem to be quite a few of you for a routine criminal inquiry."

"No one said it was routine, eh, Gordon? The thing of it is, we really should talk to Sir John before something goes into print that shouldn't. Maybe the squire can put this right for us, clear up any misunderstandings. You wouldn't want a misunderstanding on the front page."

"Front page? This?"

"It may not seem much to you, not in the grand scheme of things, but it is, as I say, a juicy story, a real mystery in the grand manner. You know how the reading public loves their true crime: Sweeney Todd, Jack the Ripper, Dr. Crippen—"

"This hardly seems of the same caliber, Mr. Owen." Fordyce drew a gold watch from his trouser watch pocket, opened the watch cover, then closed it with his thumb, slowly. The click echoed in the high-ceilinged vestibule. "Sir John will be home shortly. Perhaps you should speak with him. This way, please."

We were led to a large, bright solarium at the back of the house, overlooking a slate veranda and thereafter the gravel paths and fallow beds of a garden nearly half as wide as the house. As we entered, Harry caught up with me and held out his hand for the note I'd sent Fordyce. Fordyce pulled a bell rope to summon the butler. "I think you'll be comfortable here. Alden, take their coats, and I think some morning refreshment would be in order for our guests." Then poor little Alden departed, struggling under the weight of our coats and headwear; Gordon Fordyce followed him out, closing the high glass doors behind him.

The Yanks had all done a fair job of maintaining their composure up until then. The grins blossomed.

"Well, day-um!" Woody Kneece blurted. "My momma taught me not to brag, but I'll tell you that back home, we live all right. I thought our house was something. But this . . ." He turned toward Ricks, now lighting up a cigarette on the settee. "As I remember from doing some homework on you, Lieutenant, factually speaking your family lives pretty good, too. The law pays good out there in the Golden State."

"Captain, there's money and there's money." Ricks let his unbandaged eye roam round the room.

"And this is *money*!" Kneece agreed. "You wonder why with this kind of dough this fella doesn't get himself a secretary with better-looking legs. Eddie, where do you know this Fordyce fella from?"

"A professional encounter."

"That was no love note you sent him," Ricks said.

Harry turned the note over to Ricks, then faced me with a puzzled smile. The note read:

What's the going price of peace in our time?

I parked myself in a winged wicker chair across from Ricks and cadged one of his cigarettes. "It was the fall of 1938," I began in my best once-upon-a-time sonority, "right after Chamberlain had returned with the Munich Pact. You remember . . . 'Peace in our time.' In commemoration of continued amity on the Continent, Sir Johnnie hosted a celebratory soirée here at Belleville. His good chum Ambassador Kennedy was in attendance, the Astors were here, and—"

"That Cliveden set you were telling me about," Harry said.

"Aye, all saluting Chamberlain's triumph over the warmongers. Well, obviously, it was quite the *fête soignée*, as our little froggy *amis* across the Channel might say, fair game for my society column colleagues. I managed entry on the coattails of the lady who scribbles my paper's column and she has yet to forgive me for that night."

"This sounds like it's going to be good," Kneece said.

"So, there arises that time in the evening when Sir Johnnie feels the call to raise his glass and toast the renewed peace. Some sentimental lass bemoans the fate dealt out at Munich to the poor Czechs, and Sir Johnnie says, with grave sympathy for our eastern brothers, ' 'Tis a pity, but peace comes at a high price.' Perhaps I'd too much to drink, or perhaps I was simply galled at how serenely they'd all written off the Czechs. In any case, I couldn't let such an opportunistic choice of imagery go unused. I raised my hand: 'Um, pardon, Sir John, a question? Purely a financial concern.' 'Certainly, lad, let's have it.' 'Sir John, this price of peace: Is that a fixed fee? Or will we have to give Adolf another slice of Europe at a later date to keep pace with inflation?' Of course, that went over so delightfully, I couldn't leave off just then. 'Or is this an installment arrangement? Will we be giving Adolf a fresh slice of Europe every first of the month?' "

"Should've quit early," Ricks advised. "You started to beat it to death there."

"Mr. Fordyce sicced two rather bulky doormen on me to escort me out. 'Sir John! Sir John! The next payment to Adolf—will you ask for volunteers, or will they be conscripts like the Czechs?' "

"I'm surprised they let you get all that out," Harry said.

"They were pushing me toward the door, but I had two good legs under me then. However, after that last bit, they became positively rude and out I went. Tore the sleeve on my dinner jacket, ended up costing me another ten quid to the chap at the to-let shop. Wasn't long after that my boss thought it might not be a bad idea if I spend some time at one of the foreign bureaus. And *that* is how I wound up in Singapore." I patted my wooden leg.

Alden returned just then, pushing a tea cart ahead of him. He told us to help ourselves and exited. We served ourselves, and I lingered over the cart with Harry.

I pointed out to him the freshness of the melon and strawberries. I dabbed my fingertip in my mouth—"Pardon my poor manners"—and touched it to the contents of the full sugar bowl, then licked my fingertip. "It's not saccharin."

I knew he was thinking of the contents of the burned-out C-47 hulk back at Kap Farvel.

"Hey!" Kneece called from the windows. "Is that him?"

"No," I said.

From a far wood topping a knoll descended a horse-drawn wagon and a pair of outriders. As the party drew closer I could make out the features of the men on horseback: Both looked to be in their thirties, one dark, the other fair, both possessed of the same square-jawed good looks. On the bench of the wagon sat a man and woman. As they drew up to the far side of the garden, Gordon Fordyce hurried toward them from the house. While one groom took the two saddle horses after the riders had dismounted, another held the dray horse while two more slid a large fir from the back of the wagon. Fordyce grabbed the fair-haired man and pulled him aside.

At first, Fordyce seemed to be doing all the speaking. The other man stood by, head bent, as if listening and considering intently. He said something brief to Fordyce which agitated the secretary. The fair-haired man waved a good-bye to the other members of his party and began moving toward the house. Fordyce interposed himself again.

"Do you recognize him?" Harry asked me.

I shook my head, but was no longer quite sure.

The man flashed Fordyce a comforting smile, patted him soothingly on the shoulder, but the look on his face remained firm. Fordyce stepped aside to let the man by, then followed him toward the house.

"I don't know about you fellas," Kneece said, "but I'm curious."

We heard their footsteps in the hallway, then the door to the solarium opened. Fordyce stayed by the door as the younger man entered. His wide, handsome face was lined and tanned from weather, but in a way that gave him a vital, athletic air, emphasized by his riding wear, the smile of even white teeth, the broad but light step of his walk.

"Good day, sirs!" he declared jovially. "My friend Gordon Fordyce tells me you are here for Sir John." There was a slight accent in his speech, a sibilance on the *s*'s, a hardness to the consonants. "I am Erik Sommer. There are so many of you. To whom do I introduce myself first?"

I stepped forward and took his outstretched hand, introducing myself. "Mr. Sommer, have we met?"

"Not that I recall," he replied, but I saw something in his eyes, the same doubt I was feeling, the same vague tickling of familiarity. "I am rarely come to this country, and most always as Sir John's guest. But"—a good-natured shrug, and that beaming smile—"who knows? And your friends, Mr. Owen?"

I introduced the others. Sommer went from one handshake to the next, but took an extra moment with Peter Ricks, his light blue eyes drawn to the square of gauze over the lieutenant's eye.

"Not so serious, I hope?" he said to the lieutenant, still holding his hand.

"Getting better all the time," Ricks answered.

"Ah, good. This was an accident? Or no? You have been in the fighting?"

"The lieutenant's on medical leave from Italy," I said.

An odd considered look crossed Sommer's face, but it was fleeting and the smile returned. He clasped a second hand round Ricks's. "It is good you are back safe and feeling well."

"Thank you," Ricks said.

"That also is from Italy?" Sommer pointed at the bandage on Woody Kneece's forehead.

"Travel mishap," Kneece said.

Sommer gestured toward the tea cart. "I see that Gordon provides for you. Very good. That is how Sir John would prefer. Do you mind if I share? Warm the blood?" He poured himself a cup of coffee. "Gordon! Where is the chocolate? I know it is a gift for Sir John, but I think he would offer it to his guests. Especially on this chill day."

As Fordyce rang for Alden, there was some fuss in the hall. Through the open solarium door we could see two grooms wrestling seven feet of fir tree from the wagon down the main hall.

"A Christmas tree?" Kneece guessed.

"Ah, yes!" Sommer said. "It is something, a good feeling here"—he thumped his chest—"when you bring the tree down yourself. It was Sir John's suggestion. 'Go, find a tree, Erik,' he says. 'Get the winter air in your lungs! It is good to make the body work!' Do you know Sir John?"

"Not personally," I said.

"Ah, *professionally*," he said, as if this were some sly conclusion. "He never grows old, Sir John. He knows: Make the body work!"

"As we'd say in my part of the United States, Mr. Sommer, you don't sound like you're from around these parts," Kneece commented.

It took Sommer a moment to decipher the statement. "Pardon? Oh, yes, I see! No, no, not from these parts. My friends, they as well are not from these parts."

"Mr. Sommer and his party are guests of Sir John," Fordyce interjected.

"All these rooms," Sommer said, indicating Sir John Duff's mansion, "and he gives us our own house!"

Again Fordyce amplified: "They have guest rooms in the carriage house."

Past his shoulder I saw Kneece and Harry exchange a quick word between themselves, finalized by a short nod of agreement from Harry.

"Um, excuse me, Mr. Fordyce," Kneece said. "You know, it was a long ride out here and I think maybe I drank a little too much of your coffee. Is there someplace where, as the saying goes, I can freshen up?"

It was another turn of phrase that took Sommer a moment to interpret. When he did he laughed. "Yes, yes! 'Freshen up'!"

Alden had appeared. Fordyce whispered some instructions, then the butler led Kneece out.

"Where is that young man from?" Sommer asked. "His English is like music!"

Harry told him.

"He comes a long way, this young man," Sommer said, nodding thoughtfully. "All this way to talk to Sir John? It must be very . . . what is the word? Grave? Gordon says you are here for some trouble with Sir John."

"Just a few questions," I said.

"In what regard, may I ask?"

"I don't think it's our place to share that with you," Harry put in. "If Sir John wants to tell you, that's one thing—"

"Ah, I see, quite discreet." Sommer nodded approvingly.

"Oh, come now, Harry!" I declared. "We've just finished telling ol' Gordon here that this may all very likely wind up on the front page of my rag! No sense being all sly and tricky now!"

"The newspapers?" Sommer was as good at the game as Gordon Fordyce. There was no alarm to it, no indication of more than a casual curiosity. "It must be quite important."

"Oh, not so important," I said. "But the sort of news that brings a few pence 'cross the counter. But I think your chum Gordon and I would probably agree that based on what we know, there's nothing for you to be worried about. Eh, Gordon? It seems obvious, the matter doesn't concern Mr. Sommer, eh?"

"I only worry for Sir John," Sommer said. "I do business with Sir John, but I think myself also a friend, you see? So I do have the concern."

"What kind of business would that be, Mr. Sommer?" Ricks asked.

"Steel. My friends and I, we represent several makers— What is the word, Gordon? Manufacturers? Yes, several manufacturers of steel. In Sweden."

"I thought that was all tick when Norway fell," I said.

" 'All tick'?"

"Done in. Finished." I turned to Harry and Ricks. "When Sweden declared its neutrality at the beginning of the war, the understanding accepted by all sides was that Sweden would continue to sell steel both to us and the Germans. The closest port to the Swedish steel mills was Narvik, up in the Norwegian hinterlands. But when Jerry took Norway, well, it's become something of a one-way arrangement since then, between the Swedes and the Germans. I trust that's a fair and unprejudiced way of explaining the situation, Mr. Sommer?"

"It is your country, Mr. Owen. However you choose to say."

"If you're not doing business with Sir John anymore, what brings you to England?" Harry asked.

Gordon Fordyce stepped forward. "Mr. Sommer is a guest, gentlemen, and as such, there's no need for him to be pestered with your inquiry."

Sommer held up an assuaging hand. "Thank you, Gordon. But I understand. These men have a job, yes? In their job they must be thorough."

"No stone unturned," Ricks agreed. There was a certain barb to it that Sommer either missed or ignored.

"So I ask again," Harry began, "Mr. Sommer, if you're not doing business with Sir John anymore, what brings you here?"

"The holiday! Sir John and I are long friends. Sir John should not sit in this big empty house by himself on Christmas!"

"It's nice Sir John has such good friends," Ricks said.

"I am curious," Sommer said, "if you permit; this problem for Sir John, have you made any progress? Are you learning?"

"All the time," Ricks replied.

Sommer set his coffee cup down and studied the lieutenant. His smile seemed to take on the same barbed edge as Ricks's pronouncements. "Mr. Owen, you were going to say to me about this story your newspaper will have."

"Ah, yes, well—"

We all froze. As if on musical cue, a single piano note drifted through the air from somewhere far off in the house. There followed a second, then a third, tentative initial notes all, then they began to flow with increasing smoothness in a gentle, bittersweet melody.

Gordon Fordyce closed his eyes and took a deep breath, as if restoking his infinite patience.

I saw Harry smile. "Woody," he said.

We followed Fordyce out into the vestibule. Something ahead froze him and he moved deferentially to the wall. Beyond him we saw the open front doors of the house. Outside, parked beside our Army sedan, was a Bentley, its chauffeur standing by the open passenger door. On a bench across from an open door that led off the vestibule sat John Duff. There was a small smile on the baronet's craggy face, a smile as bittersweet as the music issuing from the room across the hall.

Though Sir John was in his seventies, there was nothing frail or failing about him. He may have had a thickened middle, but his chest was broad, his shoulders straight. The sweep of hair atop the leonine face was chalk white but full; the small green eyes surrounded by puffy folds of skin penetrating.

The music ended, the echo of the last notes hung in the hallway, then Sir John rose from the bench and entered the room across the hall. Gordon Fordyce closed the front door and followed him into the room. So did Harry, Ricks, and I.

It was some sort of salon, elegant with its antique chairs and sofas, brocatelled walls, and coffered ceiling, but uncluttered enough to avoid the Victorian stuffiness that afflicts so many of the great old English estates. In one corner of the room the grooms had cleared a space to mount the fir tree. At the far end, above the mantel of a pilaster-framed fireplace, were three portraits, nearly life-size. The center canvas displayed a woman, fortyish, plump but pleasant-faced, sitting in that very room, adorned in the type of high-collared garb common thirty years ago. Flanking her on the left was a picture of a handsome young man, wearing casual riding wear, posed among what looked to be the grounds aback of the house, with a roan pawing the turf behind him. To the right, a canvas of another lad no older than the other, dressed in the tweeds of a young gentleman, posed against a bank of the house's casement windows.

Tucked in a corner of the room, almost hidden, was a small keyboarded instrument, its compact box wrapped in gilded designs of vines and grape leaves. Perched upon its bench was Woody Kneece.

No one seemed to know quite how to begin until Harry stepped forward: "I didn't know you played the piano."

Kneece grinned self-consciously. "Factually, it's what they call a spinet. Although it's not a true spinet. The originals were really bitty harpsichords. Right or wrong, Sir John?"

Sir John had still not lost his smile and was shucking off his coat as Gordon Fordyce came up behind him to catch it. "Frankly, lad, you're better versed in the matter than I. What was that you were playing?"

"Cavatina. My mother likes it a lot."

"My wife saw that thing at an estate liquidation and fell in love with it," Duff said. He pointed to the woman's portrait above the fireplace. "Never learned to play worth a damn, though."

Kneece fingered the yellowed pages of sheet music. "*Somebody* played."

"My elder, Raymond, though I must say he had more enthusiasm than talent. Didn't matter. 'Make a joyful noise' it says somewhere in the Good Book, doesn't it? Raymond did. It was a wonderful noise to fill the house."

Woody Kneece studied the portraits. "He was the rider?"

"Yes."

"You still keep a nice set of horseflesh, Sir John."

"They saw us riding up," Erik Sommer explained.

"I hope I wasn't out of line," Kneece said. "I was using the, you know, the *facilities*, I saw this as I went by, I couldn't resist."

"No problem, lad."

Kneece pointed to the third portrait. "Your other boy?"

"Calvin. Two years behind, but they were inseparable. Calvin didn't play, but when Raymond sat at the keys he would . . . well, one doesn't dare call it truly *singing*. It was all in fun, you understand. Calvin would be like so . . ." The older man pointed his toes out at a ninety-degree angle, hands clasped below his heart, elbows jutting out. ". . . as if he were Jenny Lind or something. Raymond would bang away and Calvin would begin the most god-awful caterwauling . . ."

Woody Kneece, caught up in the spirit of the moment, began a spirited playing of "The Lambeth Walk." Sir John began to sing along in a *faux* operatic style that soon reduced the two of them to laughter.

"A joyful noise!" Kneece declared.

"Yes," Sir John said, wistfully, as he sat on the bench alongside Kneece.

The captain again reached for the keyboard, but this time the tune was plaintive, and in a low, quiet voice, he began to sing:

> *"The minstrel boy to the war is gone*
> *In the ranks of death you'll find him;*
> *His father's sword he has girded on*
> *And his wild harp slung behind him . . ."*

Sir John joined in, his voice a rich baritone that I'm sure was the envy of his parish choir.

> *" 'Land of song!' said the warrior bard.*
> *'Tho' all the world betrays thee,*
> *One sword, at least, thy rights shall guard,*
> *One faithful harp shall praise thee.' "*

Kneece put his hands in his lap. "I don't think there's a sadder song in all the world."

"I think not," Sir John agreed. "I'm afraid I'm forgetting myself." He held out a hand to Kneece. "John Duff."

"That's Captain Kneece of the American Army's Criminal Investigation Department," Gordon Fordyce spoke with perhaps more emphasis than was required.

"Corps," Kneece corrected. "Criminal Investigation Corps."

Fordyce seemed not to have heard. "This is Major Voss of the Judge Advocate General's Corps. And that's Lieutenant Ricks."

Sir John went from shaking hands with Harry to Ricks. He nodded at the lieutenant's bandaged eye. "I hope that's less uncomfortable than it looks, lad."

"Should be coming off any day, Sir John."

"Good, good. And what department are you from?"

"I'm just along for the ride. I had a chance to see an honest-to-God knight's house. How could I pass that up?"

Sir John chuckled, shaking his head. "Americans."

"And this," Fordyce said, pointing to me, "is Mr. Owen." He named my newspaper.

"I know you, don't I?" Sir John said as we shook hands.

"The dinner party after Munich, Sir John," Fordyce supplied.

Sir John chuckled again. "Ah, yes. It was not your point I objected to that evening, Mr. Owen. Certainly history has granted your view more vindication than mine. But it was a social engagement. I thought there were more suitable occasions for such a discussion."

"Fair enough, Sir John. Then I apologize . . . retroactively." We exchanged good-natured smiles to signal that it was all past and forgotten.

Except perhaps by Gordon Fordyce. "They're here about that business on Orkney," he said.

"The soldier who was found dead?" Sir John asked. "He was American, then?"

As if in answer, Woody Kneece drifted through a few more bars of "The Minstrel Boy."

> "The minstrel fell but the foeman's chain
> Could not bring that proud soul under . . ."

Sir John looked back to Kneece at the spinet, then to the portraits over the fireplace. He turned back to us with a broad, hospitable smile. "You'll stay for lunch! We had planned only something simple, sandwiches and light refreshment, but still, I insist."

"As long as you insist," Harry said.

"Sir John," Fordyce interceded. "It might be difficult to accommodate the extra guests."

"Oh, bosh, Gordon! We can use the dining room. I prefer to save all that folderol for formal occasions, but there's certainly enough room there."

I leaned toward Harry's ear and whispered, nodding at Gordon Fordyce: "Methinks the fairy queen is jealous."

"I think it will just be us for lunch, Sir John," Erik Sommer said. "I'll ask the others, but they seemed quite tired after the morning's ride. I have the belief they will want to rest."

"Oh, well, then, it's simple again. Where's Alden? Alden, we'll lunch in the library. Gentlemen, shall we adjourn and let these good men tend to the tree? By the way, Erik, fine choice on this tree. Alden, we'll need extra chairs. Have the chaps lend a hand. Gentlemen, if you'll follow me . . ."

He led us across the hall. Fordyce lingered behind to close the salon's door behind us, shutting it with an unnecessary firmness.

The library was a smaller, cozier room than the salon; the chairs had been selected for comfort, not fashion. There was a pleasant, manly smell of brandy and cigars, of leather book bindings and wood from the oak shelves and paneling.

"Ahhh, the patriarch's private sanctum, eh, Sir John?" I said.

"Something like that." Sir John gravitated behind the massive desk set by the casement windows.

"My daddy has a library kind of like this," Woody Kneece said. "Smaller, of course. He inherited it with the house. I don't think my daddy's ever read anything more than cotton quotes and the bloodlines for his racing stock. But that was Daddy's corner of the house. When that door closed behind him, you left him alone. He might just be only sitting looking out the window, but if he was in that room . . ."

"When my boys were alive I never closed the door," Sir John reflected. "Even when they were small. If I had business to conduct, well, then, some poor guest suffered them climbing about him like monkeys. But I never closed my door to them. Calvin used to like to roost here under my desk. He would be under there moving his little toy autos about, making little purring noises, even if I had someone in here. I used to keep toffees in my desk I would slip to him."

"I'm sorry I missed those days, Sir John," Erik Sommer said.

"Beautiful books," Harry observed, moving along the floor-to-ceiling shelves. "I envy you having the time to read them, Sir John."

"Major, I must make a confession. As with the good captain's father, I inherited them. They came with the house, most of them."

"But not all." Harry pointed to a shelf of books clearly not as old as the rest of the library. "Not these."

Sir John shrugged.

The food arrived on a cart with Alden at the helm. On a sideboard, he laid on a buffet of finger sandwiches, a compote offering fresh fruit and nuts, and a pot of tea. While he did so, I joined Harry by the shelf he'd pointed out to Sir John. There were many histories, from Gibbons to

Wells, even Caesar. As for the fiction: Hemingway's *A Farewell to Arms*, Crane's *The Red Badge of Courage*, Remarque's *All Quiet on the Western Front*.

I knew what Harry was thinking: the oddness of a man who had lost so much to war studying it in such detail. But Sir John was no different from the doctor who sets himself to learning all there is to learn about a disease to better understand the mechanism that took his children.

As we availed ourselves of the buffet, Peter Ricks indicated a small statuette on the library mantel. It was not a particularly good rendering, the kind of thing one buys more for sentiment than aesthetic appreciation. It featured a youngster in period costume, something medieval, a lute under one arm, bent under the great weight of a broadsword strapped to his back. Ricks caught my eye; we both looked at the statuette and nodded in recognition: The Minstrel Boy.

As we ate, Sir John sat close to Woody Kneece, who regaled him with tales of South Carolina life. Kneece typically displayed a modesty and discomfort with his family's comfortable circumstances, sentiments that Sir John obviously found admirable.

In the meantime, Ricks, Harry, and I found ourselves seated with Erik Sommer. Gordon Fordyce positioned himself in an isolated corner. His cool gaze kept drifting from our little group to the pairing of Sir John and Kneece.

Sommer made polite conversation with the Americans, asking them about their homes, comparing Harry's Newark and Ricks's San Francisco to Stockholm and Sweden's more northern climes, where the steel manufacturing centers were located.

"That's a pretty good deal you have there," Ricks said. For all the hospitable warmth the Swede maintained, Ricks had, since their first introduction, regarded him with a caustic eye.

"Pardon?" Sommer said. " 'Deal'?"

"That neutrality deal. It works out all right for you people, doesn't it? I mean, you get to keep doing business, make some good money from the war, and nobody's bombing your factories, your businesses—"

Gordon Fordyce cleared his throat. "Lieutenant Ricks, you are here at the forbearance of Sir John. You may have business with him, but Mr. Sommer is a guest."

"It's all right, Gordon." Sommer waved soothingly in Fordyce's direction. "In the lieutenant's place I would feel the same, I imagine. I can only say to you, Lieutenant Ricks, that I am not my government. I did not say 'This is our policy.' I am not the owners of my company. I did not say 'This is who we will sell to.' "

"You're just some guy trying to make a living."

"I have my job. What else am I to do?" Sommer bowed his head for a moment, then he put a hand on Ricks's forearm. "This may mean nothing to you, but I am sorry for the war."

Which I thought a curious statement.

"Perhaps the Swedes would have taken sides if they could have been assured Britain would have protected them better than they did the Norwegians," Fordyce said.

"Gordon, please." Sommer said it gently. "As you say, I am a guest. These men are guests as well."

"How is it you get back and forth between here and Sweden?" Harry asked. "Air? Sea?"

"Ship, mostly."

"You don't worry?" I asked.

"You mean, is it dangerous for us? We fly the neutral flag, yes?"

"Still. You must remember that incident last summer."

Sommer nodded gravely. "Sad, very sad."

I turned to Harry and Ricks to explain. "I'm sure you remember, Harry. Jerry shot down a commercial plane flying Lisbon to England."

Harry nodded. "That actor was in it. The guy from *Gone With the Wind*. The goofy-looking one Scarlett was in love with."

"It was Leslie Howard, and were he still alive, he would join me in objecting to your referring to English panache as 'goofy.' "

"People even thought maybe the Germans attacked the plane because Mr. Howard was a spy," Sommer said.

"I think too many people saw *Pimpernel Smith* too many times," Ricks said disparagingly.

"Still," I said to Sommer, "you must worry."

"My wife at home, she worries, but here I am," Sommer said philosophically. "My friends are here. You saw: One even brings his wife. To come see our good friend Sir John . . ." He shrugged; surely their friend was worth the risk?

Sir John called for a platter of light pastry for dessert. He offered tea and coffee and some of the hot chocolate brought him as a token Christmas gift by Erik Sommer. And, for those more inclined, he offered a fine brandy and cigars from his humidor.

Peter Ricks and I took our rich-smelling cigars from their packing tubes. He smiled slightly and at my questioning look held up the band from his cigar: Cohiba.

"Gentlemen," Fordyce announced. He shifted in his seat, adjusted his trousers, and carefully crossed his legs at the knees. "I hate to be the taskmaster here, but I think, perhaps, we should address the reason for your visit. While we appreciate the seriousness of the issue, Sir John does have guests who have come a long way and whom he is now neglecting."

Sir John nodded in Fordyce's direction. "See what he does for me? If it weren't for good old Gordie, I sometimes think, the whole machine would grind to a halt. You're quite right, Gordon, thank you. I know several of you spoke with my man up there, Mr. Bowles. You, Major? And Captain Kneece? Yes, well, I don't know what I could add. Mr. Bowles was the fellow 'on the scene.' That's the correct parlance, Mr. Owen? 'On the scene'?"

Harry had produced his little notebook and reading glasses, and was flipping back and forth through the scribble-covered pages. He scratched his head and frowned. "About Mr. Bowles . . ."

"Teddy Bowles is a trusted, long-time employee, Major. Beyond that, I know the man personally. He's an all-round good chap."

"I'm sure. You know, that place where he's living isn't that far from where they found the dead officer. We were a little surprised Mr. Bowles hadn't heard anything."

"Good God, man!" Fordyce sighed. "Teddy Bowles is as old as Methuselah. I'd be surprised if he knew what was going on outside his front door."

"That's not how he came across to us," Woody Kneece chimed in.

"I haven't seen old Teddy . . ." Sir John mused. "I had just assumed . . . When was it, Gordie? When was I up there last?"

"Not since the beginning of the war. Fall '39."

"Maybe . . ." Kneece began. Sir John and Fordyce looked to him expectantly. "I don't want to cast aspersions about somebody, well, I can see you like the old fella . . ."

"But?"

"Maybe Mr. Bowles has a reason to be selective about what he sees up there."

Gordon Fordyce rose. He crossed to Sir John's chair, standing close by him. "Before you arrived, Mr. Owen alluded to some sort of misuse of the Orkney property."

"There are signs," Kneece continued, "that some kind of 'traffic' has been going through there."

"Traffic?" Fordyce echoed. "Of what sort?"

"That's something we can't say right now," Harry said.

"But you're sure?" Sir John asked.

"Yes." Harry said it firmly.

Erik Sommer cleared his throat. "Sir John, perhaps this employee of yours is involved in some side business? Something of his own?"

"Old Teddy? Hardly."

"Still," Fordyce said, leaning close to Sir John's ear, "we should have some of our own people look into this."

"By all means, Gordie. Good thinking! I'd hate to think Teddy Bowles is up to something he shouldn't be." Sir John rubbed his jaw thoughtfully. "If there is something to this . . . what does it have to do with the American soldier who was killed?"

"Maybe nothing." Harry flipped to another page of his notes. "You say you haven't been up there since the war began?"

"That's right," Gordon Fordyce said.

"Orkney seems like an out-of-the-way place for a factory. That's why you bought that stretch of land, right? That's what we were told: to build a factory."

"It was that very out-of-the-way nature of the place that attracted us, Major," Sir John replied. "At the outset of the war, we were quite nervous about the safety of our manufacturing centers here in England. We'd heard a lot about how capable the Luftwaffe was—"

"We were looking for a site out of German bomber range," Fordyce said.

"But you never built the plant," Harry pointed out.

"As you say, it was out of the way." Sir John shrugged.

"The difficulties of providing resources," Fordyce put in. "Enlisting personnel, providing electrical power—"

"I tend to think those kinds of things would've been obvious from the beginning," Harry said.

"It was a frantic decision made in frantic times." Fordyce said it coldly.

"Understand, Major Voss," interjected Sommer, "Europe was falling. You cannot understand how it was to look at things in those days."

"So you bought the land to build a factory, you didn't build the factory, but you kept the property?" Harry persisted.

Gordon Fordyce's lips flicked in what I assumed was a smile— pinched, brief, and superior. "The market for real estate is hardly booming at the moment. The British agencies that investigated this matter saw no need to raise any of these issues, Major."

"I am confused as well." Erik Sommer was frowning. "I do not see how this is something to do with the poor dead man."

"I imagine they're just being thorough, Gordie," Sir John said.

Harry looked up from his notes. "You said you haven't been to this Orkney site in how long?"

"You keep asking that," Fordyce said peevishly.

"With the war it must be three, four years," Sir John replied. "Eh, Gordie? Three to four years? Autumn '39, isn't that what you said?"

"Something like that."

"No need to visit, really," Sir John explained.

Harry put his notebook away and began to fold up his glasses. "You have a boat, don't you, Sir John?"

"You named it after your sons," Woody Kneece said.

Sir John smiled. "How did you know?"

Kneece smiled back. "*Ray*-mond. *Cal*-vin. *Ras-cal*."

Sir John nodded. "They never saw that boat. I bought it after the war, the first war. In answer to your question, Major, yes, I have a boat."

"Where do you keep it?"

Sir John's thick white brows closed ranks, and he rubbed his jaw with his knuckles again. "Oh, well, let's see. We keep slips for it at Brighton and Cardiff, and even one up the Thames at Richmond Landing for when we're in the London office."

"What about your place in Scotland?"

"Yes, of course," Sir John said after a moment. "I'd forgotten about the lodge. It's been some time since I've used it."

"Where's the boat now?" Harry asked.

"Oddly enough, I don't know."

"That *is* odd," Harry commented.

"The boat hasn't been out since the war," Fordyce explained. "What with the petrol rationing, and there's hardly a safe stretch of water outside the Irish Sea—"

"We can check on that for the gentlemen, can't we, Gordie?" Sir John said. "The whereabouts of *Rascal*, I mean."

"Yes, we can check on that, Sir John. There might not be an answer until late tomorrow or the next day."

"And, as Gordon said, we'll be sending some of my people to sniff about up to Orkney, see what we can find out for you chaps. Even if everything with Teddy Bowles is aboveboard—and I'm sure it is—with all respect, gentlemen, Teddy might be more willing to say something of note to one of his own."

Erik Sommer leaned forward. "Major Voss, do you have *any* idea about this American's death? You have all different questions. I don't see what it is you are trying to learn. Do you have any answers?"

"A few," Harry said. "But nothing we can talk about. You understand."

Sommer nodded, his eyes calculating.

"If that's all, gentlemen," Gordon Fordyce announced, "Sir John has been more than generous with his time, I think you'll agree. Now he needs to spend more of it with his guests. Mr. Owen, I think you know enough at this point to see that any mention of Sir John in connection with this story would be gratuitous."

"I would agree, Gordie, based on what I know at this point." What I left hanging unsaid, and what Gordon Fordyce seemed to understand behind his narrowed eyes, was that perhaps I simply didn't know enough yet.

Fordyce summoned Alden and called for our coats. As we waited for the butler to return, Sir John turned to the tall windows behind him. Woody Kneece joined him, and for that short while they discussed horses. Alden returned, and as we pulled on our coats—

"By the way," Sir John called to Kneece. "If you don't mind—this dead chap. What was his name?"

"Sir John," advised Fordyce, "there's no reason you—"

"I would like to know the boy's name, Gordon," Sir John said firmly.

"Grassi," Harry said. "Lieutenant Armando Grassi."

"Did the lieutenant have a family? Was he married—"

"Sir John!" Fordyce admonished.

"A mother," Harry answered. "A father."

Sir John nodded a deep nod. "Family enough. Safe home, gentlemen."

"Maybe you missed it, Mr. Owen," Woody Kneece said dryly, "but we've just been talking to the *real* guy. In the flesh."

He was referring to my endless sifting through the file on John Duff. "Ach, there I was thinking American wit had died with Will Rogers."

"You still think you know that Sommer fella?"

"I *know* I know him, and I know it had something to do with Sir Johnnie Duff." I remembered Erik Sommer's look, his ice-blue eyes fixing me through the window of Sir John's library as we had climbed back into the Army sedan. "And Erik Sommer knows I know him, too."

"But you can't remember *how* it is you know him?"

"Laddie, come see me in twenty years and we'll compare memories." I closed the folder with an unsatisfied finality. "You're quiet back there, Lieutenant," I said.

Peter Ricks was slumped against the rear door, his unbandaged eye blind to the Canterbury scenery slipping by, a cigarette dangling from his lips. "I'm contemplating."

"Were you contemplating at Sir Johnnie's as well? You didn't seem to have much to say there either."

He held up his little finger. On it sat a cigar band.

"Oh, indeed, I quite enjoyed his cigars."

"Cohibas, weren't they?" Kneece asked. "They cost a pretty penny. I know; my daddy gets them. So?"

"Lieutenant," I said, "you are in a country where people get in line for a tin of Spam. What we were presented with this afternoon represented more rations than most families see in a week."

"And top-of-the-line smokes to boot," Ricks added. "The hard life seems to end at Sir Johnnie's front door."

"Aye." I turned back to Woody Kneece. "You didn't just happen to find that piano, did you?"

Kneece grinned. "Spinet."

"With those enormous front windows, you must have seen Sir Johnnie's car coming up the drive. You staged that whole scene, didn't you? This is quite the showman you've brought along, Harry."

From the moment we had climbed in the car, Harry had either been scribbling notes in his little book, or flipping through its pages, oblivious to the presence of his traveling companions.

"I say, Harry—"

"Yes, he is," Harry said without looking up from his notations. "He sings, he dances. I'll bet he even does magic tricks."

I turned back to Kneece. "How'd you know about that 'Minstrel Boy' business?"

Kneece continued to revel in his aura of mystery, but an answer came from Peter Ricks: "He saw the statue."

"You'd already been to the library?" I asked.

"Back in that room like a fishbowl—"

"Solarium," I said. "Or, if you must, sunroom."

"—that's what I went up to the major about. I wanted him to keep that Sommer fella talking while I poked around."

"So you never made it to the loo?"

"The what? Oh, the can, well, yeah, I did. Hey, Major, if you think the rest of the house was impressive, you should've seen this guy's crapper."

"Spare us those details," Harry said.

"I get to the door, I tell the butler I'm probably going to be a while, and after he toddles off—"

"You begin snooping."

"Mr. Owen, you may be an ally and a friend of the major's, but need I remind you that I am an officer with the Criminal Investigating Corps of the United States Army. I do not snoop. I—"

"*Investigate*," Harry proclaimed.

I turned back round to Harry. "You've been awfully studious since we left."

He slid his pen into his jacket pocket with a sigh. The car turned a bend in the road, and for a moment the low sun flashed in the lenses of his reading spectacles. "They're all lying. I'm just trying to figure out who's lying how much about what. And why. 'I want to know the boy's name'—isn't that what he said? He didn't know Grassi was an American, but he knew he was *young?*"

"Figure of speech?" I offered.

"Hell," Kneece said, "he's got his own man up there. I'll bet Old Bowles told him everything there was to know, down to the size of Grassi's boxer shorts."

"And there's what he *didn't* say," Harry persisted stubbornly. "He *didn't* say 'What in hell is an *American* doing in Orkney?' "

"You figure they're all in on it?" Kneece asked, then began to provide his own answer: "Well, darling Gordie, that makes sense, he's the big mucky-muck's right-hand man. But Yon Yonson there, the Swedish guy—"

"He's dirty," Peter Ricks said.

"You sound pretty sure," Kneece said.

"For a guy with nice manners, he seemed tactlessly interested in what we were digging up on his friend Sir Johnnie, didn't you think, Mr. Owen? He even invited himself into the Q and A with Duff."

"Tripped up by good manners," Kneece said. "There's one for Sherlock Holmes."

"That thing Sommer said to me about being sorry for the war," Ricks mused.

"It did seem right queer," I said. "Why should *he* be sorry?"

Ricks nodded, satisfied to discover he was not alone in his suspicions. He sat back and extracted his silver flask.

"Sir John's brandy wasn't enough?" Harry meant it to sound casual, but I could hear the touch of remonstrance.

Ricks smiled in my direction, and there passed between us some sad sort of kinship as he held the flask up in salute. "There's never enough, is there, Mr. Owen?"

"Never quite, Lieutenant. Never quite."

Joe Ryan sat behind his desk, his eyes lost in the warming fire in the hearth behind him, his hands cupped round a brandy snifter.

Sitting across from him, Harry reread the text of the memorandum. It was addressed to Colonel McCutcheon from the military liaison's office of the U.S. Embassy at Prince's Gate, with copies to SHAEF and several British governmental and military offices in Whitehall. The body of the missive read:

> We have conferred with the relevant UK authorities as well as with the appropriate liaison offices at SHAEF and in Washington. All are in agreement on the following points:

1. *As the incident in question evidently occurred on British soil within proximity to British military installations, the investigation should properly fall to British jurisdiction;*
2. *We accept the assurances of our British ally that as far as is ascertainable neither British nor American military security has been breached or threatened, nor is there any indication at this time that this is a security matter of any sort.*

The pertinent British authorities have informed us they will continue to investigate the incident as a criminal matter and will keep interested U.S. and British offices apprised of their progress. We feel that this constitutes an appropriate and satisfactory disposition of the matter.

Formal orders from the involved agencies will be forthcoming, including those from Washington CIC discontinuing their avenue of investigation.

Harry removed his reading spectacles. He looked up to see Ryan sitting on the front edge of his desk holding out a second snifter of brandy toward him.

"Your young pal is sitting over in McCutcheon's office reading his copy right now," Ryan told Harry.

"This stinks."

"Don't look at me. I agree with you."

"You have no idea what a great comfort that is," Harry said. He stood, letting the memorandum slide to the floor, and moved toward the windows overlooking the Court. He heard a rustle of paper as Ryan picked up the page and set it on his desk, then the colonel followed him to the window still holding out the second snifter. When Harry continued to refuse it, Ryan poured its contents into his own glass.

"They're stepping away from this and dumping it on the Brits," Harry said. "And the Brits aren't pushing it."

"Let it go. Harry, I don't know what you think you've gotten hold of, and I don't know what it is you're doing that's getting everybody's nose out of joint—"

"And you don't want to know."

"You're goddamned right I don't want to know. All I know is Armando Grassi isn't worth it."

"You mean worth risking this!" Harry swept his arm at the posh accoutrements of Joe Ryan's salon-cum-office. "Just what is it you do here, Colonel Ryan? What's your job? It sure as hell isn't the law."

Ryan's face colored. "Simple tactics, Major. I don't see the good in burning myself up fighting a fight I can't win. I tried to explain that to you back in August—"

Harry turned his back and headed for the door.

"Wait a minute! Harry, I said wait!" Ryan put himself between Harry and the door.

"I'm leaving."

"Sit down, Harry."

"Is that an order?"

Ryan could have made it so, but said nothing.

"All right," Harry said and dropped into the nearest chair.

"Harry, I didn't blame you for the way you felt back in August. If I'd been in your shoes I probably would've felt the same way."

"How understanding of you."

"Jesus, you and I practically go back to the womb together. You don't think I felt bad about it? It's eaten me up every day since then. Do you remember that time I came home from Fort Dix after Pearl Harbor?"

For the first time in Ryan's office, Harry began to feel defensive. "Is this about old debts? If I've forgotten to thank you for everything you've done for me—"

"Knock it off, Harry. You wanted to go your route, try to milk something out of that lousy little private practice of yours, that was your business, fine. I respected that. No, seriously, I really did. With Cyn and then the kids, it took more guts than I had. I thought you were nuts trying to go it that way, but I respected it. I know you thought I was just taking the easy out, going in the Army. It wasn't about hard and easy, Harry. It was about eating."

"You seem to be eating pretty well these days."

"You're goddamned right I am. Back to the original question. You remember when I came home that time?"

"In your big, brand-new, shiny Buick."

"When did you ever see a car like that in our neighborhood? Maybe Richie the Boot had one, and the other neighborhood wise guys, but one of us? I was a major then, remember? With the Army picking up the room and board, that's good money. I'd socked a lot away since I first went in. Buick started running those ads that with all the factories retooling for a possible war, the bet was the '42 Buick Super would probably be the last new car anybody saw for a long while. The minute that baby hit the showroom floor in November I was there. I plunked down twelve hundred bucks cash—*cash*, Harry. Then, after Pearl Harbor, my first leave I came home. I was thinking if I got sent overseas, well, who knows what's going to happen? This might be the only time the Ryans get to have things nice.

"So, I threw Ma and Da in the backseat and took them to lunch at Vittorio Castle. *The Castle!* Joe DiMaggio eats at the Castle, Frank Sinatra eats at the Castle, the local mob guys hang out there, but nobody from our block. Except that day. Then I took them downtown to Macy's. I bought my father six two-dollar shirts. He didn't believe there were shirts that cost that much money. You know that poor dumb mick was afraid to wear them? My mother says they're still in his drawer with the original pins in them. I put five bucks down on a brand-new Coldspot refrigerator." Ryan shook his head at the memory. " 'Where does the iceman put the ice?' Ma kept asking me. I had to explain three times it wasn't an icebox. Six cubic feet in that thing, Harry, she didn't know how she was going to fill it. I gave her twenty bucks and said, 'Go to the A and P. Pack that thing full, Ma. Meat. Buy beef. Get Da a steak!' "

It had come out in a rush, Ryan leaning forward, hammering Harry into the back of his chair with his vehemence. Now he took a breath, and leveled a finger in Harry's direction. "I don't apologize for that and I don't apologize for this." He nodded at his office. "And then what happened while I was home, Harry? Do you remember? You came by and practically begged—*begged*—me to help get you in. And that wasn't because you were all gung ho about going off to war. You weren't asking me to get you into *combat*. You were looking for that fat allotment check going home every month."

"Are we done?"

"You want to be pissed at me for what happened in August? OK, fine! You want to trot around on your moral high horse? Have a nice ride! But goddammit, Harry, I earned at least a little appreciation."

"I'll tell you what: I owe you for getting me in, but August makes us even, OK? Everybody goes home with a clear conscience."

"Oh, you do love to play the martyr! You don't see it, do you? You're that blind? Jesus, Harry, you owe me more for August than for anything else!"

"Owe you for *what*?"

"You, Grassi, and Ricks made a lot of brass hats mad back then. *Real* mad! When it was over, Peter Ricks wanted to put in for combat duty in Italy? 'Get this guy expedited out there!' they told me. They're figuring with luck some kraut'll put a bullet in his brain and that'll be that as far as he's concerned. Grassi? They buried him in the deep freeze. But what happened to you, Harry? You were the guy who started all the trouble. To them, you were the mastermind, the ringleader who was the real pain in the ass. Where did you get to go?"

Don't say this, Harry was thinking. *Please . . .*

"Some of them were talking about sending you to the Pacific. One of them said Burma. *Burma*, Harry! 'Let's see how he does out in *that* shithole!' How'd you think you would've done, Harry? Malaria put a nice yellow color in your cheeks? Maybe a little dysentery take something off that waistline of yours? No. You got to go *home*."

Oh, God . . .

"I told them, I said, 'Look, trust me, right now nobody wants this done with more than Harry Voss does. Send him home, he'll be so happy he won't be any trouble. And that's how it's been, hasn't it, Harry? You didn't get home and go squawking to some inspector general down in Washington about what happened, did you? You didn't go running down to the *Newark News* and spill it, did you? No."

Harry pushed himself from his chair and started moving toward the door. His face felt hot, he could feel himself sweating inside his tunic. His head was throbbing, harder than when it had rebounded off the side of Jim Doheeny's aeroplane back at Kap Farvel.

"Jesus," Ryan muttered. "You *did* know!" The colonel bolted from his chair to grab Harry by the arm. "That's why you came here, isn't it? *That's* why you came back?"

Harry snarled, "If you want to find out how Armando Grassi got his jaw broken, leave your hand right where it is."

Joe Ryan let go of his friend's arm. Harry left, not bothering to close the door behind him.

"It doesn't make sense," Woody Kneece muttered into his cup of coffee.

"From where they're sitting, I'm sure it makes *perfect* sense." Peter Ricks poured a quick splash from his flask into his cup. "What was it they told you, Kneece?"

"You want it again?"

"And again and again."

"I feel like I'm being interrogated."

"You are."

The tones were getting sharper.

"Behave," Harry said, without looking up from his work. "And keep your voices down."

Harry had taken several mimeographed copies of the canteen's daily menu, torn them into index-card-sized pieces, and now sat at the far end of a table in a corner of the dining hall notating the blank rear sides of the paper sections. Woody Kneece and Peter Ricks sat at the other end of the table. Whatever collegial sense had developed between them over the course of the day was swiftly evaporating.

"They told you what?" Ricks pressed.

"I was given authorization to go wherever I thought I had to go, to talk to whoever I felt I needed to talk to, in order to find out—"

"To find out who killed a third-rate second looey that nobody liked! *That's* what makes shit sense, Kneece."

"They said they were worried about the security angle."

"That's complete crap! Security is counterintelligence's territory."

"CI was already on it!"

"Then why bother with you? Why'd they pick you, Kneece? What's so special about you they came to you for this?"

"How the hell do I know? Maybe they like my smile."

"What're you not telling us, Kneece!"

"It's *Captain* Kneece, Lieutenant, and before you go sticking that finger in my face again, you better remember who's got the most brass on his collar."

Harry Voss put down his pen and began to set down his scribbled-upon pieces of paper, slowly, like a pensioner at the solitaire table. "What're you so hot about, Pete?" he said calmly. "As I recall, you're not in the JAG anymore." His eyes flicked over to Kneece. "Can I ask a question, Woody? When you came to see me at my home, one of the first things you asked me about was what happened here in London last summer. You thought maybe it might have something to do with Grassi's death."

"And I was wrong. We already know that, right?"

"What I want to know is, how did you know Pete and Grassi worked with me on that case? The only people who knew they did—along with all the paperwork on the case—are here in London. But you knew *a week ago* in New Jersey. How is that?"

"It was part of my briefing when they assigned me the case."

"What did they say to you at that briefing?"

"About what you'd expect—"

"What *exactly* did they say to you at that briefing?" Harry insisted.

"They told me Grassi had been killed in the Orkneys. It was an evident homicide but we had no real details, no ballistics or autopsy report, just word of a gunshot wound to the head. They told me he'd been last assigned to a post fifteen hundred miles from where he was found. They went over his personnel file with me. They told me the word was this was a guy who made a lot of enemies."

"And that maybe he'd made some in London. In August."

"Nobody pointed me in that direction. Hell, Major, you know the file on that case is sealed."

"But they did mention that two other officers, along with Grassi, had been expressed out of England at the same time. From that you drew an obvious conclusion that something must have gone bad on that case."

"It was obviously suspect—"

"It was never an investigation." Harry sighed, scooping up his note cards and shuffling them into a neat pile.

"Oh, really?" Kneece was riled now. "Just what was it, then?"

"They sent out a plumber with a mop and bucket to check for leaks."

"Come again, Major?"

Ricks nodded, understanding. "You were suckered, Captain. They knew Grassi's murder didn't have anything to do with August."

Harry slipped his notes and reading glasses inside his tunic. "What they were worried about was that poking into Grassi's murder, somebody might butt into the August case. Or maybe they were worried that once Pete and I heard about Grassi, we might think it had something to do with August and that might push us to say things they didn't want said to people they didn't want us talking to. Or maybe it just gave them a cover to check whether any of us had let anything slip about it since they'd sent us on our separate ways." Harry rubbed tired eyes. "But they didn't give a damn about you finding Grassi's killer."

"Now you're the one who's reaching," Kneece snapped.

Harry put an elbow on the table and parked his chin in the palm of his hand. He seemed almost reluctant to give Kneece the bad news. "What did you say in that report you turned over to McCutcheon last night?"

"I sealed it before I gave it to him."

"I hope he didn't cut his finger breaking that seal," Peter Ricks muttered, and took a deep swig of his laced coffee.

"You think everybody's in on this?"

"What did you say in your report?" Harry repeated. "Did you say anything about—"

"I never mentioned your August case," Kneece said adamantly. "That was a suspicion I had, but I had nothing to tell them."

"What did you tell them? What did you say about Duff?"

"I never mentioned his name."

"But you did report what you found up in Orkney?" Peter Ricks asked.

"The major here's always telling me we don't know who back in the States might be involved, so I song-and-danced. Even though I agree with the major that this probably isn't some black-market thing, I used that as a cover. I said we found signs in Orkney that maybe Grassi had stumbled across some smuggling thing—"

"Which," Ricks interrupted, "if somebody at CIC-Washington is in on this, would've been enough for him to figure out you meant Duff."

"Even if they're not," Harry said, "and their interest is more parochial, it still would've been enough for them to know it had nothing to do with the August case. Don't you see, Woody? The minute you put down on paper that they were clear on the August incident they closed you down. They don't give a damn about a third-rate second looey that nobody likes."

"You know," Peter Ricks mused, "maybe McCutcheon isn't the one who finked. Maybe this whole thing was about putting somebody they could trust on the scene."

Woody Kneece was a rather quick-witted fellow, and Peter Ricks did not even have to finish his thought before Kneece rose in his seat, snarling: "Wait a minute wait a minute *wait a minute!* Major, you've seen the way I've been pushing this all along! Do you—"

"Watch your tone, Woody. Sit down."

Kneece blinked self-consciously, noticing the eyes of the other officers in the canteen swinging his way. He forced himself back into his chair and his tone into more moderate registers. "Do you really think—" He fell silent. Then he said, "You fellas are really something."

"I don't doubt you, Woody," Harry said serenely. "I'm just looking for any sign as to whether or not I *should.*"

"Like what kind of sign?"

"Until you get orders from your immediate superior terminating your investigation, that heavy-caliber travel authorization of yours is still in effect. Get us on the first, fastest transportation to find Coster."

"Coster? Major, by now you know I don't have a problem bending a rule or tiptoeing over a line here and there. But now you're talking about straight-out disobeying orders, and before I get my ass hide nailed to the barn door—"

"You wouldn't be disobeying orders, Woody. Not if you move fast."

"McCutcheon stood right in front of me while he made me read that memo from—"

"You don't report to McCutcheon. You don't report to the Embassy. Your direct superior is at CIC-Washington. It even says in that memo that your orders haven't come through yet. Until they do—"

"That's thin, Major. *Real* thin."

Harry leaned forward, his voice low and even. "You almost got Jim Doheeny and his crew killed back in Greenland because you were so goddamned good and determined to find out who murdered Armando Grassi."

Kneece stared. Then he shook his head, smiling, partly in resentment, partly in admiration. "Beautiful." He turned to Ricks. "Was he always this good?"

"He seems to have gotten better."

"You in for the ride, Lieutenant Ricks?"

"In for a penny . . ."

Woody Kneece sat silently for a moment, watching a pair of mess boys working their way round the dining room stringing Christmas garland along the walls. With a deep, sighing breath he rose. "Let me see what I can get us," and he walked out of the canteen.

"You *have* gotten better at this," Ricks told Harry.

"You don't have to be a part of this, Pete."

"Like I said, old habits die hard. Besides, you're going to need a guide out there."

"OK." Harry stood to leave. "There's something I've got to do before we go. And I've got another little chore for you. Do you know anybody you can ask about Kneece?"

Ricks pondered a moment, both the gravity of the request as well as the possibilities. "I don't know how fast we'll hear back. It won't be before we leave."

"Do it," Harry said.

Not far from Rosewood Court, buried deep in the earth under the Georgian grace of Grosvenor Square, was the shadowy labyrinth of linked cellars and newly dug tunnels that was home to the Americans' military intelligence unit; what the arcane system of U.S. military designations had labeled "G-2." Imperator over this half-lit world of maps and charts, light tables and reconnaissance photographs, files and telewire machines was Christian Van Damm, who ruled from a glass-walled sanctum deep within the maze.

Those who had attended press briefings conducted by Van Damm usually saw a spindly, underfed young man possessed of a death's-door pallor, looking barely capable of rising to speak, let alone lord over the acutely analytical minds of the American military's London staff. To underestimate Van Damm was fatal; inside that funereal body was a keenly vital and droll tongue that showed little mercy on those too slow-witted or protocol-bound to keep up with his own sharp directness.

Nonetheless, there was nothing at this particular moment that seemed vital or sharp-witted about Christian Van Damm. The sergeant escorting Harry through the underground complex had bade him wait outside the sanctum. The sergeant knocked gingerly on the door, then with equal caution opened it and entered. In the triangle of light through the open door Harry saw a litter of papers, and the midriff of a blanketed form draped across five wooden chairs lined up to form a functional if uncomfortable bed.

He heard the deferential mumble of the sergeant, then a sleepy grumble of response. More mumbling, then, more piercingly, "Who? Jesus, well *yeah*, show him on in!"

The lights flicked on in the cubicle; the sergeant beckoned Harry in.

The office was a blizzard of maps, paper, memos, and photographs tacked to walls, strewn across the floor, blanketing the desk. The stale air in the room was heavily flavored with body odor and the rank perfume of bad cigars. Christian Van Damm had thrown off his blanket and was sitting upright, clad in a rumpled uniform but shoe- and stocking-less. His bleary eyes squinting against the glare of the overhead light, he scratched at his unshaven chin, and pulled his mouth into a sleepy smile. "Like I told the man; Jesus! Voss! What're you? The Ghost of Christmas Past?"

"Major Van Damm."

Van Damm flicked at the silver oak leaves on his collar tab. "That's 'Lieutenant Colonel, sir, may I kiss your ring, sir,' you peon."

"Santa came early for you."

Van Damm held out a hand. "Don't just shake it, Voss, haul my ass up!"

Harry tugged and Van Damm rose. The younger man brought his blanket up with him and tossed it over a map propped on an easel in a corner. Before the blanket came down Harry had a glimpse of the Italian boot, and marker-drawn arrows indicating some force in the Tyrrhenian Sea aimed at a point on the west coast between Naples and Rome. "Not for public consumption," Van Damm said.

"I remembered you keeping odd hours," Harry told him, "but this is pretty odd even for you. Is this a matter of early to bed, or late to rise?"

Van Damm dropped into his desk chair, a ridiculously plush thing—wing-backed and covered with embroidered greenery—Harry guessed had been commandeered from one of the Georgian town houses above. "It's our busy season." Van Damm reached into a desk drawer and came up with a cellophane-wrapped cigar, a Tampa Nugget. He started to unwrap the cigar, then stopped. "I seem to remember you're not too keen on these. You gotta forgive me, Voss, they're like coffee for me. Tell you what; join me outside? I haven't had a breath of outside air in two days."

They found a bench on the green of the square. For a time they said nothing, looking out on the hushed island of withered shrubs and dry grass surrounded by blacked-out buildings. Though it was barely eight o'clock, the streets round the square were quiet and empty.

"It's almost going to be a shame when the lights come back on and there's enough gas for all the cars." Van Damm lit his cigar and took a deep drag that spurred a deep, rasping cough.

Harry made a face at the rank odor of the Tampa Nugget.

"It's this fresh air that'll kill you, Voss. Didn't you know that?"

"I was surprised to find you here. The last time I saw you, you said you were scouting a location—Where was it? Kensington, I think it was."

"Eisenhower thinks a headquarters staff goes stale if they get too comfortable. Now he's off in Algeria, wants to be close to Italy."

"How'd you miss out on that move?"

"I explained to my good friend Ike—"

"Oh, he's your good friend?"

Van Damm held up two intertwined fingers. "We're like this. 'Ike,' I said, 'you're in the commanding-general racket; you have to go where the action is. Me, well, I'm in the intelligence racket. It's kind of hard to make critical intelligence evaluations when all your background information is constantly in a file cabinet on a truck going somewhere.' So, we agreed we'd send some G-2 people along with him as liaison with the home office. We drew straws to see who'd get to live with the sand fleas."

"And you drew long straw?"

"Voss, I am now a lieutenant colonel! I do not draw straws! I rig the drawing!"

They laughed, then fell quiet again.

"I never got a chance to say to you I was sorry about how that business turned out last summer," Van Damm said.

"You've got nothing to apologize for. You did your job. The case wouldn't've gotten as far as it did without you."

"And why is that a good thing?"

Harry shrugged.

"Well, it worked out, anyway," Van Damm said.

"How do you mean?"

"They got what was coming to 'em, right? That way or the gallows, what's the dif?"

"That's one way of looking at it, I suppose."

"And you, I heard you got to go home."

"Yup. I got to go home."

"You must be here about Grassi."

Harry smiled. "How'd you . . . ? What was it you used to call this? The Spy Brigade?"

"I was always telling you, Voss: it's our job to know what's going on. Although I'll tell you the truth—there was no Spy Brigade stuff to it. It was more like the grapevine passed the word. I can't believe they dragged you all the way back here for Grassi."

"Actually, it's not my case. I was just asked to come along and help out."

"Who's doing the snooping? CIC?"

Harry nodded.

"Not that it's not nice to see you again, but what have I got to do with Grassi? I'm not a suspect or something, am I? I only met the guy that one time with you. That was enough to tell me I didn't ever want to take a long car ride with him."

"You're not a suspect. You know where they found him?"

"Orkneys. What was he doing up there?"

"That's one of the things we were looking into."

" 'Were'?"

"They're going to turn the investigation over to the British."

"Orkney is their turf, that makes sense."

"But it looks like the British aren't pressing too hard. They're writing it off as a criminal case and even at that, there's a lot of questions it seems they're not asking."

Van Damm scowled. "I know a lot of people over at Brit MI. A lot of them taught me my stuff. They're usually a pretty thorough crowd."

"Do you know who Sir John Duff is?"

Van Damm thought for a few seconds, then made an odd groaning noise signifying the name was indefinably familiar.

"He's a big businessman over here," Harry said. "A lot of defense contracts, very big with the local horsy set."

"Gee, I can't believe I haven't bumped into this guy in my circles. I should have him over for tea."

"They found Grassi near a place Duff owns in Orkney."

"You think because this Duff is like some Great Oz or something, maybe they're backing off?"

"I don't know what to think. But I'd like to know why."

"So you'd want me to ask my MI pals what's the skinny on this guy?"

"I'd appreciate it if you were a bit less direct than that."

"Gotcha. Be discreet. Cards close to the vest. All that crap."

"All that crap," Harry agreed.

Van Damm nodded. "No biggie. I can do that. But you want something else," he educed.

"This CIC guy and I talked to Duff. That's where we picked up that the British authorities were soft-shoeing. Duff has some houseguests, four that we saw. They say that they're Swedes, that they're from some steel companies Duff dealt with before the war. They say they're just visiting for the holidays."

Van Damm's expression was that of a man told the most incredulous story, something on the scale of Moon men or lost Inca treasure. "All this way to share some eggnog and Christmas cheer?"

"They say they're *good* friends."

"If Jesus had had friends like that he would've lived to be a ripe old man. Needless to say, you figure something stinks about these Swedish pals of the Great Oz. You figure it's connected to what happened to Grassi?"

"One of these Swedes seems awfully interested in how the investigation is going."

"And when I get caught stepping on the toes of my British colleagues, thereby causing disharmony between allies, what is it I'm supposed to use as an excuse when I get called out on the carpet?"

"No excuse, Colonel. An American officer dies near a top British military installation, and a big British military contractor has got foreigners poking their noses into it. Now that screams security crisis, and yet the Brits don't seem to want to do much about it."

"It doesn't scream, Voss. But it is a voice raised in concern."

"Just find out if Duff's houseguests are who they say they are. One of them gives the name Erik Sommer. The rest . . ." Harry shrugged.

Van Damm puffed steadily on his cigar. Then he took it from his mouth and spat tobacco juice onto the ground. "I don't know about finding out who they are, but it shouldn't be too hard to find out who they aren't. That much I can probably do without drawing attention."

Harry stood and held out his hand. Van Damm rose and shook it.

"I'm going to be out of town for a few days," Harry told him. "I'll come back to you then and see what you've got."

"If I come up with something hot, is there any way to get in touch with you?"

"I doubt it. We've got to talk to somebody who's off in Italy."

Van Damm's lips pursed. "Where in Italy?"

"Somewhere up on the front line. Listen, Colonel—if you don't hear from me in a few days, you might want to save yourself possible headaches and just let this drop."

"I'll hear from you, Voss. Just keep your head down over there."

Harry smiled a thanks and started walking away.

"Hey, Voss! How long are you going to be in Italy?"

"Like I said, I'm guessing a few days."

Van Damm seemed to mull something over, then he nodded resignedly. "Don't dawdle."

He was an intimidating figure, a wall of a man looming over my desk as I entered the newsroom that Monday morning. Though he was dressed in mufti, I knew only a veteran flyer would be in possession of such a well-worn leather flight jacket. He seemed amused at my reaction to his appearance. I guessed he was used to instilling such trepidation.

"Mr. Owen? I'm Jim Doheeny." He extended one of his enormous paws. "Harry Voss sent me."

"Ach, well, then," I said, marveling at how my hand seemed lost in his, "Mr. Doheeny, won't you sit? I'm supposed to meet with Harry this—"

Doheeny wasn't paying attention. He looked uncomfortably round the maze of desks and tables; the ebb and flow of my chatting colleagues, copyboys and their whiffling cargoes of paper, the jangle of phones, clatter of the telewire.

"Is this something private?" I ventured.

"Harry didn't say. But that was my sense."

I nodded for him to follow me. As we passed through the newsroom I saw Himself through the door of his office, peering up over his glasses in my direction, curious at this ursine thing trundling behind me. I smiled at him to let him know I was in no danger, then led Doheeny out to the tea room down the corridor, a small chamber where the serfs could rest weary eyes and wash down aspirin with tea from the pot always simmering on an electric stand in the corner. At present, the room was empty. I closed the door behind us, beckoned Doheeny to a seat, offered him tea, which he declined.

"Harry's gone," he said bluntly. "He sent me to tell you that."

"Gone?"

Doheeny handed me an envelope. Scrawled across the front in block letters was simply EDDIE. By the handwriting I guessed that the note had been written in great haste:

> E—
> *after Coster.*
> *if not back cpl days let it drop.*
> *thnx for evthing.*
> *u HAVE been a friend.*
>
> —H

I carefully folded the small square of paper. "When did he give this to you?"

"I got a call in the middle of the night to meet him at an airfield down in Sussex. I got there just before him and these other two guys—"

"Was Kneece one of them?"

"They were just climbing aboard. They were on a C-87—that's a long-range cargo plane. Is Harry going to Italy?"

"What makes you think so?"

"They took off on a southern heading, which could mean North Africa. But I heard a lot of traffic has been going through that field lately heading for Italy. And there's this." He took another envelope from his jacket pocket. "He told me if I didn't hear from him by the end of the week to mail this."

He let me hold the envelope for a second. It was addressed in full to Cynthia Voss.

"If I have to, I won't mail that," Doheeny said. "I'll bring it to her. I think that's, well . . ." He shrugged. "Why's he going there, Mr. Owen? I mean, I know you can't tell me about what he's working on even if you know. If I was supposed to know, I figure he would've told me by now. But why *him*? He doesn't belong out there."

"None of them do," I replied.

PART THREE

TEETH OF THE THEBAN DRAGON

CHAPTER EIGHT

CHARYBDIS

u HAVE been a friend.

I'd lent a sympathetic ear. I'd gotten him to Sir Johnnie. I'd done nothing. But now, having been given the rank, I felt obligated to earn it.

"Daniel, you spry young thing, hop to it, laddie! Earn your keep!"

One of the paper's recurring bon mots was that they must have built the building up round Daniel Brooks. Only that could account for both Brooks's decrepitude and his uncanny ability to locate any file, photo proof, clipping, and back-filed notebook amongst the rows and rows of stored material in the paper's library/morgue. If you were wanting something obscure or obtuse, you prodded plump little Daniel from his torpid half-sleep and set him off on the hunt.

"Daniel! Danny-boy!"

He roused himself from his desk, his round form even more spherical inside its two sweaters.

"Who's that, then?" he said and pushed his glasses closer to his eyes. "Ah, Mr. O making all this noise, eh?" He moved with arthritic stiffness to the counter as I pushed the Sir John Duff folder across to him. " 'Danny-boy,' eh? Afraid you were going to start singing, I was. What is it I can do for you, Mr. O?"

"A return and a withdrawal, Danny. Here's the return. Before you go lightning off, what I'm after is a picture that's not in here."

He squinted at me through his thick lenses. "Not in there, eh? If it's not in there, Mr. O, how do you know there's a picture?"

"I know that when the photo fiends descend on their prey they snap more than these few in the folder."

Daniel nodded. "If he's a freelance, he'll have all his proofs to himself, tucked home safe they'll be. But if he's staff . . . Let me check."

"Don't go nodding off back there, Danny," I called as he waddled off into the stacks. He may have appeared an old and doddering codger, but in his work he was as true as a magnetic torpedo. In seven minutes he was back with several manila envelopes of proofs from different occasions all featuring—as the marking on the envelope labels indicated—Johnnie Duff.

But after twenty minutes of sifting through the various envelope contents, even old Daniel's watery eyes could see the frustration on my face.

"No joy, then, eh, Mr. O? Are you *sure* there's a picture to find?"

"I was hoping."

"Ah, the wishful thought. It taunts us, eh?"

"That's most philosophical of you, Danny."

"The end product of spending one's hours with history. It occurs to me there's another possibility. . . . You asked for Sir John's file, and all those photo packets are for Sir John. It's possible that the picture you're looking for wasn't an assignment concerning Sir John."

"I am intrigued, Daniel. Go on."

"What I mean to say is if the assignment was for some other subject, some other person, or for an event at which Sir John was in attendance, well, the material would've been filed by the assignment sheet."

"Danny, if something ever happened to you this paper would be doomed. Let me see what you have on Mr. Joseph P. Kennedy."

Daphne St. Claire had survived three marriages—one by widowhood, two by divorce—benefiting substantially each time. Her greatest acquired asset was the surname "St. Claire." Daphne St. Claire made for a far better byline on our paper's social column than her maiden Daphne Ruggle.

We sat by the tall, arched window of a Mayfair restaurant whose finery was far beyond both my taste and means. But Daphne would not be denied, and she seemed to quite enjoy the idea of eating me through a week's pay in an hour.

Although in her fifties, she remained a strikingly handsome woman, with a deft sense of style, her only foible being a tendency to overapply her makeup. She was, at this moment, wearing one of those odd women's hats, a wee impractical thing sporting a spotted veil that I presumed to be another attempt to shave a year or two off her appearance. She was also equipped with a dangerously long cigarette holder to which she was currently fitting a Gauloise, an affectation designed to give her a flavor of the exotic. The story went that she had a closet full of Gauloise packets hoarded in her flat, spirited out of France before Dunkirk and trotted out only for certain occasions in the hopes her cache would outlast the war.

"Oh, yes, that was a lovely evening," she was saying as I leaned over to light her cigarette. "Made all the more special by your intrusion."

"I didn't intrude, Daphne. I was your guest."

"You were a fraud, Eddie. You asked that I take you as my escort, and the next thing I know—"

"I apologized then, Daphne, I apologize now."

"I wasn't invited to another ambassadorial function until Mr. Kennedy was replaced."

"Daphne, I don't know how many times I can apologize."

"You may apologize, Eddie, but you hardly look apologetic. If you had warned me beforehand that you were going to take advantage of my largesse—"

"It was a spontaneous impulse. Once Sir Johnnie made that bloody silly toast, how could I sit silent?"

"Like this, dear boy." She sat bolt upright and pinched her lips tightly closed. "See how easy it is? I'd always been under the impression you Scotsmen were a flinty, tight-lipped sort."

"A flaw in my character. Me mater was a gabby Englishwoman."

"Tosh. Englishwomen are not gabby. They're *conversational*." Her small smile hinted that her feelings were not completely venomous, but she was Daphne St. Claire and there was a protocol to be followed. "I intend for this to cost you dearly, Eddie: retribution. I'll be ordering the priciest thing on the menu, darling, and I shan't eat a bite of it. Not a nibble. Ah, here's the waiter! First, I'll have another of these divine champagne cocktails, my compliments to the wine steward, by the way. Considering the war and all that, you have an excellent cellar. And let me start with the prawns."

"Prawns?" I didn't have to look at the *carte* to gulp at the cost.

"Then we'll see afterward. Off you go." After the waiter left, she exhaled a jet of eye-watering Gauloise smoke in my direction. "This may even cost you another meal, Eddie. Perhaps tickets to the theatre."

"Good God, Daphne, I—"

"Oh, am I so hideous, Eddie? It would be so unbearable to spend the evening in my company?"

Daphne St. Claire was possibly the only middle-aged woman I knew who could still carry off the air of a young coquette. "Daphne, you could never be considered even mildly repugnant."

"That hardly has the poetry of some of your columns, but you are a dear. Now, what is it you want, naughty boy?"

"Daphne, everybody at the paper knows you're practically a living *Burke's Peerage*: Sir John Duff."

"First you insult the man at his little soirée for Ambassador Kennedy, now this. You are beginning to seem positively obsessive about the gentleman. Any particular reason?"

"I just go for a man with a title."

She made a face at my not sharing. "You *are* a dirty bird, aren't you? All right, then—Sir John. Where to begin?"

"Start with the general portrait. I know he rubs elbows with his ruling-class brethren. If I turned to his entry in *Daphne's Peerage*—"

She laughed at that. "Well, for starters, he's not really of the blood, dearie, not a true baronet at all in the historical sense. Not to the manor born, as the saying goes. Which makes it all the more remarkable that he's so well integrated into the club. I mean, *Windsor*, for God's sake! None of that looking-down-the-nose at Sir John."

"That's the respect a pile of loot can buy you."

"Oh, dearie, you think that lot gives a tinker's damn about money? It impresses them, but they'd have more respect for a pedigreed earl without a copper in his pocket than someone who actually *earned* his money! Sir John has done a fine job of polishing the silver, if you get my meaning."

"I don't get your meaning."

"You've met him, yes? A charming, personable fellow, knows which fork to use, a credit to the class."

"So how did he gain entry to the club? Was his title one of those trinkets the Crown gives away on the King's birthday?"

"Truth be told, Sir John was actually suggested for one but he turned it down. Politely, mind you, but those titles are not ancestral; they do not pass to the heirs. And *that* was what he wanted: something for his family they would still have after he was gone."

"He *bought* his title?"

"One of the less savory aspects of our monarchy. The original baronet was one of those wastrel inheritors not unlike my second husband. Remember him?"

"Albert?"

"Allan. Mind, he wasn't round long, I'm not surprised you've forgotten."

"Large front teeth?"

"Never mind."

"Like a rabbit—"

She gave me a cross stare and I let it go. The waiter returned with her second cocktail and the prawns. "I can't wait to watch them shrivel and rot," she said. "Will that pang poor Eddie's pocket?"

"Deeply."

"Good. Now, where was I?"

"The original baronet."

"Oh, yes, one of those silly fools who frivols the family fortune away on gambling or women or drink or some other indulgence. I believe in this particular case, it was a bit of everything on the buffet."

"So John Duff acquired the title, the lands—"

"The whole blue-blood birthright. It was some time ago, long enough that few remember, but it was one of the first pieces I wrote, sort of an introduction of the new baronet to the world."

"A first-class piece of journalism I'm sure it was."

She blew another puff of smoke at me to let me know what she thought of my opinion. "John Duff loved his sons, dearie. Positively doted on those two boys. Very working-class in that respect, betrayed his roots there. None of that 'I say, Junior, good show on the cricket field, well done, now off with you.' Adored the whole lot, mother and children. Married her when he was still nearly a boy, you know, childhood sweets and all that. Miriam her name was, if I recall properly. Never a whisper of scandal about either of them. For his part, he was devoted to her like a priest to a church. It was absolutely brutal on him when he lost them."

I idly reached for one of her prawns and she rapped my knuckles with her cigarette holder. "Order your own," she said.

"I can't afford to. Duff's boys, he lost them in the war, didn't he?"

"Sir John didn't want them to serve. What with all his contacts in Whitehall, all his factories making this and that for the Royal Army, the Royal Navy, it would not have been all that difficult to gain them some sort of exemption; vital to the war effort at home and so on. But those lads would have none of that. Wouldn't even tolerate headquarters duties. The oldest boy—"

"Raymond."

"Oh, bravo, someone's been doing his homework! Yes, Raymond, he enlisted first, that August when the guns first went off. Calvin was too young then, but he followed in '15, soon as he was of age."

"Sir John said they were close."

"Oh? You've been talking to Sir John?"

I smiled, as if helpless to undo my silence.

"I've half a mind not to tell you a word more until you promise to share."

I took her gloved hand. "Daphne, this is not something you want to share."

She may have played the effete, silly society butterfly, but there was sterner stuff underneath. She had been in the newspaper game long enough to sense when something of heft was afoot.

She smiled approvingly, then returned to the attitude of condescending lecturer. "Raymond was gassed at Ypres, and the little one, poor Calvin, he was lost at Passchendaele. Then the mother, she was always a frail sort, and every day the boys had been in service took a toll on her. Miriam was taken in the influenza pandemic after the war."

She had snuffed out her cigarette—thank God—and was now picking at the prawns.

"I thought you weren't going to eat anything."

"I'm ignoring you, dearie." She popped a glob of pink flesh into her mouth. "See? Completely oblivious."

"If Sir Johnnie was as close to his family as you say, well, you said it was brutal on him."

"Oh, quite."

"He's not exactly playing Miss Havisham down there in Belleville."

"For a few years he was. Oh, these are quite good! You really should order some for yourself! I'd share, but then there'd be less for me! As I was saying, yes, he did spend some time brooding behind closed curtains, and there was a worry that the whole Duff business thing would collapse and the Defense Ministry would have lost a major supplier. Up pops Gordon Fordyce. You know him? He was there that night you insulted Sir John."

"I didn't insult him. I merely asked—"

"He was the one who had you thrown out."

"I remember."

"Despite Gordon Fordyce's shortcomings of personality, Sir John took quite a shine to him. More and more, he let 'Gordie' lead him back to some semblance of a living life. Indeed, I think Gordon Fordyce may be as close to an heir apparent as Sir John has."

"I want you to look at this picture, Daphne." The particular picture I laid on the tablecloth for her showed the host's end of a dinner-party table. A laughing Sir John sat at the head. On his right sat Gordon Fordyce wearing a cool, polite smile. On Sir John's left sat the man I'd been introduced to as Erik Sommer. Scattered among the guests at that end of the table were the woman and other two men I had seen ride up outside Sir John's house with the Christmas tree–laden wagon the day before.

"Please look at the picture, Daphne. These are the people I'm interested in. This bloke, this one, and this couple."

"Oh!" She chomped down on another prawn. "The Germans!"

I'd not had a drink since the brandy at Sir John's. Right then, I wished I could've afforded to order a double scotch from the restaurant bar. "Excuse me?"

"The Germans."

"They're *Germans*? *All* of them?"

She seemed puzzled at my emphatic reaction. "Being they're from Germany, that's what I call them: Germans. What do they call them in Scotland? Kumquats?"

"Sometimes I find it difficult to believe anyone invites you and your tart tongue to anything."

"I'm always on my best behavior in the dining salons, dearie. The scorn I reserve for you."

"All right, these Germans. Who are they?"

"Business associates of Sir John's. Very chummy, actually. As a matter of fact, if I remember correctly . . ." A prawn hovered in front of her mouth as she bit her lip and closed her eyes.

"Yes?" I prompted.

"I'm *thinking*, dearie. Perhaps if I fuel the gray matter . . ." In went the prawn. "Yes, well, Sir John had been dealing with them for a bit by then, and he'd even introduced them to the ambassador."

"Ambassador Kennedy?"

"That's why they were there that evening, dearie. All chums, a League of Nations of Business."

"Do you remember their names? This one, this bloke. Does the name Erik Sommer sound familiar?"

"It does sound familiar, but . . . It was Erik *something*. Hm. Stahl! Erik Stahl. And this one I remember . . ." She touched a face I'd not seen at Belleville the previous day. Like the others he was in his thirties, handsome, confident.

"Him?"

"Oh, yes, there were five of them, dearie. A regular little Germanic cabal. I remembered Erik because he was something of the ringleader, spokesman, whatever you want to call him. Likable. Married, I'm afraid. Oh, don't make a face, dearie, you're hardly a Puritan."

"There does seem to be an age difference, Daphne."

"Given the choice, wouldn't you prefer a peach fresh from the tree over one dried and shriveled on the ground?" She smiled, and I got an uncomfortable peek at her tongue running along the inside of her teeth.

"You were saying," I prodded.

"Ah." She sighed. "Well. This one I remember because he died recently."

"When?"

"This past summer. He was on that aeroplane from Lisbon, the one with poor Leslie Howard. That was tragic about Leslie, wasn't it? Although I never forgave him *Gone With the Wind*. He made Englishmen look like simpering twits."

"He was playing an American."

"Then maybe it was the Yanks who shot him down. You don't think it's true, do you? That Leslie was some sort of spy?"

"Spies don't simper. This fellow, this German, what was his name?"

"That's why I recall it because at first no one knew he was on that plane. He was under an assumed name, incognito and all that. I suppose he was trying to sneak out of Germany. No one really knew who he was until Sir John showed up at the War Ministry asking that if the body or any effects were recovered, he'd like them turned over to him. One question led to another and that's how they found out: Anton Vogler."

I had my notebook out and jotted them down: Erik Stahl. Anton Vogler. "And the others?"

"Oh, let me see . . . Dearie, this was eons ago, you understand that? I remember the wife was Leni something. . . ."

I opened the file, the thick collection of pieces on Joseph Kennedy during his three-year tenure at the Court of St. James. "Here's the clipping, Daph, your story. Can you put the names in the piece to the faces in the picture?"

"You'll notice they didn't run the photo. That was because of you, you know."

"I didn't know that."

"The story, for reasons of which you should be painfully aware, came up a bit short—*too* short to warrant a photo was the editorial decision. All right, let's see. The couple, that's Rudolf and Leni, the Emmerichs. Rudi and Leni, I called them, because they were so cute together."

"Cute."

"And that was Albert Lindz."

"You said they were German businessmen? What kind of business were they in?"

"Dearie, I'm there to see how beautiful they are and how fashionably they dress. That these people may actually *do* something is another department. I thought that was your department, in fact. Is it true what you said earlier? Or were you simply cozying up to me to make me cooperative?"

"Was what true?"

"That you don't mind your fruit . . . a little seasoned."

The look in her eyes was unmistakable and I laughed. "God, Daphne, don't you ever get tired of the game?"

The look changed, became weary. "You're quite pleasant company when you're not making an utter ass of yourself, Eddie. I'm at the point where I'm more interested in good company than anything else."

"I hear terriers are nice."

"I take it back. You're a complete ass even when you *are* being pleasant company. Just for that, I'm calling over the waiter. I understand they have an absolutely extravagant suckling pig, and I want to hear what the most expensive desserts are. I may order two . . . and not eat a one!"

"I see you had lunch with Daphne," Bertie Welles said.

I had only a passing interest in what he had to say just then. My attention was focused mainly on the apple—Bertie's routine midafternoon snack—he was slicing into six precise crescents on a kerchief he'd spread on his blotter.

"Aye. Well, Daphne had lunch. I sat and watched."

"I hadn't heard there was anything between you two."

"Nothing to hear. Strictly collegial."

He sighed.

Bertie Welles and I had come on the paper together eons ago, had even shared a desk as novices. These days, he was penning *Bertie's Well*, which was something of a curio in the financial section of our paper. Bertie was less interested in stock indices, wage/price controls, and the other arcane business minutiae than in the obvious but oft-ignored fact that behind all business are people. *Bertie's Well* was a twice-weekly portrait of some business wizard or another and how the wizard's personality manifested itself in the subject's commercial operations. Hardly fodder for *The Economist*, but that's what I liked about Bertie.

"I thought perhaps you were getting yourself back in the game," Bertie said.

"With *Daphne*?"

"She's not a bad-looking bird for her years. Who was it that said older women are grateful?"

"Are you going to eat all that apple?"

"I'd intended to, yes. I should warn you that if you're going to be

trysting about with Daphne St. Claire—well, old boy, I doubt your current financial structure could stand the strain."

"It wasn't a tryst and I don't think I'll be eating again until next payday."

He looked mournfully down at his apple, like a general sending his
troops off to bloody battle, then passed two of the crescents to me. "Chew
them slowly and it'll get you through tomorrow."

"I need some background help, Bertie, and it's right in your line of
country. Sir John Duff."

"Something brewing with Sir John?"

"As I say, it's simply background material. I'm just trying to learn the
lay of the land. What have you got?"

"You know he's not a real baronet?"

"I've gotten most of the personal particulars from Daphne."

"You've already been to Daphne about this? Are you *sure* there isn't
something here for your chum Bertie?"

"Positive."

He tried to gauge if I was simply being hoggish. We may have been
old mates, but a good story was a good story. But after a moment, he saw
this was something else. "To think I'm sharing my apple with you and
getting nothing in return."

"I'm a swine, forgive me."

He smiled, rose from his desk, turned to the row of file cabinets behind him and returned with a folder. It made a substantial thud when he
dropped it on the desk. I began to flip through the clippings and notes
about Sir John Duff.

"His people like to present Sir John as a Horatio Alger tale, particularly
that gnat that's always hovering about him."

"Gordon Fordyce?"

"You know him? I'm Mr. Numbers; you're the wordsmith. Isn't there
a word 'unctuous'?"

"It means oily, smooth, greasy."

"It's a perfect word for Fordyce, don't you think? It even *sounds* like
him. *Unctuous.* Well, Fordyce takes great care with Sir John's public image,
and that's the angle he likes to tout."

"From what I see in this file, that's not quite accurate."

"Sir John has certainly built up quite the little empire for himself, but
he got a nice start from Daddy. Daddy owned a shoe factory in
Coventry."

"That must have cost dearly when the Germans erased Coventry."

"The factory was destroyed in the Blitz, but Sir John was long out of
the shoe business by then. But that shoe factory was the start of the family
fortune. During the Boer War, Daddy made a right treasure through a

contract supplying the Army with boots. John Junior was his daddy's right hand, then. He saw the possibilities, got Daddy to diversify, buying other garment manufacturers with the Boer War profits. They turned that boot contract into a series of contracts supplying uniforms to the various military branches. Daddy died in 1911, control passed to John Junior, then the Great War came along and Johnnie's plants couldn't make uniforms fast enough. In no time he was up to his eyes in sterling."

Bertie wiped his fingertips on the kerchief, then pulled a photograph from the file showing a young Sir John Duff posing outside a brick factory bearing the sign, DUFF & SON SHOES LTD. On either side of Sir John were the two young men whose portraits I'd seen at Belleville: Raymond and Calvin Duff. In the background of the photo, on a scaffold suspended from the roof of the factory, painters were adding an s to "Son"—DUFF & SONS SHOES LTD.

"He could've made twice as much and I doubt he'd've felt it compensation for losing those boys," Bertie said. "You know about them? And the wife? Left the poor old boy devastated. For years he just let things run themselves and the business began to unravel. He was sitting down in that place he has near Canterbury and wouldn't pick up the reins to bring it to order. There was a fair bit of concern about that in Whitehall; Duff was a leading military contractor."

"That doesn't sound like the Sir John I met."

"Oh, you've been down there, have you? Talked to the old man, eh?"

"He seems to be carrying on bravely."

"You have to credit Fordyce there. I grant you, he's hardly the bloke most would care to share a pint with, but Sir John liked him right enough, and he's not just some leech living off Duff . . . at least not completely. He's got a bit up here." Bertie tapped the side of his noggin. "Fordyce not only got Sir John out of Canterbury and back in the office, but he was the one who guided him into the subassembly business."

"The what? Sir John makes submarines?"

Bertie Welles smiled and shook his head. "Damn, mate. You are just completely at sea, aren't you?" He noticed I'd finished my two slivers of apple while he had one left. He pushed it across the desk to me.

"Subassemblies. Small pieces of big machines. Say you're Vickers. You make very nice machine guns. But whenever one part of the world isn't shooting at the other, the demand for your product tends to go down, and if all you make is machine guns, then your business suffers. Gordon Fordyce had Sir John get out of the uniform business and into factories that make precision machinery parts for contractors who make the whole item. Look, here's a Duff factory that makes the recoil mechanism for Vickers, and that also makes the bobbin system for mechanical sewing machines. War comes, and he can convert the sewing machine half of the factory to making machine-gun parts without the massive retooling required to convert a whole plant."

"And when people would rather sew than shoot each other—"

"He reverses the conversion. It paid off amply for Sir John between the wars, and these days, well, yes, there's Vickers as well as Supermarine, Hawker, Rolls-Royce, Avro . . . There's a lot of the old boy around."

I showed him the same dinner-party photograph I'd shown Daphne St. Claire. I pointed to the Germans. "Do you know these men?"

"Oh, yes! Let's see, that's Erik Stahl, that'd be Vogler . . . You know the poor sod died this past summer? Went down with—"

"Leslie Howard, yes, I know."

"Did you like his movies?"

"Simpered too much for my tastes."

"Simpered?" He shook his head, puzzled, and returned to the matter at hand. "I even did a story about them and Sir John!" He pulled out a clipping that included a photograph of Sir John with the Germans and Joseph Kennedy toasting one another in Sir John's library. The headline for the story ran *Duff Signs with Germans, Yanks for Transatlantic Venture*. The dateline for the story was March 1938. "The idea was they'd create a financial pool to invest in projects that took advantage of their respective resources, and then turn it out in the three markets: America, Germany, and the U.K."

"I'm surprised Whitehall allowed a principal military contractor to deal with the Germans like that."

"There was a concern. But Chamberlain was still on about appeasement in those days. And the arrangement did have the imprimatur of a Crown endorsement."

"Windsor."

He smiled at my insight. "As you obviously know, he was a chum of Sir John's. The expressed hope—from the duke, from Sir John, even from Ambassador Kennedy—was that the venture would demonstrate the possibilities for the various major powers to deal peaceably and profitably together. These were not starry-eyed idealists, mind you. At least in part, Sir John was sincerely motivated by the loss of his sons. And Mr. Kennedy, I'm sure, had a concern about something similar happening to his boys. But even with that in mind, let me tell you that these men—all of them—are intelligent, practical men. What they were promoting was an intelligent, practical paradigm."

"But then came the war and that was that."

"Quite. Do you remember a *Bertie's Well* I wrote back in '37? The one that got Himself in such a huff he spiked it? There was quite a to-do about it, even a call from the PM's office to the publisher."

"We were still on the appeasement tack then, and the thinking was your piece was not fostering understanding between the nations. You were instructed, as I remember, to stick to writing about business instead of bylining agitating editorials."

"It *was* a business story! It was a simple financial deduction that there could be no incentive to keep Mr. Hitler from eventually going to war. He'd dedicated the whole German economy to war matériel. To hang an entire national economy on a single product is fiscal madness. I made the case that it showed Mr. Hitler to be someone *not* interested in sound financial policy nor money matters. He was not a practical man, nor in many ways particularly intelligent. Mr. Hitler, I concluded, is a madman."

"These Germans, Stahl and the rest, what do you know about them?"

Bertie began rooting through the folder again. "I had some background material on them in here when the announcement was made. Yes, here it is. Hm, I'd forgotten about that."

"What?"

"Vogler was with Krupp, but the others worked for German subsidiaries of American companies. Stahl and Emmerich were managers at Adam Opel, which is a subsidiary of the American General Motors Corporation. Lindz was at Ford's Cologne subsidiary."

"How powerful were they? Senior management? Executive level?"

"Hardly."

"Then who were they to be dealing with the likes of Sir John Duff and Joe Kennedy?"

"Well, the material I got at the time positioned them as young talents on the rise in German industry."

"Next generation of management. Managers of tomorrow."

"Quite. If you want to be flowery about it."

"Nazi?"

Bertie shook his head. "But not anti-Nazi either. When Ford-Germany offered Hitler a million marks on his birthday back in '39, a lot of the management tried to be part of the giving to curry favor with The Chief. But Lindz stayed out of the fray, notably so considering he was being groomed for future advancement with Ford. None of these four men has ever openly supported the Nazis or openly criticized them, even early on, before the war."

"Very careful of them."

Bertie's face twisted, unsure. "Perhaps, like Sir John, it's a mix of the practical and the altruistic."

"How so?"

"At the time the joint venture was announced, I spoke with Erik Stahl. Charming enough young man, not what one would expect. German factory manager, one tends to think of a human machine, all facts and figures, Teutonic efficiency and all that rot."

"But he wasn't."

"I asked him what, if anything beyond simple profit, motivated him into this joint venture. He said he felt a certain empathy with Sir John. You see, Stahl lost his father in the first Great War."

I sat back in my chair, musingly sucking on my apple-flavored fingertips. "Where are they now? The three who are still alive: Stahl, Emmerich, and Lindz?"

Bertie shrugged. "Building trucks and tanks for the Wehrmacht, I should imagine."

"What was Vogler doing on that plane from Lisbon?"

Another shrug. "He was traveling under a phony passport. The guess at the time was he must have been trying to get himself out of Germany."

I rose and thanked Bertie for the apple and the information, then withdrew to my desk to type up our conversation as notes.

"Eddie?" Bertie called. "Whatever this is, be careful. Sir John has many friends. I doubt any of them are friends of yours."

"Here now, are we burning the midnight oil?"

Cathryn could do more with a raised eyebrow than Leslie Howard in three hours of emotive simpering. That brow, raised barely a fraction, telegraphed surprise, annoyance, nostalgia, anger, and apprehension.

"Eddie. How did you get past the sentry?"

"Press pass, my sweet. Have you forgotten what it is I do for a living?"

"Ah, as it happens I do remember. You pester people. And here you are a-pestering."

"So, these are the new digs?" The ante-office was very much her: organized clutter about her desk; a dainty vase containing a half-withered bloom; several little reproductions of Arles on the wall behind her.

"Ah, still fancy your van Gogh, I see," I said, perusing the reproductions.

"I don't know what worries me more," she replied. "That you might be here on business . . . or not."

"I can't say I care for the defensive frame of mind government work has given you, love."

The door to the inner office swung open. He was a middle-aged man, waspish, not too bad looking in a chinless, thinning-hair sort of way, just pulling on his coat. "I'm off, Cathryn. There's no need for you—" He saw me and froze. "Oh! Pardon. I wasn't aware you had a visitor."

"No visitor, Mr. Berwyck. This is my—"

"Eddie Owen, Mr. Berwyck," I said, shoving my hand into his and pumping like a fiend.

"Owen?" He looked to Cathryn.

"That's me," I said, now taking his hand in both of mine and continuing to pump. "That's me, the old ball-and-chain."

"Sorry?"

"I'm Mr. Owen. The husband."

"Ex-husband," Cathryn said.

"Husband, ex-husband, a rose by any other name, eh, Berwyck?"

He managed to extricate his hand, but there was nothing to do about his comprehensive state of puzzlement. "Yes, well . . ."

"Just here making Christmas greetings, Berwyck old man," I said. "Didn't mean to disrupt operations. Carry on, don't mind me."

"Oh, no, fine," he said. "We're closing up shop for the evening, anyway. Ex-husband, was it?"

"In a manner of speaking," I said.

"In a civil-law manner of speaking," Cathryn said.

"Yes, well . . ." He produced a polite smile, still unsure if he'd come into a situation where he'd rather not be. "Yes, well, as I say, I'm off. Cathryn, there's no reason for you to stay, nothing that won't wait until tomorrow. Mr. Owen, it was nice meeting you." He tendered his hand reluctantly, but this time I let him off with a gentlemanly shake.

"The pleasure's been all mine, Mr. Berwyck. Happy holiday, safe home, cheery-bye!"

He was still looking over his shoulder toward me as I hung in the office doorway, waving ta-ta to him as he passed down the corridor.

"You can be incredibly mean," Cathryn said.

"I thought I was rather charming."

"That's when you're meanest."

"I noticed he doesn't wear a wedding ring."

"Neither did you."

"Anything I should know about? A little late-night dictation, perhaps? Chasing you round the desk and all that?"

"Mr. Berwyck is—and has always been—a perfect gentleman. Besides, I believe he still lives home with his mum."

"Oh," I said. We both smiled.

But her smile became guarded. "Why *are* you here, Eddie? I hope it is not in some grand romantic gesture on the eve of the holidays."

"Eddie Owen? Grand romantic gestures? Hardly."

I looked for signs of disappointment in her eyes but saw none.

"Business, I'm afraid," I told her. "Purely professional."

She began closing her desk drawers with a protective firmness. "No."

"You haven't even let me—"

"No! Mr. Berwyck is a perfectly nice man. He's been damnably decent to me, and I've no reason to suspect him of any of the kinds of things you're always poking about—"

"Calm, love, calm. I'm not here about Mr. Berwyck. I'm certain he's a perfect angel. Even on first meeting, my heart filled at the sight of him—"

"Stop."

"I'm not even here about any misdoings at your lovely little ministry. *Are* there any misdoings I should know about?"

"Other than that the sentries seem terribly undiscriminating about whom they let in . . ." Her desk was now neat and tidy, her coat and purse on her desk waiting to be donned.

"All right, then," I conceded. "As I recall, at our last meeting you mentioned, in passing, between the divorce decree and the forever-farewell, your employment here. By the way, did I mention that this is very nice? Your cubby? Delightful. Enjoying your job, are you?"

She remained stone-faced.

"You deal with land leases for the military. You must have some sort of background file on available lands, lands for purchase, all that sort of thing. I want to check on some land that was acquired up in the Orkneys a few years ago. I'm sure you must have some information on it."

"Possibly. Probably. But all that information is confidential."

"As well it should be, and no one ever need know where I got it."

She was uncommitted, but curious. "What is it you want to know?"

"This was on Orkney Mainland. Since that's where Scapa Flow is, I'm sure that one or another of the military agencies would have vetted any significant land acquisition on the island."

"Land acquired by who?"

"Sir John Duff."

She sat expressionless for a full count of five before she laughed. "You're after Sir John—"

"I'm merely trying to find out about a land purchase."

She shook her head, still smiling. "First, you want me to violate this ministry's confidentiality, and secondly, you want to pillory Sir John Duff. If you can manage to run over Winston Churchill's favorite dog on your way home, you'll have had a full day. What is it you think Sir John has done?"

"I don't know that he's done anything. That's what I'm trying to find out."

"You're after some fair-sized game, Eddie." She bowed her head contemplatively. "Maybe I *have* forgotten what it is you do for a living." Facing me again, her eyes hard and fixed: "Mr. Berwyck *is* a nice man."

"I'm sure he is."

"I would not take it kindly if he were somehow dragged into your newspaper—"

I put a hand on my heart. "No reason that he should be."

It was still another minute before she sighed, as if disappointed in herself, then drew some keys from her desk and bade me follow her down the corridor. "We keep those records in the vault," she explained.

I followed her first down one hallway, then another until we reached a cul-de-sac terminated by a large, metal door. When she said "vault" I had pictured one of those massive bank vault doors of black-painted steel. This was merely a heavy metal door painted the same lifeless beige as the corridor, and opened with one of the keys on her ring. She reached inside and flicked on a light. I saw a cramped compartment stocked with rows of locked file cabinets, and metal shelves laden with tied-shut portfolios and tall ledgers bound in green baize. I made to follow her inside but she turned and stopped me with a fingertip firmly applied to the tip of my nose.

"You stay out here," she declared. She reached inside the vault and dragged out a wooden chair, which she placed outside the door by the corridor wall. Like a reprimanding schoolteacher she pointed me into the chair, then went inside. I heard her rattling about, unlocking file drawers, shuffling through folders. I lit a cigarette. "When was this?" she called out.

"Sometime around the beginning of the war, I should think."

"Hm. Are you sure about the date?"

"No."

"Is that a cigarette I smell?"

I noticed the NO SMOKING sign near the door and hastily stubbed the fag out on the floor. "Someone must have passed by," I said.

I heard another hm. "There is an inquiry here from Sir John's offices about the possibility of acquiring property on Orkney Mainland, but it's dated December 1940."

"That must be it."

"And yes, there was a query raised by the Defense Ministry. There was some question about letting Sir John set up shop so near a major RN anchorage." She leaned her head out. "I thought Sir John did a lot of work for the military."

"He does. It's a little complicated."

She retreated back into her hole and I heard her continue to leaf

through her papers. "Somebody vouched for him, though. Oh, *Eddie* . . ."
Again she put her head out. This time the raised eyebrow conveyed the
reproving pity one might display toward someone who had volunteered
they were willingly about to leap into the gaping maw of a sizzling vol-
cano.

"Let me guess," I said. "The Duke of Windsor?"

"You knew?"

"Informed guess."

"The Duke of Windsor, Eddie? Sir John? You don't need to run over
the PM's dog. You've pretty well gone the limit." I thought I detected a
certain grudging admiration on her face, but that may have been a
Christmas wish on my part.

"So Windsor writes to the military joes, tells them Sir Johnnie is all
right in his book, and that's the end of it."

"Not quite," she said, and there was more shuffling. "There's another
query from the Navy that following July. It seems Sir John never got
round to building whatever it was he had originally told them he was going to build there. The Navy wanted to know what was going on. It looks
like they were still concerned about the security reliability of Sir John.
Let's see, ah, this must be the response. A letter here going on about the
unanticipated difficulty in building and maintaining some sort of manufacturing plant on Orkney. You would think that would've occurred to
them beforehand."

"One would think."

"And then there's some polite language that essentially tells them to
leave Sir John alone."

"Also from Windsor?"

"No. Odd. Again it's somebody vouching for Sir John, but . . ."

"But?"

"It's from the Foreign Office. It's a security issue; I would've expected
it to be addressed by one of the military or intelligence offices. I can't
imagine what interest the FO would have in this. Eddie, whatever are you
getting yourself into?"

"I'm not quite sure I know."

I could see it in her face, the old instinct to warn me off, to behave
myself, to do anything to make my life a little safer and saner. But by this
time she knew better. She went back into the vault to put things away,
back safely under lock and key.

"Cathryn?"

"Yes?"

"When we were together . . . What did you think of what I do? I
mean, you know: the job?"

Her movements ceased for a moment as she paused to think. "I assumed it was like this. You flitting here, flitting there, prying round—"

"No, no. You misunderstand. What did you think *about* my job?"

"You mean my opinion?"

"Aye."

I heard a file drawer close, the key turn in the lock, then the vault compartment went dark and Cathryn was in the corridor, pushing the heavy door closed and locking it. "What does it matter now?"

"I'm curious."

"All right, then. Sometimes I thought you were no better than one of those sex criminals who go peeping through people's bedroom curtains. Most times I thought you were something akin to a ghoul."

"Oh, well, I suppose that's a step up from bedroom peeper."

"Do you remember when you were gadding about in Mexico, back in the twenties?"

"Covering the Civil War."

"On your way home your route took you through America. You stopped at some small speck of a place, in Texas, I think it was. They had lynched a Negro the day before. Men in white hoods, they'd beaten the boy and hung him by the road leading into town. No one knew why, at least no one would say. You wrote about that. Not a news item, really. I suppose you'd call it more of an essay. I still remember the headline: *Rule of Fear in the Land of the Free*."

"The headline wasn't mine. A little much, I thought."

"I was very proud of you then, Eddie. There were other times as well. Even now. I still read everything you write."

I began to open my mouth but she seemed to know—or at least fear—what might come. She shook her head. "It was never what I thought about you and your job, Eddie. You could have been off to uncover the Great Truth of All Things. But I would have been home, just as lonely."

I don't know how many times I walked the span of Westminster Bridge before I finally stopped mid-river and lit a cigarette. London was lost out there in the night. Either end of the bridge disappeared into darkness. Below where I was leaning against the balustrade, I could hear the water lapping at the columns of the supporting arcade. I thought it odd how only now, in the middle of the second Great War, was it quiet enough for me to hear those licks of water. In peacetime, the traffic would have been heavy enough that I'd never hear a drowning man cry out for help.

Bedroom peeper. Ghoul.

It was cold out there on the bridge. I flicked my cigarette away. The red tip dwindled until it was swallowed by the blackness. Even way up there on the bridge I could hear the quick little hiss of the cigarette's dying.

Himself and his missus lived in a neighborhood of tidy little row houses out in Notting Hill; all small, white-trimmed, a square of garden in front, a slightly larger square in back for a yard, both winter-withered and flattened in the miserably cold rain that had been pouring down all day.

"I should sack our damn meteorologist, don't you think?" he said as he admitted me. "Light snow was the prediction. Snow for Christmas, he said. By Christmas we'll be needing a boat, not a sleigh."

The rooms were as neatly kept as the outside of the house, except for a corner of the parlor where a small paper-strewn desk sat. He was alone.

"The Missus is off with her mum," Himself explained. "Christmas tidings and all that."

"The old dame is still alive?"

"Just to spite me. So, we're bachelors for the night, eh?"

He cracked a half-dozen eggs and we supped at the kitchen table, the conversation remaining innocuous throughout; a few tales from the office, a nostalgic anecdote or two.

"I'll tend to the washing up," he said, "and you see to a fire, eh?"

I poked round the parlor fireplace until I got a comfortable blaze going, then settled into one of the well-worn chairs, watching him through the doorway as he puttered over the kitchen sink. He was still the same looming figure he was at the office: bulky and thick-waisted, the large head with those baleful eyes focusing on one over the top of his spectacles. Yet, bent over a sink of suds, clad in a tattered cardigan I'm sure his wife would have gladly consigned to the church jumble sale, he seemed almost pitiable. It was an air enhanced by a spate of coughing that doubled him over.

"All right in there?" I called, starting to climb out of my chair.

He waved me back down. "Just swallowed wrong. Will it be coffee or tea?"

"Let's be civilized. Tea."

As he set the pot on, he rummaged in the cupboard and held out a bottle of Black & White. "Or . . . ?"

I shook my head no.

"Taken the pledge, have we, my son?"

"I'm just off it for a bit. I've no intent to make a passion of it, though."

He smiled and turned to put the bottle back on the shelf. He hesitated a moment, studied the bottle, then I saw his shoulders rise and fall in a sigh and he put the bottle away. He brought the tea out on a tray with a plate of biscuits.

"The missus bakes those herself. Hope your teeth are in good shape, my son. Personally, I use them to knock the pigeons off the eaves. Ah, now," he said, settling in his chair alongside me in front of the fire, "isn't this all nice and snug?"

Actually, compared to my bare little flat, it was quite nice.

"You've been quite the foxhound of late. You were a regular dervish yesterday, first to old Danny Brooks, and Daphne St. Claire, and then Bertie Welles. By Christ, you won't work that hard when I want you to!" He smiled without mirth. "What is it about Sir John Duff that so intrigues you, my son?"

I couldn't help but show my surprise, but even before I could ask how he knew, he was already giving me an admonishing look. Of course he knew; he was The Boss Himself.

"Or perhaps you are not at liberty to say?"

"You wouldn't be warning me off, would you?"

He chuckled. "If I could warn my lads off of big game so easily, they wouldn't be my lads. In fact, it's been good to see you on the hunt again. It's been a while since I've seen you do it . . . as if you mean it." His lips pursed thoughtfully. He was always a man who knew his own mind; I could not recall ever seeing him hesitate to act once he saw a course of action. "You know I've never been one to meddle in the personals of my people," he said finally.

"You say this to me over tea in front of your fire?"

He chuckled. "Yes, well. I suppose longevity breeds a certain . . ." He frowned, looking for the word.

"Intimacy?"

He winced. "Let's say familiarity. Jesus, my son, I know you longer than the missus. I've been worried."

"About me? How thoughtful. You *are* a love, love."

"Sip your tea and shut up, thank you." He set his cup down on the side table, looking away from me, unnecessarily busying himself with the doily on the table. He mumbled something.

"Eh?"

"I said," and he turned to me, "perhaps it's not my place. You've been back on your game all nice and regular the last day or so. Perhaps you've turned the corner. Or perhaps it's just . . . I'm worried it'll pass and you'll be back where you were."

"I think it's just this business with Cathryn—"

"We all come into this profession with the passion of new priests. All of us. Even the ones more interested in their byline than a story, the dirt-diggers who work for the tabloids trying to find some MP in *flagrante delicto*—at some level we all believe we've joined the same priesthood. We're the elite that's privy to The Truth with capital T's. That's quite exciting. My God, what we put on paper can change the world!"

"Impassioning."

"I'd run my pencil through prose that purple, but yes. Then some years go by and we come to that unhappy moment when we realize it's not the gospel we're delivering. We work ungodly hours, we humiliate ourselves to court contacts, we sacrifice. Wives, families." His eyes, in a very deliberate manner, settled on my artificial leg. "Sometimes more. This is what we give to bring The Truth to our loyal readers. And what do our loyal readers do with it? The men'd rather read the rugger scores, the ladies Daphne St. Claire. Both are more interested in some Dr. Crippen sex criminal than in poor conditions for the miners in South Wales.

"Still, we keep on. We cultivate this very cynical, very world-weary air because, after all, we are the ones in the know. We know the world in a way all the little blissfully, conscientiously ignorant misters and missuses out there"—he nodded at the rain-splattered window—"can't see. But you still come to the day when you wonder: Why did you willingly give up so much? To what end?" He reached for a cigarette box on the side table and offered me one.

"Should you be doing that?" I asked. "Won't the missus smell it when she comes home?"

"I'll tell her it was yours. 'That bloody Scots bastard filling our home with his filthy soot!' She'll have your liver on a plate." A deep draught set him coughing. "Some keep on simply for the pay," he continued. "One gets used to eating and having a dry, warm place to live. Hard to argue with that. Some keep on because it's all they know. But they're all like priests; the passion dies, they keep themselves going through the motions by nipping at the sacramental wine." His eyes turned to the flames with a softness in them I'd never seen. "I would tell anyone in that situation . . . *anyone* . . . that it's time to leave the Church. Better to start all over than go on like that. You've not a lot of time; that's no way to waste it." He took a brightening breath. "Then there's those who pass through it. They find religion again. Somehow."

"All this, all what you're saying . . . Did you go through it?"

"Anyone in this work who says no is a liar. Or deranged."

"You passed through it."

He shrugged modestly.

"How did you find God again?"

He turned to me and he was his old self just then, the condescending, all-knowing smile. "You accommodate, my son. The front-page sex crime pays for the page-three story on some MP's fiscal malfeasance."

"Which our loyal readers skip over on their way to the sports scores or Daphne's latest tale of what fat grande dame wore what at some high tea. Why bother, then? *They* don't care, so why bother?"

"*They* don't have to care, you silly ass." He took a sip of his tea and gave me that same smile. "Only I do."

CHAPTER NINE
EARTH-BORN MEN

HARRY YAWNED HIMSELF AWAKE, TRYING TO make himself comfortable amid the crates he'd formed into a little cubby. He took the cigarette Ricks was holding out to him, then looked out the waist window of the C-87. Below, the Mediterranean was a rippling gold lamé in the afternoon sun. "Where are we?" he asked.

"We turned off at Bizerte about ten minutes ago. We should see Sicily in about twenty minutes, be on the ground ten, fifteen minutes after that." Ricks held out a light for Harry. "I'm going to get on the horn and set things up for us."

Ahead, almost lost in the glare on the water, Harry could make out the sparkles of wakes turning in the sun, each curl of glitter topped by the black oblong of a ship. The C-87 began to ease down and the stocky forms of a dozen Liberty ships became clear. Patrolling round them, like herding dogs, were three escorting corvettes. The C-87 passed over the convoy low enough for Harry to see the upturned faces of the men on the decks, their hands fluttering in hullos.

When Ricks returned, he found Harry staring at a small square of paper: the ID photograph of Armando Grassi.

"Where'd you get that?"

Harry nodded forward to where Woody Kneece was ensconced in the Perspex nose of the aeroplane. "When he first came to see me," Harry said and slipped the photo into his pocket. "He must've forgotten it."

"Like hell."

A C-87 is a cargo conversion of the four-engined B-24 Liberator bomber. Having been designed to carry bombs rather than passengers, it lacked even the elementary comforts Doheeny's ship had offered, and with its narrow fuselage and lower silhouette, there was little room to move about, a fact complicated by the ship's being packed with medical supplies.

Ricks brooded over the stacks of crates and their attention-getting red crosses. "Something must be cooking for them to be in such a rush for this stuff they can't wait for the regular convoys. Man, I hope we're not walking into something."

Thirteen hours in the cramped cargo plane had left Harry Voss, Peter Ricks, and Woody Kneece logy and stiff, particularly the young captain. He'd spent most of the trip in the C-87's claustrophobic nose compartment, where he could take in the horizon-to-horizon vista of such enthralling sights as Gibraltar, the swaying palms of the African coast, the dull, arid bluffs of the Atlas Mountains behind. "Oh, *man*, somebody get me some binoculars! I think I can see guys on camels down there! *Camels!*"

They stumbled arthritically out the fuselage hatch at Palermo. Before the propellers stopped windmilling, a fuel lorry lurched up to the aircraft, and a "deuce-and-a-half"—two-and-a-half-ton cargo lorry—had backed up to the loading hatch.

"C'mon c'mon c'mon!" barked the sergeant in charge of the ground crew, clapping his hands, spurring the chain of men passing cargo from the ship to the lorry bed. "I got three more o' these pregnant cows comin' need this slot! This crate's gotta be off the ground ten minutes ago. Let's *go!*"

The entire airfield was similarly energized, C-47's and 46's from North Africa, and C-87's from England constantly clanging down onto the metal runway matting, deuce-and-a-halfs rumbling up, rumbling off. Beyond the swarm of men busying themselves with Harry's particular ship, a rangy-looking sergeant atop the hood of a jeep waved at them with a clipboard.

"Major Voss and party? You better climb in, sir, there's not a lot of time. You must be Lieutenant Ricks, got a radio message for you, sir, got to sign for it."

While Ricks signed the chit and quickly scanned the message, Kneece turned to Harry with a mockingly castigating eye. "This is *your* party now?"

Harry pointed to Ricks. "He made all the calls."

"Always play your highest card," Ricks explained as they climbed in the jeep.

"Say, Sarge, where's your mess hall?" Woody Kneece asked. "Factually, we've been on that plane a loooong time, and I wouldn't mind—"

"No time, sir, sorry, don't even know you got time to piss, got you gentlemen on a transport pulling out with a Naples convoy in two hours," the sergeant rattled on efficiently. The jeep smoothly navigated the bustle of the aerodrome. "Found you a platoon of replacement tanks heading to the same sector, piggyback your way practically all the way you got to go, make sure you tell 'em you're JAG priority 'cause that's the only thing gettin' you outta here so fast."

Harry frowned at Ricks while the grinning CIC captain silently mouthed, " 'JAG priority'?" Ricks looked away, ignoring them.

In minutes the speeding jeep was vaulting its way down a frighteningly narrow road snaking out of the Monte Pellegrino hills. Harry had only a glimpse of Palermo's red tile rooftops shooting up toward them, and the busy harbor beyond, before they were winding through the tight, cobbled streets of the city. Palermo was a jumble of buildings clinging to the hillsides that led down to the sea. Some of the streets were no more than alleys, choked still more by a stuttering flow of bodies—most in American uniform—and military vehicles. There was a brief burst of daylight as they broke through into the Piazza della Vittoria, roared past the Royal Palace where Patton had made his headquarters when Palermo had fallen, and then back into the shadows of the labyrinth. The claustrophobic vias fell away at the waterfront, and before them lay a panoramic view of the harbor, filled with milling naval vessels, all tinged with the crimson of the lowering sun.

The quay was thronged with men, vehicles, supplies. MP's stood atop crates, their faces red from constant use of their traffic whistles, and beach-masters blared instructions over Tannoy speakers to the LST's and smaller craft filing up to the quay for loading.

"What the hell is going on?" Ricks asked the sergeant as the jeep pulled to a stop. "This isn't reinforcing. This is a buildup."

The sergeant shrugged. "You know how it is, Lieutenant, there's all kindsa poop floatin' around, we're gonna hit the boot up north and take Rome from the sea, we're gonna land in southern France. Who knows? This is as far as I go, sirs—you're lookin' for a tank platoon under a Sergeant Angstrom. Even in all that mess a tank platoon can't be too hard to find."

Harry and Kneece climbed out but Ricks slid into the seat next to the sergeant. "You two go ahead. I'll meet up with you. Sergeant, where's the Quartermaster's?"

As the sergeant whipped the jeep into a turn, Harry called after Ricks: "What do you think you're doing?" Harry wasn't quite sure he correctly heard what the lieutenant shouted back to him. He turned to Woody Kneece.

Kneece looked equally puzzled. "It sounded like he said something about 'proper attire.' "

As the sergeant had predicted, it was not hard to find the platoon of Sherman tanks, like a string of rocks poking above foaming rapids. The four Shermans were parked in a line, facing rearward toward the bay. A seaman in Navy denims used signal flags to guide an LCT into the quay. The front ramp of the LCT clanged down onto the centuries-old stones, the craft's diesels revved, the propellers stirred foam at the stern to hold the vessel in place.

Harry looked unhappily at the bobbing landing craft. "I thought that sergeant said we were going on a *ship*," he moaned. "Isn't that more of a *boat?*"

"Factually, I think he used the word 'transport.' "

"Which is double-talk for *little* boat."

A Landing Craft Tank is a hundred-foot-long version of the smaller Higgins boats used to carry troops to beach landings. A drawbridgelike ramp at the front led into an open-topped cargo well. Aft, where the helm for a Higgins would be, sat a small superstructure housing the engine compartment and topped by a cramped bridge.

Harry went up to the nearest Sherman and called up to the sergeant standing in the commander's hatch. "Are you Sergeant Angstrom?"

The tank commander pointed to another sergeant conferring with the signaling seaman.

Just then, Angstrom twirled his gloved finger in a "wind-'em-up" signal, and the four 460 BHP Chrysler engines coughed and backfired noxious blue clouds until they settled into a dull roar. The seaman and Angstrom began to help guide each Sherman as their clanking steel treads carried them rearward down the loading ramp into the LCT's cargo well. As the last tank eased its way into the landing craft, the seaman noticed Harry and Kneece standing anxiously nearby.

"If you sirs are goin' aboard, now's the time."

"We're waiting for somebody," Harry said.

"Sir, you can wait for 'im here, or you can wait for 'im in Naples, but this cigar box is leavin' in one minute."

" 'Into the valley of Death rode the six hundred,' " he heard Kneece recite as the captain followed him down the ramp. "Since the lootenant made all the arrangements I guess you don't have any idea what we're supposed to do when we get to the other side?"

"Not a damned clue," Harry muttered, glumly watching the seaman signal to the LCT's bridge to start the ramp winch. The ramp had just begun to rise from the quay when the seaman signaled for a halt and a wheezing, red-faced Peter Ricks, laden down with two packed seabags, several webbed belts tossed over one shoulder, two M1 rifles slung on his other, and three helmets hanging by their chin straps from one forearm, came skidding down the ramp.

"You cut that a little close, Lootenant," Woody Kneece commented.

"Captain, Major, with all due respect—get naked."

"Right here?" Harry asked.

"Why not?" Kneece cooed, affecting the face of a mooning lover. "The music is soft, the sunset romantic, the sea air sweet . . ."

Peter Ricks emptied the seabags. "I couldn't get full outfits, but this should do. I had to guess at sizes." He handed out combat fatigue trousers, shirts, boots and leggings, windcheaters such as the tankers favored, and the little woolen beanies worn inside helmets. "Is this familiar to you?"

Kneece took the rifle, snapped to attention, held the weapon at inspection arms, and slickly thumbed the breech open. "The Garand M1 rifle is a gas-operated, semiautomatic—"

"Thank you, Captain," Ricks cut him off as he handed him a webbed belt carrying canteen, bayonet, first-aid pouch, and ten magazines for the rifle. "You were moaning about being hungry." From the seabag he tossed him a boxed K ration. "There's a couple more in here, but make them last. We don't know when we'll get a chance to stock up again." He handed another belt to Harry; this one held a holster with .45 automatic and spare pistol magazines. "I had a feeling you wouldn't want a weapon, but where we're going I'd be a lot happier if you had something. You know how to use this?"

"Sure," Harry said. Ricks looked doubtful when Harry couldn't even figure out how to adjust the webbed belt.

Ricks turned to Angstrom, who was instructing the tank crewmen to stretch shelter halves between the parked tanks. "Hey, Sarge! You Angstrom? This your platoon?"

Angstrom was what the Americans refer to as a fireplug: short and sturdy. He was nearly thirty, with a full, light mustache and serious blue eyes so light they seemed to glow in the darkening shadows of the cargo well. There was a seasoning to him the other tankers didn't have. The others—their commanders included—were younger, chattering and bouncing about like children on a first campout. But Angstrom moved up and down the rank of Shermans, quietly issuing his orders, looking to be sure that nothing was left undone or overlooked.

Ricks introduced himself, Harry, and Kneece, then offered the sergeant a cigarette to show that the formalities could be set in abeyance for the moment. "What're your orders?"

"We're replacement tanks, supposed to fill in a tank company up around someplace called Minga-something."

"Mignano."

"Yessir, that's it. I got the extra rocker"—a reference to his five stripes as tech sergeant—"so I'm supposed to baby-sit 'em 'til we get there, and then they'll split us up."

"That's where I was until this bought me a vacation." Ricks pointed to his bandaged eye. "We're heading up to the same sector. Mind if we hitch a ride with you once we land?"

"You're more than welcome, Lieutenant." Angstrom saw the apprehension in Ricks's eyes as the lieutenant watched several of the youngsters chase each other round one of the tanks. Angstrom pulled off his tanker's football-style helmet and rubbed fretfully at his matted hair. "Yeah, I know; they're kinda green. They all just come over a coupla weeks ago."

"How about you?"

"Got my arse kicked at Kasserine, but this is my first time back in the show since I been out of the hospital."

"Well, I don't want to be the one to tell you your business—"

"Sir, the first time one of those kraut 75's went whizzing by my head at Kasserine, I learned nothing was like they taught us at Fort Riley. If you been up to the line and got some gems of wisdom to share, sir, I'm happy as hell to hear 'em."

"You'll probably get this all again from the skipper. Put a man on each tank's turret .50-caliber as an AA watch. Soon as the sun goes down, nobody smokes unless they're under cover. And except for the man on watch, keep your crews out of the tanks until we're ready to land. If something happens to this tub, those guys'd have a hell of a time getting out."

As Angstrom hurried off to give the necessary orders, Harry asked Ricks, "Are you just being careful or can it really get that—"

"Bad? You know Bari? Port town on the east coast of Italy. Three weeks ago, a kraut air raid hit the harbor. They put seventeen merchant ships on the bottom."

The convoy—ten LST's, four LCT's, escorted by two Navy destroyers—formed up in an assembly area off Cape Gallo just after sunset, and started across the Tyrrhenian at about twelve knots, which would put them in Naples late the following afternoon or early evening. The tankers gathered atop the hunch-shouldered hulls of their Shermans to watch the last bloody streaks of light drain from the evening sky.

A pale Harry staggered out of the LCT's small, foul-smelling head. Ricks took him by the arm and led him to a seat on the afterdeck. The shallow draft of the vessel meant it dipped and listed with the slightest wave, and each motion threatened to send Harry back to the loo.

"You should've had some crackers," the lieutenant told him. "Would've settled your stomach."

The thought of anything edible made Harry clutch his stomach and moan. "Where's Junior?"

Ricks chuckled. "He went up to see if they'd let him on the bridge. He thinks this boat trip is a bang and a half. Maybe it reminds him of his yachting days." At Harry's puzzlement, Ricks fluttered a wireless message he'd received at Palermo. "You wanted me to ask about him. This was forwarded from London."

"And?"

"Daddy's got dough. A lot of dough. One of the richest families in South Carolina. Daddy's got a lot of political pull, too, very big in the state political machine. Daddy greased Sonny's way to those captain's bars and also his assignment to CIC in Washington instead of a combat tour. He ever tell you anything about his civilian police experience?"

"I think he referred to himself once as a plain old country cop."

"Our Woody did two years with the South Carolina State Constabulary before he joined the service. That might have a nice rustic sound to it, but it's what other states refer to as the state police. And he earned himself a pretty hot reputation in those two years. Your friend likes to play his game close. Are you going to call him out on any of this?"

"Not unless I have to. We're here on his ticket. You like to lead with your high card. I like to save it." Harry looked up at the star-speckled sky. "I wish I could enjoy this the way Woody is. It's a beautiful night."

One of the Coast Guard deckhands stopped to pick up their seabags and overheard Harry's remark. He grunted. "Pardon me, sir, but it rained every fuckin' night 'til tonight, and I wisht it would fuckin' rain this fuckin' night!"

After the grousing crewman disappeared into the aft superstructure, Harry turned to Ricks. "What do you think is his problem?"

"His problem is they don't drop bombs when it rains," Ricks replied.

Several of the tank crews were huddled under one of the shelter halves. They giggled, they joked, there was the rustle of boxed rations being opened, the clatter of canned C rations. Harry heard the hiss of a portable stove, smelled freshly brewed coffee. They invited Ricks over, queried him about life on the line.

"Hey, Major!" Angstrom called out on seeing him. The sergeant was atop the lead tank, pulling the wireless whip antenna over. "Want to give me a hand here?" Still a little queasy, Harry climbed up on the bogie wheels and pulled himself onto the rear deck of the tank. "Just hold this thing down for me," Angstrom asked.

In the feeble moonlight Harry noticed the words stenciled in white paint across the back of the Sherman's turret: Irma's Boys. "Who's Irma?"

"My wife." Angstrom reached into the commander's hatch and pulled out several small objects hanging from ribbons. "My kids made these for me in school. My wife sent them to me for Christmas. You can't see it, it's too dark, but they each put their name on the back: Donny, he's the oldest, nine, he did the tree, and then the twins—that's Tim, and this one's from Stevie." He held them up for Harry to see in the moonlight. They were wooden cutouts, one shaped like a Christmas tree, the other two like Christmas ornaments. Angstrom began to tie the ribbons to the top of the antenna. "I thought, you know, what the hell, maybe for luck. You can let that go now."

The antenna sprang back to its upright position; the three little ornaments rattled against each other in the breeze.

"How much you want to bet some hard-ass officer makes me take 'em off?"

Harry clapped a hand on the sergeant's shoulder. "He's going to have to outrank a major."

Angstrom brewed some coffee over a portable stove under the shelter half behind Irma's Boys. He and Harry spent the evening exchanging stories about their families, displaying wallet photographs by the light of Angstrom's Zippo lighter. It was enough to take Harry's mind off the movement of the LCT and as the night wore on he grew drowsy. Angstrom drew two sleeping bags from inside his tank and offered one to Harry. They stretched them out on the deck of the cargo well, and after a few last words about home both drifted off to sleep.

The swaying on the LCT that had sickened him now rocked Harry to sleep. His body so craved the rest that even the jarring peal of the LCT's general quarters alarm was slow to rouse him.

"C'mon, Major, up!" Angstrom shook him, none too gently.

"Major, are you in here?" Now Ricks's head was poking under the shelter half, and Harry felt the lieutenant grabbing at him.

"What the hell's—"

"General quarters!" a voice blared over the Tannoy system. "General quarters! All hands to battle stations! Destroyer radar picket has incoming bogeys, course three-four-zero, range twenty-five miles."

"Out of the northwest," Ricks told Harry. "They'll be krauts. We've got about five minutes." He jammed a helmet on Harry's head and pulled him out into the cargo well between the Shermans and the hull.

Angstrom scrambled onto his lead tank, replacing the antiaircraft gunner standing watch. "Look alive, people!" he called to the other gunners. Each pulled back the heavy bolts on their .50-caliber guns to chamber the first round, then grabbed the heavy guns by their twin grips, swinging them skyward.

"Radar picket reports friendlies on intercept course. Bogey targets range fifteen miles."

"How're you doing, Major?"

Harry found Kneece huddling behind him. "I wish I was somewhere else right now," Harry replied.

"You and me both, brother," came an unknown voice out of the dark.

"You're the veteran," Woody Kneece said to Ricks. "What do we do?"

Ricks shook his head; there was nothing to do.

"Friendlies report interception on bandit formation, altitude six thousand, range ten miles."

Bulky in his helmet and life jacket, an LCT crewman came squeezing by, life belts draped over his arm. "Major, you got a belt? Here, just tie it on like this. Who else doesn't have a belt? Hey, you, meathead! Ditch the cigarette! Anybody still think we're havin' a gorgeous fuckin' evening?"

Through the vibrating deck plates Harry sensed a change in the pitch of the LCT's engine, felt the craft pick up speed, crashing harder through the waves. Over the sound of the throbbing engine, GQ gongs and Klaxons went off on the other convoy vessels.

Ricks climbed up on the rear deck of Angstrom's Sherman. "Don't wait until you see them," he advised. "The minute you see those destroyers putting up fire, let go!"

"Let go at *what?*" the nervous sergeant asked.

"Just let *go!* Put as much steel in their way as you can."

"Range five miles. Bandits now at three thousand feet."

"Out there at ten o'clock!" a spotter on the bridge called out. Ricks pointed up into the night sky to their left. Harry climbed up on the Sherman next to him and followed the lieutenant's directing finger.

The night sky was patched with luminous, fluffy clouds, limned in moonlight. Flickers of light danced across the sky, lost speed, then arced slowly earthward, dying out before reaching the black sea.

"Tracers," Ricks explained. "They're duking it out with our fighters."

The far clouds lit up briefly—a bright orange flash that dwindled into a smoldering fireball tumbling toward the water. A cheer went up from the bridge crew.

"Let's hope it was one of *theirs,*" Ricks said quietly.

"Maybe they'll get them all?" Harry asked.

Ricks smiled sadly. "Some'll get through. Some always do."

The LCT's engine changed pitch again; the ship seemed to veer violently first to one side, then the other.

"He's taking evasive action." Ricks nodded at the Tannoy speaker, expecting an announcement.

"Heads up on deck! Bandits coming in!"

Harry followed Ricks as he leapt back into the darkness of the cargo well. They rejoined Kneece against the side of the well. From beyond the gunwales Harry saw gun flashes, then tracers spraying up into the sky from the escort destroyers that had positioned themselves between the convoy and the incoming attackers. Neither the hull of the LCT nor the growl of the vessel's engine muted the chaos from the destroyers, an atonal symphony of pumping 40-mm cannon and clattering 20-mm guns. Then the antiaircraft guns on the LST's joined in: The blast of individual guns was drowned in a roar of fire. Flaring orange blossoms of flak burst so densely Harry couldn't imagine anything airborne surviving.

"Start putting it up, Sarge!" Ricks called up to Angstrom.

The four .50-calibers on the tanks began their own staccato chatter. It echoed deafeningly within the metal confines of the well.

Harry risked a glance upward. He saw nothing in the night above him other than the hail of tracer fire, could hear no engines above the din. But then, low at first, then knifing through all the other noise . . . a scream.

Not human. Not mechanical. Something alien. Something designed for the sole purpose of adding the element of terror to impending death.

"Stukas!" Ricks hissed it as if it were a profanity.

The approaching whistle stabbed Harry with a cold pain in his bowels and he lowered himself to the deck with the other men, hunching in, his arms going round his legs as he curled himself into a ball because the scream told him *I am hunting you . . . I am coming for you . . .*

The scream of the Stuka grew louder, and he could feel the movements of the LCT grow sharper, as if the man at the helm, in his evasion, was growing more desperate.

Then, another sound, a soft, almost gentle high-pitched whistle detaching itself from the howling scream of the dive-bomber.

Harry'd suffered enough bombing raids in London to know the sound of a falling bomb, yet he'd never felt a gut-wrenching fear like this. He'd borne out the London raids in some kind of shelter: a cellar, an Underground, *something.* But here, there was no cellar to climb down into, no place to run. The level bombers that had devastated London made it seem a random process, but the Stuka had picked his ship, had sighted him—*I am coming for you. . . .*

He looked up again. *If you're coming for me, I want to know.*

In the flashes of the .50-calibers he spotted the frantic face of one gunner, his expression a mixture of raw terror and rabid hate. Another gunner hammered at the jammed bolt of his weapon. Behind him, Kneece crouched, his face also turned to the sky, his mouth agape, his eyes hypnotized by the macabre beauty of the tracers floating through the dark. Then above, a ghost of an image, something barely separated from the night by the moon glowing against the ugly broken-winged silhouette descending on them, its fixed landing gear outstretched like talons.

Harry heard other bombs whistling down among the convoy ships, the crash of their explosions, the hiss of displaced sea.

But the most frightening moment, the most terrifying sound, was the small voice coming from the dark well—he never found out whose—that muttered a resigned "Uh-oh."

The roar of the detonation was deafening, so loud that Harry was sure the 1,100-pound bomb must have landed square in the cargo well. But then the ship dipped into a heavy starboard list, away from the blast, the deck canted so sharply that Harry and the others went skidding across the deck only moments before a cascade of seawater drenched down upon them.

Harry wasn't sure if he'd lost consciousness or was simply so dazed that the next moments passed without registering. He found himself suddenly aware that the firing had died out across the fleet, and the voice on the Tannoy was ordering the tankers to cease sending tracers up into an empty sky.

"You OK, Major?" Kneece helped him to his feet. The same seaman who had distributed the life belts squeezed by, stopping periodically to flash a lantern at the hull and deck, sheltering the light with hand and body. The seaman turned to the bridge and cupped a hand to his mouth: "This looks like it all came in over the top! She's still tight!"

Harry looked round for Ricks, and found him on one of the tank turrets helping the gunner with the jammed .50-caliber clear his weapon. Ricks clambered down to the deck. "Jesus, Major, you're soaked to the bone. Let's get you dried off before you catch your death of cold. *That* they don't give Purple Hearts for."

The placid, sapphire-blue bay set against the semicircle of white beach had once offered one of the most beautiful vistas in the Mediterranean. Buildings centuries old jostled with the new on a parade of bright stucco down the verdant inland hills to the bay, held back from the water by a tree-lined boulevard populated with touring cars and horse-drawn cabs.

There had been no pitched battle when Naples fell, but with Teutonic efficiency, the withdrawing Germans had seen to it that the Allies would be deprived of the city's militarily prized assets. At the rail yards and at every siding, whatever rolling stock that had not been removed had been torched, the warehouses and service buildings alongside razed, the tracks blown up. The port had suffered even more grievously: demolition teams had been unleashed on dockside storehouses and cranes; merchant ships had been scuttled at the docks and throughout the bay to block Allied deep-draft cargo vessels.

These obstacles the Americans had addressed with characteristic ingenuity. Bridging equipment had been used to extend the harbor's piers, running them hundreds of yards into the bay, even across the exposed decks of the ships the Germans had scuttled, their hulks serving as pilings, out to where the Liberty ships could safely moor. Nor had the Germans anticipated the tonnage of men and matériel that could be delivered directly onto the beach by LST's and their smaller brethren. These devisings would suffice until the never-resting engineer units rehabilitated the city's vitals.

Yet all this hivelike activity only degraded the city: Naples had the unattractive bustle of a factory town—the bay choked with drab naval vessels; the piers and beach aswarm with engineers and cargo handlers; stores piled on the beach; the unending, unstopping parade of deuce-and-a-halfs and other vehicles trundling down the shorefront promenade carrying men and munitions to the battlefront some fifty miles north.

Harry's LCT threaded its way past the ships riding at anchor in the bay and through the maze of scuttled merchantmen under the pall of a leaden sky. An unbroken blanket of dark clouds sent down a steady rain that sucked the color from even the once gemlike bay. The only break in the monochrome scheme was the crimson glow cast against the clouds by Vesuvius, a furnacelike radiation enhancing the factorylike grimness.

Harry sat with Ricks and Woody Kneece atop the turret of *Irma's Boys*, each shrouded in a rain slicker Ricks had produced from his seabags, along with musettes for each of them containing extra rations. The lieutenant had one other item of equipment to add to their kits. He reached inside his rain gear and came up with two packets of prophylactics. He handed one to Kneece.

"Am I going to really need this?" the captain asked. "Doesn't look like there's much fun left in this town."

Ricks tore open his own packet and rolled the pouch down over the muzzle of his M1. "Keeps the rain out." He then slowly began to peel the bandage from his injured eye.

"Should you be doing that?" Harry asked.

"This may not be the time," Ricks answered, "but it *is* the place."

The LCT skipper tooted his vessel's air horn in salute to another landing craft passing by, heading away from shore. The LCIL—Landing Craft Infantry, Large—was another expanded version of a Higgins boat. A tarpaulin had been stretched across the top of the LCIL's cargo well against the rain. Between the gap of gunwale and tarp, Harry saw an interior lit by Coleman lanterns. The deck of the cargo well was a solid carpet of men on stretchers, their myriad bandages bright in the lantern light. The LCIL was heading for a hospital ship anchored far out in the bay.

"You OK?" Ricks asked, noticing the shudder pass through Harry.

"Just a chill."

The ramp of the LCT went down. The three officers held tight as Angstrom's driver fired up the Chrysler engine and took the Sherman down into the mild surf, then up onto the oil-streaked sand.

A slicker-clad figure on the beach waved them to a stop, climbed up the bow of the tank, and introduced himself to Angstrom in a tired and cracked voice. "Corporal Schuyler. You Angstrom? I'm supposed to guide you and your tanks on up to the line."

In the gloomy afternoon light, with the rain dripping in a curtain off his helmet, there wasn't much to see of the corporal. Harry could pick out only red-rimmed eyes, a thick stubble, a sodden cigarette drooping unlit from his lips.

Angstrom introduced the three officers. "These gents are supposed to hook up with an infantry battalion up in the same sector."

"South of Route 6," Ricks explained. "Near Mignano."

"What unit?"

Ricks told him.

The corporal nodded. "I gotta stay with these tanks all the way to their dispersal point," Schuyler said, "but we'll run close by there. I'll point you in the right direction when we get close. We're gonna be headin' out right now, though, straight from here to the line, so I hope you guys got all your gear with you."

Military traffic monopolized the city's *vias*. MP's were placed at nearly every intersection to channel it smoothly to the roads winding northward out of the city. At each intersection clusters of signs erected by the American engineers pointed the way to every major military unit in operation between Naples and the Main Line of Resistance. Among the signs were placards warning GI's about the hazards of venereal disease, and asking them, *Is Your Tent Clean?*

When the column was stopped by MP's to let cross-traffic through, Italian civilians materialized out of the gray veil of rain and clustered about the vehicles. Women wore sodden tatty aprons over sodden tatty dresses, rain draining from sagging, wide-brimmed straw hats. Some were old, others merely looked old. They offered up baskets of apples and hazelnuts for sale.

At one stop Harry saw a woman looking even more worn out than the roadside marketeers offer a handful of change to one of the applemongers. The woman with the apple basket shouldered her away, and when the other woman persisted, kicked at her, the other vendors joining in with curses until the woman withdrew.

"They won't sell to their own," Ricks explained. "She can't pay what we can. And if those women don't want their families to starve, they need what we can pay."

They joined the endless train of vehicles on one of the roads running among the low hills of the coast. In the fading gray light Harry saw a strangely undisturbed countryside of farms and groves crowded round the endless hills. Ten steps away from either side of the road the war disappeared.

Ricks leaned close to him, speaking confidentially. "If anything pops, get clear of the tanks."

"If something happens, I was figuring on hiding behind one of these monsters," Harry said.

"Major, if anything pops, it's the tanks they'll be going for. There's a reason they call them Purple Heart boxes."

With a top speed of little more than twenty miles per hour, the four Shermans periodically had to pull aside to allow knots of vehicles behind them to pass. When the last of the daylight had gone, the vehicles in the column fearlessly turned on their headlamps.

"No choice," Schuyler told them. "These goddamn guinea roads twist around like spaghetti, you got all these trucks runnin' like there's no tomorrow . . ." He didn't need to complete the equation. "They kill the lights when they get up to the combat zone." He grinned. "Hell, sirs, it ain't like the krauts don't know we're here."

They passed through villages, clusters of stone and stucco-covered buildings. Hollow-eyed civilians watched from their lightless windows. Skinny children stood by the roadside, dressed in rags and cast-off—or pilfered—articles of German, Italian, British, and American uniforms. All were spattered with mud, their hair matted from the rain. Sunken-cheeked and red-eyed, the children carried themselves with the jauntiness of any combat veteran, brazenly running alongside the column with begging hands out.

"Hey, GI, GI, *mange*, GI, chocolate, GI, hey, GI, Hershey, GI, hey 'mericana . . ."

Harry began to reach into his musette for his K rations.

Ricks laid a restraining hand on his arm. "Unless you're going to feed them all . . ." he cautioned.

As if to illustrate the point, the tank commander behind them tossed a C ration to the gaggle of little ones. Instantly, the smiling children turned vicious, clawing and pulling at one another as they scrambled on the dirt for the tin. One of them, a wiry little thing lost in a Wehrmacht officer's tunic, came up with it and scampered into the darkness with his prize.

"What're all these rocks?" Kneece pointed to a section of wall standing erect in a field of rubble.

"Now?" Schuyler said. "It's shit is what it is."

Ricks explained: "We shell the hell out of these places to chase the krauts out. Then the krauts shell the hell out of them when we move in. At the end of the day, there isn't much left."

The rain managed to find its way inside their slickers, snaking down the collar, in through an upturned sleeve. As the night deepened, the rain grew more chill, and they began to chafe at their increasing discomfort and the tedium of the journey. In Harry's case it didn't help that he hadn't had a full night's rest in three nights. The heat from the Sherman's Chrysler engine helped sap him, created a lulling damp warmth inside his slicker. More than once he was shaken alert by Schuyler, Woody Kneece, or Peter Ricks, lest he topple unconscious from the rear of the tank.

"You take a tumble, Major," warned Corporal Schuyler, "and you're gonna be road goo 'fore them jokers behind us can hit the brakes."

A complete cessation of motion finally stirred him from sleep. This was not one of those times when the Shermans had pulled aside for the sake of the vehicles behind them. The line of cat's-eye headlamps extended for miles. The entire column was stopped. From ahead he heard cursing voices, the impatient honking of lorry horns, an MP's angry whistle.

Schuyler was gone; Ricks and Kneece stood with Angstrom atop the turret, trying to peer through the rain and darkness ahead.

"How long have I been out?" Harry called up to them.

"Maybe twenty minutes," Woody Kneece said.

"How long have we been here?"

"A little while. Schuyler went up ahead to see if he could find out what's going on."

Peter Ricks climbed down and sat on the edge of the turret, rubbing his chin in worried thought.

"What's the matter?" Harry asked him.

"I don't like this," the lieutenant said. "We're close to the line."

The rain and narrow slits of light from the cat's-eye covered head-lamps revealed little. On Harry's right, the road bank rose steeply. To the other side was a roadside shrine, a life-size wooden carving of Jesus on His cross, sheltered under a small awning. The crosspiece was draped with dozens of hastily run strands of telephone wire, so many it looked as if someone had rested a cape across Christ's shoulders.

In the spill of light from the road he could make out wet, shadowy shapes headed south toward Naples. He leaned forward, squinting, and saw what he first took to be horses, then belatedly realized were mules, a long string of them, each carrying a dark oblong pack across its back.

"The trucks can't get up into these hills," Ricks told him. "They use the mules to bring supplies up . . . and bring the bodies down."

Harry counted twenty animals, and the string had yet to end. He was grateful when Schuyler returned.

"The road's a mess up there," the corporal reported. "You got a deuce-and-a-half up to its axles in mud. Even if they pull 'im clear, nobody's gettin' through 'til they get some engineers up here to do somethin' 'bout this road."

"You have a map, Corporal?" Ricks asked. "Let's borrow the back of this guy's truck and have a look at it."

They climbed into the dry rear of a lorry stopped just ahead of them. Harry saw the flash of a torch in Schuyler's hand, the map spread out on the floor of the lorry bed. Ricks and the corporal talked for some minutes. There was a lot of pointing at the map, and then into the space around them. Then Ricks returned.

"You two feel like a walk?" the lieutenant asked Harry and Kneece.

Kneece looked out into the wet night. "Walk where?"

"A couple of miles that way, we pick up an access road that takes us straight to the battalion headquarters we're looking for. It's either hoof it or sit out here in the rain all night."

"It's black as the inside of a duck's ass out there."

"I've never had my head up a duck's ass, so I'll take your word on that," Ricks retorted. "I've got a compass. We just head due north and we can't miss it."

Kneece shrugged. "I can take a couple of miles stretching my legs."

Both younger men turned worriedly in Harry's direction.

"Sure," Harry told them.

"Don't say 'sure' unless you're sure, Major," Ricks said.

Harry's answer was to climb down from the Sherman.

They were all less sure about Harry's certainty—including Harry—minutes later. Unable to find the footing on the slick grass of the bank that his two younger mates had found, Peter Ricks and Woody Kneece had to haul Harry up to the crest. At the top he dropped to his knees wheezing more than the two men who'd dragged him up.

"I'll be fine once we're moving," Harry gasped, urging the now hesitant Ricks on with a nod.

Ricks reached under his slicker for a dressing from the first-aid pouch on his belt. He stuck the square of white gauze under the camouflage netting at the back of his helmet. "I'll take the point. Let me get far enough ahead where you can just about still see this. The lines up here are pretty stable but that doesn't mean there isn't infiltration, so keep your eyes and ears open, your mouths shut . . . sirs." To Kneece: "Easy on the trigger. You're behind our lines; the chances are anything we bump into is going to be ours." Ricks glanced at the luminous dial of his compass, snapped the cover shut, then led them away from the road.

With only the dullest moonlight seeping past the never-empty rain clouds, the surrounding terrain was no more than a pencil sketch of open fields. The horizon ahead of them and the road behind them were obscured in a velvety curtain of blackness and rain.

As the din of the traffic-laden road subsided, they heard rumblings near and far, all along what Harry imagined was the front line. His first thought was thunder, but the detonations were too sudden, too percussive, strings of them too close together: artillery. At times he would see distant bursts of light—a muzzle flash, or the explosion of an incoming round—and there would be a brief presentation of a silhouette: shoulder of a hill, copse of trees, some lone outbuilding.

The field gave way to the ordered ranks of an olive grove.

"Careful," Kneece whispered over his shoulder, and Harry followed the captain in skirting a large, muddy shell crater littered with the splintered limbs of olive trees. A blast had punched a twenty-foot hole in the latticed canopy.

Harry walked with increasing weariness as the wet grass dragged at his legs. He fell into a dazed trudge, his head beginning to loll forward. Benumbed, he didn't realize their little column had halted until he stumbled into Woody Kneece.

Ahead, Ricks was signaling them to stay put, then he vanished into the darkness. In a moment, he was back, waving them forward. "There's some kind of shed just up ahead. It's empty, looks like a good place to be dry for a few minutes."

"Shed" had been a generous description. The structure was a windowless four walls of scrap wood hammered together into an eight-by-eight-foot square with a roof of rusting corrugated tin. But it was dry.

Ricks flashed his torch about the musty interior, the beam playing across rusting pruning shears and cobweb-adorned farm implements. He closed the creaking door, lit a candle from his musette, and set it in the middle of the floor. Harry found a bare corner and dropped to the dirt floor. Off his feet for the first time since they'd left the road, he worried he might not be able to regain them. He took off his helmet, relieved to be rid of the constant rattle of rain on his "pot," although the drumming on the shed's roof may have been even worse.

"You should eat something, Major," Ricks said.

"I'm too tired to eat."

"All the more reason you should."

Harry pulled a K ration from his musette, but only picked at the crackers and tin of cheese, washing them down with a swig of metallic-tasting water from his canteen.

"Crap," Kneece said, rooting about in his own musette. "All I have is breakfasts."

"I didn't have time to shop," Ricks said without apology. "Here, I've got a supper. I'll trade. Major, take this. Make sure you eat it all."

He tossed Harry a D ration, the so-called "energy bar" troops were issued for emergencies: six hundred highly concentrated calories of chocolate, oat flour, and skim milk powder in a four-ounce bar.

"Hey, Kneece," Ricks called, "I'll bet right about now you're thinking you should've listened to Daddy and stayed in that nice, warm office back in Washington."

"Why, Lootenant Ricks!" Kneece said pleasantly. "You've been *snooping!*"

"Let's just call it turn-about-fair-play, Kneece."

"It's *Captain* Kneece, Lootenant, and it's not quite the same thing. I was pursuing an official investigation."

"Pete, I'm not sure this is the time or place to get into this," Harry cautioned.

"You're wrong, Major," Ricks said evenly. "This is the *perfect* time and place. Where we're going, we may have to share a foxhole with this guy. I'm wondering how safe my ass is going to be, covered by somebody who keeps secrets from the people he's supposed to be working with."

Kneece bowed his head and put a hand over his heart. "I am sincerely sorry for the agitated state of your ass, Lootenant."

"That's enough," Harry snapped, dragging himself to his feet. "From both of you. I'm making it an order, Lieutenant: Move out."

But it was Kneece who held up a hand. "No, Major. He's making a fair call. Lootenant Ricks, if you figure my daddy pulled some strings to get me these captain's bars and a cushy job in D.C. where the only bleeding I do is from paper cuts . . . you figure right. See, I'm the only male heir; I'm the last one carrying the family name. In my part of the country, that's real important. At least to my daddy. If my daddy could've done anything about it, I wouldn't be in the service at all. Hell, he didn't even want me to be a state constable! But don't call me to account for his doings."

"That all being the case," Ricks said, "we come to the sixty-four-dollar question: Just what in the hell are you doing here, Kneece?"

"Back in London, you and the major smartly made a case that I've been used. I resent being used."

"You know you're going to catch all kinds of hell for this junket when you get back. Or are you just that cocksure Daddy's still going to be able to protect you?"

"I doubt he would if he could. I expect nobody's going to be more irate over me being here than him." Kneece pulled open the door and pointed to the rain-filled night. "Do you see my daddy protecting me now? My whole life—no matter what I do, no matter what I got for myself—everybody looks at me and I hear 'em thinking the only reason I got what I got is because Daddy bought it for me. Well, factually, nobody's daddy can buy diddly up here, no matter how much money he's got. Here, I either cut it on my own hook or I don't. If you still have a problem with me at your back, Lootenant, I'd be obliged if you'd let me walk point."

Ricks extinguished the candle and stuffed it back in his musette bag. He stood at the open door, looked at his watch, checked his compass. He looked at Harry. "Ready, Major?"

And with Peter Ricks in the lead, they started off into the rain.

They slogged on for another hour before they stepped out onto the access road.

Harry thought the going might be easier than stumbling over the roots of the olive grove, but the road was no more than a river of deep mud churned to a sucking mire by the heavy vehicles that had left their tread marks.

It was nearly another hour before a voice barked at them from the darkness up ahead: "Halt and identify yourself!"

Ricks waved at Kneece and Harry to stay behind. He stepped forward, his rifle held up over his head.

"Do you think this is it?" Harry asked Kneece hopefully.

Kneece sniffed at the air. "Smell that?"

It was something more edible than boxed rations simmering on a stove.

"Uncle Ray used to say any hot food on a cold day smelled like home to him."

. . .

The *podere*—as those squat Italian farmhouses are called by the natives—sat at the end of the road in a clearing, near the base of a low hill. Outside the farmhouse, a petrol-fed generator *put-putted* away. The farmhouse served as the battalion command post, and the clearing as home for the battalion's headquarters company.

Hidden under the branches of olive trees, and further concealed by twig-filled camouflage netting, were a parking area for trucks and jeeps, the battalion supply point and its piled crates of munitions and fuel drums, an aid station marked by red crosses in circles of white, and the battalion's Heavy Weapons company of 81-mm mortars. Near the edge of the clearing, providing the welcoming scents that had wafted toward them, was a field kitchen. A dozen soldiers stood in line in the rain, mess kits in hand, filing by two petrol-fueled stoves to have their tin plates filled from tasty-smelling pots.

"They're serving a late supper," Kneece commented.

"They rotate the men back in squads," Ricks explained. "Gives them a chance for hot food and a break from the line. It can take all night to get through the roster."

It didn't seem much of a respite to Harry. There was nowhere for the men to go with their meal. They simply dropped to the ground under the meager shelter of the olive trees, trying to wolf the steaming food down before the rain dampened its heat and flavor.

After identifying themselves to the sentries, Harry, Ricks, and Kneece were admitted into the large room of the *podere*, which normally served as kitchen, dining room, and parlor. Now that space had been divided in half by blankets hung on a line strung across the room. Under the light of strings of bare bulbs, a squadron of clerks busied themselves with paperwork and typewriters, a switchboard buzzed, a pair of wireless operators twiddled with their consoles. In its ad hoc way, the room seemed no different from any administrative office back home, even down to the smell of fresh coffee from the pot kept warm on a portable petrol heater. Harry found the domesticity of the scene disorienting.

Ricks took it all in with hard eyes. Harry could see a corner of the lieutenant's mouth twitch in barely repressed disgust.

They had been standing there only a second or so before an angular twenty-something captain emerged from behind the blankets. He had fragile, doll-like features, and had only half-successfully managed to subdue a head of curls with a thick coat of pomade. "Major Voss and company? I'm Captain Joyce, battalion exec. Major Porter's been waiting for you fellows." To one of the clerks: "I need that corporal from Love

Company. You'll find him over at the mess tent." Back to Harry and company: "Gentlemen, won't you please step this way?" Captain Joyce lifted the blanket to allow them to pass.

The battalion CO rose from behind the farmhouse dining table he was using as his desk, coming forward to shake Harry's soggy hand. Major Conrad Porter was a stubby, round fellow, a touch of premature gray at his temples, a face full of dimples when he brandished his too-broad smile. "Major Voss! And this must be Captain Kneece and Lieutenant Ricks." He gestured to some folding chairs set near the cheery blaze in the broad hearth. "Why don't you gentlemen get out of those things and dry off. Joyce, grab their rain gear, won't you? And maybe get them some of that coffee I smell out front?"

As they sat by the fire, Ricks's eyes rested on the major's boots, their polish shining in the firelight. Harry looked at his own footwear: He was caked in mud to the top of his leggings.

Porter held out a pack of Lucky Strikes. Peter Ricks declined with a slight nod of his head. "We didn't know when to expect you guys. I was on the verge of turning in myself."

"Sorry if we kept you up," Ricks said.

"It's not that. It's just we were beginning to worry. Ah, here's Joyce with the coffee. All we've got is powdered milk, I'm afraid, but the sugar's the real thing. Looks like you fellows have had a long, hard pull. Can we get you something hot from the kitchen?"

Harry and Kneece were about to voice an enthusiastic yes, but Ricks cut in: "No, thanks, Major, we're fine."

"Joyce, where's that bottle? The captain found a bottle of this incredible brandy the locals drink. Maybe you'd like some with your coffee? Made from fruit, I think, isn't that right, Joyce?"

"*Grappa,*" said Harry.

"You've heard of it?"

"Some friends back home introduced me to it."

"The most incredible stuff! Joyce, why don't you get these gentlemen that bottle and pour a few—"

"Thanks again, no, Major," Ricks said. "We really should—"

"The lieutenant's speaking for himself," Woody Kneece cut in. "I think he's a Mormon. But being a lapsed Baptist myself, I wouldn't mind a snort."

"How long will you be with us?" Joyce asked, pouring a small splash into a canteen cup for Kneece. He offered the bottle to Harry, but Harry shook a smiling no. "Maybe you can spend the night drying out before you go on up to the line? We've got a spare bunk upstairs."

"We really should get straight on up to this guy," Ricks replied, then turned to Harry. "Don't you think, Major?" He turned back to Porter. "Our information is that Lieutenant Coster was assigned to your unit as some kind of forward observer, to a company commanded by a Captain DeFrance—"

"Well, he *was* assigned to Captain DeFrance," Joyce said.

Ricks scowled. "Don't tell me something happened to him."

"Not to Coster," Porter replied. "To DeFrance. Wounded several days ago, on his way home as we speak. A shame. Good man. One of the platoon leaders has the company now. What was the name, Joyce? Beam?"

"Lieutenant Brahm, sir."

Porter shook his head and smiled in a self-mocking manner. "This thing with DeFrance happened so fast I still haven't had a chance to orientate myself with the new company CO. He's a good man, though. Hell, they're *all* good men, my company commanders. They wouldn't be in my battalion if they weren't! Now, the message I got from you—" Porter started to search through the papers on his desk.

A piece of paper materialized in Joyce's hand where he stood by his smaller, folding table across the room. "Here, sir."

"Ah, yes! This message I received from you requests we put you in contact with Lieutenant Coster. It doesn't give— Well, gentlemen, I don't mean to pry, but the man is in my command and there's nothing here about the whys and wherefores." Porter smiled nervously. "I mean I know you have your protocols and the like—"

"It really doesn't concern you or your command, Major," Harry said comfortingly. "It has to do with a matter prior to his assignment here, when he was still flying cargo across the Atlantic."

Porter seemed relieved. "Then it's all the lieutenant's worry, eh, Joyce?"

"I do have a question for you, though," Harry said and saw Porter's nervousness return. "I'm curious about what Coster's orders were when he arrived. Specifically."

"I'll have Joyce pull those for you. Nothing to them, really, just that we were to use him as a forward air controller. They're still developing this practice of close-in air support and they said, as I recall, that Coster was a kind of, oh, I don't remember the word—"

"Experiment?" Ricks offered.

"They said they'd be monitoring his performance, work up some kind of evaluation."

"Who's 'they'?" Harry asked.

By then Joyce was back from the clerical side of the blanket wall and presented Harry with a typed order that said, in military verbiage, what Porter'd just told them. As for the question of who "they" were, there was no answer: "These orders come from G-3 in London. There's no mention of who's supposed to supervise this project."

"And we haven't heard from anybody about this since Coster arrived," Joyce said.

"Did Coster have anything to say when he got here?"

"Beyond making it very clear he didn't want to be here," Joyce replied, "not much."

"How's he worked out?" Kneece asked. "As an air controller?"

"Frankly, we thought that's why you were here." Porter seemed reluctant to go further, looked pleadingly to Joyce.

"Lieutenant Coster has been a little . . . *zealous* in calling for air strikes," the battalion exec explained gingerly. "I'm afraid some civilians have been hurt unnecessarily."

"Relax, sirs," Kneece soothed. "We're not here about that."

Ricks set his coffee down unfinished. "We should get moving," he told Harry.

"Not yet!" Porter said. "You need your— Ah, here he is!" He gestured at the dripping figure shuffling through the blankets. "Gentlemen, this is—"

"Dominick!" Harry was out of his chair like a shot, setting his coffee down so hastily it spilled.

"Signor Roosk! I guess I'm supposed to salute and call you 'Major.' "

"I take it," Captain Joyce observed, "that you and Corporal Sisto are acquainted?"

"A little bit," Harry said, and he and the corporal chuckled.

Dominick Sisto had the lithe build of a boy; there was barely enough of him to wield his bulky Browning Automatic Rifle. The whiskers on his unshaven chin had the patchy, downy quality of an adolescent's. But set in his youngster's face were old eyes, red-rimmed and wary.

With a happy suspicion, Harry turned to Kneece. "Is this your doing?"

Kneece drained his *grappa* as if it were an earned reward. "I remembered the name from that very concerned woman I met at your home. When I knew we were coming here, I looked him up. Turns out this was his unit, I got to thinking he might be a useful . . . liaison."

"And guide," Porter said. "The corporal is from Love Company, and that's where you'll be going." He beckoned them to the map. "Behind this house is Hill 465. Love Company's CP is just the other side of the hill. My rifle companies are dug in along here, about two hundred fifty meters further on. The MLR runs along these hills looking down on them. Now, this space between Love's CP and their front line, you'll have to be careful there. That's all open space and is heavily mined. Corporal Sisto, has that area been cleared yet?"

"No, sir. Krauts like to shoot the engineers in the day, sir. Engineers don't like to clear mines in the dark, sir."

"Well, gentlemen, I wouldn't worry. I'm sure Corporal Sisto and Lieutenant—"

"Brahm," Joyce supplied.

"Yes, Lieutenant Brahm and the corporal'll get you to your man all in one piece."

"Piece o' cake," Sisto promised. But with a smile that told Harry, *Then again, maybe not.*

It seemed as if the whole of the olive grove lit up in a series of blinding flashes, each accompanied by a detonation that Harry felt in his chest and that sent a tremble through the earth under his feet. The volley subsided, the noise rolling off across the grove like fading thunder. Sisto headed them out of the clearing and along a path circuiting the base of the hill.

"Jesus . . ." Harry gasped.

"What the hell was that?" Kneece demanded.

"Don't worry," Ricks said. "Outgoing."

Sisto grinned back at Ricks. "You been around, Lieutenant?"

"We're practically neighbors, Corp. Third Battalion."

"No kidding! You oughta come over and visit. Word is we got much better mud than you guys. Ours has a nice, slow ooze. I hear you guys got that runny shit."

Runny shit. Harry remembered Dominick Sisto the altar boy, afraid to even say "damn" lest his mother hear him, and spank him all the way from home to the confessionals at St. Lucy's Church.

A second artillery volley illuminated the olive grove.

"Heavies," Ricks said.

"They got a battery of 155 'Long Toms' dug in half a mile northeast," Sisto told them. "They like to shake the krauts up at night. 'Course, then the krauts want to do it back. Hey, Cap'n Kneece, I really wanna thank you for hookin' me in here. This means somethin' when you're over here, to see somebody from back home. Signor Roosk and me, we go back. I think maybe I was even his youngest client, isn't that so, signor?"

Harry chuckled at the memory. "I think so."

"I was what? Ten?" Sisto turned to Kneece. "It's summer, and in that building you can really bake when it gets hot."

"Like an oven," Harry amplified.

"So, my bedroom, the window, it looks out on the airshaft on top of ol' Mr. Mayer's store. I say to myself, lemme get a little air, I go walkin' around out there, it's dark, I trip, I fall through ol' Mayer's skylight. Somebody hears the noise, they call the cops, next thing you know the whole neighborhood's outside that store wantin' to see who the son of a bitch is broke into Mayer's store. Out I come. I'm all scratched up from the fall, I look a mess. Well, my ol' lady, she comes runnin' right down when she heard all the noise. You know how all those little ladies are, right, Signor Roosk? Gotta have their nose in everything? She comes runnin' down, didn't even know I was missin' she's movin' so fast to get the gossip. She spots me come out the door and she has a conniption. She doesn't know whether to faint 'cause I'm all cut up or whack the hell out of me for breakin' into ol' Mayer's store. I'm tryin' to tell her I didn't break in, I fell in, but now she's finally decided to start whackin' me—"

"For breaking into the store?" Kneece asked.

"No, for practically givin' her a heart attack. Well, she's not listenin' to me, the cops want to haul me off to the station—it was that ball-buster O'Rourke, Signor Roosk, 'member? That fat mick bastard was always bustin' balls in the neighborhood. They drag ol' Mayer out of bed, O'Rourke's beatin' his gums at him to file a complaint, and then along comes Signor Roosk. He talks all nice 'n' quiet, gets everybody calmed down. He tells my mom, 'Look, signora, you know Nicky's a good boy. If he says it was an accident, you know it's an accident.' He tells ol' Mayer, 'Mr. Mayer,' he says, 'you know Nicky, you know the Sistos, you know me. The kid had an accident. You let him work off the damage and call it quits.' Ol' Mayer says fine, that fat O'Rourke's pissed 'cause nobody wants to file a complaint, and I got my—whatchacallit? An acquittal?"

"More like a plea bargain."

"So, what're you doin' here, signor? I 'member Mom writin' me months ago you were back home. Lucky bastard, I'm thinkin'. No offense. That's just like this fuckin' Army. You get your ass home safe and they drag you back."

"It wasn't the Army, Nicky. Business."

"Boy, I thought I had a shitty job. How's Mom? You seen her, right?"

"Just before I came over. She's worried, Nicky. She hasn't heard from you in a while."

Dominick Sisto shrugged inside his rain slicker, like the little altar boy shamed by a lapse in good conduct.

"You should write to her," Harry said.

"I will."

"I'd leave out some of the grittier details."

"Sure. I know Mom, she's probably havin' kittens as it is. Don't worry, I'll leave this stuff out. Besides, who'd believe it?"

They heard distant explosions, a muffled fusillade of them.

"Somebody's catchin' some serious hell," Sisto said.

Between the dark and the rain, Harry couldn't make out much; yards of open field to one side, the base of the hill to the other. Twenty minutes later, Sisto stopped them at the edge of the olive grove.

"OK," he said, "it gets real nervous now." He nodded at the field behind him.

"Didn't the major say the CP was in a farmhouse out here?" Kneece peered into the rain. "I don't see it. Are you sure we're in the right place?"

"It's there, Cap'n," Sisto said. "Just not much to look at. See, the major, he's got his house 'cause he's got this whole fuckin' mountain between him and the krauts. We go out there, there's nothin' between us and the krauts but . . ." He held out his cupped hand to catch the rain. "So, from here on out . . ." He put a finger to his lips. "I'll take point, Lieutenant, you got the back door if that's OK with you. You sirs"—Harry and Kneece—"you follow in the middle, keep some distance between you."

One by one, walking five yards apart, they followed Sisto out of the trees and across the field. Harry felt . . . he couldn't find the word. Afraid, certainly, but something else.

Fragile. That was the word. Harry walked across the sodden field as if he were made of glass, the enemy—the whole world—invisible beyond the small circle of grass and mud he could see.

Sisto had been right about the house: There wasn't much to see, even close up. A part of an outer wall here, the planking of the floor, the rest of the house blown away into rubble.

"Peach," Sisto called out in a loud whisper.

"Pit," came the countersign, and the security squad huddled behind the pitiful segment of wall waved them in. A shell crater some ten feet across occupied the back of the house, had eaten away at the flooring and into the cellar. A ladder ran down the muddy side of the crater as a walkway. Sisto led them down the ladder and past a shelter half, draped across the opening into the cellar.

The cellar was a bare cave roughly hewn out of the ground under the house. Water seeped through the flooring above; the packed-down earthen floor was slick, the air dank and chill. Shadows ebbed round the pools of light from two hissing Coleman lanterns. A wireless operator dozed by the company's two pack radios, one tuned to the battalion frequency, the other to the company's platoons. A folding table held the company clerk's typewriter, and some huddled shapes were snuggled deep in their sleeping bags nearby. Harry heard snores.

The nearer lantern sat on a table draped with maps covered in grease pencil markings. Nearby, propped against the dirt wall atop his sleeping bag, was a soldier wearing a second lieutenant's gold bars on his collar. He was unshaven, his thick brown hair filthy and matted. Harry couldn't tell the man's age. The lieutenant's eyes were closed. "Y'all my relief?" The lieutenant barely moved his lips when he spoke.

"Excuse me?" Harry'd thought the man was asleep.

The lieutenant's eyes opened slowly, small, sad, and tired. "Any a' y'all my relief?"

"No. Sorry."

A ghost of a smile. "You're sorry?" He pulled himself to his feet, reached for a pair of wire-rimmed spectacles on the map table. "Coffee? It's not very warm." He nodded at some open Marmite cans nearby. "Somethin' t'eat? There's some left. Don't know what kinda shape it's in. Must be cold now." The lieutenant sipped the cold coffee, looked down at the Marmite cans, and sighed. "They been sendin' us an awful lotta hot food lately."

"You sound like you're complaining," Kneece said.

"You usually get a lot of good food before a push," Ricks explained.

"Fatten up the sheep," Sisto added.

The lieutenant studied them again, blinking as if he was seeing them for the first time. "Any a' y'all my relief?"

"You already asked," Harry said. "I'm afraid not."

The lieutenant shook his head. "Did I ask you if you wanted coffee? I thought I did. What time is it?"

"Oh-one-forty," Ricks told him.

"Who are you?"

Harry introduced the group.

The lieutenant seemed mildly interested. "You must be here 'bout the nutcase. The flyboy."

"Captain DeFrance had been informed we'd—"

"They took DeFrance outta here a coupla days ago."

"We know."

The lieutenant shuffled to a canvas folding stool by the table and lowered himself into it with a grunt. There was a postal box on the table, the small, sturdy kind used for mailing breakables. The lieutenant flipped open the box and Harry saw a flattish cake, pieces gouged out of it, the rest crumbling much like the house above them. "Yup, we were settin' here eatin' powdered eggs. Said his wife made better eggs, he was gonna go home for breakfast, walked out inta the minefield 'n' got his leg blown off." The lieutenant broke off a piece of the cake and popped it into his mouth. "I hope that lady makes *damn* good eggs."

"Are you Lieutenant Brahm?" Harry asked.

The lieutenant nodded mutely at the corner near them. Harry looked down and was startled to see a body almost at his feet, its rain slicker covering all but the muddy boots. "Sniper," the lieutenant said through his mouthful of cake. "This mornin'. I guess Porter ha'n't got 'round to readin' his mornin' mail. You sure you don't want coffee? Got cake, goes good with the coffee. Came for the cap'n yesterday. From his wife. All the way from—where was it?" He fumbled with the wrapping paper. "Eau Claire, Wisconsin. Not bad. She even wrote 'Happy Birthday' on it." A fresh leak started through the planks above the lieutenant. Without rising, he slid his seat a few inches out of the way.

"Who's the senior officer here?" Harry asked.

The lieutenant smiled grimly as he patted the pockets of his field jacket, looking for something.

"He's the only officer," Ricks said, understanding. He offered the lieutenant a cigarette, lit it for him.

"You say that like a lodge brother," the lieutenant said, nodding a thanks for the cigarette.

"Third Battalion," Ricks told him.

"Lieutenant Robbie," the lieutenant said, introducing himself.

"Sorry about Lieutenant Brahm," Harry said.

"Why? Did you know him?"

"Major Porter said he was a good man."

"How the fuck would Porter know? He ain't stuck his nose 'round that mountain since he set hisself up in that farmhouse." To Sisto: "Hey, Dominick! How's life back there at the Waldorf?"

"Nice," Sisto said. "Dry."

"Betcha miss it awready, huh?" Robbie took a deep pull on the cigarette, spurring a series of racking coughs.

"You all right?" Kneece asked.

"If you were my relief, I'd be fuckin' fine." Robbie laughed, triggering another series of coughs. "Did you boys say why you're here? Somethin' 'bout that flyboy? You come to pull 'im outta here?"

"We're just here to talk to him," Harry said.

"Too bad."

"Why?"

"I don't know what he'd been through 'fore he got here, but he'd pretty much had it when he showed up. Been a pain in the ass ever since. They put 'im up on the line with a field phone, Coster's supposed to coordinate close air for us. Crazy bastard's been droppin' bombs all over fuckin' Italy. He's so flak-happy he hears mice in the night he calls in bombers. I don't even pass his mission calls on no more, less'n I get it confirmed from my people on the line. You're not gonna take 'im with you?"

"We're just here to talk to him."

"Shame. Why don't you take *me* with you?"

Harry smiled in sincere sympathy. "Could we talk to Coster now?"

"I ain't stoppin' you."

"He's in a nice deep hole about three hundred yards on," Sisto told them, pointing toward the front line. "He don't come out."

"Not for nothin'," Robbie emphasized. "You wanna talk to 'im, you're gonna have to go on up there. Personally, if it was me, I'd just mail 'im a questionnaire. Dominick, you think you can get these fellas up there with nobody gettin' hurt?"

Sisto shrugged. "We'll see."

"You fellas be careful," Robbie warned. "That squirrel hears noises in the dark, he'll just as soon take a pop at you as anythin' else. Iff'n this rain lets up, you wanna be back here 'fore sunup, otherwise there ain't gonna be no gettin' crosst that field 'til nightfall. You're lucky, maybe I'll see y'all for breakfast."

"Rain's lettin' up," Sisto observed unhappily.

They were kneeling in the shelter of the one standing wall of the farmhouse—or rather the few truncated feet of it that were left—along with the CP's security squad.

Harry shifted uncomfortably. His tired legs ached.

Ricks pointed to the diffused glow behind the rain clouds. "Looks like the moon's ready to break."

"Yeah," Sisto said. "We want to be across before that happens."

"That's it out there? That's where the krauts are?" Kneece burbled.

Harry couldn't see the captain's face, but his voice was tense, his breath coming in short pants. Not fear. Excitement.

Ricks hushed him.

"OK, listen up," Sisto said. "You see out there, those little stakes with the white tape on 'em? You stay just to the right of 'em. That's the way through. Don't step nowhere you don't see me step, otherwise you're gonna be in the mines. When you get up to the line, remember the sign is 'peach,' countersign is 'pit.' You bump into anybody in the dark, you say 'peach,' and you don' get 'pit' back, you start pullin' the trigger. Awright, let's go. And for Chrissake, move quiet." Sisto fished his dog tags out of the collar of his slicker and held them in his mouth. Ricks followed suit and indicated Harry and Kneece should do the same. "So 'ey won' ma'e noise."

Sisto led off, holding himself in a crouch, moving quickly though not at a run. They followed at intervals: Ricks, Kneece, Harry.

Harry stayed so close to the ground markers he almost tripped over them. His eyes kept racing from Kneece ahead of him, trying to make sure he followed the captain's footsteps, to the muddy field round him, wondering which of those puddles and mounds might be a mine, wondering if his feet were pounding the spongy earth too hard and might set one off. As the rain lightened, Harry saw a copse of cypress trees just ahead, nestled together round a hump of ground. Sisto signaled them to halt, and they all dropped to one knee.

"Hey, in the bunker!" he heard Sisto whisper. "Peach. Peach! Hey, asshole, *peach!*"

There came an explosive *pop*, and it was only when Harry saw the other men in the file drop facedown into the mud that he realized it'd been a gunshot.

Jesus . . . and he put his face to the wet earth. *No place to go . . . this is worse than that damned boat. . . .*

"You OK, Signor Roosk?" Dominick Sisto called back.

Harry nodded he was fine.

"*Stunat!*" he heard Sisto fume. "We're *Americans*, you stupid fuck! Peach! *Peach!*"

The beam of an electric torch lanced out from the earth mound and picked them out one by one.

"This guy's unbelievable," Ricks said. "We should nail this guy for being a prize fuckin' moron."

Sisto was charging toward the source of the beam. "Put out that light, dumbshit!" The corporal stumbled his way into a hole at the rear of the mound, grabbed the torch away, Harry heard a body hit the mud. "What the fuck is the matter with you?" Not waiting for an answer, Sisto wheeled and urgently signaled the rest of them to follow.

In the dark, Harry tripped down the hole, which turned out to be the muddy entryway into some sort of dugout, low-ceilinged, he painfully learned when he tried to stand up. It was also cramped. Bodies kept rubbing against him. He heard the rubbery rustle of a rain slicker; an elbow thumped against his helmet—Ricks's voice, "Sorry, whoever you are"—then the slicker was held up across the entryway and Harry heard someone tucking it tight round the edges of the portal.

The flick of a match, the flare of Peter Ricks's candle.

It had been Ricks who had stripped off his rain gear. He took off the outside shell of his helmet, planted it in the earthen side of the dugout, dripped some soft wax onto the metal, then set the base of the candle in the wax. They were a sight, helmets, faces, and slickers glistening with mud. Sisto was holding the torch and a .45, both confiscated from the guilty party.

"Where is this prick?" Ricks seethed.

Sisto stepped out of the way and pointed to a figure curled in a corner behind him. Ricks reached down, grabbed the man by the front of his leather flight jacket, and flung him closer to the candle.

"Je-Je-Jesus I'm sorry I-I-I'm sorry I'm so-so-so-so-sorry I didn't know it was you these fuckin' krauts, the fu-fu-fuckin' krauts, they come around all night, they fuckin' *infiltrate* all fuckin' ni-*night*—"

"What the hell kinda crazy bedbug is *this*?" Peter Ricks demanded. The cringing figure pushed away from them, looking like he sought to push himself into the dirt wall.

Second Lieutenant Andrew Coster was a stunning testament to how even a short time under fire could age a twenty-four-year-old man. He hadn't shaved since he'd been flown out of the naval air station at Narssarssuaq three weeks earlier, nor, by the rank smell in the dugout, bathed in as long. His face was gaunt, wan; his entire body trembled uncontrollably. His brown eyes, swallowed in shadowed, puffy flesh, were set in bloodshot fields.

It was the eyes that registered with Harry. Not the flaming sleeplessness of them, but the wild, darting look that, even after seeing and knowing he was surrounded by fellow Americans, never faltered, never eased. Andy Coster wasn't just afraid; he was consumed with terror.

"C-c-can I have my gu-gun, huh, can I have my gun, oh, Jesus, oh, Jesus, do-do-don't take my gun for Christ's sake in the name of C-C-Christ c-can I have my gun?" The words tumbled out over each other, the trembling lips moving so fast Coster had no time to swallow. Spittle bubbled up at the corners of his mouth.

Peter Ricks's anger abruptly subsided. "Major—this is what you've been chasing since Greenland?"

"Factually, he *is* a little anticlimactic," Woody Kneece murmured.

"How 'b-b-b-bout my gu-gun, f-f-fellas, huh, my gu-gun don't leave me without a gun what the fuck is the ma-matter with you guys leavin' me without a f-fucking gun?" In the space of a whimper, Coster seemed to go from crippling terror to angry desperation.

Ricks knelt by the flyer, reached out a hand to his face.

"N-n-no!" Coster reached up to fend off Ricks, as if fearing a blow. Ricks batted the hand away and held Coster's eye open wide.

"Son of a bitch," Ricks muttered and stepped back from him. "You're not going to get anything worth a damn out of this guy anytime soon.

He's all wound up on Benzedrine. Looks like he's been eating them like gumdrops. Where are they, Coster?"

"G-g-gimme my gun I'll t-tell you you gimme my gun."

Ricks pulled Coster upright, patted him down until he found the envelope of pills in the flyer's breast pocket. He pushed Coster away and headed for the door.

"N-n-no no no!"

Coster flung himself at Ricks, who easily pushed him off, then laid a sound punch on the flyer's chin that left him sprawled and unconscious on the muddy floor.

Dominick Sisto applauded.

Ricks scattered the pills outside. "Let him sleep this off for a while. Then maybe we can get something out of him. That rain's gonna stop. This bozo should have a set of field glasses here somewhere."

They bumped against each other in the small chamber. The observation post, which, from the amount of work done on it, obviously predated Coster's arrival, had been scooped out of the earth to a depth of five feet. A web of heavy tree branches formed the base of a domed ceiling, over which had been thrown a tarpaulin and then a covering of earth and shrubs as camouflage. There were observation ports facing the MLR, but they had been blocked with sandbags.

They searched through the litter on the floor: K ration boxes, C ration tins, a sleeping bag and a grid map trampled into the mud floor. They found the glasses near a field phone by the blocked ports.

Ricks blew out the candle and had Sisto help him pull the sandbags clear of the ports.

The rain stopped.

The OP had been well sited on a slight rise that gave it a nearly 180-degree unobstructed view of the terrain in front of it. The American line ran along the low side of a shallow dale. A winding stream curled through the bottom of the valley, now rain-swollen past its banks, leaving the grassy expanse on either bank shining under the cloud-diffused moon. Even a military amateur like Harry could see how inhospitable the American position was: the far side of the valley was marked by a line of higher, steep-sided hills, looking down on the American positions.

Ricks silently scanned the hills with the field glasses.

"See anything?" Kneece asked, his voice tight.

Ricks shook his head. "But they're up there. Corp, how often do they probe around here?"

"Whenever they can," Sisto replied. "Anything to keep us gettin' a night's sleep."

"How far apart are the other foxholes?"

"Maybe every ten yards. There's also an empty hole on either side of us inside these trees to support the OP. Nobody's in 'em; nobody wants to be around this nutcase." He gestured at Coster, who hadn't moved since Ricks struck him.

"Corp, why don't you set up shop in here? I'm going to take the hole on the right."

"What about us?" Kneece asked.

"You two stay and guard your witness, and hope when he comes to he makes some sense. If he does, come get me. If anything pops, you two stay here. This is your position."

Whatever ravages the war had inflicted on the hillsides and fields along the MLR were invisible in the night. The clouds broke up, a crescent of moon appeared, and the sodden landscape lit up in a thousand glittering points, every droplet, course of water, and puddle a twinkling sequin. The bombardment they'd heard off to the southwest had slowed to a few sporadic explosions, then nothing. Standing by the entryway they could look off to where the noise had been and see a scarlet glow pulsing in the dark.

Harry pulled the steel shell off his helmet and set it down on the floor as a stool. "So what's with this corporal business?" he asked Sisto. "You're coming up in the world."

"Well, it's not like being some fancy-schmancy JAG major."

"Trust me; that's not all it's cracked up to be."

"I was up to buck sergeant for a while. Was even runnin' my platoon. 'Course, at the time, the platoon wasn't much bigger than a squad."

"What happened?"

"I coulda used you then, Signor Roosk. You coulda spoke for me like you did that time with ol' Mayer."

"Uh-oh."

"All I did was use my initiative. They were always givin' us all that use-your-initiative guff back in basic, so that's what I did."

"That's what you did."

"We were bivouacked outside of Avellino. There was some kinda big house there, like an estate I guess you'd call it, some rich guy's place. My initiative told me maybe that place hadn't been properly reconnoitered, maybe something of military value had been overlooked."

"Like?"

"Did you know all these big places in Italy got these wine cellars?"

"Oh, brother."

"We took no prisoners, Signor Roosk. Not a bottle was left standing. Unless it was empty."

Kneece laughed with them.

"Pipe down in there!" Ricks hissed at them from outside.

Woody Kneece stood by Sisto at the observation port. "This may sound crazy, but I almost *want* something to happen."

"Not crazy," Sisto said. "You think like that 'til your first time. Then you don't want anything to happen anymore."

"Jesus, I could use a cigarette."

"You do it like this." Sisto crouched low in the dugout. He lit a match, covering its flare with his body against the wall. Once the cigarette was lit, he kept the glowing tip inside his cupped hands. He handed the cigarette to Kneece, who did likewise.

"You said you were at Avellino?" Harry asked. "A lot of the people in our neighborhood come from around Avellino," he explained to Kneece. "A lot of them still have relatives here. How was it?" he asked Sisto.

"Pretty banged up. Mom told me to try and find our people. She said we had aunts, uncles, cousins, but all I found was this kid. Maybe twelve years old. I couldn't understand him too well. The Italian we talk back home isn't exactly like what they talk here. But if I got him right, he's some kinda cousin to me. He spent six days living in a drainpipe until the shooting stopped. He was all I found. Didn't know where his mom and pop were. Some of the people still in town told us a lot of people took off into the hills. Maybe they came back, I don't know. I think that's why I don't write to Mom so much. She always asks, and I don't know what to tell her. I mean, Signor Roosk, that used to be her *village*." Sisto went rigid. "Shhh."

Kneece extinguished his cigarette. They could hear someone running along the American line of foxholes in their direction.

"Peach." It was Ricks.

"Pit."

More footsteps toward Ricks's position, a quick, hissed conversation, then a pair of legs running by the observation ports to continue on down the line. Ricks stuck his head by the port.

"What's the poop?" Sisto asked.

"Listening post thinks they heard something moving about two hundred yards to our right. Maybe they scooted over in the rain and now they can't get back. If this pops, you hold fire unless it moves this way. You wait for me to call it, understand?"

Sisto nodded and Ricks returned to his position. "You may get your wish yet, Cap'n," he told Kneece as he moved his BAR to a port that angled toward the right flank. "Probably in there." Harry joined him at the port, followed the younger man's pointing to a train of small boulders and shrubs marking a rill sliding down the front of the American heights into the stream at the bottom of the dale. Sisto stripped off his slicker, the better to reach his ammunition bandolier. "You got a weapon under that, Signor Roosk?" He meant Harry's slicker.

"A .45."

Sisto chuckled. "Wyatt Earp." He cocked the bolt of his BAR and adjusted the rear sight for the range. "You guys better unhook your chin straps."

"Why?"

" 'Cause if somethin' goes off close by, it's gonna blow your helmet clear and take your head with it."

It was only minutes—long minutes—that they stood by the port, studying the shadowy line of rocks and brush. Harry could hear those short pants from Ricks again, and in the feeble light he could see the captain's eyes were wide.

"Peach!" Loud, from the American line.

"This is it," Sisto whispered.

"Peach! I said peach, goddammit!"

A pause. Then, from the shadows below the foxhole line: "Tree."

"Tree my ass you cocksucker!"

Before the epithet ended, a .30-caliber machine gun stammered, sending a stream of tracers ricocheting among the rocks. Simultaneously the rattle of M1's followed along the stretch of the line immediately above the intruders.

"See 'em?" Sisto asked. Harry could see the corporal's finger flex round the BAR's trigger.

"Is that them?" Kneece's tongue kept running round his lips as if no sooner had they been dampened than they dried. *"Is that them?"*

Harry did see them—shadows almost indistinguishable from the dark humps of the boulders, only they were moving, darting here and there on their way down the hill. They would stop, turn, there'd be the flash and bark of a Mauser, then the scramble down the shallow defile would continue. One of the Germans broke from the shadows for the stream. Shimmering geysers of water spurted up round him. The figure seemed to lose its balance, stagger along off-kilter before falling facedown in the water. It didn't move again.

The Germans across the dale, up on the hills, answered with machine guns of their own, MG42's, faster-firing than the American .30-calibers, the bursts ripping roars echoing across the dale, the flickering muzzle flashes radiating streams of tracers, arcing over the stream, covering the withdrawal of their *Kameraden.*

Then came the thudding *whumps* of mortars behind them, and the dale filled with the brilliant, dead light of parachute flares lofted up by the 60-mm mortars of Love Company's Heavy Weapons platoon. The flares sputtered and hissed, shed sparks, their flickering light painting the countryside in bleak chiaroscuro.

Dominick Sisto followed the Germans down the defile with his sights, but held his fire. More than once Woody Kneece raised his M1, and more than once Sisto restrained him: "Hold your fire!" And then it was one restraint too many for the captain.

Kneece rushed out the dugout entryway. Through the observation port Harry saw him run past Ricks hunkered down in his hole just a few yards away. Kneece ran to the outermost cypress tree, raised his rifle, and began snapping off rounds.

"Kneece!" Peter Ricks bolted from his foxhole, yanked Woody Kneece's M1 from his hands with one hand and grabbed his collar with the other, dragging him back to the dugout. He thrust Kneece through the entryway. "I told you not to fire!" Ricks screamed, his enraged face twisting in the unearthly light of the flares.

"I didn't come all this way not to be a part of this!" Kneece shouted back.

"Down!" Even as he yelled, Sisto was already diving, pulling Harry down with him.

They hugged the floor as one of the MG42's across the dale raked the cluster of cypress trees. Bullets thunked into the dirt and branches of the dugout's roof.

This was no longer some grotesquerie Harry could watch, in rapt horror, at some remove. *They're trying to kill me . . . they're trying to kill me. . . .*

But the burst of fire was short-lived, as if it could find little hidden among the cypress trees to keep its interest; soon it returned to the steady flashes of the weapons trying to kill its mates down by the water.

"*Asshole!*" Ricks spat at Woody Kneece. He threw Kneece's rifle to Harry. "Don't give that to him!" He turned and ran back outside to his position.

"Oh, fuck . . ." Dominick Sisto muttered. "Get down deep, signor."

Sounds of mortars, but more distant, from behind the hills across the way. Harry heard a high, violent flutter, like the panicked burst of birds from the brush, then a volley of mortar shells crashed along the American line.

Harry pressed closer to the dugout floor, his nose filled with the smell, his mouth the taste, of the churned mud beneath him. He felt the impacts through the ground, felt them pound deep in his chest. His fingers clawed at the wet earth as if he could bury himself deeper.

Then a falling flutter, painfully, shatteringly clear in his ears . . . *Jerry,*

Ricky, I'm sorry . . . coming in close . . . Jesus, Cynthia, Cyn, I'm—close enough that when it hit the impact bounced him off the ground, a torrent of dirt and sod vomiting through the ports on top of him.

It had taken minutes for that first machine-gun burst to escalate into a mortar duel, but even more swiftly it was over. Scattered rifle shots, and finally nothing, not even echoes. There was nothing left to shoot at.

"I think I'm bleeding." Harry felt it on his face, tasted it in his mouth. *You're fine you're fine if it was bad you'd be hurting you're fine* but not once, in his gut, did he believe it.

"Let's see." Sisto helped him sit up. He found Coster's torch, and, sheltering the light with his torso, quickly checked Harry over, then flicked the torch off. "You're OK, signor. Just a bloody nose. Must've been the concussion. Next time, put your arm under your head. It'll soak up the shock."

Ricks was back in the dugout. "Corporal, take my place outside."

After Sisto left, Harry helped Ricks replace the sandbags in the observation ports. He took a last look down into the dale. He saw the silhouette of the man who'd fallen in the stream, and farther beyond, in the fen on the other bank, another crumpled shape. *That's them; the krauts, the Germans, The Enemy. All that noise, all that fire, and that's how it ends; those two lumps.*

He slid the sandbag into place and sealed the view away.

Ricks relit his candle. The dugout had not survived unscathed. Some of the branches serving as beams had buckled, and a square of tarp flapped, its dirt cover bleeding onto the floor. Ricks tucked the tarp back into place.

Woody Kneece sulked in one corner. "I'm *sorry*. Is that what you want to hear?"

"I don't want to hear a fucking thing from you!" Ricks seethed. "In fact, you open your goddamned mouth just once and I'll fucking shoot you myself." And Harry never once thought—then and forever—that Peter Ricks didn't mean every word he said.

A moan, a stirring from the other end of the dugout: Coster.

"OK, Major, you wanted to talk to this guy?" Ricks shook a splash of water from his canteen onto the flyer's face, then another until Coster's eyelids began to flutter. "There you go, Major. Talk to him. I just hope whatever you get is worth it."

Coster's eyes lapsed into their frightened, darting mode. "Was it a dream, did I have a dream? They came at us, didn't they? They hit us, didn't th-they? Didn't they?"

"Just a probe," Ricks said.

Coster's fear immediately turned to rage. "A *probe*? Fuck that! They come crawling up here like ants at ni-night, e-*every* night! Those aren't no fuckin' probes!"

The flyer was a stewpot of emotions, each bubbling up violently, almost instantly replaced by another. How would he deal with the boy without using a whip and chair, Harry wondered. "Coster."

"You were here before, weren't you? All you guys? Where's my gu-gun? Did you see my gun? I had a gu-gu-gun, did one of you *fuckers* steal my fuckin' *gun*?"

"Coster!"

The sharp snap of Harry's voice silenced Coster immediately. He squinted about him in the flickering candlelight. "Who are you guys?"

"I'm Major Harold Voss, Judge Advocate. That's Captain Derwood Kneece, Criminal Investigation Corps."

Coster slumped, as if inwardly collapsing. "Oh, Jesus. You're here about the c-crash, you're here about the plane the plane the crash—Who're *you*?" He peered suspiciously up at Peter Ricks.

"Never mind me. Worry about them." Ricks pointed to Harry and Kneece.

"Nononononono." Coster was staring at Peter Ricks. "*You're* the one to watch the scary one y-y-you—" Coster began to sob. "I kn-kn-knew it always always knew it from the top the start from the b-b-beginning, I used to t-tell him, 'How long?' I used to say, 'H-how long do you think this is gonna g-go on? S-s-sooner or later,' I s-said, 's-s-sooner or later—' "

"Who did you tell?"

"M-Mac, M-M-Mac, who else do you tell?"

"McKesson?" Kneece asked. "The pilot who commanded your transport?"

Coster's eyes closed tightly, battling a memory. "Oh, Jesus J-Jesus M-Mac." Then the tears were gone, the anger back on all burners. "I t-told him! I s-said, '*Asshole! Asshole!* Sooner or l-later.' " The voice turned small and plaintive. "Are you guys gonna get me outta here? Please? Gonna t-take me outta here?"

Ricks sat on his helmet and rubbed wearily at the scabs around his eye. "I'm getting a headache from this jerk."

"What do they call you?" Harry said soothingly. "Andy? All right, Andy, try to listen to what I say, OK? Concentrate? Let's go through this very slowly, one piece of it at a time. We know about the X-ray flights, OK?"

"Oh G-God they *know*! You sonofabitch! You didn't give a shit! He didn't care, M-Mac didn't care, he needed a copilot is all he c-cared about—"

"Coster, do you remember me socking you?" Ricks cut in impatiently. "If you don't get hold of yourself I'm going to lay you out again. Now: Forget the footnotes and just answer what this man asks you."

"Andy," Harry said. "How did you get involved? Who brought you into this?"

Coster's lips trembled, the tears welled up again, the momentary control evaporated, but then a threatening look from Ricks shored him up. "OK," he said, taking a shaky breath, "OKOKOK." Another breath. "We were in flight school, flight school—"

"You and McKesson?"

"—kinda b-buddies even though Mac was an instructor, OK? An instructor this is in Oklah-homa, flight instructor, then he's off somewhere, he gets transferred off somewhere, I dunno dunno wh-where, and I'm b-bakin' my ass down in T-Texas—"

"How did he bring you in?"

Coster seemed astonished that Harry didn't know the obvious answer: "He asked me."

"Asked you."

"He c-came to me."

"When was this?" Kneece asked.

"L-last year, early f-f-forty-two, Mac shows up in T-Texas, says he's on leave, wants to talk to me about this thing this th-thing, this job do I want in, c-clean, he says, it's clean, n-no worries. No worries. *Look at me! Look at this shit!* N-no *worries?* You *know* why I'm here why they put m-me here oh Christ . . ."

"Hey!" It was Sisto in the entryway. "They can hear you guys in fuckin' Naples. They won't need no recon to find us next time."

"What did McKesson tell you?" Harry asked Coster. "What did he say about what you'd be doing?"

"We were gonna be flying some stuff, 'goods,' 'the goods' Mac called 'em, goods to England, under the c-counter. He didn't say what, some stuff, some goods for some people is all he says to me, I f-f-figure it's b-black m-m-market or something, I guess, I dunno, what else could it b-be, right? He s-says, look, he says, you get your legit flight pay, nobody's gonna call you up for combat action, on top of that under the c-counter you get a hunnerd b-bucks, a *hunnerd bucks* every time you make the trip." He saw Ricks lighting up a cigarette. "C-can I have one of those?"

"No."

"Who brought McKesson in?"

"S-s-somebody brought him in, how else how else do you—"

"Who?"

But Coster suddenly went still, now wanting to hoard what he knew.

"Who brought McKesson in?" Harry pressed.

"Look, before I go givin' up names—"

"We already know," Harry said. "But I want to hear you tell the story." Coster squinted warily, then turned smug. "You d-don't know sh-sh—"

"Lieutenant Colonel Edghill," Kneece pronounced, "handled the American side out of his office in Washington."

Coster's smugness turned to alarm. "If you know Edghill, you don't need m-me—"

"We want to hear it from you, Andy," Harry said. "Tell me."

"Awright, fine yeahyeahyeah, Edghill, this guy, this colonel, Edghill's the big shot, some D.C. big shot—"

"How did Edghill get to McKesson?"

" 'G-get'? He didn't 'g-g-get' to him, they're buddies, all the way from school, all real hoity-t-toity up in Harvard together, b-before the war they're up in Harvard these two b-brainy guys, Mac tells me the story, they're real whizzes these two, he says they s-see the war's comin', no way 'round it, we're gonna g-g-get dragged into this mess so let's g-go in the service early, get the jump, get to p-p-pick their spots, everybody's gonna wind up in, Roosevelt's gonna drag everyb-b-body in, but who wants to get killed just 'cause Roosevelt's got a thing for the limeys? Fuck 'em, f-f-fuck 'em it's their war—"

"So they both go into the service," Harry cut in. "Then sometime later, after the war starts, Edghill gets McKesson to make these X-ray flights."

"I d-don't know when they started, but ye-yeah, I g-guess like that—"

"And then McKesson brought you in. How many X-ray crews are there?"

"I'm n-n-not sure, I dunno, I never met any of 'em, not 'til I got flown over here oh Christ hereherehere—"

"The crews, Andy," Harry said.

"I'd hear things s-sometimes make me think us and one other crew, sometimes I think maybe two, three altogether rotating, I g-guess."

"And the crews were all brought in the same way? Somebody knew somebody?"

"I dunno, I didn't know anything about the other crews, just ours. Marquez, he was somebody Mac rem-membered from somewhere he was stationed, we needed a radioman so he got Marquez, we needed a flight engineer he doesn't know anyb-body he asks me m-me he asks, somebody you can trust, Andy, who c-can k-keep his mouth shut, this guy I knew from Texas . . ." The name stalled on his lips.

"Sergeant Bell," Harry said.

Coster's face squeezed painfully closed, his fists thrown up to his eyes. "Did you *see* him? All b-b-burned up like th-that? How do you *live* like that, all—"

"You don't," Kneece said. "He's dead."

The flyer went rigid. He wanted to doubt; couldn't.

"The doctors wanted Bell to stay in Greenland until he was well enough to travel," Harry said.

"But your friend Edghill wouldn't wait," Kneece said.

"They brought him back to the States on the next X-ray return flight and he died."

Coster fell back against the muddy wall of the dugout, wailing. "Oh, God, oh *God, G-God!* I brought him in I brought him in!" He sat bolt upright. "That fuck McKesson!" Then, just as upset over McKesson as Bell: "Did you see M-Mac, poor p-poor Mac, like you step on a bug can't even tell what it is anymore."

"Andy, Edghill managed the U.S. side of the X-ray flights. How did it work on the other side?"

"It was a timing thing, always g-gotta be there a certain t-time, after d-dark, come in just about on the d-deck, Mac, Mac, he used to scare the c-crap outta me he'd take it soooo d-down I thought we'd end up in the drink is how it was"—anger—"how he did stuff, always pushin' a limit, that's how he got 'em all how Marquez and Bell—"

"Andy! The English side. You'd fly into the Orkneys, there was a field set up for you. Then what?"

"—I t-told him let's just w-w-wait the w-weather out but Mac l-laughs, he says, 'My ass sticks to the t-toilet seat here it's s-s-so c-cold,' he says, real smartass, always with the wise remarks, 'I st-stick to the toilet seat, I'm not stayin' here no longer than I have to' and we go and he pushes it—"

"Coster!" This time, Kneece cracking the whip. "How did it work when you came down in the Orkneys?"

"I d-dunno who any of 'em were, we got t-told when to come d-d-down and wh-where but nothin' about who, so we come in and there'd be these limeys to unload the plane, I d-dunno where the stuff, the 'goods' went from there, these limeys, all in civvies— You're sure 'b-bout B-Bell, 'bout him bein' d-dead?"

Harry nodded. "After the crash in Greenland, an Army officer came down from Godthåb to talk to you: Lieutenant Grassi."

A new emotion for Coster: annoyance. "Little pain in the ass."

"That's him," Ricks commented.

"I figure, I think he m-musta seen what was l-left of the c-cargo," Coster said, "figured somethin' out, he was always in my ear."

"Definitely Armando," Ricks muttered.

"I d-didn't say anything to him, I say anything I kn-know it's over f-for me, no more g-gravy train *gravy train!*" Fearful eyes ran round the dugout. "This is where the train stops, guy, this this th-this!"

"What happened with Grassi?" Harry pressed. "How did he wind up on that plane with you?"

"*It wasn't my fault!*"

"Coster!" Ricks put a finger to his lips.

"He tells me, this Grassi, he says he's with JAG—"

"Slight exaggeration," Kneece said.

"—and he's always on me, even in the hospital, in my ear, what's goin' on, what's all this stuff, who's involved, what's goin' on, who's involved, over and over—"

"I guess his style hadn't mellowed up there," Peter Ricks told Harry.

"—then I get this message from Edghill, 121 X-ray—"

"The makeup flight," Kneece said. "You'd lost the cargo, they were sending in another one—"

"—and they say, 'You get on that plane!' and that's goin' *east*, not home, they're not b-b-bringin' me h-home . . . *east*. I didn't know what that meant, I didn't know it was gonna be th-this shit, but I know it's not gonna be good 'cause it's f-fuckin' *east!*"

"The flight came in, Andy, and you and Grassi got on it."

"He s-says to me, he t-*tells* me, 'Andy, they're gonna try to fuck ya,' he says and they're sendin' me *east* so maybe he's ri-right, and he wants on that plane *on* that plane, you he-help me, he s-says, and it's b-better for you and I'm helpin', right? Helpin' you, right? You kn-know what they want why they s-sent me out here—"

"You got Grassi on the plane?"

"I say to the c-crew another m-message came in maybe they d-d-didn't receive it or some bullshit that Grassi's supposed to come wi-with me, I dunno what he thought he was g-gonna do when he g-got there—"

"That, sadly, also sounds like Armando." Ricks stubbed out what was left of his cigarette.

"The plane landed in the Orkneys," Harry went on. "Then what?"

Coster looked at him, helpless. "They got spooked, I g-guess, they saw him, d-didn't know what he was do-doin' there, somebody pulled a g-gun . . . I didn't have anythin' to do with—"

"I know, Andy. Did you see the man who shot Grassi? Can you identify him?"

"They put me out here to die you know that dontcha out here to fuckin' *die!* They said they're just gonna tuck me someplace 'til stuff dies down but they want me fuckin' *dead!*"

"Andy, you said Edghill brought in McKesson, and McKesson brought you in. Who brought Edghill in?"

"What makes you think anybody did?" Ricks asked Harry. "How do you know this isn't all Edghill's own brilliant idea?"

"Because I don't see how a G-4 transportation officer in Washington came to do business with our friend with the title in Canterbury. Who, Andy?" Harry pressed.

Coster was guarded now; frantic eyes settled down enough to show the calculating going on inside the pep-pill-addled brain. "I heard a name. A *big* name. That was the c-carrot, all the w-w-way at the beginning that sonofabitch M-Mac said, 'Andy, do this right and when this is all over we'll n-never have to worry 'bout a job.' "

"What's the name, Andy?"

Coster smiled, deviously, maliciously. "N-n-n-*no*!"

"Andy—"

"You find this guy that shot Grassi, I'll f-f-finger him for you. I'll he-help you run down the 121 X-ray flight crew. I'll g-give you the name *the name*!" The bargaining collapsed into a pleading sob. "But you gotta get me outta here. I c-c-can't b-*be* here! *I don't belong here!* I didn't kill that guy, I g-g-got into all this to stay *away* from all that! Get me outta here and I'll give it all to you all to you *all to you*!"

Peter Ricks rose with a disgusted grunt, dropped his helmet back on his head, and headed out.

"Stay with him," Harry told Kneece, meaning Coster, and went after the lieutenant.

Outside, he found Ricks huddled by the trunk of the outermost cypress tree with Dominick Sisto. Harry found the empty foxhole on that side of the OP and slid into it. In the distance, somewhere down in the dale, Harry could hear a voice; faint, weak. German: "*Bitte . . . Amerikaner Kameraden . . . nicht schiessen . . .*" Then: "Americans . . . help me, please . . . I wounded . . . please . . . *bitte . . .*"

Harry saw Sisto point to the base of the defile the Germans had used for their withdrawal. Ricks came back and slid into the foxhole beside Harry.

"Will they come out to get him?" Harry asked.

"The krauts?" Ricks shook his head. "He's too close to our line."

"How about our people?"

"Nobody's going down there in the dark."

"What if he's still alive at daybreak?"

"We'll see then."

"*Amerikaner* . . . I have hurt, please . . . *Bitte . . .*"

Ricks nodded at the OP. "I hope you're not thinking of taking Mr. Section Eight with us?"

"Why not?"

"Because you won't get him any further than Porter's HQ. Do I have to remind you about the shell game you played with Captain Dumb-ass's orders to get us out here? You and Kneece are already so far above your authority I'm surprised you don't have nosebleeds. Hell, I'm supposed to be at a convalescent hospital in London right now. I'm going to be lucky if I don't get busted down for going AWOL when we get back."

"That won't happen," Harry promised. "I'll tell them—"

"Nothing." Not harsh or angry; simply final. "I made my choice, Major; I'll deal with it."

"Bitte, please to have help . . . American friend, please . . ."

"You saw the kind of guy Porter is," Ricks said. "He's got cover-my-ass stamped all over him. You show up with this Looney Tune and he's going to send a message back to G-1 in London that says, 'Please inform whoever it is wants this crackpot out here so badly that some legal people just took him into custody.' And because Porter is a cover-my-ass kind of guy, he's not going to let you go anywhere until he gets an answer, Major. You won't even get Coster as far as Naples."

"What am I supposed to do?"

"For now, leave him until you can arrange some kind of bullshit reason to pull him out of here. The guy's nuttier than a bag of pistachios. You should be able to pull him out on a psycho."

He saw Harry's look of concern toward the dugout.

"You don't want to tell him?" Ricks said. "Fine. I'll give him the bad news. I don't mind. You want to pity him, have a ball; but for him, I'm dry."

"I'll tell him," Harry said. "He's right, Pete; he *doesn't* belong here."

"Fuck him," Ricks snarled. "Nobody belongs here." He looked at his watch. "We've got about two and a half hours of dark. You've been going all night. Why don't you sleep for an hour. That'll still give us plenty of time for me to have you around the back of that hill before sunup. Hey, Corp! Inside. Catch some sack time before we head out."

"What about you?" Harry asked.

"I'll be all right."

"*Amerikaner, bitte* . . . Baseball, Roosevelt. You help, *ja*? *Bitte*?"

"Lieutenant," Sisto called, still at the cypress tree. He nodded down into the dale. "This guy's gonna keep this up all fuckin' night. Hey, it's not like they don't already know we're here."

Ricks gave a nod.

Sisto squeezed off three quick bursts from his BAR.

The dale went quiet.

Sisto slung his BAR on his shoulder and started for the OP. "Maybe now we can get some fuckin' sleep."

Inside the dugout, Kneece asked Harry, "What was that shooting?"

"Shut up," Harry snapped, and sat down to talk to Coster.

•   •   •

As they started back down the path through the minefield, Harry stopped
and looked back at the hump of the OP. He was just able to make out the
shadow of Coster standing in the entryway.

"You come back for me," Coster said. The Benzedrine was gone now,
the voice tired and feeble. "Please."

Harry raised a hand, then turned and headed across the field.

Major Porter assigned Captain Joyce to drive them back to Naples. Even
the jeep with its four-wheel drive couldn't negotiate the boggy, rutted
road, so Joyce took another route, an ad hoc jeep trail through the groves
that brought them back onto the road they'd followed out from Naples,
only at a point much farther north than where they'd left it the night before. A few minutes' travel and they were stopped by MP's directing traffic
off the road, along a detour that ran through a field.

The road ahead, for a length of some two hundred yards, was pocked
with shell craters. This was the site of the explosions and the glow of
flames they'd seen the previous night. A half-dozen lorries lay smashed,
crumpled like lead foil, gutted by fire, canvas covers burned away, leaving
the ribs exposed like the blackened bones of a fire-consumed dinosaur. A
squad of engineers with shovels worked in support of a Hough loader
piling dirt into the craters to put the road back into usable shape. Other
engineers attached the first of the wrecks to the hook of a Diamond "T"
recovery vehicle to haul it clear of the road. By the roadside, a dozen
blanket-covered bundles lay in a neat line as a Graves Registration unit
loaded corpses onto a lorry bed.

Among the wrecked lorries Harry saw the burned-out shell of a
Sherman tank. In the field were several more lorries and another stricken
tank, hit as they'd tried to make for the concealment of the olive groves
some yards off.

Harry told Joyce to pull out into the field. He climbed out of the jeep
and started for the blasted Sherman.

A human body that dies by fire is a grotesque nightmarish stick-
figure drawn in charcoal. The muscles contract, pulling the face back in a
hideous grin; the skeletal arms and fingers and legs curl inward. It was
these rigid, twisted shapes another Graves Registration detail—with ker-
chiefs tied in place over their mouths and noses against the stomach-
turning smell of seared flesh and burnt petrol—was trying to wrestle
clear of the charred hulk.

Harry walked round to the rear of the tank. Much of the paint had been burned or blackened away, but some of the white stenciling along the rear of the turret still survived: ma's Boys. Above, hanging from the tank's radio antenna by a blackened strip of ribbon, was a lump of charred wood, shapeless, like a lump of Christmas coal.

"You shouldn't've gotten out of the jeep," Peter Ricks said softly behind him, steering him back to his seat.

CHAPTER TEN

KRONOS

"AND WHAT IS IT YOU WANT me to do about this flyboy, this Lieutenant Coster?" Ryan busied himself about the fireplace, poking the embers uselessly.

"Work out a ploy to bring him back from Italy."

"From Italy." Ryan set down the poker. "A ploy?"

"So that no one knows why he's being pulled off the line."

"Which is?"

"He's a witness to Armando Grassi's murder."

Ryan came round the front of his desk. He leaned against the glossy oak, the polished toe of his shoe nudging at the flakes of dried mud left by Harry's boots. "He told you that?"

"And that he can name the names of some of the other people involved."

Ryan sighed. "Coster's not a witness, Harry."

"Don't do this, Joe."

The colonel flinched as a gust of wind accelerated the patter of rain against his office windows. "Harry, you have a guy who's in a place he doesn't want to be, who—by his own admission—was a participant in a criminal enterprise as a way to avoid combat duty, and now he's offering some uncorroborated fairy tale to get himself off the line. I've got no authority out there, Harry, and you've got even less. For me to reach fifteen hundred miles to pull this guy off the line, I'd probably have to take it up with 5th Army Headquarters. There's no way I'm going to tangle with Mark Clark's staff armed with as little as this."

"You're not even going to try?"

"Try *what?*" Ryan withdrew to his chair behind the desk, dropping to the seat with an exasperated huff. "It's *over*, Harry. It's *been* over! You weren't even supposed to be in Italy!"

"Be a lawyer for five minutes and do this."

"Let me remind you: You're only here on Captain Kneece's coattails, and your invitation expired when the CIC terminated the investigation. This was never a JAG case, Harry! Even if this office *were* called in, you're not staff here! You're Fort Dix, remember? You do not belong here! *You do not exist!* Can I make it any plainer than that? Oh, Harry," Ryan said, pained, "what the hell were you doing out there? God forbid something happened to you, what was I supposed to tell Cynthia?"

"I wouldn't want *you* to tell her a thing."

The colonel stiffened at the rebuke. He reached for the brass cigarette box on his desk. "You're out of here, Harry," he said as he flicked his Zippo aflame. "Captain Doheeny and his crew have already been notified and are standing ready at Duxford. As soon as this weather clears—which should, I'm told, be late this afternoon or early evening—you and Captain Kneece are on your way home. That's an order, Harry, straight from Prince's Gate. You've got some hours to kill, so why don't you have yourself a nice hot shower and a shave, the canteen's still serving break-fast, get some hot food in you, have a little Postum and take a long nap." Ryan exhaled a stream of cigarette smoke into the air. "With a good tail-wind and you don't stop to pee, you should be home for Christmas."

Harry wearily pulled himself from his chair and headed for the door.

"You're welcome," Ryan called as Harry banged the office door shut behind him.

Harry felt too tired to fight blowing rain, too tired to do anything. He lowered himself to a bench in the entry hall, not sure if the creaking he heard was coming from the wooden seat or his bones. The rain against the leaded panes of the entry hall was a monotonous finger-tapping. He tottered on the abyss of sleep.

A break in the weather in the Naples sector had allowed Harry, Kneece, and Ricks to fly from Italy directly to England. While that made for a faster return transit, it also meant a half-day of enervating air travel still wardrobed in the combat kits they'd been wearing for forty hours. Ryan had had an Army saloon and driver waiting to hurry them to

Rosewood Court—Harry to be immediately ushered into Ryan's office; Woody Kneece to McCutcheon's, the CIC senior officer.

His eyes closed and he saw Dominick Sisto, the boy he remembered playing kick-the-can on brick streets, now grown up and emptying his BAR into the night; "*Bitte* . . . please . . ."; the obscene caricatures of an incinerated Angstrom and his crew.

The memories might fade, he knew, but he also knew they would never leave him completely. A day in Branch Brook Park with his boys, an embrace from Cynthia, a summer afternoon basking on the back porch of his tenement—everything would be poisoned after this. There would, forever after, be a part of him his family could never know or understand, and that he could never explain.

And this also came to him: It was over and he'd failed. *Again.*

"Major? Major! Y'all got canned, too?" It was Woody Kneece, dripping with rain. "I hope it was nicer than the reaming I got from McCutcheon. There ought to be a law against that kind of abuse."

Harry hadn't the energy for more than an acknowledging nod.

Kneece shrugged prosaically. "Well, hell, I made a choice. I just didn't figure— Well, until that first time you go to the dentist, you don't really know how bad he can hurt you." He shrugged again, this time a hopeless designation for the material in his hands.

"What's that?"

"Irony." Kneece held up a large manila envelope marked:

EYES ONLY   CONFIDENTIAL
TO: CAPT. D. KNEECE.
C/O CID LONDON

"It's that stuff my Washington contact got me on Edghill. And these were waiting in our room when I got there." He handed Harry three wireless messages:

FROM: LT CMDR G ZAGOTTIS
         CO NARSSARSSUAQ AIR STATION
TO: MAJ H VOSS
         C/O JAG LONDON
DATE: 12-22-43
RECD RADIO COMM THIS AM TO EXPECT 132 XRAY THIS STATION
1500 HRS GMT STOP THOUGHT YOU SHOULD KNOW STOP PLS
ADVISE END MESSAGE

FROM: LT CMDR G ZAGOTTIS
        CO NARSSARSSUAQ AIR STATION
TO: MAJ H VOSS
        C/O JAG LONDON
DATE: 12-22-43
132 XRAY ARRIVED THIS STATION 1520 HRS GMT STOP DEPART
DELAYED DUE TO WEATHER STOP EXPECT DEPART LATE AM 12-23
STOP PLS ACKNOWLEDGE ADVISE ASAP END MESSAGE

FROM: LT CMDR G ZAGOTTIS
        CO NARSSARSSUAQ AIR STATION
TO: MAJ H VOSS
        C/O JAG LONDON
DATE: 12-23-43
132 XRAY EN ROUTE ICELAND ETA 1320 GMT STOP ACKNOWLEDGE
STOP GUESS ITS YOUR PROBLEM NOW END MESSAGE

"How come he sent these to you?" Kneece asked Harry. "Factually, this is—was—my investigation."

"I'm prettier. If this is like the other X-ray flights, it'll hold up in Iceland until it can time its arrival in the Orkneys for after nightfall."

"This is like salt in the wound," Kneece groused. "Ya know, Uncle Ray used to say—"

"I hope he said get me a car."

"What?"

"A car, a jeep, I don't care."

"Major, we are *done*! McCutcheon made it clear to me that after this any ideas I have about a career in the Army I can pretty much kiss—"

"Kneece, for all I care you can sit here picking your nose if you want *after* you get me some transportation, but right now get me something with wheels and a motor now, *now, NOW!*"

Harry very nearly pushed Kneece out into the rain before turning to the corporal at the entry-hall reception desk and reaching for his phone.

"Sir, you can't—"

Harry smiled coldly, pointed to the gold major's leaves on his collar, put the same finger to his lips, then used it to dial the G-2 complex at Grosvenor Square.

"I wouldn't mind just once going someplace where we sit in something warm," Kneece grumbled.

Harry, however, was oblivious to everything but the contents of Woody Kneece's manila envelope. He flipped through the pages, reading by the gray light as runnels writhed down the jeep's plastic windows.

Dear Pecker-Wood—

Do you owe me big for this!!!! I am in so much trouble because of you! Every day I've been on this Colonel Brass Ass keeps coming in here asking me what it is I'm spending so much time on instead of the casework I'm SUPPOSED to be on. You damn well better crack open that little black book of yours when you get back and share. I don't mean those crows you're always trying to pass off when you're hooked up with the pretty sister. No, sir, my ration book is all used up on "nice personalities"—ha-ha. You start sharing the GOOD quiff.

There's not much straight poop to dig up on Lt Col Wilton Cary Edghill. The files are still off limits, and this has been Edghill's Post of Command since before most everybody else got here so nobody remembers the hows, whens and whatevers of him coming on. But this guy's none too shy showing off his college ring—Harvard class of '37. Whoop dee doo. From what I hear he lets you know that Harvard is the brain factory of the world and no matter what school anybody else went to if they didn't go to Harvard you're some kind of 4-F moron (I seem to remember YOU didn't go to Harvard, ha-ha). What I find out from calling around at Harvard is Edghill's pop is good pals with guess who? Forget it; you won't guess—Joe Kennedy. Yeah, THAT Joe Kennedy! Edghill Sr. is some kind of big deal $$$$$ guy up in Boston so he deals a lot with old Joe, and they're both supposed to be big with the local Dem machine. Edghill Jr. was some kind of fellow dorm rat at Hah-vahd with Joe K. Junior. Edghill Jr. even took time off from school to work for old Joe when he was working for FDR in '36.

This is the kind of b.s. artist Little Wilton is—ask anybody in his area and they'll tell you he's always going on about how the limeys and the commies played FDR for a sucker getting him into a war that's none of our business. And then he goes and works The Chief's campaign.

Edghill came out of H with a business degree, which people tell me is some kind of license to steal so with old Joe as a pal he's keeping the right company. The poop at Hah-vahd is Little Wilton's aiming for a political career and figures a few years in uniform won't hurt, or showing the Dem party bosses what a good boy he can be (which explains him working for FDR). Now here's where it gets REAL curious—

Little Wilton comes out of OCS and in a couple months he's got his captain's ladders and a special job at G-1 here in D.C. Two bars, his own department, and nobody gets to ask him BOO about what he does. And this is AFTER he was investigated by CID and Army Intel as a possible security risk because of all that prop wash he dished out about Roosevelt and the war.

The rumor mill says old Joe pulled a lot of strings with his Dem party chums to get Edghill into G-1, a favor to Wilton Sr. keeping his son from ending up someplace where he can get his head blown off. It's also old Joe doing a favor for himself by putting Little Wilton where he can see Joe still gets all his little treats while he's serving the flag at Prince's Gate, *even when the rest of England is starving. This last part isn't a guess—there was flak about old Joe using military transports—or I should say MISusing them. FDR gave old Joe the sack in '40 but funny enough LittleWilton doesn't lose his job. Here it gets REAL curious AGAIN—*

Old Joe is back in the States,Wilton Jr.'s enlistment is almost up, everybody's smelling a war, so when the kid's hitch is up he should head for the hills, but the kid re-ups. Go figure.

And while you're figuring, figure why he's still got this office nobody's supposed to stick their nose in, and he gets bucked to major and a year later he makes light colonel. You sniff around you get the impression Joe K. is still pushing LittleWilton, but I can't dig up a WHY.

But I'll let you worry about that. I eagerly await your return, the opening of O Blessed Black Book, and the deliverance of a few numbers and addresses.

The jeep drew to a stop in front of the G-2 building. Harry shoved the pages at Kneece. "Do some cramming while I'm inside."

"You want me to wait—"

"Right here. I'll be out as soon as I can."

"It's cold out here! Can't I wait in—"

"No!"

And Harry was gone.

"I'm real curious about just what in the hell you've gotten yourself into, Voss." Christian Van Damm closed the door of his smoky kingdom behind Harry and went round the windowed cubicle drawing each set of blinds.

"I don't know what I've gotten myself into," Harry replied honestly. "You're supposed to tell me what I've gotten myself into."

"I don't know exactly what it all means, but I don't like any of it." Harry couldn't remember ever seeing the G-2 man's eyes so awake. "Remember before you left, I said the circumstances didn't scream, but justified a voice raised in concern? I'm thinking about letting out a scream." Van Damm sat in his throne behind his desk and reached for one of his rancid cigars.

"I wish you wouldn't."

Van Damm studied Harry: his drawn face, his mud-splattered combat kit. With a nod that betokened respectful deference, he set down the cigar. "We went back a month to see if there was some kind of immigration record on an Erik Sommer. Nothing. How long can he have been here, I'm wondering? So we went back two months. Nothing."

"How far back did you go?"

"A year."

"And still nothing?"

Van Damm grinned slyly. "I didn't say that." He flipped open a file folder. "Take notes, Voss, because you don't walk out of here with this. I don't need black-and-white proof floating around that I've been doing something I shouldn't be doing. OK. Keep in mind, the Brits keep a pretty close eye on whoever comes into the country these days, neutral or not. But going backward from December, they don't have anything on an Erik Sommer until July of this year: coming into England by air—via Lisbon."

"Portugal?"

"How many Lisbons do you know? A Swede coming into England via Portugal—that's a hell of a long way around. And Sommer's not alone. You go back over the rest of the year and five names—all supposedly Swedish nationals—keep showing up on the flight manifests, over and over, the same bunch of names: Sommer, a guy named Bjorg"—he pronounced it *Ba-jorg*—"another guy named Thulin, and a husband-and-wife number. The Nykvists. Maybe these little jaunts go back further than a year, but we had to back off because people are starting to nose around wondering why *we're* nosing around. The Lisbon joyrides stop in August. You remember that civilian passenger plane the krauts shot down in August? Flying up from Lisbon?"

"I remember."

"That actor was on it, Leslie Howard. You like him? He was a little too Englishy for my taste."

"He was no Hoot Gibson."

"Down into the drink goes Leslie Howard and everybody on the plane with him, including Mr. You-Don't-*Really*-Believe-I'm-Swedish Thulin."

"You think Thulin's why the Germans shot that plane down."

"Maybe they just didn't like Leslie Howard a whole lot. But, like I said, that ol' gang o' mine stops taking the plane after that. I had our people in Stockholm do some snooping. They may not have been coming in by plane, but they were still coming. Once each month since August, one or another of these question marks has been coming to Merry Old England by boat."

"I thought you said there was no immigration record—"

Van Damm sat back in his plush chair, a smug look-at-the-magic-I-can-do smile on his face, his fingers laced across the front of his stained shirt. "They didn't come in by commercial ship. They applied to the Swedish government for permission to travel here by private vessel—"

"A yacht," Harry said. "It wouldn't happen to be called the *Rascal*, would it?"

"Maybe in England it is," Van Damm mused. "In Sweden it's the *Bifrost*."

"The what?"

"That's Swedish."

"For what? Twice as icy?"

"Damn, you're an uncultured son of a gun, Voss." Harry glared. "OK, I looked it up. The Bifrost is the rainbow bridge between Asgard—that's where all the Viking gods are supposed to live—and the earth, which ain't as nice a neighborhood. Especially lately."

"Wait a minute, you did say there was no immigration—"

"I said there's no record of them coming into this country. But there are records of them leaving Sweden. There's no record of the Bifrost coming into any port in the U.K. But the harbormaster at Göteborg records the Bifrost leaving Sweden for England four times since August, the last time being a week ago: December seventeenth. You want to hear something else that'll put your eyebrows up around your hairline? Our people did some peeping into Swedish shipping registries—"

"No Bifrost."

"We're not talking about some six-foot rowboat, either, Voss, not if this thing can handle open water from Göteborg to someplace down here. That's the North Sea you're crossing there, my friend. The Swedish shipping registry should have it listed. Now let me put your eyebrows up behind your ears. The Swedish state department has no record of issuing a passport or any kind of travel papers to Sommer, Thulin, Ba-jorg-whatever-the-hell-his-name-is, or Mr. and Mrs. Nykvist." Van Damm again reached for his cigar, and, again, Harry dissuaded him with a look. "You're killing me, Voss."

"Better you than me."

"You know what I'm thinking, and if you're half as smart as I like to think you are, you should be thinking the same thing."

"They're Germans."

Van Damm nodded gravely. Unconsciously, he reached for his cigar, caught himself, and jammed it in a desk drawer out of tempting sight. "That explains why they were coming through Lisbon. Franco may like to call himself neutral, but Spain's the friendliest—and fastest—route out of occupied Europe: to Lisbon, and then to England. And you'd have to be a German—and a well-thought-of German to boot—to move around as freely as these guys seem to."

"If they started by coming through Lisbon, wouldn't it have been a better cover for them to pretend to be Portuguese?"

"My guess is they figured their Aryan good looks wouldn't've mixed too well with Portuguese names. What's keeping me up nights is trying to figure out what they're up to. They're not refugees: They keep going back and forth. And they're not agents."

"You're sure about that?"

"Unless they're the dumbest spies Admiral Canaris has ever put in the field. Their covers are rank amateur and I mean rank as in stink—that's why it was so easy to pick 'em apart. But here's the real kick-you-out-of-bed-at-night: The Brits know about 'em."

Harry blinked. "You're talking about the British authorities. British Intelligence, British immigration, British—! How do you know?"

"Thulin died in that plane crash. It wouldn't've taken much homework at all to figure out he wasn't who his ID said he was. So, you know who went to the Brit Foreign Office and said 'if you find the body I want it'? Your pal Sir John Duff. Here's a guy who's a big shot in British arms, he's got a tie to a dead somebody who ain't the nice, safe neutral he says he was, and the Brits just let it go. No follow-up, no nothing. There's more." Van Damm paused, shaking his head, as if he couldn't believe it himself. "The different Intelligence groups don't always know what all the other groups are doing. Every once in a while, maybe one of our operations bumps into one of theirs. But we're a pretty collegial bunch. Something like that happens, I get asked over to MI 6 for tea, I sit with my opposite number, and it's all, 'Pip pip, old bean, good show, but you're treading on our toes, eh? That's our joe you're poking at with a stick, so be a good chap and back off, eh? Good fellow, pip pip!' So I asked around over there. Don't get your shorts in a bunch, Voss, it was all real informal, real friendly, off-the-record, and your name didn't come up once. But I didn't get my cup of tea this time, Voss. What I got was a real informal, real friendly 'Butt the hell out, Yank!' No explanation, no nothing, just a big, blank wall with 'Do Not Enter' all over it."

"Have you ever come up against something like that?"

"It happens. Maybe something is so classified only the big mucky-mucks know about it. But I don't like this, Voss. Four krauts having tea and biscuits with a wheeler-dealer in British armaments is what I do call a screaming security risk. Listen, Voss—I know this started out as a favor, but it just turned into something else. This is bad with a capital B, understand? What I should do is go up the T.O., flag my senior at SHAEF. Even if this is some tip-top-secret classified job, him they'll tell, at least enough for him to feel safe and happy and come back to me with something to make me feel—"

"Safe and happy."

"Yeah."

"Wait on that."

"Why?"

"A day. Eighteen hours. Just until tomorrow morning."

"Voss, let me repeat: *Why?*"

Harry flipped his notebook closed and slipped it into his breast pocket, then folded his reading glasses. "I have a chance to find out what this is all about."

"And if I make noise, everybody goes to ground, is that it?"

"Tomorrow morning, I don't care if you stand out in front of Buckingham Palace and tell the world that Sir John Duff and Fatso Goering double-date. Just give me until 0600. By that time, this may all be academic . . . and you'll be kept clear of this, which, I'm starting to feel, will be a very good place to be."

"For me," Van Damm agreed with a certain amount of unease. "But what about you?"

Harry was already on his feet. "I am touched by your concern, Colonel. Give me until tomorrow and I'll buy you a box of those filthy weeds you smoke myself."

Van Damm closed his eyes, shook his head. "I'm gonna hate myself in the morning, but how can I refuse an offer like that? By the way: How was Italy?"

"See Rome and die."

"Where's Peter Ricks?"

"Don't you want to get in out of the rain?" Kneece asked.

Harry remained standing by the driver's door of the jeep. "Where is Ricks?"

"At the hospital, I guess. That's still his billet. What'd you find out?"

"Later," Harry said, "helping" Kneece out of his seat into the rain by tugging on his elbow.

"What're you doing?" the captain asked unhappily, hunching up his shoulders as rain splashed down his collar.

"Go find Ricks," Harry replied, climbing behind the wheel. "You both go to the Rose and Crown and wait for me. I'll be there as soon as I can."

"Did you happen to notice all this rain coming down on my head?"

"Don't whine, Woody." And Harry sped off.

I'd been finishing one of those airy-fairy items Himself referred to as a Stiff Upper Lip piece: one of these bits of morale-propping propaganda masquerading as an anecdotal bit of color. This particular column featured a dotty old bird living alone in a row house in the Blitz-savaged South End, eccentric in an adorably English way. She talked to her cats, set tea for them in the overgrown garden in her yard. The garden, a tangle of brambles and untamed flowers, had gotten quite out of hand ("I keep meaning to get to it," she apologized in her birdlike little chirp—or so I wrote), but finally the yard was tackled by sympathetic neighbors who chipped in— also, in that adorably English way—and put her garden straight for her. Lo and behold, as they hacked away at the brambles, they found a 250-pound German bomb buried in the dirt up to its stabilizing fins. The UXB squad that came in to remove the bomb guessed it was a stray that had been sitting there since the Blitz. The moral of the story is—so I wrote— "Tend your gardens regularly!!" (I knew Himself would never tolerate that second exclamation point; I added it just to taunt him.)

The only undoctored truth to the tale was the bit about the bomb. The facts were that she was a sour old spinster who had let her garden fall into the same state of disregard as her seedy little home. She had a "bugger 'em all" attitude regarding the sensibilities of her neighbors, smoked like a chimney, drank like a fish, swore like a sailor, and dressed like a ragpicker. The huggable pack of kitties were actually feral felines feasting on the horde of field mice that had found a home in the tangles of brambles. The generous neighbors had been moved less by sympathy than by the health threat posed by the zoo garden next door. I doubt many a tear would've been shed along that street had that 250 pounds of TNT detonated square on the old bird's noggin.

I was just finishing my rewrite, trying to incorporate Himself's one-word editorial comment—"Soften!!!" (only He was licensed to indulge in superfluous exclamation points)—when my phone rang. "Can you get out for an early lunch?"

"Who is—Harry? Harry!"

"How's the Rose and Crown sound?"

"By Jesus, where are you?"

"In a jeep out in front. Hurry up. I'll treat."

"Good Christ, mate, you've touched my flinty Scot's soul."

I grabbed my hat and coat, and in a minute I was hobbling as fast as I could to the jeep at the curb. I stopped halfway through the door, frozen by the sight of Harry in his mud-daubed kit, his eyes ember red and sitting atop gray pouches. "New uniform?"

"All the kids are wearing them."

I slid in and the jeep lurched off. "Harry, it's good to see you, and intact, more or less. I was worried. Your friend Doheeny—who strikes me as a royally decent sort—that visit of his, that business of The Last Letter . . . That was a bit of melodrama I could have well done without, mate."

"Do you know where I was?"

"Doheeny guessed Italy, which made me guess you've seen Coster."

"Yeah. I saw Coster."

There was a heaviness to the way he said it, not just in his voice, but in the haunted look behind his eyes, and it pained me to see it. What pained most was that, by experience, I knew what it was. There's a bit from Ecclesiastes, I think: "*In much wisdom is much grief: and he that increaseth knowledge increaseth sorrow.*"

Like all the other public houses in England at the time, the Rose & Crown was open only a few hours in the afternoon and then again in the evening, as a means of stretching rationed liquor supplies. It was still an hour from the afternoon opening, but for the fiver Harry supplied Lil, she gave us run of the room, and for another few quid from Woody Kneece provided a piping pot of tea and a plate of nibbles.

Harry ensconced himself in a booth alone. He laid out his little pieces of paper—wrinkled and dog-eared veterans from the trek across the North Atlantic; new ones made on a borrowed bar tablet. He made his notes, shifting the pieces of paper this way and that, peering hard at them through his reading spectacles. I sat over my cup of tea, fascinated.

"Not bad, huh?" Kneece was standing with his back to the dartboard, bent over so far rearward I thought he'd fall on his arse. In this fashion he was lobbing the darts and had actually managed to stick a few into the cork.

Ricks sat apart from us, elbows on knees, hands closed round a cigarette, head hung forward, as if the most important concern in his universe just then was the puddles forming round his boots.

Harry glanced at Kneece briefly over the tops of his glasses, sighed, and turned back to his paper puzzle. Harry's shuffling of paper ceased as he saw something that turned his face . . . not so much hard as committed. He began to gather up his bits of paper one by one into a neat deck. "I'm going up there."

I think all three of us—myself, Kneece, and Ricks—froze for a moment, unsure we'd heard correctly, or that we'd understood what it was we'd heard, or afraid that we *had* heard correctly.

Harry tucked his papers inside his windcheater. "Tonight. I'm going up there tonight."

"Going up *where?*" Kneece asked, but he already knew.

"To do . . . ?" I asked, not really wanting to know.

Harry sighed, resigned. "I'm going after that night train."

Woody Kneece laughed derisively. "Major, you *are* truly something! You don't give up!"

Peter Ricks threw his cigarette away—apologies for the mess, Lilith— and slid into the booth bench across from Harry. "You can't win," he said flatly. "There's big people behind this, people we don't know about. There *have* to be, running interference for Duff on this side of the ocean, for Edghill back in the States. And people big enough to do that—"

"We're not going to get any authority to move on it the way this case is sitting," Harry told him. "Right now, we've got nothing but some rumors and gossip and a couple of informed guesses. It's too easy to pretend that what you can't see isn't happening."

"Out of sight, out of mind?"

"Exactly. So you drag it out where everybody can see. You stand there with one of their bootlegged planes in hand, a bootleg cargo, a pile of coconspirators. . . . I don't care how big a mop they have, they can't put spilt milk back in the bottle."

"You're starting to sound like Uncle Ray," Kneece drawled. "Only I understand him."

"They're going to be real mad," Ricks told Harry.

"My heart goes out to them," Harry said.

"Y'all can't be asking us to join this *posse* of yours!" Kneece went from mockery to incredulity. He turned to Peter Ricks. "And y'*all* can't be thinking of going up there with him?"

"I'm not asking anybody to do anything," Harry said. "I'm telling you what I'm going to do."

"Even if we pull this off," Ricks pointed out evenly, "they'll crucify us."

"Maybe."

"You didn't learn anything from what happened to y'all back in August!" Woody Kneece protested.

"Oh, no," Harry said. "I learned a lot."

"Last question," Ricks persisted. "Is Grassi worth all this? You *are* the guy who broke his jaw, aren't you?"

Harry reached inside his windcheater and came out with the cracked photo of Grassi. He pushed the photo in Woody Kneece's direction. "You left that with me, remember, Woody? In my kitchen back home. That wasn't an accident, was it? Now, *you* take a look. He wasn't just a picture. He was as real as anybody here. He was a pain in the ass and any other way you want to say not a nice person, but he was killed for no good reason and nobody seems to give a damn. If the only reason you put that uniform on was to make a point to Daddy, fine, you made your point: Go on home."

"There's a lot of boys—a *lot*—who are dying every day for no good reason," Peter Ricks said.

"I can't do anything about them," Harry replied solemnly.

Peter Ricks picked up the photo. He sighed. "Pain in the ass." He handed it back to Harry and smiled good-naturedly. "I don't know what

I'm worried about. You saw that buildup in Italy. They're getting ready for a push. So, as far as I'm concerned, I can get it in Orkney, or get it in Italy, so I might as well get it here. At least here I have some kind of say in my own destruction."

"You need me." I wondered who'd made that insane statement and then realized it was me.

Harry shook his head. "Eddie, this isn't your—"

"You *need* me, Harry." *Stop your blathering, you,* I scolded myself, but I kept talking: "You need someone outside the family. I'm a civilian, and a journalist. They can't send *me* off to some frontier outpost in Italy or the Arctic."

"Factually," Woody Kneece said wryly, "as I recall, didn't you tell us you pissed off Mr. Sir John Duff and got your British arse sent all the way out to Malaysia?"

"It's a Scottish arse, Captain, and my story still ran. If I'm witness to this, I'm your leverage against them: I'm your guarantee this can't remain invisible."

Peter Ricks groaned. "I don't like this."

"Lieutenant, I appreciate your being concerned for my well-being, but it's a bit misplaced. I have more experience under fire than anybody in this room save you." In an unfair emphasis I knew he would never refute, I punctuated the statement with a knuckle rap on my wooden leg.

"I still don't like it," he said. But his tone was resigned.

Woody Kneece picked at the plate of nibbles, took a bite of a slice of Spam, made a disgusted face, and threw the remainder back on the plate. "Well, well. What's the worst that can happen? If they bust me, I can always get a job working for my daddy." He beamed a broad smile: "And y'all could always get a job working for *me!*"

"See?" Harry said to Ricks. "We don't have a thing to worry about!"

Kneece put his hands in his pockets and came to stand over Harry's table. "All right, Major. You got your posse. Let's go tip over some milk bottles."

The flight mechanic slammed the hatch of the Dakota and took a seat in the cargo cabin across from Sparks and the copilot. The only noise was the drumming of the rain on the aluminum hull.

The copilot rapped knuckles on the bench. "With all present and accounted for, I hereby call this meeting of the He-Man Woman-Haters Club to order!" The crew chuckled, desperate to dispel the oppressive seriousness.

Doheeny smiled. "Major Voss asked something of me . . ." The smile disappeared. "Well, what he asked, it's not really for me to say yes. Maybe I better let him explain a bit." Doheeny turned to Harry. "They're all yours, Harry," and he stood away.

"I'm sorry for dragging you guys out into the rain like this," Harry began, "but I thought we should have the privacy. You guys must've been wondering why you've been lugging Captain Kneece and me all over the North Atlantic, especially after that little 'mishap' at Kap Farvel."

The copilot raised a hand. "Yeah, well, sir, we did take a little umbrage at that!"

Another spate of nervous chuckles.

"OK, here it is," Harry went on. "There's a kind of smuggling ring running between the States and someone on Orkney. I say smuggling, but this isn't just about somebody making a few bucks moving black-market nylons and booze. You saw that wreck back in Greenland. Three of the men on that ship were killed. A U.S. Army lieutenant on Greenland got wise to what was going on just a few weeks ago, and he was murdered—they put a bullet through his head—to keep their operation quiet." He looked at their grave faces to see that they'd absorbed the story thus far. "The people involved in this business have some pretty powerful friends. So, the people who should be doing something about it are sitting back, and the people running the operation are so confident they're not going to get touched, they're not even waiting for things to cool down; they're moving another load into the Orkneys tonight, right into the same place where they killed the Army lieutenant." He cleared his throat. "Since nobody else wants to do anything about this, Captain Kneece and I, and some other fellas, we want to go up there tonight and try to put a stop to it."

"Major," the copilot asked, "are you asking us to grab pitchforks and torches and go on after these bad guys?"

"That's not your job. Your job is to fly this aeroplane. That's what me and my people need: transport to the Orkneys."

"So we fly you to the Orkneys," Sparks said. "We've flown you just about everywhere else; so what?"

"It's not that simple, fellas," Doheeny pointed out.

Harry went on: "Because these people have powerful friends, and because going there would be a violation of a direct order sending us home . . . this could mean trouble for everybody involved." He looked at the copilot and Sparks sitting together. "For you civilians, I don't know what that would mean for your careers, now or after the war. And you, Sergeant, you're Army—"

The flight mechanic's head bobbed in agreement. He looked at the sergeant's stripes on his shoulder and waved his fingers at them: "Bye-bye, stripes."

"At the very least," Harry agreed.

"Harry—that is, Major Voss—he asked me to fly him up there," Doheeny told his men. "But we've all been flying together a long time, too long for me to put your necks on the line for something like this unless you want to. This is purely voluntary."

The copilot fidgeted in his seat. "Cap'n, look, I'm just the meter reader up there in the dummy seat. If you want to ferry the major up, just say the word—"

Doheeny was already shaking his head. "It's got to be your decision. Each of you. I need a crew to fly this crate. That means if one of you says no, nobody goes. Nobody's going to hold that against anybody: not me, not the major. To make sure none of you feel pressured into this, I thought we'd do this by secret ballot so nobody'll have to worry about—"

They had already been exchanging looks, their familiarity with each other precluding the necessity for any spoken dialogue.

"Cap'n, with all respect." The flight mechanic stood, tugging at the duck-billed cap in his hands. "You need a crew . . . we're your crew."

I stood in the doorway of her office for some time. Even then she didn't notice me until that little chinless wasp Berwyck did. He'd come from his interior office to hand her some papers.

"Cathryn, be a dear and retype this when you—oh! Mr. Owen!" He didn't seem to know what to make of my rough clothes, hardy khakis of the sort I'd last worn on my jaunt to Malaysia.

That's when she looked up. Surprised. Unpleasantly.

"Hello, Berwyck old man. How goes the war, eh? Working the slaves to the nub, are you? Is he treating you all right, Cat? No floggings, I trust. Tell me, and I'll thrash this member of the oppressive proletariat!"

He began inching back toward his office. "Sorry?"

I came up to him—which made him flinch—and threw an arm about his shoulders. "A joke, Berwyck, a gibe, a jest!"

He smiled weakly. "Of course. Well . . . ." He wriggled out from under my arm with an admirable politeness. "We do seem to be seeing quite a bit of you lately."

"An aberration, Berwyck. Fear not. I'll soon be retreating to my previous anonymity. Hope I'm not a bother."

"Oh, no, I didn't mean to imply, well—"

"Mind if I have a word . . . ?" I cut him off mercifully—the poor blighter did seem to be foundering—nodding in the direction of my wife.

"Yes, why, certainly. Cathryn, this is nothing urgent I've left you.

When you have a chance. . . ." He stepped back farther into his office, keeping me in sight all the time as if concerned that once he turned his back I might pounce. "Nice to see you again, Mr. Owen."

"Always a pleasure, Berwyck. Toodles."

He closed the door behind him, which I thought curious, as it hadn't been closed when I got there.

"We *are* seeing a terrible lot of you lately," Cathryn said. "I'm seeing more of you now than when we were married."

I clutched my heart as if struck by an arrow. "Spot on and deadly, my dear!"

"How long were you standing there?"

"I was dumbstruck by what my eyes beheld: Still Life—Woman and Typewriter."

"You're a depressing sod." She leaned forward, whispering: "I've helped you *once*, Eddie! Not *again*! If you've come back to—"

"Nothing of the sort, Cat. Can we go somewhere?"

She took me by the hand to the landing of the main staircase.

I offered her my pack of Players.

"No." Then she remembered herself: "Thank you. You know, you torment that man unforgivably."

"Who? Old Berwyck? I love the little bugger, Cat. I think he's an absolute delight."

"Little boys who pull the wings off flies think the same thing about the flies. Now: What is it you want this time?"

I held out my latchkey to her.

Her eyes narrowed. "What's this about?"

"Key to my flat, dearie. I'm off for a few days."

"And I'm to feed the fish and water the flowers?"

"Cat, you should know better."

"Ah, yes, any living thing in your flat would have long since died of neglect."

"Or sued for divorce. Sorry. It was a bad joke."

"You've been off before without leaving me your latchkey." She had yet to take the key.

"It's just in case you need to get in while I'm gone."

"With no flowers or fish, why should I need to— Oh, no." Her eyes widened in dismay. "This has to do with why you were here the other day."

"I'm just off to do a little research—"

"Sir John, Eddie? Sir John?"

"A little louder, dear, I don't think they can quite hear you down to the street."

"I shouldn't be surprised, not after the other night. Research?

Bollocks! Think a little better of me than that! This is your grand gesture, isn't it? This, this *expedition* of yours! And *this*"—she waved a hand at the latchkey—"is your hero's farewell. I won't have it, Eddie. It was enough to be married to you and worry if you were coming home—"

"Cat, dear, how sweet! You still care!"

"I should knock you over this banister. It would serve you right to have that haggis between your ears dashed all over the foyer." She had vented, and now sagged back against the wall, drained. She held out a hand, snapping her fingers impatiently until I handed her a Players and lit it for her. "Eddie, I won't try to talk you out of this. I learned long ago there's no getting sense into that Scottish noggin of yours. What is it about heroic self-destruction that men find so appealing when they start questioning themselves?"

I lit my own Players off the same match. "It is a puzzlement, eh, lass?"

"Bollocks." She held out her hand for the key. I handed it over.

"It's just that I've been thinking—"

"A mistake for you."

"Aye. But I have to admit to not being all that impressed with myself."

"You of all people, Eddie. You've done your bit. Even if you only ever wrote *one* important story—"

"I've written a million words, Cat, and gauging by the front page of the morning edition, none of them seems to have done much good by anyone. Just once, I would like to . . ." I wasn't sure what it was I did want to do, but I knew she understood even better than I.

"Merry Christmas, you silly bastard," she murmured, gave me a sound slap on the cheek, then a peck where the blow had left my face hot, before she turned and hurried down the hall, back to her office with my latchkey in hand.

It is on such paradoxes that great philosophers and poets better than I dwell.

The plan was simple. Leaving from Duxford rather than the usual ATC terminus at Prestwick allowed Doheeny to cheat his course eastward. Filing a flight plan that kept him over land as long as possible—a prudent enough maneuver prior to a North Atlantic crossing—brought his path even closer to Orkney, sending him up the east coast of Britain before heading out into the Atlantic across the mouth of Pentland Firth.

From several canvas equipment bags Peter Ricks meted out cold-weather gear. One bag, however, remained untouched. As he was moving it out of the way I heard the clatter of metal and wood. "Something special Santa left under the tree," he told me, "for later."

It was nearly six P.M. when we crossed out over the sea. In those northern climes, and it being December 24th to boot, it was already quite dark at six P.M. A sliver of moon flashed intermittently through clouds onto the black waters. Enough moonlight came down to bring out the shadowy hump of Hoy passing a few miles by our starboard windows. But then the clouds closed and Hoy disappeared into blackness as the Dakota drew farther from land, northwest out over the Atlantic.

Doheeny came back from the cockpit to sit with us.

"So when do we do this?" Harry asked him.

"I was going to suggest now. We're out far enough to where anybody can see it makes more sense to route us into Orkney than back to Scotland. We also just got a radio alert there's a squall line bearing southeast. I don't want to be in a one-engine race to the barn with a storm out here."

"I thought the engine failure was to be a bit of playacting," I pointed out.

"If it's going to look good, I'm going to have to kill the engine before we land at Kirkwall. We'll be fine. Without cargo, one of those engines could carry us all the way to Iceland. I just wanted to warn you it might get a bit bumpy back here." Doheeny went back forward. "Hey, Marconi," he flagged Sparks, "send your Mayday." He slid back into his seat. "OK, Tonto, pull the plug."

The copilot pulled back the throttle and propeller control, cut the fuel feeding to the engine, then struck a red button overhead. The engine feathered. As the Pratt & Whitney's roar stuttered, then stilled, the Dakota yawed heavily to starboard, beginning a listing, downward slide. We braced ourselves in our seats, suddenly seeing the dark and inhospitably cold waters of the North Atlantic through the windows across the cabin. The copilot killed the ignition switch to the engine, then addressed the settings for the port engine, boosting its power. At the same time, Doheeny's right hand danced among the tab controls while his left wrestled with the control yoke until the ship came back into trim, but now less than a thousand feet above the ocean. The pilot began a slow turn back toward Orkney. "Fellas!" he called back to us. "You've got about thirty minutes until H-hour."

Woody Kneece turned round in his seat and grinned at Harry. "Makes you wish you'd stayed home in bed, huh, Major?"

"I tried that," Harry replied. "It didn't work."

"You lied to me back in Italy, didn't you?" Ricks asked. He nodded at the weapons arrayed on the Officers Mess billiard table. "You really *don't* know how to use these."

"Basic training was a long time ago," Harry apologized.

"We've only got time for a quick refresher. Mr. Owen, you should sit in on this." There followed some quick instruction about safeties and magazine releases. "Got all that?"

"What about aiming?" Harry asked.

"If something pops, just put out as much fire as you can. I'm not so much worried about you hitting something as in putting out enough lead to keep them from getting a good bead on you."

Ricks turned at the sound of the Officers Mess door opening. He picked up one of the .45's from the billiard table, made sure it was loaded and cocked.

Astin Moncrief came into the Officers Mess with Jim Doheeny.

"Ah, Major Voss!" Moncrief smiled a polite welcome. "Good to see you again, though I'm sure you and your mates'd just as soon be on your way home, eh? Bit of luck there, just beat this snow in, good-o!" The RAF major prattled on, but bit by bit, he noted the arms on the billiard table, the combat trousers extending below parka hems still carrying a bit of Italian mud, the look in Peter Ricks's eyes every bit as cold and unforgiving as the muzzle of the pistol he held by his side. The polite blather became a desperate ramble, as if the longer he could talk the longer he would put off an unwelcome event. "Seems someone's up to a bit of a to-do, eh?" He went dry, his voice giving out before five hard faces. "Might I ask what this is all about?" he squeaked.

From icy stillness into sudden action, Ricks was explosive, quick-stepping across the room, grabbing Moncrief by the front of his bridge coat, and flinging him into one of the seats by the fire so hard the lieutenant had to put a boot on the seat to keep it from toppling over. Ricks grabbed a telephone from a nearby lamp table and dropped it into Moncrief's lap. "I'm sure you have a pretty good idea what this is all about, Major."

"I'm afraid I don't—"

Ricks set him back into the seat with a push that was nearly a punch. "Major, try to get out of that chair again and I'm going to hurt you." He picked up the telephone receiver and thrust it into Moncrief's hand. "Now be a nice guy, get us some transportation, something we can all fit in. A command car would be nice. And then all of us are going to take a ride." He placed the muzzle of the .45 against Moncrief's forehead. He pushed the pistol hard against the skin, pushing Moncrief's head against the seat back, burrowing the rim of the barrel in the flesh. He thumbed back the hammer of the pistol. "I won't ask twice."

Harry pulled Doheeny aside. "Jim, we don't know who else on this base might be involved, so there can't be any alarm. Go back to your crew. If anybody asks if you've seen Moncrief, if you know where we went—"

"The last time I saw you, you were all having a friendly chat here at the club."

"If anybody wants to change their mind," Ricks announced, hanging up the phone for Moncrief, "this is their last chance."

Doheeny unhappily watched us strap on our pistol belts, sling on our carbines and bandoliers. He exchanged a look with Harry, Doheeny's eyes pleading that Harry be the one to change his mind. Harry merely smiled a sad smile, patted the flyer on his shoulder, then sent him out into the freshening snowfall.

My leg made it simplest for me to ride up front alongside Ricks at the wheel, while Harry and Kneece in the rear squeezed Astin Moncrief between their parka-clad bulks. Even without my leg, I think Ricks would have preferred the arrangement. All through the flight I had noticed Ricks and Kneece kept a distance, both physically and otherwise, always cool to each other, never saying more to each other than they needed to.

My gloved fingers flexed round the barrel of the carbine propped between my knees. I was sure I could feel the cold steel through the gloves.

Over the course of my twenty years on the job, I have been shot at with weapons of all calibers, from pistol to cannon. I have been threatened by blade and blunt object, assaulted by fist and boot. I have been bludgeoned, beaten, bombarded, and bombed, and climactically dismembered. One never ceases being afraid; one can even grow accustomed to being afraid.

But being afraid to die is one thing. And killing is something else again. You would think it an easy enough thing to do, there being so much of it about. What did it require? A few pounds of pressure on the metal crescent of a trigger. But now, faced with the possibility . . .

We passed the cottages of Stromness. I glimpsed a woman tending the blackout curtains, two boys gawking at the command car bounding past, a white-maned gentleman—pipe clenched in his teeth—contemplating the falling snow. Perhaps it was the aftereffect of all those toddies, but they all looked beautiful to me.

"This is where they found Armando," Harry said a few minutes later, and Ricks slowed the car to a halt.

Beyond the sequined curtain of snowflakes, the frozen beach where Grassi's body had lain was invisible in the dark.

> "*The minstrel boy will return we pray,*
> *When we hear the news, we all will cheer it.*
> *The minstrel boy will return one day,*
> *Torn perhaps in body, not in spirit . . .*"

It was Woody Kneece, singing softly.

"Knock it off," Harry said.

"Would you prefer another song? I do a mean 'Don't Sit Under the Apple Tree With Anyone Else But Me.' "

"I prefer you shut up. Pete, the road you want is just up ahead. Turn here."

Ricks slipped the car into gear and started along the track of frozen mud that followed the head of the beach.

Woody Kneece leaned forward and pointed through the snow-splattered windscreen. "You can pull off right up there and I can show you where I made a hole in the fence. We can slip in there."

But Peter Ricks did not pull off the road. Instead, the car began to accelerate, and in moments we saw the gate rushing toward us.

"Pete . . . ?" Harry asked.

I don't know which of us cried out "*Jesus!*" Perhaps we all did. The toddy-fueled journalist in me prevented me from completely closing my eyes, wanting to note every detail, as the protective cage over the command car's grille hit the gate square on, the chain holding it snapped, and the gate rebounded against the fence with a metallic twang. The blow shattered both headlamps, and I wondered how Ricks vaulted the car up the rutted path in the snowy dark without hitting any of the trees lining the route.

He skidded the vehicle to a halt in front of the cabin and bounded out of the car, carbine in hand. Old Teddy Bowles was already in the door, shotgun in one hand as he hastily pulled on his mackintosh.

"Mr. Bowles!" Ricks called out. He had the carbine at his shoulder, leveled at the old man. "Either you or that weapon goes on the ground *now!*"

"Please, Teddy!" Moncrief called from the car. "Drop it!"

It took Bowles only a second to make a sage decision.

Ricks nudged Bowles inside the cabin with the muzzle of his carbine. "Major Voss, would you mind getting his weapon? Mr. Owen, please escort Major Moncrief inside. Captain Kneece, I'd appreciate you pulling the car around back out of sight."

No peat-burning stove could compete with the Orkney winter, but after the wind-whipped ride in the command car, the inside of the cottage was comparatively cozy. I gravitated to the glowing stove, warming my hands before the grate. Kneece reached for the pot of coffee simmering atop the stove.

"Don't," Peter Ricks said curtly. "Unless you want to pee on yourself once you're outside." He took in the pride of felines dotted about, almond-shaped eyes fixed curiously on the newcomers filling the room. "What's with all these goddamned cats?"

Harry nodded Teddy Bowles and Astin Moncrief to chairs, then perched on the edge of the table, looking down at the two men.

"Major Voss," Moncrief ahemmed, trying to reassert some composure, "I don't know what you think you're about, but you are making a horrible mistake."

"I kind of thought we were overdue for this tune," Kneece said.

"Major Moncrief, please," Harry said dismissively. "We know about the X-ray flight coming in tonight. We know it's going to set down on Sir John's land. We know the cargo will be transferred to his yacht and be taken down to his lodge in Scotland. What we need are details."

"I don't know what this X-ray rubbish is you're spouting on about," Moncrief blustered, "but as soon as I can get word to my sergeant-at-arms, you and your men will find yourselves under close arrest, and when I contact your superiors in London—"

"Yell loud," Ricks suggested, fingering the grip of his carbine. "I strongly urge you gentlemen to see the error of your ways. Decide to be heroes, help us out, and maybe you'll get a break on the back end."

"They said there'd be no troubles, is what they was always sayin'," Bowles protested shakily.

"They were wrong, Mr. Bowles," Harry told him. "Right now I can stand in the well at the Old Bailey and make a case against both of you not only as parties to all this smuggling, but as accessories to the murder of an American Army officer. But that's not how it has to be."

"Ye want me t' do foul by Sir John 'n', noope, I won't 'elp ye make yer lies against him."

"Lies?" Peter Ricks said it with a biting iciness. He nodded at Bowles and Moncrief. "They're going to waste time, and we don't know how much time we have."

Harry regarded the hard eyes of the lieutenant, gave a glum, almost imperceptible nod, then stepped away.

Ricks's eyes settled on a pear-shaped tabby seated at the far end of the table. He raised his carbine, holding it out toward the tabby in his outstretched hand like a pistol, and squeezed off a shot.

The room exploded in cats dashing fearfully this way and that.

The dead set of Ricks's face had not changed, nor did it as he swung the still-smoking muzzle toward the shocked faces of Teddy Bowles and Astin Moncrief. "You guys have a choice. You either help us, or you do not see the error of your ways and I blow your fucking brains out. Look me in the eye, gents; I am not bluffing." Moncrief turned away as the carbine muzzle hovered just in front of his eyes, blinking against the sting of the tendrils of smoke curling from the black hole. "If I don't get some cooperation by the count of three, somebody is going to be dead. Onetwo—"

"All right!" Moncrief spat.

Like Moncrief, I had looked into Peter Ricks's dead eyes: I was nearly as relieved as the British major when the lieutenant lowered his weapon.

"One loves a penitent man," I said. "Inspiring."

"What time do the X-ray flights touch down?" Harry asked.

"It's never the same," Moncrief gasped. His chest heaved, his body sagged. The last few seconds had utterly unmanned him. "It depends on what can be worked with the patrol schedules."

"What about tonight?"

"It should be around 2200 hours. A little after, perhaps."

"You're not sure?"

"There isn't constant communication with the flights. I'm only told when they've left Reykjavik, then I estimate."

"That gives us about two hours," Kneece said, regarding his watch.

"What about the boat?" Harry continued. "When does the boat get here?"

"Tonight, there's a one-hour gap in the patrol screen. They should arrive anytime during that period, a half-hour either way of 2100."

"Mr. Bowles," Ricks said. "How many men crew the boat?"

Teddy Bowles's eyes were on the spray of blood and brain matter at the far end of the table.

"Mr. Bowles!" Ricks poked the old man in the chest with the barrel of his carbine. "How many men are on the goddamned boat?"

"Hm? N-not always the same, noope. A half-dozen maybe, sometimes I seen as many as ten."

"Which of you two is here when the boat comes in?"

"I'm never here," Moncrief said. "It's safer for me not to be directly involved."

"*Was* safer," Ricks corrected. He turned to Bowles. "Are you always here when the boat comes in?"

"No. I mean it's oop to when the plane comes down, isn't it?"

"How's it supposed to work tonight? The plane is coming in at ten o'clock, the boat before."

"I'd be out at the field fer the plane. I gots to light off the smudge pots, don't I? So the plane can see the field. I brings the spare petrol so they can refuel."

"So if you're not here, the people on the boat wouldn't worry."

" 'Ey'd be thinkin' I'd be at the field, wouldn't they?"

"What would they do then?"

" 'Ey'd go to the barn, eh? I leaves the barn open, I does, there's a lorry there, 'ey'd roll 'er out 'n' starts for the field."

Ricks nodded approvingly and lowered his weapon. He looked round, spied the open door to the storeroom, and disappeared inside. In a moment he returned with a length of rope. "Captain Kneece," and he nodded in the direction of the dead tabby. Kneece went into the bedroom, came back with a pillowcase. He knelt down out of sight, came back up with a bundle soaking dark red through the linen. Kneece carried the bundle outside.

"Mr. Bowles," Ricks said, "I'm going to put you and Major Moncrief in your storeroom. Since there's no lock for the door I'm going to tie your hands and legs. I'm not going to gag you, but if either of you make the least little noise, I'm going to come in there and both of you are going to join your little furry friend. Mr. Owen, why don't you help Mr. Bowles and the major get comfy in back."

When I closed the storeroom door on Teddy Bowles and Moncrief, I found Ricks by one of the front windows, gloved finger to lips in thought as he studied the ground outside. Woody Kneece returned.

"What'd you do with it?" Ricks asked.

"Burial at sea. I threw it in the water."

Ricks nodded. He picked up a poker and began to break up the fire. "I don't want smoke coming out of the chimney," he explained.

"A lot of ground to cover," Kneece said, "here and the landing strip."

"Fuck the plane," Ricks replied. "The worst that happens is they beat it back to Iceland. By the time they land we'll be in a position to call for MP's to be waiting for them when they touch down. We need to give the boat crew the idea that Teddy's off dealing with the plane. The way I see it, some of the crew come off, go for the barn to get the truck. Some will stay with the boat. Major, Mr. Owen, I'm putting you two here in the house. Mr. Owen, that'll be your position there. Major, you take that front window by the door. If something pops, depending on how things break, from there you can direct fire either at the barn or at the boat. See those rocks on the bank by the north side of the dock? I'm going in there. That'll put the guys going for the barn in a crossfire. If somebody starts shooting, they'll fall back on the barn. You told me that door is the only way in or out of the barn, so we'll have them bagged."

"And me?" Kneece asked.

"I'm putting you in those rocks on the south side of the dock. You'll be able to either support my fire on the barn, or lay down suppressing fire on the boat as needed."

"Factually, once things start to 'pop,' unless those fellas on the boat are somebody's idiot cousins, they're gonna cut and run," Kneece pointed out.

Ricks shrugged. "That's that many fewer of them for us to worry about. It doesn't matter if Moncrief has anybody in the local Navy group in on this with him. We show up back at Kirkwall with those guys in the barn and nobody'll want to be on record as refusing a request to intercept that boat." He went round the room, turning down the Colemans that lit the cottage. "Major, Mr. Owen, you should leave those windows open. If there's a fight, you don't want to have to worry about flying glass. Here's the big thing: No matter what happens, nobody does a thing, nobody makes a move, nobody opens fire unless I do. I make the first move. Understand?" He turned to Kneece. Even in the darkened room, I would not have wanted that invisible glare turned on me. "Do you understand this time, Captain? Let me hear you say it."

"I understand," Kneece said.

"Major, Mr. Owen, you two keep your heads down until you hear me give the word." Peter Ricks paused to consider if he'd left anything undone or unsaid. "I guess that's it, then."

"Just a moment." They all turned to me. I shrugged. "Seems we should say something heroic, don't you think?"

I thought I heard a breathy chuckle from Ricks's direction. "Amen and give 'em hell," he said, and stepped out into the eddies of snowflakes.

Kneece followed. The door closed.

I don't know how long Harry and I sat there, growing colder with each tick of the clock, listening to the wind draw sighs from the rafters of the cabin. Whatever glow I'd retained from the toddies flickered out; I was feeling grimly sober. In the shadows of the unlit room I could just make out Harry, head bowed. . . . In thought? A prayer? Perhaps dwelling on the still-strong smell of cordite in the room.

"Harry? Harry!"

"Hm?"

"Point that the other way, if you please."

He'd laid his carbine in his lap, unthinkingly leaving the barrel canted in my direction. "Oh. Sorry." He stood the weapon on its butt, leaned his forehead against the barrel. "How long's it been?" he asked after a bit.

"It's too dark to see my watch. Harry, I have to ask."

"Ask what?"

"I don't mean to question your altruism, but . . . Maybe I'm just jaded, turning into a surly old sod."

"What's your question?"

"I didn't know Armando Grassi very well, but what I knew of him . . . I just can't believe you've gone through these last two weeks for him."

"So everybody keeps reminding me." He flexed the hand he'd fractured on the lieutenant's jaw four months previous.

"Why, then? Ach, you should be home where it's safe"—I shivered theatrically—"and warm. I have a suspicion."

He nodded at me to go ahead.

"You feel some fault lies with you for what happened last summer, aye? And you're looking for some way of balancing out the scales."

He was silent for a long moment, as if considering. "Maybe. In part."

"The other part being?"

Another moment. "Did I ever tell you how I got into the service? Joe Ryan pulled strings. Look at me, Eddie. Do you think I could've passed the physical without someone pulling strings for me? Once he got me in, he greased my way to my majority. He brought me with him to England and fed me the good cases to pump up my record. Eddie, I was in England for nine months. I lived like a king in Rosewood Court, sleeping on clean sheets every night in a four-poster bed." A sigh. "I needed to earn it, Eddie."

"Earn what?"

"Nine months of that and a failed case. For that I got a ticket home. I don't know how to live with that, Eddie."

In a world gone insane with indecency, the man had enough conscience in him to shame a pope. It made me feel small. It also made me feel what a great tragedy it should be for the shoddy state of the world to lose that last good soul.

I heard a deep rumble out of the east, becoming more distinct as it grew nearer. "Aeroplane?" I asked Harry.

He nodded.

"The X-ray plane?"

He was looking skyward, judging. "Doesn't sound like a C-47. Sounds bigger. Maybe one of those big flying boats that do the patrols. I wouldn't think any of them'd be going up until this snow clears."

"I thought Moncrief fixed it so none of them'd be about at all."

Harry shrugged, as puzzled as I.

The engine noise grew louder—the aeroplane must've been quite low—setting crockery and cookware rattling, the windowpanes fluttering in their frames. It faded, its drone drifting in and out of the rising and falling wind like a distant bee.

Then another noise, similar, an engine—I thought, for a moment, the patrol plane might be circling back—but this one had a different, deeper pitch, a slower, more muscular rhythm.

Harry rose, just enough to look over the sill of the window. What moon there was was dulled by the clouds and swirls of snow, but we could make out the foot of the dock, the rippling surface of the water. The far end of the dock, however, was lost in darkness. From somewhere beyond that, someplace out on the water, came this second, nearing engine.

"I think this might be them," I said. Surprising how hoarse even a whisper can be.

A flashing spear of a light—small, probably nothing more than a torch or Aldis lamp—came out of the dark, swept this way and that, finally settling on the end of the dock. We could not see the yacht, only the glowing disc of the lamp, the pilings silhouetted in its beam. The engine dropped, revved, dropped again as the helmsman tried to sidle the vessel up to the dock. The engine died, we heard some voices—barked commands—the thud of boots as a crewman jumped across to the dock to moor the boat.

A call from the boat: "Oy! Teddy-boy! Are ye about, old Ted?"

A few murmurs, then the cadence of several pairs of boots trudging our way along the dock.

Harry and I slid back down to the floor.

"Good luck," Harry said softly. I gave a tight nod I hoped he could see.

I brought the carbine to my chest and slid my finger round the trigger. In the cabin's cold I felt sweat trickle into my eyes.

We heard the footsteps—couldn't tell how many—leave the planking and crunch across the snow and frozen mud in front of the cabin. One set of steps paused:

"Oy! I say, Ted-o!"

A mumbled consultation with his mates, then several sets of steps crunched toward the barn, and a single set toward the cabin. We never found out why: a search for hot coffee, a pack of cigarettes, maybe he just wanted a moment out of the cold.

Perhaps from my vantage it was easier to discern the parting of the group. I looked to Harry to see if he recognized it as well, but he signified nothing from his crouch below the front window. I waved in his direction, but there was no response. I turned my carbine on the front door, toward which the single pair of boots seemed to be heading.

"Hold it right where you are! All of you!"

Woody Kneece.

"Goddammit!" Harry hissed.

"This is the United States Army! Throw down your weapons and surrender or we will open fire!"

It began with a single shot that hugged the snow-filled air round the cabin for an incredibly long moment, coming—so it sounded—from the man who'd been heading for the cabin. Then a flurry of shots from Woody Kneece's position. A flurry answered from the barn.

"Now!" Peter Ricks yelled. "Nownownow!" and the crackcrackcrack of his carbine.

I rose and saw the two shadows near the barn, each armed with a rifle, their forms flashlit by muzzle flares, firing toward Peter Ricks as they backed their way to the barn.

I didn't aim, didn't even raise the carbine to my eye—I just tucked it in my shoulder and began squeezing the trigger.

A burst of automatic fire, a Sten, from the boat.

"Woody! Woody!"

It was Harry. He was standing in the window, the carbine forgotten in his hands. Then a noise from deep inside him—a cry, a scream, something of anger, something of pain, all commingled in one horrible, inhuman explosion. His carbine came up and he began firing, even as he screamed, firing, pulling the trigger even when the weapon had nothing left to spit out.

"Reload, Harry! Reload!"

I was scrambling to push a fresh magazine in my own weapon. Loaded and cocked, I turned back to the barn. In the muzzle flashes I saw a figure on the snow-dusted ground. The other man had made the barn, was snapping off shots at Ricks through the open gap of the door.

Then the whole of that side of the island filled with the ghastly, flickering light of parachute flares, drifting down in a line following the shore. Peter Ricks exposed himself, jumping to the top of his cluster of covering rocks, waving his arms in mad signals into the sky.

Those heavy engines came down, so low the whole cabin vibrated, so near I thought the cabin roof would be torn clear.

"Stay down!" Ricks yelled to us, then jumped into the rocks.

It came down like rain in hell, a cascade of tracers from the machine guns of the thundering Sunderland overhead. The guns raked the length of the dock, flinging up a shower of splinters, scything their way toward the yacht. I saw figures jump clear of the boat as the deluge of machine-gun fire tore away at the varnished wood and brass fittings until some of those fiery little lances managed to burrow deep enough into the hull to find the petrol tanks.

The blast sent a gust of warm air through the room. Again the cabin rattled. The yacht rose up nearly clear of the water as the aft section dissolved in a swirling, ugly, mottled ball of flame.

In just seconds the boat settled to the bottom, leaving only the shattered, smoldering bridge above water amidst a stinking halo of floating, burning petrol.

Peter Ricks had dashed out from the rocks onto the dock, waving an all-clear at the Sunderland, still rumbling about unseen behind the glare of the flares.

I charged out of the cabin, forgetting my leg. By the dying light of the flares I saw two staggering figures on the end of the dock. Ricks advanced toward them, carbine up and ready.

"Lie down on your faces! Hands on the back of your head!"

He signaled me to move on the barn. The man who'd hidden himself there advanced toward me. I raised my weapon.

"Not me, mate!" he called out, tossing his rifle to the ground and then raising his hands. "I'm done!"

"*Goddammit!*" Harry. Partly an oath, partly a sob.

I swung round. He'd clambered up the rocks where Woody Kneece had stood, and was now sliding back down to the bank.

"*Goddammit!*"

Harry took his carbine by the barrel and smashed it down on the rocks, again and again and again: I heard the walnut stock splinter.

The flares died, the flames at the end of the dock dwindled, the hovering Sunderland drew back up into the snowy sky.

The rest, as Hamlet said, is silence.

CHAPTER ELEVEN

GREAT PAN IS DEAD

IT TOOK QUITE A BIT OF rapping the brass knocker, pounding on the door, and yanking on the bellpull before a bleary-eyed Gordon Fordyce, clad in silk pajamas and dressing gown, his hair an oily tangle, pulled open the door. "Major Voss!"

Harry pushed past him into the entry hall. "Do you mind? It's raining."

Fordyce peered outside to see if Harry was alone, saw only the empty jeep parked in the drive in the early-morning grayness. It was a chill rain, quickly poisoning the warmth of the hall. Despite the damp, Fordyce remained by the open door, his hand still on the knob, an unsubtle suggestion that Harry was welcome to leave. "What're you doing here?"

Harry shucked off his sodden parka, shook the rain off his crushed officer's cap, made a show of scraping fresh mud from his combat boots along the edge of the varnished oak step. "You're up awfully early, Gordie."

"I don't sleep through the night. Insomnia."

"Guilty conscience?"

"What do you want? Never mind, it doesn't matter. I want you out. This is an absurd hour, whatever the reason. If you wish, you may make an appointment—"

"I'm not going anywhere, Gordie."

"Don't call me that."

Harry strode over to him, pushed the door free of his hand, and slammed it closed. "Get your tail upstairs, wake up your boss, and get his fat arse down here."

Fordyce took a step back. For the first time he took in the ruffled American, his unshaven face, bleary eyes, filthy combat fatigues. "I don't know what your particular madness is, Major, but if you don't leave immediately, I'll ring your superiors. To hell with that—I'll ring the police and have you arrested."

"I'm asking you nice to go get the chief, Gordie, and I wish you'd do it. I've had a long, bad night. I'm not in the mood for a lot of discussion."

Fordyce picked up the receiver and began dialing. "Enough of this. I am calling the police! I've given you fair warning—"

Harry moved with a suddenness unexpected from someone who appeared asleep on his feet. He grabbed the receiver out of Fordyce's hand and yanked the telephone wire free of its wall connection. Going to the door, he opened it, and tossed the phone out into the rain. "There! Now we won't have that distraction."

"You *are* mad!"

"Mad, Gordie? I'm downright pissed."

"Gordon!"

They both turned to the staircase. Sir John Duff stood there on the landing in his velvet dressing gown.

"Sir John, this man—"

"It's all right, Gordon," Duff said, making calming motions with his hand. "I take it you're here to see *me*, Major? Gordon, why don't you start a fire in the library?" Fordyce hesitated. "Now."

As Fordyce disappeared into the library, Harry pointed through the archway of the salon where the Christmas tree, now heavily adorned with ornaments of foil and crystal, stood.

"Pretty," Harry said. "But I wouldn't count on Santa leaving too many presents under there tonight. His sleigh got hung up in the Orkneys last night."

"I'm not sure I get your meaning, Major."

Harry studied the aristocratic face looking down at him. "Are you that good a liar, Sir John? Or is that Gordie's job—dealing with the dirty work?"

Duff's face remained serene. He walked slowly to the bottom of the stairs. "Would you like to meet more comfortably?" He indicated the library.

"Why don't you invite your houseguests? They always seem to have an interest in things that aren't any of their business."

"As it happens, my guests have departed."

"Really."

"Called away. Personal matters."

"No kidding."

He again motioned toward the library. "Please, Major."

Harry scooped up his parka and trudged into the library. Gordon Fordyce had the beginnings of a blaze going in the fireplace. "Why don't you sit here by the fire?" Duff suggested. "Would you care for something to eat, Major? From the looks of you, I doubt you've had breakfast. No? Coffee perhaps? Gordon, bring us a pot of tea, please. Don't wake Alden, he needs his rest. Tend to it, won't you, Gordon? There's the good fellow." Duff waited for Fordyce to leave. "Please, Major, sit down before you fall down. Good lord, you look utterly done in!"

Harry dropped into a chair, letting his parka drop to the floor beside him.

"Better, eh? Let me get this fire up a bit for you. If you'd like, I can provide you with a bath. Perhaps you'd like to rest a bit, use one of the spare rooms. We can always have this discussion later today."

"We could. But it's fresh in my mind now. You know how that is."

Duff juggled the fireplace logs about with a set of tongs until the fire crackled warmly. "Ah, there we go! You were saying something about the Orkneys?"

"Why don't you ask little Gordie about it? He's the night crawler, he must've already gotten the call. I'm sure he didn't want to disturb his lord and master. Or maybe that's what his job is—to keep you insulated."

Duff lowered himself into the plush chair across from Harry. He drew one leg across the other, tucked his dressing gown primly closed. "Again, Major, I'm afraid I don't follow. Are you saying you've just come from the Orkneys?"

"I went up there last night, flew back early this morning."

"Good lord, no wonder you're such a sight."

"Major Astin Moncrief is under arrest. Mr. Bowles is under arrest. We're holding some of the men who brought your boat into your dock on your land."

"My boat? Did you hear that, Gordie?" Fordyce had appeared in the doorway, tea things on a silver tray in his hands. "He's talking about the *Rascal*, aren't you, Major? The major says—"

Fordyce set the tray down on a table by the fireplace. He poured two cups of tea. His hands were trembling.

"Gordon had just been looking into that for you, Major," Duff went on. "When was that, Gordon? Just yesterday, wasn't it?"

"Just yesterday. Milk, Major? Sugar?"

"Remember, Major? When you were here last we said we'd look into that for you. We have some troubling news, I'm afraid."

"Somehow I'm not surprised," Harry said.

"Tell him, Gordon."

Fordyce handed Harry his cup. "It seems the *Rascal* has gone missing."

"Do tell," Harry said.

"Evidently, it's not the first time, either. There was an ex-employee of Sir John's, a man named Carlyle Booke. He was, at the time, a very trusted member of the household staff at a lodge Sir John keeps in Galloway." The ever-so-smallest bit of a smile: "Perhaps you know of it?"

"I've heard of it."

"Sir John moored the *Rascal* there. Booke had open access to the lodge grounds and the boat. In fact, it was his responsibility to care for the boat."

Harry set the teacup down on the table, untouched. "Let me guess: You fired Booke."

"Several years ago, in fact. I can't remember the reason at the moment. Some form of misconduct."

"I'll bet that was around the end of 1940."

That little smile again. "It may have been, yes. How did you know?"

"I'm clairvoyant."

"It seems that Booke never quite turned in all his keys, that he's actually been availing himself of the grounds and the boat for some time. We didn't know, because—"

"You haven't been up there since the war." Harry yawned. "Well, you don't have to worry about your boat anymore. Or Mr. Booke. Your boat—what's left of it—is on the bottom at the edge of your dock. Eight men came in on the boat. Five are dead. Carlyle Booke is one of them."

"Good lord!" Sir John Duff gasped. "Gordon! Did you know about this?"

"First I've heard."

Harry made an unimpressed clucking sound with his tongue. "I suppose that's your way of telling me you have no idea what Booke's been doing with your boat?"

"It's a *yacht*, actually," Gordon Fordyce said.

"It *was* a yacht," Harry reminded him.

"Mind yourself, Gordon," Sir John snapped. "Major, are you implying that *we* might somehow be involved?"

"What could be going through my head to make me imply that? I must be deranged."

Sir John shook his head, quite stricken by the news. "It's so much to grasp. You said . . . you said Old Teddy was under arrest? Yes? Was he connected to all this? And Major Moncrief?"

"I'm afraid that's how it looks, Sir John," Harry replied.

"I never would have thought that of them. Of *any* of them. I mean, we were forced to let Booke go, but I hardly thought . . . And Old Ted, of all people . . ." Sir John shook his poor trouble-plagued noggin.

"What's the world coming to?" Harry pondered.

"Quite," Gordon Fordyce said.

Harry drew his Lucky Strikes from his blouse pocket and extracted the last cigarette. He crumpled the empty package and tossed it on the table, then lit his cigarette. He took a long drag, sighed out a stream of smoke. "Woody Kneece is dead, Sir John. To refresh your memory, he was the young captain who was with me on Sunday—the one who played your whatchamacallit in the other room."

"Captain Kneece?"

"Yup."

"Dear God. Do you hear, Gordon?"

"Yes, Sir John." While Duff digested this latest bit, Fordyce removed the crumpled cigarette packet from the table and tossed it into the fire.

"Major Voss," Duff said, "all this, this affair, this business up at Orkney . . . is all this connected to the death of the American officer you first came to see me about?"

"Yes."

"And you've been through all . . . all this because of that dead officer?"

Harry shrugged. "Sure."

"Extraordinary. Was he a friend of yours?"

"Couldn't stand the man."

"As I say: extraordinary. Off to bed with you, Gordon."

"Perhaps I should—"

"Leave us."

If he was peeved, Fordyce concealed it superbly. He rose without another word and left, closing the library door behind him.

Duff waited a moment, studying the closed door before turning to Harry. "Major Voss, I apologize in advance for being presumptuous, but I get the impression you have a great deal more to tell me."

"Funny you should say that." Harry wriggled in his chair as if preparing himself to deliver a ripping good yarn. "Let's go back to those heady days of appeasement before the war. There's you, your good pal the American ambassador to the Court of St. James—Joe Kennedy—and your buddies from across the Channel. You all see an opportunity to make some money together and also teach the world a lesson in profitable co-existence in the bargain. But despite your shining example, here comes the war. Kennedy gets the ax and is sent home, and your other friends go back where they came from: You call it Sweden, I call it Germany, but let's not quibble.

"You all agree this is too good a partnership to break up just because of some silly old war. Kennedy knows a young Army officer named Edghill willing to do him some favors he shouldn't, and Joe Senior still has enough muscle left in Washington to muscle Edghill into a position to do those favors—specifically, the transporting of goodies to his business buddies back in England. Those goodie-carrying planes need a place to land, so you pick out a place up in the Orkneys and get another of your good friends—the Duke of Windsor—to use his pull to see that the land-buy goes through.

"But then one of Edghill's flyboys gets sloppy. There's the crash in Greenland: Enter Lieutenant Armando Grassi. Grassi hitches a ride with the only crash survivor—a pilot named Coster—on the replacement flight. There was a plan for Coster: Hide him at the Italian front until things cooled off. And because you *are* the civilized guys who tried to prevent the second Great War, nobody said it out loud, but the hope was there that if some combat misfortune should come down on Andy Coster's head . . . well, you'd owe Fate a thank-you note.

"But Grassi was a surprise, and somebody at the landing field panicked. And from such acorns do mighty oak trees grow."

Duff took a deep breath, made as if to speak.

"Extraordinary, I know," Harry said.

Sir John Duff stood, poked at the fire, and drew open the blackout curtains. He looked out across the rain-sodden lawn and scowled at something outside. "Do you know why I keep that obscenity out there?" He pointed to the gutted B-17 ploughed deep into the heather by the estate's drive. "You must have wondered," Duff continued. "Your Air Corps wanted to take it away, even brought round equipment. I chased them off. I *ordered* them to leave it. Do you know why, Major?"

"Not a clue."

"There was an RAF officer, someone from one of the ministries, an American officer as well. They wanted me to give over some of my land for some sort of military post, an aerodrome, I think. I don't really remember. But what I remember is they sat here, in this room, right where you are, and the RAF man quoted me *Henry V*. At that very moment, a flight of bombers flew over. I don't know if these men had timed their visit to coincide with a mission, or the aeroplanes were a planned part. No matter. The planes roared over and he sat there quoting: 'Gentlemen in England, now abed, shall think themselves accursed they were not here'— and so on. I suppose the idea was to inflame my patriotism"—Sir John pounded a fist over his heart—"to make me hunger to be part of the great adventure. It is very easy to be captured by the heroic spirit of the moment, Major, particularly a moment built as exquisitely as that. And that is why I leave that hideous thing out there. To remind them—to remind me—as to what the great adventure truly is." He gestured out at the blackened hulk. "Those happy few didn't look so happy when I saw their burned bodies dragged from that monstrosity. Those heroes will not be showing their scars and saying, 'These wounds I had on Crispin's day.' "

"But you help build those monstrosities," Harry said. "You help build the guns and the bombs."

"As you somewhat wryly pointed out, Major, my friends and I tried damnably hard to keep this war from coming. Now it's here. Whatever I can do to end it as swiftly as possible, I'll do."

"You're rationalizing."

"Perhaps. But now my primary concern is to see that this war is the last war."

Harry took a last puff on his cigarette and tossed it into the flames. "I believe you believe all this crap, Sir John. Did it ever occur to you you've been played for a sucker by a bunch of people who just want to make a buck?"

"Major, did you know that the Chinese were buying Coca-Cola in Shanghai back in the twenties? As much as a million cases per annum, even while China was at war with the Japanese for control of Manchuria."

"Maybe I'm just tired, but now it's time for me not to see your point."

Duff smiled. "Major, I lost all my illusions twenty-five years ago. I don't trust in the altruism of others. I think the current state of world affairs is evidence enough that heroism has died an ugly death. But commerce—base self-interest—I had hopes there, Major. My friends, my houseguests, they have a saying where they're from: 'One crow does not peck out the eyes of another.' Ironic, eh? My faith was in their greed. Their very rapaciousness would be the salvation of the world. How can you possibly consider that to be naïve?"

Harry stood and pulled on his parka.

"Leaving, Major? Why did you come here?"

"I'm wondering."

Duff followed him to the door. As Harry crossed to his jeep, Sir John called out to him: "You'll extend my condolences to Captain Kneece's family? He seemed quite a decent sort of young man. I liked him."

Harry halted, stood there in the rain, his right hand dropped into the pocket of his parka. "Does it still hurt that your sons are dead?" Harry asked.

"Certainly."
"I'm glad."

It was an ignored cul-de-sac not far from Rosewood Court: drab shops peddling bric-a-brac, and at the end of one walk a dark, worn cubby of a pub called the Old Eagle. Of little interest to most of the Americans billeted at the Annex, the Old Eagle had always provided Harry and Joe Ryan relief from the constant sight of the American uniforms filling London, as well as a respite from the Annex canteen fare.

This rainy afternoon, every shop in the cul-de-sac was boarded up, abandoned, including the Old Eagle. A massive bomb crater ripped the cobbles at the end of the street, reaching almost from curb to curb. The blast had collapsed several buildings, blown out the glass and scarred the faces of all the others. The street had been nearly lifeless before: the bomb had been its death blow.

Harry stood across the street from the pub. The boarded door had been pried open, and in the darkness beyond Harry could see a small circle of flickering warm light. He carefully navigated the rim of the bomb crater and stepped inside.

At a far booth, Joe Ryan sat huddled in his trench coat. The light came from a candle he'd planted on the table. Also on the table rested a thermos and a small linen bundle. At the creak of the door Ryan looked up. "Bring back any memories?"

"You don't want to be tickling my memory."

"Are you going to just stand there?"

"You had a message waiting for me at the Annex to come here."

"I had a message—and a car—waiting for your plane at Duxford. Where've you been? Nobody knew where you—"

"I'm here. What do you want?"

"Right now I want—I'd like you to sit down. Jesus, Harry, you look awful."

"Some people think I'm pretty cute."

Ryan unscrewed the top of the thermos, poured out a mug of steaming coffee, and set it in front of Harry. He fumbled with a briefcase on the bench beside him. "I've got powdered milk and saccharin in here if you—"

Harry was already sipping at the mug.

Ryan unknotted the bundle: a napkin from the canteen containing three breakfast rolls. "I snitched these on the way over. I thought maybe you hadn't had time to get anything to eat this morning. They're cold now. Sorry." From the briefcase, a pack of cigarettes and matches. "How're you fixed for butts? Never mind, just take 'em."

Harry remembered Dominick Sisto: *Fattening the sheep.* He lit a cigarette. *Isn't that what the firing squad leader does? Doesn't he offer you a last cigarette?*

"So," Harry said. "Do I get court-martialed here? Or back in the States? Or is it going to be that old trick of shooting me off to some far corner of the world?"

"Oh, no. You'll be going home. As a matter of fact, a C-87 with Captain Kneece's remains on it'll be flying you out tonight. There'll be a few days' leave so you can enjoy what's left of the holiday season, then, by the time you report back to Dix, there'll be a letter of commendation from the Judge Advocate General waiting there for you. Sometime after that, you might even be trading those gold oak leaves of yours for silver ones."

"Commendation?"

"There'll also be one sent to Captain Kneece's family, and one for Ricks, an official thanks to that snoop Owen, Doheeny and his crew, too. And there'll be some noise about cooperation between allies and a tip of the hat to those RAF maniacs who sank Duff's yacht. By the way, Harry, who the hell *are* those guys? Mac-something and—"

"Macnee and Donlay. Jim Doheeny'd met them the first time we came through the Orkneys."

"How'd they get drafted into serving the cause?"

"Evidently, I cut a less-than-inspiring warrior figure. Doheeny saw us marching off armed to the teeth, thought I was getting in over my head . . ."

"I can see where he would. How'd he know he could depend on those two?"

"He knew they weren't involved—after all, these were the guys who'd found Grassi's body. And you only have to talk to them for five minutes to know they're crazy enough to take off in bad weather without filing a flight plan on an unapproved mission. They actually thanked us afterward for breaking up the boredom. I also think there was something about the brotherhood of airmen and that kind of crap. Now: What's this baloney about a commendation? Commendation for *what?*"

Ryan took a moment as if steeling himself. Then he put on the broad, practiced smile that had oiled his way from Newark street urchin to JAG colonel. "For smashing a smuggling ring."

Harry closed his eyes, pained. "Smuggling."

"I don't know what the exact language of the commendations will be, but something along the lines of the risks—professional and personal— you and your plucky little group took to bring down this band of vile profiteers."

"Who are they saying are the vile profiteers behind this 'smuggling' ring?"

"Edghill and Moncrief."

"Of course."

"The story they're dishing out is Moncrief brought in this old coot Bowles, and Bowles knew somebody named Carl Booke—"

"Carlyle."

Ryan looked at him curiously, then shrugged it off. "Moncrief is going to be demoted and transferred to some black hole of the British Empire. I heard they're considering someplace in the CBI Theater like Burma, which is going to make him wish they *had* thrown him in the jug. Edghill will probably spend the duration shoveling snow in the Aleutians. As for Bowles, it seems you made the old guy some kind of offer about going easy if he cooperated? Our British colleagues feel bound to honor that commitment—"

"Noble of them."

"—so Bowles will be charged, undoubtedly convicted, but there'll be no jail time. Hell, Harry, at his age the old bastard won't live long enough to see the end of this business."

Harry wrinkled his face the way one might over a child's outlandish tale of monsters beneath the bed. "Moncrief would know Bowles from them both being on Orkney Mainland, and Bowles would know Carlyle Booke because they both worked for John Duff. Anybody happen to mention how it is Edghill and Moncrief came together?"

Joe Ryan's smile twisted wryly. "They haven't figured that out yet."

"I'm sure they'll think of something." Harry drained his mug. Even before he set it back on the table, Ryan poured him another cup. "That was Duff's boat," Harry persisted, "pulled up at Duff's dock by Duff's cabin. How come I don't hear Sir John Duff's name getting mentioned here?"

"Gordon Fordyce made a statement to the British authorities this morning. It seems—according to Fordyce—this guy Booke—"

"Stole the boat."

Joe Ryan blinked. "How'd you know that? Wait a minute: Do I want to know how you know that?"

"They're going to buy this fairy tale about the stolen boat?"

"It may not be very believable, but it *is* credible; that's all they need. Unless Edghill, Moncrief, or Bowles fingers somebody, that's where it ends."

"Hang some jail time over their heads and maybe they will."

Ryan's smile faded. "It's been decided, Harry. This is the way it's going to happen."

"What about the other men from the boat?"

"They're just a bunch of dockside goons. According to them, Booke would hire a group of them every time he had to make one of these Orkney runs, as many as he thought he'd need, not even the same ones each time. They only dealt with Booke. As far as they knew, this was Booke's show. One of them says he was there the night Grassi flew in. He says—"

"Booke killed Armando Grassi."

"How'd you know that?"

"Educated guess. This is all wrapping up very neat." Harry tore off a piece of breakfast roll, then reconsidered and tossed both pieces down on the napkin. "Coster's promised that he'll talk. Coster can name the names."

Ryan's eyes dropped to the table. "Andrew Coster's dead, Harry."

"Oh, Christ . . ."

"I got the word right after you left yesterday. A kraut mortar took out his OP an hour after you left him."

The two weeks of near-nonstop traveling, the nights with little or no sleep, Woody Kneece, the sudden pointlessness of it all . . . Harry wanted to close his eyes, climb on top of the table, and cry himself to sleep. "Somebody's been protecting these guys all along. Somebody still is."

"And you want to know why?"

"You're goddamned right I do."

Ryan chuckled.

"If you think that's funny, Joe, you should hear my story about the major who beat the colonel to death with a thermos."

Ryan waved a calming hand. "It's just that this is how I told them you'd be. I said this guy has got to know. Because even with his commendation and a lieutenant colonelcy, Harry Voss'll keep pushing until he does know."

"Flattering, real sweet of you to say. Now: Why?" Harry's palm came down on the table hard enough to topple the candle.

"Easy, Harry! You'll burn what's left of this place down! They never really protected anything. It was more like they turned a blind eye—"

"Who turned a blind eye to what?"

Ryan let a moment go by; enough for Harry to know he was only going to be told so much, and that what he would be told would not necessarily include all the whos and whats and whys.

"Harry, the war's going to end one day."

"That's the rumor."

"There's Nazis who are going to find themselves at the end of a rope when it's all over, or in prison, or on the run. The ones left behind are, at the very least, going to lose their jobs."

"Won't that be a crying shame?"

"The Nazis'll be out. The Gestapo has already gutted their opposition. That means that once the shooting stops, there's going to be a power vacuum in Germany. The only people Churchill hates almost as much as the Nazis are the commies. He hates them so much he keeps lobbying Eisenhower for a landing in the Balkans, even though everybody tells him it would be a disaster. He's worried about cutting the Russians off before they advance into Europe."

"What the *hell* are you talking about?"

"The next generation of leaders in Germany, Harry. The people who are going to hold the public offices and run the businesses. The way the Brits see it, Sir John is cultivating people they believe are a pro-British, pro-democratic bunch of pro-capitalists."

"Is that our side's take on it, too?"

Ryan shrugged. "Roosevelt thinks he can work with Stalin more than Churchill does, but that doesn't mean FDR's not worried about what might happen in an unstable postwar Germany. And it's a way of protecting American business interests. Some of Duff's friends worked for companies that had American parents before the Nazis seized them. Joe Kennedy provided a conduit to the American parents to monitor their German operations, and connections to the people that will help them pick up the pieces and get their shops back in working order after the smoke clears."

"Eleven men are dead."

"Nobody's happy about that, Harry."

"Eleven. Men. Are. Dead!"

"And that's why the powers that be are happy you brought all this to light! They looked the other way when Edghill and Moncrief were doing favors for Kennedy and Duff, but they didn't know—they're *saying* they didn't know—how out of whack the whole operation had become: planes, crews, then what happened to Grassi—"

"Goddammit, Joe, it's not just Grassi. I realize that these days, eleven corpses may not mean much—"

"C'mon, Harry, do you really give a damn about those bone breakers last night? And that crash in Greenland, the way I hear it that was because a lousy pilot made a lousy call. We're all lucky that guy was flying booty instead of troops or bringing home wounded. Besides, I'm told they were all a bunch of shirkers, Coster included."

Jesus God I am so tired! "Armando Grassi's dead, Joe. And so is Woody Kneece. Make me feel better about that."

"I can't." In one of those rare moments spread thinly over all the years they'd known each other, Harry heard Joe Ryan speak with candor. "All I can tell you is if Grassi hadn't been murdered, this business would still be going on. He was the price of uncovering it. Woody Kneece was the price of stopping it. You won, Harry. This operation, this ring, it's over. Finished. And the guy who killed Grassi, he's dead. The guy who killed Woody Kneece, he's dead. That's all you're going to get, Harry, and I hope to God this time you learn to live with that."

Harry pulled himself from the bench. He walked idly about the shadows of the barroom, kicking at the litter on the floor, glass crunching underfoot. He stopped at the threshold, watching the rain pepper a muddy pool in the bomb crater outside.

"It's more than anybody else could've gotten, Harry," Ryan said. "It's more than anybody else would've pushed for."

Harry pulled Armando Grassi's photograph from inside his jacket. He touched his cigarette to it and the paper began to smolder, then burn. He flicked the burning square of paper into the rain. "Can you do me a favor, Joe? Doheeny should fly Woody back to the States. And I should take him home."

"Are you sure?"

Harry nodded.

"Yeah, I can arrange that. I was hoping to have you with Cynthia and the kids by tomorrow. There'd still be Christmas leftovers in the icebox."

"Even a late Christmas'll be a better Christmas than the Kneeces are going to have."

Joe Ryan gathered up his thermos and mug, left the bread for the rats, and snuffed out the candle. "You did a hell of a job, Harry. It's just that it's not a perfect world."

Harry sent his cigarette sailing in a long arc, ending in the water in the bomb crater with a small phhht. "So they keep telling me."

I was incredulous. "Harry, you—you—went down there to—"

"What'd you ever do with that .45?" Peter Ricks asked.

Harry smiled a dopey, liquory grin. "Right here in my parka." He started to reach for it, but a laughing Ricks stopped him.

I was still shaking my head, unbelieving. "Harry, you crazy old sod, I can't believe you went down to Sir Johnnie's to—to—"

"I don't know what I was going to do," Harry said. "Not really. I thought I would know once I got there. But I didn't."

"You had it when you saw Ryan?" Ricks asked.

"Sure."

"And you didn't use it?"

We all laughed.

I'd conducted the three of us to a café I knew with inelegant food and a tolerable wine cellar (aided and abetted by the more potent contents of Peter Ricks's flask). Harry's usually troublesome stomach evidently had risen to the occasion, or else Harry had made a commitment to ignore the consequences, and got himself as pissed as Ricks and I. After the café, it was off to the Rose & Crown where, I'm afraid, we provided quite a disturbance.

We told stories, war tales of the last weeks, a few caustic memories of Armando Grassi. And then we spoke of Derwood Kneece.

"You would've thought he'd learned his lesson in Italy." Harry moped into his beer.

"Learned what?" Peter Ricks plucked Harry's cigarette from his lips, used it to light a fresh one of his own, then slipped it back into Harry's mouth. "I'll be damned: you think that kid screwed up again!" Ricks laughed, shaking his head. "Major, that kid saved your bacon!"

Harry turned his foggy eyes toward Ricks. "What're you talking about?"

"Three men came off the boat, Major. But only two of 'em went for the barn. The third one—the guy you pipped—he was headin' right for the house."

"He's right, Harry," I said. "There were only two of them at the barn."

Ricks smiled, amused at Harry's befuddlement. "You couldn't see him 'cause you were down like you were supposed to be. Where I was in those rocks, I couldn't see him either. The only person who could see him was Kneece. For him to get his sights on that guy, Kneece had to go way up on the rocks, and that left him open to the guys on the boat. He had to know that. But if he hadn't done it, you wouldn'ta seen that guy until he walked in the door, and that woulda been messy." Ricks looked down into his glass, swirling the liquor about, then held it up in salute. "Woody Kneece did all right, Major."

Lilith rang the closing bell, warned us not to end up jailed in our disgusting condition, shooed us out. The day's rain had set the stage for a bracingly chill evening. I volunteered that I had a bottle of not-too-appalling stuff back at my flat that would surely keep us warm. Harry was game, but Ricks begged off.

"I'm on a midnight flight back to Italy," he said. "The hospital told me if I'm well enough to fly off to Italy and Orkney and every other goddamn place, then I must be well enough to send back up to the line." He squinted at his watch in the blacked-out street. "Jesus, I gotta shake a leg if I'm gonna make it! Hey, Major, you better let me have that piece. If I let you keep walking around with it, I'm going to be sweatin' the whole flight that you're gonna get yourself hurt."

Harry dug the .45 out of his parka pocket, but didn't hand it over right away.

Ricks snatched the weapon out of Harry's hand and buried it in his own pocket. "Don't," he warned.

"Don't what?"

"C'mon, walk me to the train. I'm freezin' my ass off out here."

Hunched against the cold, hands jammed deep in pockets, we walked a wavering line abreast to the nearest Underground.

"Sooner or later you're gonna be thinkin' 'bout all this." Ricks took a nip from his flask before passing it round. " 'N' you're gonna be thinkin' maybe it's your fault. 'Bout ol' Woody Kneece. Well, *don't*. He made a choice like we all did."

"The man's dead, Pete."

"*One* man, Major. Let me impart some words of wisdom based on my vast military experience." Ricks stopped at the top of the Underground stairs, swaying. "That wisdom is this, Major Voss, sir: If you wanna get in a fight, expect somebody's gonna get hurt. If you're gonna fight a war, figure somebody's gonna get killed. If you don't want to pay, don't dance. Gentlemen, I take your leave. Mr. Owen, next time I read the funny papers I'll think of you."

"Thank you, Lieutenant. It's been a pleasure to serve with you."

"Pete . . ." Harry looked for words, didn't find them.

Peter Ricks grinned, took Harry's hand in both of his, then bounded down the stairs. His whistle echoed up the well, an off-key rendering of "The Minstrel Boy."

I drove up to Duxford with Harry the following afternoon to see him off. We sat next to each other in the cargo cabin of Jim Doheeny's C-47, waiting for the flyer and his copilot to return from a last-minute briefing at the Operations shack. We said little; most of it had been said the night before, and the late hours we'd kept and the drinks we'd downed had left us fagged and sullen. And even had we had a full night of restful sleep, there was still the long crate lashed to the cargo deck holding the body of Derwood Sitgreaves Kneece to brood over.

Sparks plucked at his guitar. Harry cocked his head; I thought I saw the ghost of a smile. I guessed the wireless operator was threading through one of the tunes Woody had taught him.

The flight mechanic politely suggested to Sparks—with a respectful nod in our direction—that the wireless operator lay his guitar down.

"Let him play," Harry said. "It's all right."

"Hey, Harry!" Doheeny called from outside. "I think this is for you!"

There was a jeep barreling across the aerodrome. The driver honked his horn to ensure our attention. It was Joe Ryan.

"How nice of you to come say good-bye," Harry said to Ryan.

The colonel killed the engine of the jeep but did not climb out. "Where were you last night?" he asked Harry coolly.

"Did we have a date?"

Ryan glared at Doheeny and his copilot. They mumbled something about preparing the ship for takeoff and climbed aboard.

"What were you doing last night?" Ryan asked again.

"Peter Ricks, Mr. Owen, and I went out for a couple of drinks."

"Until what time?"

Harry stepped closer to Ryan's jeep, his face wary.

"I asked you, how long were you and Ricks and Mr. Owen out having drinks?"

" 'Til closing," I volunteered. "That would've been tennish or so."

"And then what?"

"Pete had to run for an air transport to Italy," Harry said. "Then Mr. Owen and I went back to his place for a bit. I don't remember how long. It was pretty late when I got back to the Annex. You can check the sentry's log. What's this about?"

"Sir John Duff and some guy who works with him—"

"Gordon Fordyce?" I offered.

Ryan nodded. "They were found dead this morning in some place he has down around Canterbury."

I wished I was sitting down. Harry turned his back to Ryan so he could lean against the jeep.

"It looks like it happened around two this morning," Ryan went on in a tight voice. "The prepared statement is going to say that Scotland Yard is working on the assumption that Duff and Fordyce stumbled across an intruder."

"But that isn't the story," I said.

Ryan sighed grimly. "The on-scene report says it looks like they were kneeling, somebody stood behind them, held a pillow over the muzzle of his gun, and put a bullet through the back of each of their heads."

"That's an execution," I said.

"Whoever it was was very careful," Ryan continued. "He picked up his shell casings. The ballistics prelim says the slugs show rifling from a .45 automatic. An American round has people thinking an American killer. The Yard doesn't want that news getting out until they know more."

"Why create unnecessary friction between the Allies, eh?" I asked.

Ryan took a long breath. "There was no air transport to Italy last night," he announced.

Harry went rigid. "Maybe——"

"Peter Ricks didn't fly out of England last night on *any* plane to *any-where*," Ryan said coldly. "He shipped out by sea with a convoy for the Mediterranean that left Portsmouth this morning."

The three of us were quiet a long time then. I saw some large, black birds picking at something out by the tarmac. Crows, I thought, but then one began bobbing its head, letting out a laughing *toc-toc-toc* that carried sharply across the quiet aerodrome. Ravens.

Joe Ryan cleared his throat. "So, you two must be mistaken."

Harry and I exchanged a confused look.

"If Peter Ricks didn't have to catch a flight, he must've been with you guys all last night," Ryan declared. "Jesus, Harry, I'm not surprised you don't remember. You must've really been tanked. You never could hold your liquor." Ryan's foot reached for the jeep's starter. "You better get going," he told us as the motor coughed to life. "You don't want to keep your plane waiting."

"Hey, Joe!" Harry called as Ryan wrestled the jeep into gear. "I'll tell Cynthia you said hello."

Ryan smiled and nodded. "I'll see you around the old homestead one of these days."

"That'd be nice. Merry Christmas, Joe."

"Merry Christmas, Harry-boy."

Harry and I watched as the jeep rumbled away.

"You really should try a social visit one time," I told Harry. "Something not as . . . *exciting*."

He grinned. "Eddie, you *have* been a friend; a good one. Thanks."

"Stay home this time, Harry. You earned it."

"You'd miss me." He held out his hand.

I raised mine high. " 'I will never forget you. I have carved you in the palm of my hand.' "

"Shakespeare?"

"The writer's friend: the Bible." I brought the hand down into his, clasped my other over it. "Safe home, Harry."

The hatch closed behind him, the energizers whined, the engines sputtered, then roared, scattering the ravens. I watched the plane lift off and grow small with distance, finally disappearing into the northern sky.

EPILOGUE

DROPS OF AMBER

I WAS GIVEN THE DUFF STORY to write for the afternoon edition since I'd been the one who'd broken the news about the supposed black-market ring. It was an easy piece to do: a few facts from the police report, a statement from Duff's people, and the high points of his biographical file. I'd become so well acquainted with the file I hardly needed to reference it.

The Boss collapsed in his office on January 6 of the new year—by the Christian calendar, the Epiphany.

I sat by him on the floor as we waited for the ambulance. He was conscious throughout, although he looked a fright, ghostly pale, his breath labored.

"You'll miss me, you will, eh, my son?"

"You should've just drawn your holiday like everyone else," I pretended to scold him, "instead of cadging a sick leave, you lazy sod."

His hand squeezed mine. "Be good, my son."

As it read in the next morning's edition, he died peacefully in his sleep at 5:40 A.M., attended by his wife.

The associate editor was asked to take the helm for the moment. The AE asked that I write a column under his name—a tribute to the Boss. I begged off and he seemed to understand. The Boss's missus asked me to say something at the service. Again I had to refuse.

Twenty years on the job had left me quite skilled at dealing with the pain of others. But I found in myself little ability to deal with my own.

It rained the day of the burial. Cathryn stood arm in arm with me by the side of the missus as they laid him to rest. We shared a taxi taking the missus home. I said to her, "I'm glad I didn't write the tribute piece."

"Why is that?"

"He would've stood up in the grave to pencil out mention of the rain. 'Doesn't need it, my son,' he would've said. 'A bit too dramatic, eh?' "

Even the missus smiled.

They made the AE's posting permanent. He asked me if I'd mind going through Himself's sanctum to collect his personals. I set them carefully in a box: family photos, citations, and the like. And, of course, those two chipped teacups hiding in his desk drawer.

I brought the lot round to the missus. She was puzzled over the cups. When I explained them, she laughed. "That old bugger!" She handled them a moment, then pushed them to me. "They seem something you should have."

I stopped by the Rose & Crown on my way home. I told Lilith to dig deep behind the bar for her best stuff, the stuff the customers never see, the special-occasion stuff, even if it took my entire pay packet to pay for it.

It was a fine, fiery old brandy, the likes I was shocked she was even acquainted with, let alone possessed. "I've been saving a few bottles of this for their homecoming," Lil said, nodding at the pictures of her husband and son on the wall behind the bar as she poured the brandy in the cups. We drank to the Boss, to her husband, to her son, to all the husbands, to all the sons.

The buildup in Italy we'd seen that December explained itself when American and British troops landed at Anzio and Nettuno sixty miles behind the German lines on January 22nd. The U.S. Army Public Information Office described the landings as a daring attempt to flank the Gustav Line and strike deep into the German rear. In truth, the Anzio beachhead was a mammoth piece of bait. The hope was that the Germans, panicked by an Allied force deep in their rear, would draw strength away from the Gustav Line to repel the landing, leaving the line weak enough for the Allies to finally punch through.

But the Germans responded in better fashion than anticipated. The Anzio/Nettuno sector was swiftly contained and the Allied main force continued its brutal inching up the Italian boot. The hoped-for breakthrough would not occur until May.

If, as Peter Ricks had claimed, it was a headline Mark Clark and his 5th Army were fighting for, it would be a short-lived glory. The newspaper banners announcing the taking of Rome on June 5th were stale within twenty-four hours, with the announcement the following day of Operation Overlord: the Allied landings in Normandy.

Peter Ricks, wounded in the horrific fighting round Cassino that presaged the May breakthrough, missed the brief victory parade.

I received a letter from Harry the week after the Anzio landings. It was a long letter, running several sheets. Also enclosed were two American ten-dollar bills.

There were a lot of the usual banalities: bits about his family, about home, how was I faring, talk of Anzio, had I heard anything from Ricks. Trite, trivial, expected, yet good to read coming from his pen.

He told me about taking Woody Kneece home:

> I spent the trip wondering just what exactly I was going to say to these people. When I met them, I told them that Woody had died like a hero, saving a fellow soldier's life. I didn't have the nerve to tell them it was me he'd saved.
>
> Pete was right about the family being pretty well off. Their house could hold everybody who lives in my building. Still, they kept the service small and buried Woody in a family plot outside of town. Since Woody wasn't killed in action against the enemy, there was no Purple Heart or color guard, but the State Constabulary supplied an honor guard.
>
> I met the famous Uncle Ray. He's not what I thought he'd be. Remember when we were at Sir John's and Woody mentioned his father's library? It is a big one, but as you talk with Woody's people you realize his father uses it for show—Uncle Ray is the one who actually reads the books.
>
> He guessed it was me Woody had saved, but he also seemed to understand that I didn't want Woody's parents to know that. I told him about what Woody had said about being the last to carry the family name.
>
> He told me not to feel guilty about that. It's just a name, he said. The dinosaurs died out, the dodo died out, the Kneeces would die out, he said. The only people who care about that are the Kneeces, he said.
>
> I didn't get home until a week after Christmas. In the beginning Cyn asked me about what happened but I couldn't tell her much and she stopped asking. It's bad enough one of us knows.
>
> Philip Mayer knows. You'd like him. He's your kind of people, which I hope doesn't require much more of an explanation. Without my even saying anything, he seemed to know what happened. I was out on the front stoop one night having a cigarette and he was just closing up his store, which is right next to our building. He called me in and we sat around drinking this horrible sweet wine of his.
>
> It's funny how you can say things to some people you won't say to your wife. I didn't

want to tell him anything, but once I started talking I couldn't stop. I talked about Woody
and Armando and what happened last summer and about killing that man from the boat. I
started to cry. I was crying so hard I didn't think I'd ever stop.

He called me heldish, which is Yiddish for hero. I said I didn't do anything to get
called a hero. He said it was because I cried. He said he'd be more worried about me if I
didn't cry.

The twenty dollars is for you to go out and buy the best bottle of booze you can. Bring
it over to Joe Ryan and tell him it's from me.

It's possible you and me may never see each other again. Cynthia asks me how you and
me could be such good friends. We knew each other for a week back in August, and another
week in December. I don't know how to explain it to her. I'm not sure I understand it
myself. But you'll always be a friend, Eddie.

Be well and take care of yourself. Try not to cover anything more dangerous than cricket
matches. You're a good guy, Eddie Owen, even though I get the feeling you don't always think so.

Your friend,

Harry

I still have that letter, yellow and brittle now. Every so often I take it out
and pour myself a few sips of something warm into one of those chipped
teacups. "Harry," I say, and hold up the teacup, "meet the Boss. Boss, meet
Harry."

I'm ashamed to be in such good company.

The drink gone, I fold the letter and tuck it safely away, then turn in
and sleep the satisfied sleep of a man who knows that while he's never
been the man he'd hoped to be, two honorable men called him friend.
There's few in this world can say as much.

ACKNOWLEDGMENTS

As in The Advocate, I am again impressed at how much of a collaborative effort producing a novel turns out to be, and it would be an omission of the highest order not to give praise where praise is due.

First and foremost, I have to thank dear Kate Miciak. An editor in the Maxwell Perkins tradition, she is a hand-holder, rooting section, aesthetic backstop, guiding hand, tutor, and, in the truest sense of the word, a creative collaborator. She was one of only two people—myself not included—who believed I had this book in me, and helped midwife it onto the page.

The other was Richard Derus, my one-time agent and, I hope, long-time friend. In fact, there would be no story for Officer of the Court if Richard had not provided me with one.

And there's Connie Munro, my copyeditor, who once again took on the thankless, gloryless task of giving this work a consistency of style, a literacy, and sometimes even a coherence that, I'm sorry to say, does not fall naturally to me.

Thanks to all of you and the rest of the Bantam team for making Officer of the Court happen.

And also as in The Advocate, it would be unfair not to give tribute to the research and labors of other writers and helpmates whose contributions helped provide the historical basis for Officer of the Court—

BOOKS:

Allen, William L. *Anzio: Edge of Disaster*. NY: Dutton, 1978.

Ambrose, Stephen E. *Citizen Soldiers: The U.S. Army from the Normandy Beaches to the Bulge to the Surrender of Germany, June 7, 1944–May 7, 1945*. NY: Simon & Schuster, 1997.

Collier, Peter, and David Horowitz. *The Kennedys: An American Drama*. NY: Warner, 1984.

Collier, Richard. *Eagle Day*. NY: Dutton, 1980 ed.

Eisenhower, David E. *Eisenhower: At War 1943–1945*. NY: Random House, 1986.

Farago, Ladislas. *Patton: Ordeal and Triumph*. NY: Ivan Obolensky, 1963.

Forty, George. *U.S. Army Handbook 1939–1945*. UK: Alan Sutton, 1997 ed.

Gann, Ernest K. *Fate Is the Hunter*. NY: Ballantine, 1972.

Immerso, Michael. *Newark's Little Italy: The Vanished First Ward*. New Brunswick, NJ: Rutgers University Press, 1997.

Jablonski, Edward. *Airwar*. Vols. I–IV. NY: Doubleday, 1971.

Katz, Robert. *Death in Rome*. NY: Pyramid, 1968.

Kemp, Peter. *Decision at Sea: The Convoy Escorts*. NY: Dutton, 1978.

McCutcheon, Marc. *The Writer's Guide to Everyday Life from Prohibition Through World War II*. Cincinnati: Writer's Digest, 1995.

Murphy, Charles J. V., and J. Bryan III. *The Windsor Story*. NY: Dell, 1979.

Nalty, Bernard, and Carl Berger. *The Men Who Bombed the Reich*. NY: Dutton, 1978.

Pyle, Ernie. *Brave Men*. NY: Holt, 1944.

Robinson, Derek. *Piece of Cake*. NY: Knopf, 1984.

Robinson, Wayne. *Barbara*. NY: Doubleday, 1962.

Talese, Gay. *Unto the Sons*. NY: Ballantine, 1992.

Terkel, Studs. *The Good War*. NY: Pantheon, 1984.

Veterans of Foreign Wars Edition of Pictorial History of the Second World War. Vols. I, II, III. New York: Wm. H. Wise Co., 1946.

OTHER PUBLICATIONS:

"Environment." Firth. http://www.users.zetnet.co.uk/firth/environment/htm

Frank, Al. "Ladies and Gentlemen, the Terminal Is Taxiing." *The Star-Ledger* (New Jersey). Feb. 13, 2000. p. 27+.

Goldman, George. "Mariners Were the First to Go, the Last to Return." *The Star-Ledger* (New Jersey). Dec. 7, 1999. p. 20.

Gordon, William. "Victory at Sea." *The Star-Ledger* (New Jersey). May 27, 1993. p. 85+.

———. "Bygone First Ward." *The Star-Ledger* (New Jersey). Feb. 1, 1995. p. 41+.

Hampson, Stephen. "The Plight of the Neutrals." *History of the Second World War*, 1973 ed. Part 7. p. 194+.

Hays, Constance L. "This Bud's for Them." *The New York Times*. June 23, 1999. C1+.

Kemp, Peter, Lt. Cmdr. "Struggle for the Sealanes." *History of the Second World War*, 1973 ed. Part II. p. 281+.

Kershaw, Andrew, ed. 1939–1945 *War Planes*. History of the World Wars— Special Edition. Hicksville, NY: Marshall Cavendish, 1973.

Mappen, Marc. "Jerseyana." *The New York Times*. January 9, 1994. p. 19.

Marks, John. "Now, American Firms Face Holocaust Claims." *U.S. News & World Report*. December 14, 1998. p. 40.

Nichols, Mike. "Return to Base." *The Star-Ledger* (New Jersey). May 23, 1999. Section 8, p. 1+.

Orkney info. Firth. http://www.users.zetnet.co.uk/orkney/htm

Rendall, Anne. "Orkney." Scotland Gen Web Project. http://rootsweb. rendall.net/orkney, 1998.

Richards, Denis. "The Battle of Britain." *History of the Second World War*, 1973 ed. Part 9. p. 225+.

Schofield, B.B., Vice-Admiral. "The First Arctic Convoys." *History of the Second World War*, 1973 ed. Part 33. p. 907+.

Simkins, P.J. "Battle of the Coral Sea." *History of the Second World War*, 1973 ed. Part 32. p. 887+.

Swinson, Arthur. "Japanese Victory: The Conquest of Malaya." *History of the Second World War*, 1973 ed. Part 26. p. 710+.

"Today's Almanac." *The Star-Ledger* (New Jersey). June 1, 1999. p. 2.

INTERVIEWS AND RESEARCH ASSISTANCE:

Colonel Arnold Briggs, U.S.A., retired

Josephine Esposito

Vincent Esposito

Michael Gepner

Gene Gulich

Rita Gonzalez, U.S.N.

Tony Lorenzo

Lucy Mesce

Thomas Mesce, U.S.N.

Faye Palazzo

Tina Young

Marie Zanetti

ABOUT THE AUTHOR

BILL MESCE JR. lives in New Jersey with his wife and children.